THE RECKONING

OTHER TITLES BY MEGAN CRANE

The Bloodlore Series

The Reveal

The Edge Series

Edge of Obsession

Edge of Temptation

Edge of Control

Edge of Power

Edge of Ruin (The Edge Novellas)

The Devil's Keepers Series

Make You Burn (The Deacons of Bourbon Street)

Devil's Honor

Devil's Mark

Devil's Own

THE RECKONING

MEGAN CRANE

This is a work of fiction. Names, characters, organizations, places, events, and incidents are either products of the author's imagination or are used fictitiously. Otherwise, any resemblance to actual persons, living or dead, is purely coincidental.

Text copyright © 2026 by Megan Crane
All rights reserved.

No part of this book may be reproduced, or stored in a retrieval system, or transmitted in any form or by any means, electronic, mechanical, photocopying, recording, or otherwise, without express written permission of the publisher.

Published by Montlake, Seattle
www.apub.com

Amazon, the Amazon logo, and Montlake are trademarks of Amazon.com, Inc., or its affiliates.

EU product safety contact:
Amazon Media EU S. à r.l.
38, avenue John F. Kennedy, L-1855 Luxembourg
amazonpublishing-gpsr@amazon.com

ISBN-13: 9781662531545 (paperback)
ISBN-13: 9781662531552 (digital)

Cover design by Logan Matthews
Cover illustration by Christina Chung

Printed in the United States of America

To all the wolfgirls who know their worth.
This is for you.

1.

Full Cold Moon

There are banshees moaning their lullabies up in the trees while the full moon shines down. It's like she's singing along. The moonlight makes the woods around me stark and gleaming as I hurry along the old wolf path that winds its way through them. I have to look up past banshee hair on the breeze and all those gaping mouths to see the moon herself, high above the nearest mountain.

The full moon, I think as I gaze at her serene ripeness in the night, *can bite me.*

To say I'm sick of the monthly drama would be putting it mildly.

Not exactly a great look for a werewolf, but then, I've never been quite like other girls. Literally. Back in high school, way back before the Reveal set all of the Kind free to be our monstery selves when and where and how we liked, I was a werewolf walking around in teenage human girl form, blending in with the rest of them as best I could.

They didn't like me any more than my pack likes me now, no matter how many of them followed me around, because I was a mystery they couldn't solve. That was how I learned that people like questions a lot more than they like answers.

I keep picking my way through the dark woods all the same, because it's the night of the full moon and I've been back here in Oregon since the Reveal crashed through the academic plans that were my only escape from all this, however temporarily. But that escape ended abruptly along with everything else the day the old prophecy came true and I was ordered to come home. Now when duty and tradition call, I'm honor bound to answer.

Showing up for pack rituals is basic, entry-level diplomacy—not to mention, good manners—and it won't hurt me to employ some of that. I'm still a little shaky from the last couple of moons we've had this fall, and I can't really afford to be shaky. I need to show my face, little as anyone wants to see it these days. Something that isn't likely to change until I comply, which I won't be doing tonight.

That's the thing. Even before I see the fresh remains of some kind of a mammal on the path to the pack's den—though it smells like a murder instead of a hunt—I already know that tonight's full moon celebration is going to suck.

The way they all do for me these days, and tonight there's no hoping that the rise of a long-prophesized death goddess might shift attention off my various failures for a time, like it did for the past couple of months. We fought her and we won, and now I almost miss the crazy bitch, sunk back down deep beneath Crater Lake where she belongs.

Vinča, destroyer of worlds and princess of pestilence, was an excellent distraction from the narrowing window that is my life.

I'm already late. I can feel the moon's power up above me in the cold November sky, rising high and sending out its silver beckoning deep into bone and blood. The *bitten*—those turned into werewolves instead of born—will already have succumbed. They'll already be roaming down from the hills and into the places where the humans hide, in search of tasty prey.

I'm *blood*, not *bitten*, and that means I get to choose whether or not to surrender to the moon's seductive pull. My toxic trait is imagining that this means I should get to make my own decisions in other arenas too.

I think of my forbidding mother's narrow gaze and grim mouth, and sigh. This is the same female who once told me that if it were up to her (it wasn't), she would have broken my legs to keep me home where I belonged so there'd be none of what she calls—to this day—my *entitled disrespect.*

That was back when I was eighteen and leaving for college, the first wolf in my pack—in any of the packs that roam North America, no big deal—to ever do such a strange, inconceivably human thing. *The first wolf who would* want *to,* my mother said derisively.

I decide not to think about her anymore when I'll be seeing her shortly. Just like I do my best not to think about Ty either, while I'm at it, because his pull on me makes the moon's seem almost silly.

The truth is, there are very few moments in a day where I'm not thinking about Ty Ceridwen. The leader of our pack and the *Rix* of the Western Wolves. Which is an old way of saying he's the king.

He's also the bane of my existence.

Not to mention, the love of my life. The asshole.

I should hurry down the last and steepest part of the overgrown path that leads to what looks—to humans and other poor, powerless creatures—like the ruins of an abandoned mine tucked away out here in the Coastal Range that marks the western edge of the Rogue Valley, the southernmost valley in western Oregon down by what used to be the California state line. I should duck inside the dire-looking exterior, bare my teeth at the sentries though I'm still wearing skin instead of fur, and surrender to the inevitable shit show I know is waiting for me on the other side.

I should, but I don't.

I stop and investigate the carcass instead, because I don't want to face my pack on another full moon night when I don't intend to comply. And also because everything about the mess in the middle of the trail is weird.

The location, first of all. Humans might have spent centuries unaware of the fact that werewolves live this close to them in their pretty little Old West towns, where they imagined they could strip the hills of gold and steal the most fertile land, blah blah blah, happily ever after human-style. But we were always here. And the *bitten* werewolves wouldn't dare risk pack displeasure and punishment by littering their kills around. I would be able to smell the *bitten* signature scent if any of them had been that stupid tonight. Meanwhile, the other kinds of creatures who kill for fun know better than to provoke us and aren't generally foolish enough to get their kicks *right here*.

Not just in werewolf territory, but essentially at our front door.

I crouch down and take a moment to figure out the scent profile. There's so much blood that it's hard to tell what animal it is at a glance or even a quick inhale. It would be easier if I shifted into my wolf form, but I don't. I can't. The moon is too full, and it would be too easy for me to get caught up in it, this close to the den. Then there would be no avoiding the inevitable.

I swallow back the driving urge to *just surrender* that's with me all the time now, no matter how much I pretend otherwise, and rely on the pretty spectacular sense of smell that's still available to me in my human form instead. It's safer.

I take a deep breath in and realize that it's a skunk, though it didn't spray before it was killed. That's weird enough, but there's something else I don't like about it.

I frown down at the remains. *The positioning*, I think. That's what keeps poking at me. The fact that someone—or something—went to great lengths to *place* the kill here. And to leave it the way they placed it, like some grisly art exhibition in the dark November woods. When it really doesn't make a lot of sense to kill a small mammal, dissect it, and leave what meat there is in the end of a cold fall to steam into the night.

Most things that hunt and kill small mammals are hungry when it's this cold, not out to make artistic statements.

It feels like a message, and even though this is nothing but a poor, hapless skunk, I know better than to ignore the kind of message that comes with entrails.

I inhale the scent again, but it's not the smell of death that bothers me. That's natural. There's something else to it that I can't quite name. All I know is that it makes my hackles rise, which in this form means the back of my neck prickles and goose bumps shiver down my arms. I'm wearing a tank top, so I can see them. It might be December tomorrow, but I'm still a wolf. I don't get cold.

Though whatever it is about this skunk, it's making me more shivery than I'd like.

I stand up again and look around me, keeping still enough that I can hear the murmuring of the forest.

I'm not afraid of the woods. That's a human thing, and fair enough, because chances are, they would be eaten the minute they step three feet into a bunch of trees. There's no telling what lurks out here at any given moment these days, but again. It doesn't make sense that anything would be lurking *here*, specifically.

In the woods, yes. In the woods outside the wolf den where the most powerful wolf in this part of North America lives? Unlikely.

I know that *something* must be lurking, not only because I can feel that little tingle of awareness but because the kind of creatures that typically hunt and kill—and I'm one of them—might do it for fun. But they'd enjoy the snack when they were done, and no one does that in the middle of a wolf path when the moon is high.

Unless they're psycho. I can suddenly see Vinča's creepy minions in my head, plague masks and cloaks and too much blood on an altar stone.

Suddenly it seems creepier out here than before, and I decide I'd rather deal with the usual melodramatic banshees than whatever this is. I start moving down the path again, but I can't get that torn-up little creature out of my mind or the way it seemed *placed* on this path for me to find.

Specifically me, because every other wolf around here is either one of the *bitten*, who would have been turned into a terror at moonrise, or *blood* like me and therefore already gathered with the rest of the pack. I'm the only wolf who's always late. That's not a secret.

I'm also the only wolf who lives apart from the pack. I'm the only one who has to make my way over here instead of simply rolling out of my private den into the communal caverns.

Leave earlier, my frosty mother suggested the last time I pointed that out. *Or are you too addicted to making a spectacle of yourself?*

That's Johanna Hemming for you. She never bothers to lift a claw when she can use her words instead. But all of that is pack shit, and given that I'm about to walk into the greatest possible expression of pack shit there is, I need to make sure I remember to tell Ty what I saw out here.

When he's in the mood to listen to me again, that is. After the full moon it usually takes him a minute.

But now that I think about it, the way the skunk was ripped apart and splayed open reminds me a little of that black magic crap that the death goddess's freaky minions liked to play with. All those blood sacrifices and ponderous rituals that they found so important in the run-up to Halloween.

It reminds me of them—but they should be gone. Like she is.

Like she's supposed to be.

It's easier to be a wolf. You chase or are chased. You eat or are eaten. Tooth and claw, howl and hunt—wolves are simple creatures, really. Even wolves with too many *ideas,* like me.

This is what I tell myself as I make it to the old mine's entrance. It looks like a ruined, run-down piece of shit, the way it's supposed to. A derelict, blackened structure that should have fallen to pieces years ago and might still, at any moment.

I walk to the front door, or what's left of it, and make my way into the unappealing rooms within. Debris is strewn about, looking dirty and even a little dangerous. It looks like fires have been stamped out, questionable parties thrown, and there's even graffiti on the walls.

All lies, of course. Smoke and mirrors.

Any creature that dares to spend any time between these walls uninvited never leaves again. Wolves take territory seriously.

On the other side of the creaky, treacherous wood floor, I open another door and I'm outside again, in the narrow space between the godforsaken old house and the hill behind it. The old mineshaft is still propped up overhead, defying gravity with every passing second.

I don't look around for the sentries I know are watching me. I don't need to, because they make sure that I can hear them growling as I saunter by. My special little greeting from my people, so sweet.

I give them the finger and a little smile for good measure, and then, between two giant rocks that make it look as if nothing could be behind them but more rock, I slip into the shadow that is really an opening and enter the den itself.

Legend has it that the first wolves built our cave system long before the miners showed up. Then they watched and waited as the rude, foolish humans built the pack a perfect little camouflage. As a thank-you, the wolves ate the whole mining company. A celebratory snack.

We tell our young this story around the fires when we gather, embellishing it more and more each time, so that a little wolfling might labor under the impression that "miner" is another word for "meat." Something that does not go over well in human public schools, as I know from experience.

As I navigate my way into the narrow passage, deliberately unlit, I can already hear the howling and the barking from up above, high on the top of this hill that is too treacherous for anyone to climb without four legs and the sort of supernatural athleticism werewolves are all born with. It's all sheer rock and treacherous crevasses. It keeps us safe. It keeps us hidden.

It also keeps us in the Stone Age, but no one likes it when I say that.

I can smell roast meat, venison if I'm not mistaken, because on full moon night there's always a feast. For those who run, but also for those who need to stay behind. The old and infirm. The pregnant females. The young. I can hear the drums from up above. Down here, there's music. Wolves love a full moon party. I used to myself, before I was old enough to understand what it would mean for me.

The caves roll out in all directions, covering miles beneath the lush Oregon wilderness, but the main cavern is where we come together.

This is where *blood* werewolves operate our tight community and raise our families, exactly the way we've been doing since the dawn of time.

Wolves live a long time. And they don't like change.

I keep finding this out the hard way.

Inside the main cavern I see the very young, the very old, and the very, very pregnant sitting on the many couches and lying on the floor. In case I'm tempted to think it's only the more active members of the pack who resent me, the moment I step inside and everyone scents my presence, I can hear a little more of that quiet growling.

Not *loud* growling. Nothing *aggressive*. No one would actually *come for me*. No one would dare mess with something that's Ty's. They're just sending a message, like their version of an artistically eviscerated skunk.

I was born the long-awaited mate to the king himself, because that's how it goes in werewolf packs. Every king gets a fated mate. If he doesn't, he's not a real king, though there's usually a century or so of leeway on that. If she dies, he sometimes gets another. If you believe the myths, it's the moon who makes these decisions as it suits her, letting the males fight to the death for their position and then presenting winners with a worthy female to stand by their side, produce their young, and keep the den in line while the males are away.

They knew I was coming before I arrived. They could scent me on the wind.

But then they got *me*.

Expectations are a bitch.

I nod at the old ones, because it's never a weakness to show respect, especially if they're already not pleased with me. I smile at the little cubs who are tumbling around, switching in and out of their forms as they go, roughhousing it up with abandon. And I nod my head at the pregnant females—trying to make it clear that not wanting to become *just like them* doesn't mean that I think I'm *better* than them, just different.

I can see they don't believe it.

I greet them all, but I don't stop. I keep going and I climb the stairs that wind around the cavern walls and lead to a door near the top. This, too, would be easier on four legs, but I can't risk it. Two months ago I came much too close to losing my head on a different mountain, Ty and me in wolf form and that moon madness gripping me hard—

Luckily, that night there was that terrible, bloody ritual, horrible death goddess minions to fight, and the new local oracle—my friend and landlord Winter Bishop—to try to save. Enough distractions that I didn't forget myself.

Better to stay in skin tonight.

I push my way through the door. It opens onto the top of the hill, where we gather for the moon every month. The moon that makes us and marks us. The moon that guides us and watches us.

The moon who does with us as she will.

It's loud out here, and for a moment I stand near the jagged rocks that hide this upper entrance to the caves below. My pack is spread out all over the hilltop, basking in the moonlight and the cool night air. There's a part of me that loves this place and these people. Exactly as it is right now. The laughter. The carousing. The *pack* of it all.

This is where I grew up. This is where I played as a cub. These caves are where I slowly came to understand that Ty Ceridwen, so golden and powerful, and nothing short of *astonishing* even to a child, was mine.

These are my people, rough and wild.

Before the Reveal, Ty and his lieutenants—some of those being my brothers and cousins, and no, they don't support me, because loyalty to Ty and to pack comes first—hid in plain sight out there in the human world. They were outlaw bikers, causing a commotion wherever they went. They fought. They did their share of carousing. They involved themselves in all manner of things, most of it what humans consider *shady*.

Then again, it was only ever the human biker gangs who got caught and thrown in prisons.

Wolves have bigger teeth.

Out in the human world, they all looked like big, powerful men with tattoos and bad attitudes, alarmingly afraid of nothing at all. They liked loud Harleys, easy sex, and the ability to do whatever the hell they wanted, whenever the hell they wanted to do it.

They still do.

Back then they also ran protection for various not-exactly-legal industries all up and down the West Coast, from the ocean to the Rockies. Now it doesn't matter much what's legal, because there's no one around to do anything about it. After the Reveal, while many other creatures were enjoying the all-you-can-eat buffet that was suddenly on hand everywhere, the wolves were thinking ahead.

Or Ty was. He wasn't thinking about stuffing his face like everyone else. He was thinking about supply chains.

He's the reason there's food in the valley, along with most other conveniences that not only humans rely on. Him and the relationship he built with a few manky creek-side mages out in Eagle Point. He's also why other pockets of wolves across the continent are similarly positioned to weather whatever storms might come in their areas, though he couldn't do that himself. He could only share what he'd done out here with the rest of the packs.

North America is divided into pack territories. It's only in the past fifty years or so that these packs have stopped trying to murder each other and have maintained a peace treaty. This isn't just so that wolves can trot around, howling at the moon without having to fight over where they're doing it. It's also because werewolves like power. Money before the Reveal, control after, and more of both if we're not at war with ourselves.

No one's better at this than Ty, but that's another point of contention between us.

I step out from the protection of the rocks before everyone catches my scent and starts some new narrative about how *Maddox Hemming can't even come to the full moon gathering on time and then tries to hide when she does.* I move across the hilltop, the moonlight like a spotlight. I walk like I crave the shine.

The moon up above isn't quite to its highest point tonight. Not yet.

But we can all feel it coming.

On regular nights the *bitten* women hang out up here or in the adults-only parts of the caves, talking and dancing and fucking around—I mean that literally—with the full-blooded wolves. *Blood* wolves are mostly male. I was the only full-blooded female born into this pack in more than forty years, just to pile on those expectations. When male wolves want to mate, they have to depend on finding females from other packs.

They used to go on raiding parties and take the females they wanted, but we've evolved. Or so we like to claim.

These days, all the North American wolf packs gather every five years to sort out things like territory disputes, protection capacity on different routes, enemies who need a more comprehensive spanking, and mating bids. The next gathering will be here, when the Wolf Moon is new next month, and it will run straight through to the winter solstice.

Wolf week, I like to call it. *I* think I'm hilarious.

Male wolves will use the week to fight for the available females. Theoretically any female can decline a mating at will, but in practice, that would cause a pack war. It never happens.

Most female wolves are better behaved than me.

On the other hand, no one will be fighting over me, either. They never have and they never will. Everyone knows I'm Ty's and only Ty's.

So really, *I* have nothing to complain about, as Johanna always reminds me. She was stolen by my father from one of the Canadian packs, and the way she carries herself reminds me of the stories she used to tell when I was small. Stories all about the place she came from. Winter forever. Very little warmth. Sharp, overbearing mountains and ice stuck to her fur like daggers.

A lot like her gaze sticks to me now from across the hilltop, but I don't look that way for long.

Ty is sitting on the rocks on the far side of the hilltop up above everyone else, and I can't help but look at him. He's lounging on the highest rock like it's a cozy sofa, still wearing his skin, and not for the first time in my life—or even the first time *today*—I'm forced to contend with the fact that I find this man irresistible no matter what form he's in.

Man. Wolf. Both. All.

I was fucked before I was born. Full-on fated mate *fucked.*

It could be worse. At least he's hot.

Though *hot* doesn't do him justice. He's the biggest male here. He measures over six foot five in his human form, and he's much, much bigger in fur. He's wearing a ripped black T-shirt and old jeans, his feet in his favorite motorcycle boots, and the rest of him is nothing short of a festival of hard muscle. He's beautiful, covered in ink that adores him like everyone else here, all of it highlighting his dark-gold splendor.

His hair is like gold at night, long and thick when I grip it. He's wearing it back tonight, but it never stays there. His beard makes him look both less pretty than he really is, with those remarkable cheekbones that could make another man seem angelic, and significantly more dangerous even in relaxing moments like this would be if we weren't us and tonight wasn't a full moon.

His mouth is a sacrament and, like a sacrament, is often cruel. Deliciously cruel, exceptionally mobile. And usually dirty as hell.

Everyone can see that he's ripped. I know *exactly* how ripped, because I've had my own mouth on every single part of his fascinating body. More times than I could begin to count. There's no part of him I haven't climbed, worshipped, or both.

Nothing makes me feel more like the typical sweet, soft, subservient wolfling girl I'm not than Ty. He's the only thing that ever has, if I'm honest. But that's private.

As usual, even glancing at him pokes that simmering fire that's always inside of me and always about him. Ty is heat and fury, a mighty howl, and a bottomless longing within me. Before he was all of that, he was still there. As a new cub, when I was fractious, he alone could soothe me. As I got older, long before there was anything sexual between us, I still felt drawn to him.

I knew he was mine before I knew what that meant.

And even though I know he was fully aware I was here before I set foot into that falling-down building—he can feel me wherever I am, the same way I can feel him, and that's less a superpower than a curse sometimes—he deliberately doesn't look at me now.

Just a little slap to remind me of my place. Luckily for me, I like it rough. I like *him* rough, even when I know he's furious with me. Maybe especially then.

We fight fire with fire, Ty and me. We've been doing it for years.

I stay where I am, standing there outside the ring around the fire with my head slightly bent toward the rock where he's sitting. It's a show of respect, because no one can join the pack without the king's acknowledgment.

I don't mind it when he takes his time. He needs to show everybody else that he's not as pussy-whipped as the very daring have been known to suggest—though never directly *to* him, of course. No one's that suicidal.

The truth about Ty Ceridwen is that he does what the fuck he wants when the fuck he wants, the end.

In the outside world, he's all leather and threat. In these hills, he's the king, undefeated by all challengers for a hundred years. In bed—or anywhere else we might find ourselves—he's demanding. Endlessly creative. Gloriously sure of himself, and me.

Tonight, when he finally deigns to look at me, his gaze pounds into me like a blow.

He does that on purpose too.

I need to talk to him about that poor skunk, but I can tell by the way he's lounging there—his dark, brooding gaze on me like he already knows how this night is going to go and is already deciding how he'll punish me for it—that it's not particularly wise to try his patience now.

When he inclines his head just enough that I can call it an acknowledgment, I move into the crowd instead.

Males with mates are hunkered down with them, always touching, their gazes loaded with the run they have ahead of them. Full moons are the only times female wolves are fertile. And we can only be fertile in wolf form.

That's why I've been avoiding full moons with Ty for years now. Because if I run with him, he will complete the ritual that was my fate before I was born. He will claim me beneath the full moon, no doubt knock me up, and that will be that. The only wolf to ever have gone to college, learning the human world from the inside out, will be relegated to litters, nursing, demure smiles from my place behind him, and den politics ad nauseum.

That's how it's always been. That's how it will always be, unless someone changes it. And since no one else around here seems to even imagine there could possibly be a better way, I guess that in addition to requiring my *fated mate* to like *me*, personally, instead of what I represent to him—I might also have to mount a small revolution.

But that's getting ahead of myself.

Right now I have to survive the night, which is easier said than done when I can feel the moon all over me like Ty was earlier, making me want to give him whatever he wants. Making me ask myself why on earth I wouldn't when I can *feel* him still, his handprints on my ass, his bite marks on my neck, and I know that he would make all those demure smiles and tiny-stakes domestic battles feel good. Making me wonder if everyone is right and there's something wrong with me, after all—because I can't stop fighting the fate that I've always known will claim me, in the end.

The gorgeous werewolf king who's obsessed with me who I couldn't stay away from if I tried.

And it's only a matter of time before fate stops waiting and takes what it wants.

Ty too.

2.

Since contemplating my doom is such a thrill, I decide to amp the whole thing up with some overdue family time.

My three older brothers and a handful of my cousins are kicked back on one of the rocks near Ty, one of the perks of being in the group of Ty's lieutenants. His vice president, Connor, is not directly related to me, which I assume is why he's not glaring at me like all the ones who are. At the moment, anyway.

They still operate like a motorcycle club, a shift in previously long-standing pack policy that came about when Ty won his position a hundred years ago and, shortly after, recognized exactly how he could use the growing biker subculture to promote the pack's best interests. He got a lot of pushback, because there's always pushback from the other pack kings, and werewolves *really* don't like change, but he prevailed.

He always prevails.

I feel that same prickle on the back of my neck as I think that, more confirmation that I'm doing nothing but delaying the inevitable. He'll win. I know he will. That isn't the point.

I tell myself that isn't the fucking point, but I find it hard to remember when I'm here, neck-deep in pack and pack politics and all the parts of these things that I love against my will. I love them—or what they could be—so much I want to make them better, for all of us, though no one sees it that way.

Not even my own family. Maybe especially not them.

Everything in the pack is based on hierarchy. And even though I'm Ty's fated mate and everyone has always known this, I haven't actually, officially mated with him yet.

Fucking him constantly in skin and fur but without the power and seal of the full moon doesn't count.

What this means for me is that I retain my only bargaining chip with Ty. What this means to my family is that they can't claim the power and status they feel entitled to. My brothers and cousins fought their way into Ty's circle, because that's the only way to become the trusted seconds of the king. It's always about blood spilled and blood avenged. Creatures of tooth and claw require proof in red to trust anything.

My brothers and cousins view my refusal to seal the deal with Ty as disrespect.

My uncles, too old or otherwise compromised to serve Ty bodily, are waiting for my ascension so they can reclaim the bragging rights they lost when their glory days passed. My mother and aunts, on the other hand, have to wait for me to do my moon-given duty before they can assume their rightful positions in the pack. Females fight dirtier than males, and not always with their paws.

Johanna feels she has been slighted every day, by every female in the pack, because she cannot assume her rightful position as celebrated mother of the *actual* queen until I become that queen. And therefore she cannot take revenge on all the females who she feels were unkind to her when she was brought into this pack in the first place.

My mother's greatest weapons are her infallible and extremely detailed memory. And enough spite to flood this whole valley. Maybe the world.

Family time has been fraught with peril since I was young, since most of my relatives have been pissed at me since the day I bled the first time, catapulting me into womanhood according to all the old ways, and yet failed to immediately secure my place at Ty's side.

I was only thirteen.

It's really not such a big surprise that five years after that, I took the escape hatch marked *college* and bolted for the East Coast.

I thought I'd never come back.

But this place has its hooks in me. You can't choose the things you love. You can't make your heart obey when it refuses to hate the place that made you.

Believe me, I've tried.

I let the drums work their way inside me. The drums and the fire and the occasional howls of celebration, and I'm too much of a wolf not to admit that this gets to me. I might not like pack politics or my family's dynamics, and I've grown to hate the weight of the expectations on me, but there's something about waiting for the full moon to hit just right.

It makes me remember exactly who I am. It lets me *feel* the power in me. The power the moon gave me, like new blood inside me. A different, better homecoming.

I haven't run beneath a full moon in a long time.

I can feel the urge inside me the way I always do. It's a drumbeat all its own. It feels the way Ty makes me feel—and it's all wrapped up together. Longing for the change, the lightning burst into fur. Desperate to run as hard and as fast as I can, barreling through these woods and deeper into the mountains, free and whole and covered in moonlight.

The longing for him, too. To meet him in our wolf forms on a night like this and let that magic I know we have between us explode, taking us to a place I'm not sure I can really imagine.

I know that it will change us, that claiming. What I don't know is how.

Much as I like to pretend it isn't there, down deep there's that part of me that's just a girl. A wolfgirl who was taught from birth that her greatest purpose in life was to carry the king's babies and make this pack stronger.

It's not that I don't want those things. I just want them in *my* time, not anyone else's.

I feel certain a woman can have any number of great purposes.

I have to physically restrain myself from looking back toward Ty, then. I don't need to catalog his expressions when he looks at me to know how sick of my shit and my timeline and my *resistance* he is. He's made that clear.

Most recently earlier this afternoon, when he found me in the little cottage where I live, down in Jacksonville on the oracle's land, something I decided I should do back when we all believed we'd have to trick Winter into figuring out her visions of the rising death goddess.

Ty was not exactly thrilled with that choice, mostly because he knew perfectly well that the main reason I'd made it was to distance myself from the pack. From him.

Again.

When he showed up this afternoon, he held me down, pinning my wrists high up over my head while refusing to sink deep inside of me, and he got directly in my face.

Up close, no matter how pissed he is, he's even more beautiful than he is at a distance. It's truly unfair.

Tonight, Maddox, he growled at me. *I'm not playing with you anymore.*

So I bit him.

I gave him something else to worry about. He gave me a number of ways to repent for that choice. And we ended up the way we always do. Sweaty and torn open and tangled around each other like we were supposed to be fused into one from the start. Like maybe the moon got it wrong.

I can feel him watching me as I move around the fire, making my way across the hilltop. I feel him the way I always do. His gaze, the weight of it—he might as well have his hand wrapped around my throat.

I can feel that, too, and my whole body goes hot at the image. The memory. The anticipation.

Still, I don't look back.

There's too much wolf in me tonight, teeth bared and pressed *just there* beneath the surface. I'm too close to forgetting myself.

I wind my way through the crowd. And the pack might like to growl to indicate they think I'm falling down on the job of being Ty's queen—which isn't unfair, it just isn't as black and white as they'd like to believe—but they're still my pack. I'm still theirs, they're still mine.

I get smiles and hugs now that I'm within reach. Heads tipped to mine. Those already wearing their fur whine slightly and butt their snouts against me. Unlike humans, wolves touch. This is how we remind ourselves who we are. This is why this place and these people were so hard for me to leave.

This is why I came home instead of running away, every summer. This is how I entangled myself with Ty in ways that can never be undone, when the smart move would have been to get on a plane and fly to a wolfless place and let them figure it out however they could in my absence.

I missed my chance on the planes, thanks to the Reveal. Any wolfless places out there are now firmly out of reach.

When I get to where my family sits, they're lounging around in their usual configuration toward the back of the gathering. The better to highlight my family's elevated status. To indicate they're not like everyone else milling around—though not as *clearly* not like them as they'd prefer.

My uncles squeeze my hands as I pass. My aunts press their shoulders against mine. They all murmur their greetings without the hint of a reproving growl.

Up close, it's sometimes hard to remember why I go to such lengths to steer clear of these people. And it would be so easy to simply drift into the familiar, the expected, here. It would feel good. It would be celebrated.

And then, I remind myself sharply, *you'll look around one day and realize that you've made a whole life that has nothing to do with you.*

Mates of kings have status, but they're still just mates.

Wolf packs are about the males. That's the way it's always been. That's the way everyone thinks it always will be. Females are good for sex, breeding, and raising the young. They are known for tempests in teapots and other such "dramas" that the males can dismiss. Condescendingly, of course.

I learned a lot of words and phrases for this kind of environment when I was in college, but I quickly discovered that no one here wants to listen to a lecture from the one female around who doesn't have to follow the rules.

Yet, my uncle Ezra said one summer, his gaze hard on me. *You don't have to follow rules* yet, *girl, because Ty gives you too much leeway. That won't last.*

I pretend I can't remember how satisfied he looked, in advance, that a comeuppance was en route. Better to promote family harmony than the alternative, which I sometimes think might explode out of me like a comet when I least expect it.

My mother lives on spite, but sometimes I think I'm made of rage. At least we have that much in common.

Johanna Hemming rises from where she sits, the widowed mate of a celebrated high-ranking lieutenant who died in a skirmish before I was born, everything about her elegant and chilly though most wolves run hot. Even the hair that cascades down her back, inky black and straight, seems like a rebuke of my many excesses and betrayals. Not to mention my waves and curls.

She kisses each of my cheeks in turn, but I'm close enough to her that I can see how cold her gaze is. The kisses are for show. They're for the rest of the pack, not me.

"I hope you plan to stop embarrassing us tonight," she says as she pulls away. She sits down on the smooth, flat stone behind her and nods to the stone beside it, but it's not an invitation. It's an order.

And she's doing it to humiliate me. Because she and I and every other wolf in the Rogue Valley know that she doesn't hold rank over me, whether she's my mother or not.

This is the bloody, beating heart of all our problems.

If she could control me, she would have, and long ago. But I was Ty's, not hers, and that's always meant that only he can tell me what to do. Johanna has never liked the fact that, as far as she can tell from my lack of a crown, he indulges me endlessly.

Little does she know what prices he exacts for his patience.

There are some things even notoriously free and open and casually sexual wolves don't share.

I remind myself that in college, I didn't just learn how to beat humans at their own game. I also learned that the way to do that best was to remain calm above all things, and not to sweat the small stuff.

So I sit. I let her head be higher than mine, because I know it makes her feel important.

What I also know is that it makes me look like the bigger person for allowing this to happen. It makes me look like I can't be bothered to engage in power struggles, suggesting I have better things to worry about—and also that I'm not the least bit concerned about my status.

This makes me seem even more powerful, and I know it.

My degree was in political science and business, but it might as well have been in strategy.

"I'm sorry that you feel embarrassed," I murmur once Johanna has finished pretending *not* to look around to see who might be witnessing her little power play. When my aunt offers me a beer, I take it. The night all around us is cold and littered with stars, but here on the hill, it's hot. I can feel the sweat on my skin, and when I prop the beer bottle on my thigh, I can see the ring of condensation it makes against the faded denim of my jeans.

"The moon is nearly high," my mother says, as if that isn't something we can all feel like moon-shaped timepieces inside of us, ticking away.

Johanna is an imperious woman. In her skin, she terrifies the humans. In her fur, they mostly die of heart attacks before she gets around to biting them. Male wolves still sniff around her, looking for a way in—but though she'll run, she rarely lets them catch her. She hasn't changed her form yet so I let my gaze move over her tattoos, full sleeves on her bared arms and that raven on her throat. I can't see them tonight, but I know that they're all over her back and legs, too.

I have my own tattoos, incantations and wild magic pressed into the skin we only wear some of the time. Before the Reveal, humans interpreted this as threatening, no matter how many tattoos they sported themselves.

These days, they can tell who we are by the way our eyes look in the light sometimes, like gold. And all of our usually wild hair. And . . . the way we are.

Reckless by their standards. Outlaws then, monsters now. I guess it shows.

I sneak a look across the fire toward Ty. He's big and brawny, all of that dirty-blond hair that's always a little bit messy, and that beard, and when he moves he has a swagger that tells everyone and everything in a ten-mile radius that he's the alpha. He doesn't have to say a word. He just is.

Smart people have always given him a very wide berth, but me? I'm either running to him or away from him, but there's never that much space.

He catches me looking and, for a moment, there's a pulse of that blistering heat between us. I feel it curl all around me like he's pinning me to a bed again from across the top of this hill.

It's not as if it's easy to refuse the call of the moon. I don't actually enjoy pissing off my family, letting down my pack, and making Ty feel betrayed again and again.

Not that anyone ever asks me why. They just tell me what an asshole I am.

"I can feel how high the moon is, Mother," I say lightly, that ticking inside me so loud now it's all I can think about. "Can you imagine being moon numb? I think I'd rather be dead."

"It might come to that," Johanna replies, hard as fucking nails.

"I love you too," I murmur.

She turns her head to look at me, her eyes dark. I brace myself for whatever she's going to hit me with, but she doesn't get the chance.

The drums get louder. We can all feel it, that surge deep inside.

In the distance, we can hear the young cubs and the old ones howl from inside the cavern. Farther still, the thin howls from the *bitten*. Even the regular wolves join in, some of them already here on the hill with us—not exactly pets. More like companions.

This is the moment we wait for every moon. The pack begins to howl too.

I can feel it inside me, like a song I can't help but sing, flowing through me, opening me up, desperate to make me *exactly* who I'm meant to be—

But I wrench myself back. I tamp it down, and it hurts.

It always hurts. It's always hard.

I fight until I think I have it under control and when I do, I find Ty's gaze on me again from the other side of the hilltop.

Suddenly, he's all I can focus on. That forbiddingly gorgeous face of his. His mouth in a grim line. His dark eyes flashing.

All around us, the sound of the drums is replaced by the thunderclap bursts of energy as *blood* wolves shed their skin, bristling and stretching and *becoming* into their fur. When they do, they howl louder.

I can feel my body shake because it wants so badly to change. I can feel the heat between my legs, the power in my blood, and the song in me that connects me to the moon, and my pack, and most of all, Ty himself.

His eyes are dark and gleam like gold, but they have that ring of indigo at the edge, and I can feel him all over me, commanding me to do this thing at last. *At last.*

But I still don't change.

I am vaguely aware of wolves all around me. All fur and claw now, they run.

They pour down the steep sides of the hill and take off in all directions. They run for the pleasure of it. They run for the moon. I can see what they're doing in a different part of my brain, bursting out into the night, covered in moonlight and catapulting themselves into the pure joy of it all.

They will run and run until they drop. Some of them will drop together, the males mounting their females, biting down hard on their necks and then thrusting in deep. Sometimes this is simply sex, though it comes with the possibility of young, thanks to a full moon night. Sometimes this is mating between a bonded couple.

When I finally take this run with Ty, it will be a claiming. A howl to the moon, answered in the shine around us and the way he will mark me with his teeth, his claws, and when we are done, the crown tattoo he will place on my throat.

A sign to anyone who can't scent the truth that I am his.

I can feel it as if it's already happening. As if the claiming that I refuse to accept is already a part of me, a memory that hasn't occurred yet. I can feel Ty on my back, hot and heavy, and his snout in my ear, that enormous cock of his driving deep and then swelling inside me until we're stuck, tied up tight—

Once again, I have to fight, hard, to bring myself back to skin. These bones that are not a wolf's shape and that I won't let stretch, though they ache. The stone beneath me and the breath inside me and whatever the hell else I need to do to keep myself in this human form while the moon and my own desires fight against me.

It goes on and on.

It feels like an eternity. One by one, in bursts and dribbles and mad, wild rushes, all the wolves in our pack disappear into the night. The regular wolves follow.

Only Ty remains. Ty and me, his recalcitrant queen.

Neither one of us moves. He is still waiting, lounging there on that high rock that might as well be a throne. I wouldn't call it *pleading*, much as I'd like to. The way he's looking at me is too demanding.

Too furious.

I can feel my pulse like the drums that aren't beating any longer. It pounds inside my veins, and I know he can hear it too.

I still don't move. I can feel my eyes watering. I can feel my muscles aching from the force of will it takes to keep them in one place. In one body. *Here.*

We can both feel it when the moon shifts, just that little bit. Just enough.

The moment is lost.

Because the full moon run has to start at the moment the moon is at its height. If it doesn't, it won't count.

This is how we both know the very instant I've betrayed him once again.

I let out a deep breath.

Ty lets out a howl that sounds more like a roar.

Then he's on me. I don't even see him move. One moment he's across the hilltop, high on that rock, and the next he's *here.*

"You little shit," he growls, his face and that beard in my neck, his impossibly strong arms hauling me up from the stone until I'm hanging there, my toes off the ground. "Fuck you, Maddox. You know the gathering is coming up. I wanted my fucking queen before the solstice."

I want to melt. I fight instead. "Then earn her, Ty."

He doesn't like that much.

He bites me, there on my neck. And as I throw my head back—heat and desire and that slick, impossible heat rushing through me—he sets me down and turns me so I'm facing away from him. He hooks an arm around my middle and holds me back toward him, against that massive, ripped chest of his.

Then he takes us both down to our knees.

I can feel his hard, dangerous hands on my jeans. He pulls them down, out of his way, and his rough fingers find me so wet and so ready that he grunts his approval even though he's furious with me.

By the time he makes room for his cock and presses the thick tip against me, I'm sobbing out his name.

He's over my back, pressing down on me so that I'm on all fours now. He's mimicking the thing I won't give him while the moon is full, and he's doing it deliberately, and the trouble with Ty is that his punishments feel too good.

"You don't deserve it," he growls at me, his mouth at my ear. "You don't want my cock when it matters, why should you have it any other time?"

"Because it's mine," I throw back at him.

I can feel as well as hear the way he groans at that. Because the only saving grace in this shared fate of ours is that he's as powerless as I am when it comes to this. To us.

Fated means we're both fucked.

He slams himself into me, hard.

And he's not a small man. He's always big and thick and wide enough to make me feel stretched. To give me that moment of near-pain before the wild delight floods in, and it turns out, you can become addicted to that, too.

This is all the rage and longing, mad fury and desire, fate and betrayal and *go fuck yourself* that we take out on each other. This is raw and overwhelming and beautiful the way a storm is as it wrecks everything in its path.

It's not cute. It's not even the typical way he teases me, plays with me. He makes me his fuck toy tonight, and I know he thinks he's dominating me, but I like that too.

Then he groans, because I make him mine. I move my hips, I push back to take him deeper, and this is who we are. This struggle, this rush, all barbs and teeth, claws and bites and *yes*.

It's a full moon fuck, filled with a bold and battered longing for who we aren't, not yet. Who we can't be.

Who I won't let us be.

I come in a rush and he follows, scalding me from the inside out. He bites down hard on my neck, and I can smell my own blood, a coppery sheen in the air.

It makes me come all over again, and harder this time.

My throat is raw. That's how I know I was screaming his name.

In the aftermath, we're a tangle of skin and flesh and shoved-aside clothes, breathing too hard in the dirt.

I want to curl into him. I want to hold him and reassure him—and me—that we're going to be okay. That what I'm doing is the right thing, except I know that he doesn't think so.

That's why we keep coming back to this place again and again, and will keep coming back to it.

For a moment, that feels so heavy that I worry I might cry.

I sit up, wiggling to get my jeans back up and zipped. He grunts at me and runs his fingers through my hair, making a fist to hold me where I am.

"Where do you think you're going?" His voice is low, but he's not redline furious anymore.

This is the Ty I know best. The Ty I get in private. Resigned and not happy with me, sure. But still mine.

Always mine.

Nonetheless, I choose violence. It's that or sob.

"I don't like it here," I tell him, and watch his eyes blaze. "You know I don't. I came for the moon. I honored the full moon, and now I'm going home."

"Home?" His growl is edgy. Dangerous. "You don't have a home that's not with me, Maddox. You never will. Don't make me prove that to you in a way you really won't like."

3.

"Don't." I don't say that loud. It's more of a breath.

Ty doesn't back down, so I push away from him, entirely too aware that he lets me go. He watches me, his dark eyes assessing. Always appraising everything and everyone, and me most of all.

I learned a long time ago that he sees everything, and sometimes I've wished with every part of me that he didn't. Especially when the fact that he sees everything doesn't always mean he sees it my way.

He doesn't say anything as I shove the heavy weight of my hair away from my face. I sit back on my heels and look at him, still lying there, stretched out like some kind of god on a rest day in between playing games with worlds. His jeans are still shoved down, and he looks perfectly able to carry on a conversation with his cock hanging out. He is.

One thing about Ty is that he embodies the best parts of being a wolf. Part of that is having absolutely no shame. About anything, but especially his body.

Not that he *has* anything to be ashamed about, particularly not that cock of his that I can still feel—

But I can't let myself get distracted any more than I already have tonight. And when all I do is sit there and gaze back at him, he sighs. He buttons himself up and then props himself up on one elbow, still stretched out there beside me.

"Time is running out, babe." His voice is low. Serious. I can feel how serious like concrete inside me. "You know it as well as I do. You can feel it, same as I can." He doesn't look away from me as he takes his free hand and holds it over his chest, where I can feel the same longing and need in him that I have in me. "We're reaching the end of this grace period, whether you like it or not."

There's a moment here. A possibility for the radical honesty that I know he wants from me. I want it too. Or we both *say* we want it when the other one is in a different place, like that intimacy might shatter us both.

Anyway, that's what I tell myself. That's what I shy away from.

"You know it doesn't have anything to do with whether or not I like it," I say instead. I don't like the way he phrased that. Since it's part and parcel of the same story the pack likes to tell about me as it is. *Flighty Maddox. Selfish Maddox. Little Princess Maddox who takes and takes and never gives anything in return.*

Sometimes when I say things like that, it makes him mad. Tonight he sits up, reaches out, and puts a hand on my arm. "I didn't mean it like that."

I like Ty rough and overbearing. I like him wild, showing off all that power he wears so easily. I love him with his hands on me, twisting this passion between us whichever way he sees fit—and me with it.

But *this* Ty makes everything inside me . . . shimmer.

"Things have been a little intense lately," he acknowledges, still in that low, solemn way that makes that shimmering within me . . . brighten. "Death goddesses and oracles and vampires and shit. But at the end of the day, you know the only thing that matters is this. Us. I told you that a long time ago. It hasn't changed."

That hurts. He meant for it to hurt. "I know."

"This has always been a finite situation. And the shit's hitting the fan, baby. I know you know that too." His dark gaze is direct. Unflinching. "So what's it going to take? Because after all of these years, it's starting to seem like it's me you don't trust."

"That's not true."

Ty doesn't respond to that. He doesn't drop his hand, and he doesn't move closer. He just watches me, this massive, beautiful male who is already too many things to me. I can't count them all.

I blow out a breath. "It's not true," I say again. "Sometimes I think you're the only person I do trust."

His hard hand squeezes my arm, then drops. "But not enough, Maddox. Never enough."

Without him touching me, I can think a little bit better. But my heart hurts a whole lot more. I cross my arms over my chest like that will help. It doesn't.

"I'm not blind," I manage to say, though my throat feels tight. "I wouldn't be a worthy mate for the *Rix* if I couldn't comprehend the politics."

"Funny you say that." Ty's words are like bullets, and he doesn't miss when he shoots. "You had the opportunity tonight to solidify our standing ahead of the gathering of the packs, and you didn't do it. Explain that to me in a way that makes sense." His dark eyes blaze. "Because you know and I know that there are any number of motherfuckers out there who want nothing more than to crash into this valley and take me down. At what point do I stop protecting you and protect myself instead? Maybe even let you step up and offer to protect me for a change? When is that part going to happen?"

He lets that sit there for a long, long time. So long I think I almost feel the cold.

When it's clear I'm not going to say anything, he keeps going. "I've heard a lot, for years now, about what a partnership should look like. But all I see, all I ever see, is me taking heat."

My temper spikes at that, but I'm pretty sure it's just rushing out ahead of what I'm really feeling, which is shame. Because he's not wrong.

I wish he was.

"It has nothing to do with you." I grit that out.

"What I know is that you tell me that," he replies in that same implacable way that's making everything in me quiver, and not in the usual, fun way. "You keep telling me, Maddox." This time I think that dark flash in his eyes leaves burn marks all over my body and, worse, inside. He leans closer. "But I'm still the hundred-year king with no goddamned queen. I'd have to be a little bitch if I wasn't starting to wonder if maybe you don't have any intention of keeping the promises you made to me."

"I just need more time." I shrug as I say that, because it makes me feel something like helpless. I need more time because I know that it isn't the *right* time. Not yet.

I'm aware that I've been saying that for so long now. Too long now. It feels like ash on my own tongue.

"Time is running out," Ty says quietly. It hits me a lot harder than it would have if he'd shouted. If he'd come at me, wrapped his hand around my throat the way he likes to do—and the way I like him to do, to be clear—to growl straight up in my face.

Ty all quiet like this seems to settle in my bones like the kind of cold a werewolf isn't supposed to feel. Like it's already the darkest part of December inside me.

I push back and stand up, arms still crossed, but I feel restless. *Undone,* something whispers inside me, but I don't want to accept that. I look around the abandoned hilltop, empty of everyone now except the two of us. The fire still dances in the stone circle. The jagged rocks that so many of the pack use as stadium seating are empty. There's only the moon up above us, keeping her watch, and the inky dark of the night sitting heavy on the trees that stretch out all the way to the coast.

I remind myself that it really is December now, on this side of midnight. The Wolf Moon is coming. The all-pack gathering is happening. I don't need Ty to tell me that time is running out, because I can feel it myself.

Like it's been an hourglass all along and the very last bit of sand is on its way out.

"When your mother brought you to me because you bled that first time, what happened?" Ty asks, still where I left him, seemingly lounging on the ground.

He's not asking because he doesn't know the answer.

"We don't have to dredge up history," I mutter.

"Sure about that? I think we should, Maddox." There's a little more temper in his voice now, and I'm ashamed that I find it comforting.

I know what to do with his heat. It's his disappointment that breaks me, every time.

I'm now hugging myself more than crossing my arms for the sake of it. And I can't help my reflexive look toward the door that leads back down to the grand cavern, like all he has to do is bark out an order and even my memory obeys him.

Johanna wanted the spectacle. She wanted everyone to know—or to remember, maybe—that she alone had given birth to the girl who would be the next queen of the pack. She has always been exacting when it comes to upholding the old ways, especially if those old ways advance her position.

I suspect that's because she likes to think she survived the old ways more or less intact, so why shouldn't everyone else? Not that I'd dare psychoanalyze my mother to her face.

I was thirteen that night. A wolfling girl becomes a woman when she bleeds, and that's not inappropriate. Regular wolves reach sexual and social maturity a lot sooner. Humans later. Like most werewolf things, it all comes down to the blood.

Blood was the beginning and the end of it as far as my mother was concerned, and that night she herded me over from our part of the cavern to Ty's up in the front, nipping at my furry haunches when I tried to evade her.

It wasn't as if my bleeding was a secret. Everyone could scent it. Johanna wanted to make sure that the whole pack saw her delivering unto the king the queen that he was promised.

May this girl prove bountiful in all ways, my king, Johanna said with great formality, bowing down before him.

Everyone else in the cavern followed suit.

I stood there before him, not sure what the hell *I* was supposed to do.

Ty only looked at me, the biggest wolf I'd ever seen, and accepted me with a regal nod, letting me curl up there beside him for the rest of the night. It was an act of kindness I didn't have to entirely understand to appreciate.

Later that night, when the fires were low and there were the usual intimate noises in the shadows and snores from the couches, he woke me up from where I was dozing in his sleeping furs. Then he led me out of the grand cavern and back into the cave system, taking me down twisting, cold corridors until we reached his personal den.

Once there, he shifted into his human form and told me to do the same.

I remember sitting there before him in the outer room, perched on the edge of an armchair that smelled of him. I had only a rudimentary understanding of what was expected of me. My mother had pinched me and told me to *submit.* My aunts hadn't met my gaze when they'd told me that it wouldn't last long and I'd get used to it.

I could tell that they were all lying. I felt stretched thin and precarious over the top of some gaping abyss that everyone knew the contours of except me.

All I could do was sit there before Ty, who was looking down at me from his great height, and tell myself that I had to do all of those things—whatever they meant—and whatever else he asked of me too. Because everyone in my family had urged me not to embarrass them. To honor the family name.

Whatever the hell that was supposed to mean.

Ty only studied me for a moment, then made me hot chocolate.

We sat there in his living room like this was something we did all the time. It didn't feel out of character or strange to me. His den was tidy, smelling of him and the night and other good things. It lulled me the way his furs had, but then again, I'd never been afraid of him.

Do you know why they gave you to me tonight? he asked.

I hedged. *I think so.*

You've seen mating before. That wasn't a question. We were part of a wolf pack. There were no secrets, no shame. The only thing that had changed recently was that I'd begun to feel . . . *things* when I heard the noises. Or saw couples in the alcoves.

The reason that our ancestors did things the way they did is that they expected to die sooner, Ty told me. *They had no time to waste. But I don't intend to die for the next few hundred years or so. No matter what people might tell you, Maddox, there's no need for* you *to worry about anything until you're ready.*

I frowned at my hot chocolate and he saw it. Then he growled until I looked up.

You don't have to be afraid of me. You can tell me anything.

You're supposed to . . . want me, I told him. As awkward as I was serious. *That's what everyone said. That you were supposed to want me, and I was supposed to let you, and that would honor . . . everybody.*

I could see his mouth curl a little, under that beard. I remember thinking his dark gaze was like a tractor beam. I couldn't seem to do anything but stare back at him, until and unless he looked away. I had no control over it.

I do want you, he told me. Kindly.

That's what I remember the most. He told me that so very kindly. Ty, the rough-and-tumble outlaw king, was going out of his way to be careful with the feelings of a thirteen-year-old girl.

You do?

I do. He nodded at the mug I was holding. *Finish your hot chocolate. You don't need to worry about your honor. We're fine. You come to me when you're ready, Maddox. Not a minute before, no matter what anyone says.*

What if . . . I don't know what it means to be ready?

You will.

Then we sat there in what seemed to be a delightfully companionable silence until I was done with the hot chocolate. But when I went to leave, I turned back, struck by something.

My mother. She's going to need—

You can tell your mother this, Ty replied, his voice stern. *Her and anyone else. I'm a king. I want a queen, not a kid. And if they have anything else to say on the subject they can bring it up with me.*

I didn't like being called a kid, but I didn't argue. I told my mother exactly what Ty had said. She didn't like it either.

But what she really didn't like, it turned out, was that Ty meant it.

When he said that he was going to give me time, he really and truly *meant* it. He liked that I wanted to go to school. And while he maybe liked it less that I also wanted to go to college, he listened to me when I told him why. He let me give him an entire presentation about why I thought my being educated would be good for the pack. Why it would benefit the pack and promote our interests.

Sounds good. He'd been kicked back on this very hilltop after another full moon run that neither he nor I had participated in. *I like that you have a brain, Maddox. Still, I can't help thinking that the real reason you want to go away to school and play at being human for the next four years is that you're running away from this.*

I was eighteen then. All the young wolves I knew had been rolling around with each other in happy abandon for years now, but I was different. No one would touch what was Ty's. And I didn't like any of the human boys well enough to bother messing around with them, in accordance with very strict rules Ty had laid down when it came to that sort of mixing.

Control was everything. Penalties for exposure were dire. It seemed like too great a risk to take. Slip up and bite someone here in this small valley and there was no covering it up. Ty took that kind of thing very seriously.

I figured going off to college in a great big city meant I had a lot more leeway.

Staring at him that night, exposed on this hilltop in more ways than one, I could see that he knew exactly what I was thinking.

By that point, I knew better than to lie to him. It had nothing to do with his rank or mine. It had everything to do with the way he could read me.

Two things can be true at once, I said, after a moment. A long moment.

Fair enough, he replied. But he beckoned me closer and when I came, he pointed at the ground beside the rock he was sitting on, and I didn't know—then—what it was about that simple gesture that made something *click* inside of me.

What I did know was that kneeling there beside him made me feel . . . *alive.* More like me than I ever had before. I could feel my breath catch, too.

You're older now, Ty said. *We can get a little more honest, you and me.* He waited for me to nod. *We both know what's going to happen between the two of us, down the line. That's never been up for debate.*

I've never debated it, I replied.

His eyes gleamed. *Glad to hear it. But I can tell that part of why you need to go all the way to New York fucking City and live in concrete is that you want to scratch a few itches. Is that right?*

I didn't want to lie to him. But I didn't know how to tell him the truth.

He laughed, and then he took my chin in his hand and pulled my face to his.

I still remember, so distinctly, the way that touch seared through me, scrambling every last signal in my body and then setting it ablaze. Like he was flipping a switch.

You have my permission to do whatever the fuck you want, he told me, his gaze intent on mine. *Go wild, baby. You have my blessing.*

I wanted to tell him I hadn't asked for his blessing, but that wasn't entirely true. I might not have *asked* for it, but I wanted it.

Do you do . . . whatever the fuck you want, too? I asked him.

He didn't look away. If anything, his gaze got more intense. *Yes.*

I thought about that. I didn't know if I liked it, because I knew as well as he did that we were supposed to be each other's. He waited while I weighed the strange sensations working their way through me, and the even odder emotions that I'd never dealt with before.

You want to ask me about that? His fingers on my chin were like steel. I had the strangest urges, none of which I understood, so I shoved them aside. I could feel him everywhere even though he wasn't touching me anywhere but on my chin. *You can. But word of warning, I'll tell you.*

I blew out a breath. I wasn't sure that I'd ever felt so torn before. I wanted to know every single thing he wasn't telling me, because I was older now and I had a much better idea of what he meant.

But I was also pretty certain that my imagination was bad enough.

I'm good, I said.

He didn't look pleased or unpleased by that. All he did was nod, his mouth a straight line.

You do what you need to do, Maddox. I'll do the same. That work for you?

Yes. What I *felt* was significantly more complicated, but *yes* was the easiest way to express it all.

But. One small word from him and I got . . . even more still, somehow, kneeling there before him. *What I told you before still stands. When you're ready for me, you come to me. You understand?*

It was what he'd said all those years ago. And I did understand, but in a completely different way than I had then.

I nodded, then wondered if the reason I did that was so I could feel those blunt, hard fingers of his on my chin even longer.

When you do, he told me, and there was a warning in his voice then. I could see it all over that stern face of his. I could feel it, deep inside me, like the ringing of a bell I hadn't known was there. *When it's you and me, Maddox, there isn't going to be anyone else. That's when the fucking around stops. You get me?*

My fucking around or your fucking around? I dared to ask.

He tilted his head just a little, just enough to remind me how powerful he was. How foolish I was to think I could make bargains with this man. But there was also that gleam in his gaze.

If that's how you want it, babe. He'd never called me that before. I liked it. *But I got to tell you, it's going to take a lot of work on your part to keep me satisfied with some long-distance shit. You think you can handle that?*

Maybe I won't be ready for a long, long time.

He laughed at that, but it was low and dangerous, a match struck. *I've never lied to you. Do me the same favor.*

I've never lied to you, I replied, stalling.

Enjoy your freshman year, baby, he said, and I thought *baby* was even better than *babe. I suggest you enjoy it fully, because between you and me, I have a feeling that's all the party time you're going to get.*

He was right about that, too.

Now, years later, all I can think is that from his perspective, I've been a gigantic disappointment.

"I know all the packs are coming," I say, looking back at him after that unwelcome trip down memory lane. "And I know that no one understands this thing between us—"

"Including me," he growls.

I shoot a glare back at him. "You understand it, you just don't like it."

"Again, end of the line, babe." He gets to his feet then, moving much too fast and much too gracefully for someone his size. He's breathtaking, is the trouble. If I'd been fated to a goblin, my whole life would be different. I'd be on an island in the South Pacific even now. "You say you know all the packs are coming, but are you really prepared for what that means? You didn't like it that much five years ago when we were back east and no one could understand why I was letting you make a mockery of me down in New York City."

He was right. I'd hated it. "You told me you didn't care what they said."

"I don't," he shoots back at me. "But I do care about what they might *do*, Maddox. Sooner or later a hundred-year king with no queen looks like a weak-ass bitch. A liability. The fact that we managed to take down a death goddess from hell won't matter much if enough of the wrong people decide that a move against me makes sense."

"I can't believe anybody would dare."

"Maddox."

I can hear the impatience in his voice. It's all over him, and it's different this time. The all-pack gathering changes things. I should have been more prepared. I can see that he is.

He glares at me. "Stop stalling."

"I just think that there should be more than this," I say, flatly. Boldly.

I've never said it before. Not quite like that. I've hinted at it. I've come toward it but never quite got there.

Mostly because I suspected that he would look exactly the way he does now. Like I've slapped him. "What the fuck do you mean by that?"

"I mean that the world ended three years ago and everything changed, except us." I throw out my hands to encompass this hill, the den beneath it, the entire pack. "We live exactly the same way that our ancestors were living one hundred years ago. But you can remember that yourself. It was the same two hundred years before you. A thousand years before then."

"That's called history," Ty growls. "Our history."

"Is it?" I shake my head, not sure why I feel like there's an earthquake inside of me. "Why are we still hiding below ground when everyone else is walking around free? Why are we adhering to archaic rules that have nothing to do with how this pack—how *you*—can change things going forward?"

"Talking shit isn't going to change the situation."

"I'm not talking shit. You hear everything I say but you never *listen*, Ty."

That isn't fair—or true—but I don't take it back. He looks at me in that arrogant amazement that makes most people cower. I don't let myself.

I push on. "You are the smartest wolf I've ever met, and I've met a lot of wolves. Yet for some reason you think that you should be bowing your head to the old ways just because people have always done it that way. So what if they have?"

He's looking at me like I'm nuts, so I blow out a breath and give him an example. "Why should you have to negotiate with all the other North American kings? It causes chaos. It's always annoying. It would be better for everyone involved if there was only one king." I glare at him. "And it should be you, obviously, because you're the one who figured out how to take over human shit and make it ours in the first place. All the rest of them are just copying you."

"Don't talk crazy," he tells me in a low voice. "And definitely don't talk like that when the other packs are around."

"Every other king in every other pack already has a queen," I remind him.

I watch him go nuclear. "That's part of the fucking problem, Maddox."

"And what have those queens contributed to their packs?" I demand, not backing down at all. "They provide young. They create what I imagine are deeply bitchy and petty social structures in their dens, if my own mother is anything to go by. It might surprise you to learn that I think females have better things to do than play stupid little reindeer games."

"What do you think being my mate means?" He is shaking his head, looking a lot like he'd like to shake me. "Bearing the young is part of the deal, babe."

"I can't wait to have your babies," I grit out at him. "But don't you think that we have shit to do first?" When he only glares back at me, I wave my hands around, trying to take in the whole valley this time. "The vampires don't live underground anymore. Oh sure, they have their lairs, but how many vampires have you seen moving into the abandoned houses around here? Whoever heard of vampires just . . . living aboveground? There are even goblins in the half-falling-down houses off Pioneer Road, and they're not wrecking things. They're gentrifying. That's what I mean. Everything's changed, except us."

He doesn't like that, but he doesn't argue. It's why I can't hate him.

"I'm the one who lived with humans all of those years," I remind him. "I'm the one who took the time to figure them out."

"Wasted effort, it turns out, since they're nothing but snack food these days."

"Here's the thing about humans," I tell him. "I've been trying to tell you this, but you won't take it on board. They're weak. They have to build weapons to defend themselves because they don't possess the power to do it naturally."

"Like I said. Waste of time all around."

"They know how to dream," I throw at him. "Imagine what we could make of this pack if we stop living like wolves, live like the werewolves we actually fucking are, and dream like humans?"

That blazes between us, another fire all its own.

Ty doesn't shift his gaze from mine, but he doesn't come any closer either. "What I think is that you have to trust me, Maddox. It's now or never. And I don't like how *never* sounds. I don't think you're going to like how it feels."

He's blowing me off and I want to bite him, but I know where that will lead. "I don't understand why you can't trust that I have the pack's best interest at heart. Or that I might actually have learned something in the time I was away."

"Because it's bullshit, Maddox," he says, and it would make me flinch less if he shouted it. Instead, he's quiet again. It's devastating. "All this is bullshit, and it has been for years. The entire life that you've lived up until now has been an exercise of my trust in you, and what do I get back from that? Not a fucking thing. Up to and including you choosing to move out of this den like a big fucking middle finger in my face. We are literally made for each other, asshole. That's not flowery language. That's not some stupid book. It's fucking fate, like it or not."

"We can be made for each other and not ready for each other," I throw back at him, trying to disguise how *shook* I feel.

He looks like he's considering biting me himself. "You've had more than enough time to get ready."

"We can be made for each other and no fucking good for each other, too, Ty," I hurl at him. "Have you ever thought about that?"

It's one of those moments, so seldom, when I manage to hit him where it hurts. He makes a small sound, like a laugh, though not like it's funny.

I want to go to him. I want to apologize. I want to explain—except I can't explain. I've been trying to *explain* for years, and it always ends up back here.

The same sad circle, again and again and again.

"You don't think that we're good for each other, but I should trust you to do what, exactly?" He asks that in a stiff, gruff way that lets me know that I really did land a blow. And that it hurt him.

I hate myself.

But I don't stop. "You told me you'd wait until I was ready. I'm going to need you to keep that promise, Ty."

"Go fuck yourself, Maddox," he suggests, low and deliberate.

A blow in return. I deserve it.

I understand that if I don't do something about this, right now, we will stand here in this exact spot and repeat this. Over and over. Fuck and fight. Fuck and almost reach some kind of understanding—but no. Fuck again. Fight again.

But if I could do that, we wouldn't be here right now, would we?

I give him the actual finger this time, on top of the figurative middle finger he thinks my living situation is. "You first," I suggest.

This time, when he laughs, it's a warning.

I heed it. I turn and run. All the way to the steep side of the hill, and I can hear him behind me, moving fast.

I jump, and I shift midair, and when I land on the slick, steep hillside, I haul ass on four legs all the way home.

When I make it through the woods to that pretty little hill in Jacksonville, my cottage waits for me. It's nestled into the trees on the edge of the big front yard outside the oracle's house. I left the lights on to welcome me home, and once I'm in the yard—once I see them—I pause.

I take a breath, but when I scan all around me, Ty's nowhere. I can't even scent him on the wind.

I know that he let me run all this way. Let me beat him.

I know, too, that this is another example of his trust in me.

Yet I also know that no matter how much I wish it could be, it's not enough.

4.

Cold Moon, waning gibbous

It's a relief to wake up alone the next morning.

A relief that makes me feel guilty immediately, but that doesn't change it any. After a full-on pack night, I like my own space. I like my own company. I like getting to wake up in my own bed, in my own room, where all I can hear is the wind in the trees outside.

New York City ruined den life for me, but that's another conversation that starts fights I'm tired of having.

I've been renting this little cottage for about two months now and expected to enjoy the reprieve from pack politics every time I open my eyes, but it turns out I like it a whole lot more than that.

There was a lot of talk when Winter Bishop, who the Kind knew was going to be the next oracle long before she did, put out an ad for renters. Just went ahead and put it out there in the cute little newspaper that the humans distribute around to each other but that all the rest of us read too.

We still like to keep tabs on them. Old habits die hard.

There had been a lot of talk about which factions should make a run at getting in with the new oracle, but unlike most of them, I knew Winter from high school. So I was the one who nominated myself for the role, showed up on her doorstep, and won myself—and the pack—an in.

And unlike the other two renters who turned up that day to claim the oracle's three cottages, Winter knew exactly who and what *I* was.

Not a powerful sorceress in hiding like Savi Wynn, making the weather do what she likes. Not whatever the hell Briar Monroe is, who smells a bit like a dark fae but with indistinguishable magic that is distinctly *not* fae-like. I was the only one not hiding in plain sight.

Maybe that's why Winter and I became friends. Not just people who share a kitchen.

I roll out of bed. Unlike a number of my family members who like to sleep on the cold, hard ground because it's *letting the wolf lead*, I like a cozy bed. I shower in my tiny bathroom, get dressed, and head outside into the crack of a new dawn.

It's cold this morning and I like it. I can see my breath as I walk, which delights me the same way it did when I was small. The fog—natural, I'm pretty sure, not Savi's work, because it's always foggy in the mornings at this time of the year in Oregon—swirls around the pines and the madrone trees. It makes my walk across the front yard seem spooky. My feet crunch into the earth beneath me as I head toward the house that's belonged to the Rogue Valley oracle for as long as I can remember.

If anyone needed a prophecy—or a little glimpse into the future, maybe not so fancy as a whole-ass prophecy and all that might entail—everyone knew that you come up to the window around the side of this house, hand over money or goods, depending, and the wrinkled old oracle who sat in a chair by her window would show you what you wanted to see.

Or what you really didn't want to see, depending on how her cards fell.

I can't think of a single creature around who didn't end up here at some point or another.

The old oracle was Winter's grandmother and she died a month ago, killed in the big fight we had against the lovely and charming Vinča and her bloodthirsty acolytes. I'd grown to like the spooky old lady, and even though I didn't spend much time in the house proper while she was alive, I can feel her absence now.

I figure that feeling that absence is probably one of the reasons why Winter has seemed so distant over the past month. But there are any number of other possibilities. The horrendous skull-splitting visions she had, courtesy of Vinča. Then becoming the oracle herself. She also found out that her twin brother was not just a regular vampire blood addict but was being held down in the vampire dungeons—not a place with many happy endings.

Winter rounded out her eventful fall by becoming the consort of the vampire king, the infamous Ariel Skinner himself, known for his personal vampire warrior army, the fact that he was once an actual Spartan, and his brand of hard but consistent justice for the Kind who get into trouble on the valley floor.

Vampires rule the floor, werewolves rule the hills, and the sorceress keeps all of us safely tucked away from the notice of other passing threats—whether that's the sun that vampires need to avoid or the odd murmuration of the flying gargoyles. This is how it's always been here. The Reveal just made it obvious to humans, too.

Now Winter wears the vampire king's mark, a stern warning to anyone who dares go near her that the consequences will be swift and deadly if they so much as breathe on her wrong. She also plies her cards and the odd beverage at the coffee stand out on Stage Road rather than here at the house, because Ariel thinks it's safer. I'm sure it is.

Mostly what that means these days is that she's not around. I miss when she was.

Or maybe what I miss is that living here felt a bit like college again. And the truth is, if I could have, I would have stayed in college forever. Taking finals and writing exam papers was significantly less complicated than life here, neck-deep in duty, pack, and expectations.

Sometimes I almost think it's easier to miss Ty than to live with him, though that's something I'd never dare say out loud. Especially not *to* him.

I shove my hands in the pockets of the slouchy overalls I tossed on, and I wander around the far side of the house so I can access the kitchen from the back. When Winter let us move onto her land, she kept the house—and her grandmother—as safe from us monsters as she could.

Now she's one of us. Fate is a bitch.

When I push my way through the back door into the kitchen with its covered windows to keep out creatures who wouldn't dare attack anyone here, I find Briar already sitting at the kitchen table. I feel that same prickle around her I always do.

She's not right. I can't really tell what she is with any certainty, first of all, and that's a problem. Identity isn't muddy. Not among the Kind. Even monsters mixed with each other in strange combinations smell like the things that they're made of, because everyone likes to fuck, and the resulting young leave a scent trail to announce who fucked who.

Briar smells like confusion.

What I can't tell is whether she's made that way or just . . . acting that way. But hey, people are weird no matter what they're made of, and the Reveal only amped that up. All that matters to me is that while everything was going down with the death goddess and her minions, Briar was nowhere to be found. Not involved at all—and I looked.

I half expected to scent her up there in the middle of a bloody mountain ritual. Or hidden behind a mask and a cloak at Crater Lake on Halloween, but I didn't. Being a little confused doesn't make a person dangerous. Maybe she's as misunderstood as a wolfling girl destined for domestic den life who decided to go off to NYU instead.

I smile at her as I sweep inside, registering the way her eyes widen in something like shock before she drops them. So much for bonding.

I act as if I don't notice any of that and glide around the kitchen, collecting ingredients for a good breakfast. Meat. Eggs. More meat. A little bit of cheese to be fancy.

Briar, as far as I've been able to tell, would drop dead without that wool beanie she's always wearing, pulled down over her presumably fae-pointed ears. Though perhaps that's just a Pacific Northwest thing. I can handle that. It's the endless bowls of sugary breakfast cereal she consumes, which I know she can only get on the black market, that weird me out more.

"You grew up here, didn't you?" she asks.

Standing at the stove, I have to order myself not to act too surprised that she actually started up a conversation with me. Or that it sounds . . . vaguely social. I tell myself I should be nicer. I know all about not fitting in. "I did."

"You and Winter went to high school together."

"It's a small valley," I tell her. "Winter and I knew each other. Not well."

"Was it hard to have to hide?" Briar asks, with a certain intensity that makes me blink. When I turn around to look at her, she ducks her head. I'm sure I see pink on her cheeks. That makes me think she's awkward, and I can't help but soften. She's like a cub. "It—ah—it just seems like it would be hard."

"Everyone goes through adolescence thinking that they have to hide their true face," I say as I turn back to my little fry-up. "Figuring out how to go along to get along. Making sure that what makes them different, though it might also make them feel disfigured to do it, is tucked away where no one can ever find it." I flip over my meat before it gets too well done. Which is to say at all well done. "Then we all grow up and realize that being an adolescent sucks. For everyone. The end."

When I look back over Briar, she's frowning, still staring down at her cereal bowl. When she feels me looking at her, she jerks. Her head comes up and she locks eyes with me—how have I never noticed that she has rain-colored eyes—and she blows out a breath.

"I have to go," she says, but she's blushing again, and I watch her as she stands up abruptly and marches out of the kitchen. The back door slams behind her, loud enough to make the glasses in the cabinet sing a little. *Awkward,* I think.

But awkward seems kind of cute to me in the wake of a death goddess and a full moon and before all the wolves in North America descend on the Rogue Valley. I decide I'm going to make her my pet project. Something else to think about that isn't my always-on-fire life.

I'm still staring at the door she ran out of when the interior door behind me opens, all steel plates and dead bolts, and Winter appears.

"No vampire king?" I ask brightly, because the idea of Ariel Skinner himself shuffling in for communal coffee is never not hilarious to me.

Winter only smiles, like she's trying to be mysterious when I can smell him all over her.

Some in the valley like to mutter about how the new oracle might know her way around a vision but is a strange choice for an immortal vampire who has had lovers renowned the world over for their beauty. Some people in this valley will talk shit no matter what.

Winter looks both tough and pretty, even first thing in the morning. She looks like the warrior she made herself into after the Reveal, which is no doubt why she's still alive. Her blond hair is cut in a pixie style that would make *me* look like a sad, shorn sheep, but it works for her. There's a wariness in her indigo eyes, but there always is. Making it through the Reveal as a human can't have been easy.

Most didn't. I don't like to think about the human friends I had to leave behind in New York, or what likely became of them. We probably all have that distance in our eyes these days. Even though, as a card-carrying monster, I'm not supposed to think such things. I'm meant to make jokes about the all-you-can-eat buffet out there. Then pretend that I love a world without airplanes to far-off cities, excellent restaurants, and television shows to binge.

But it wouldn't be life if it wasn't complicated.

"Did I hear Briar?" Winter goes directly to the coffee machine that takes up most of the counter and requires a lot of barista shit to work right, because apparently working in a coffee stand all day isn't enough. She has to make snooty coffee at home, too.

Not that it doesn't taste good.

"She asked me about growing up here," I tell her. "About you and me being from here and going to high school together. I don't know. Maybe she's trying to make friends."

Winter looks toward the back door with an odd look on her face. "I wonder."

"Maybe she needed some time to settle in here," I suggest. I think of what Ty and I were talking about last night. "Most of the Kind live separate from each other, sometimes underground. That's how it's been forever. It's only been three years since things changed, and many creatures are going to need longer than that to catch up."

Winter frowns like she's considering that. Then she drags her gaze back to her coffee preparations.

I pile my meal on my plate, take it to the table, and pull Briar's chair back so I can sit in it. I watch Winter take an inordinate amount of time with her coffee before she comes over and sits down with me.

I take a few bites of my breakfast but then point my fork at her. "Are you okay?"

She blinks. "I'm fine." When I keep looking at her, she frowns again. "I keep having these weird, muddy dreams. That's all. So I wake up feeling that way." She lifts her mug. "Coffee helps. Coffee helps everything."

"Muddy sounds better than the piercing brain-tumor death goddess dreams," I point out. "If you have to choose."

Her mouth curves. "True. These don't hurt, they're just odd. Like I can almost remember them, but they disappear into the muck if I get too close." She takes a pull of her coffee and doesn't look at me. "Maybe I've lost them."

"Is that bad?" I watch her face as I ask it. "You're the oracle all day, every day now. Maybe your visions don't have to come to you in dreams anymore."

It seems to take her a long time to look up from her mug, but when she does, she smiles. "The last clear dream I had was about Briar. Not long after Halloween."

That surprises me, but I don't say anything. I keep my eyes on her and wait for her to tell me.

"It was clear in that I could see everything that was happening," she says, "just not what it *meant*. I had to really think about that. But it makes more sense now. I think you're right that Briar wants to make friends. I'm almost positive that the dream was telling me that Vinča was after her. Whether she knows it or not. Whether Vinča will ever rise again or not."

I sit back in my chair, and she tells me about the dream. About trailing Briar through a forest only for the death goddess to take her over and start speaking out of her mouth. I shudder with distaste. "Why would she want Briar?"

Winter shakes her head. "I don't know. And the cards have not been forthcoming. I've asked them for clarity on this pretty much daily."

I contemplate this over some bacon. "One thing we know Vinča hates is you."

"Yes." Winter takes a swig of her coffee and sighs happily. "I'm glad Briar is reaching out. That doesn't feel very death-cultish of her, so really, I don't see why *not* to be friends."

"We can all trauma-bond over being stalked by a vengeful, trapped psycho bitch," I say merrily. "We'll be braiding each other's hair in no time."

It feels like an achievement when she laughs.

Then she heaves a heavy breath, so I know she's getting serious. "How is he?" she asks, avoiding my eyes.

She means her twin brother, August. After treating him like the pawn he was, Ariel returned Augie to Winter. But Augie came home still addicted to that vampire blood. After what happened at Crater Lake on Halloween, which included Augie and Winter losing their grandmother so violently, he decided to go clean.

Except, of course, there's no going *clean* from vampire blood. Those who don't get killed for irritating their drug pushers—the vampires themselves—usually die anyway, because nothing around is supposed to meet that high.

Augie had to know that better than anyone, but he wanted to clean up. Ty told him he could make that happen—it's just brutal. And long.

"He's okay," I tell her.

I'm pretty sure she knows better than to ask for details.

Winter clearly thinks better of that. She blows out another breath. "Okay." But she sounds like she's saying it to herself. "Okay is good. More than we got some years. I'll take it."

I don't like it when my friends sound sad, so I eat those feelings. She gets up to fix herself another cup of coffee and looks more alert when she sits back down.

"Another full moon last night," she murmurs. "Would I be able to tell by looking at you if . . . ?"

"I don't actually know," I tell her. Though I know I'll have a new tattoo, at the very least. "But no need to worry about what a claiming looks like from the outside, because none took place."

I guess my attempt to sound jaunty and unbothered falls flat, because she gazes at me a little too intently, those indigo eyes of hers more confronting than I'd like. "Are *you* okay?"

I wouldn't answer anyone else on this. But I was there the night that Winter pretty much died on the top of Mount McLoughlin. There was more than one moment when I thought that I was literally holding her poor, battered body together with my own hands.

I've never been a fan of unearned intimacies, but I'm pretty sure this is about as earned as it gets.

"There's always been a time limit," I say quietly. "And we're coming up on it. Fast."

I expect her to reach for her cards, or to tell me that she dreamed about all the North American wolves who will be appearing shortly in Jacksonville, or the power of the solstice, all the usual oracle things. Instead, all she does is study me. Like I need some figuring out.

I don't like that, so I keep talking. "I'm sure it will be fine. After all, I was fated to be his mate, not his victim. So I have that going for me."

"Do you really think that he would kill you?" Winter asks, after failing yet again to smile at my attempt to lighten things up.

Again, this is not a question I would answer if anyone else dared put it to me. But this is Winter. Her boyfriend is an immortal vampire. They share blood.

In comparison, Ty and I are nowhere near as toxic. We're relatively healthy as fuck.

I wave a hand. "At this point I'm less worried about Ty and more worried about other douchebag wolves thinking they can step to him because they imagine there's some weakness in us not being fully mated."

"Is there?" Winter asks, her gaze a little too heavy on mine.

"No," I say, automatically. Maybe a little defensively. "No, of course not. It's about the perceived weakness they assume must lurk in Ty because he hasn't put me in my place. That's the only strength they recognize. And it's not that I think he can't take them if they try to fight him, because he can. He will. But it will be a whole thing, and guess who they'll all blame?"

Winter nods and drains her coffee, but even after she leaves the kitchen so she can head off to her coffee stand on Stage Road, I find myself turning what she told me—and asked me—over and over in my head.

I do my dishes, and virtuously do Briar's, too, because that's the kind of giving person I am when I'm feeling aggrieved. I tell myself it's nothing less than a goddamn olive branch toward an incarcerated goddess's intended victim when really, it's an empty cereal bowl.

I push my way back out into the yard. It's still cold, and the fog is clinging on for dear life. I let my gaze move over the old vegetable garden pen, long since gone to seed. At this time of year, the pen and the yard itself are little more than mud. The evergreens keep the woods that press in around the house from looking too bare, and I like that. I missed these cool winters of green and gray when I lived back east.

I breathe in, scenting the air, but can't smell anything or anyone out of the ordinary.

Not that I would expect to. As I once told Winter, my moving onto her land pretty much guaranteed that the pack would keep it safe. Savi renting a cottage here practically catapulted this whole hill into sanctuary status. Winter being the oracle and the consort of the vampire king means it's even safer here now.

Who would want to take on all three major powers in this valley at once?

Though now I find myself wondering if that will change once wolf week starts and all the asshole kings from the other irritating packs start throwing their weight around.

I brood on that as I head back to my cottage and get ready for the rest of my day. I want to take that glorious leap forward into the woods, shifting as I go, but I don't. If I run the way I want to, I'll almost certainly be late.

The day after another unclaimed full moon is not the day to be late. Tempers are sure to be high as it is.

I trudge out to the big old Explorer I've been driving since high school and climb in, then head down the hill. I drive down the main street of pretty, preserved Jacksonville, the human safe zone. It's still early, so there's no one around. This means I can look at the old buildings, strung with lights that remind me it's December today. And that this is the holiday season, no matter what folks celebrate.

There used to be carolers on the streets, dressed in period costumes. Maybe there still are. I'll have to remember to come and see for myself if they're doing it again this year. You never know. The chorus group could have been eaten.

Though I know perfectly well that one thing I will not have much of over the next few weeks is time. Not with the wolf packs gathering here and the role I'll have to play for them, hopefully helping to ward off any runs at Ty before they happen.

I take the road out of town, down Stage Road and past Winter's coffee stand, where there are already cars backed up. I roll down my windows despite the chilly wind so I can smell the remains of the moonlight on the acres of abandoned farmland that spread out on both sides of the road, slowly going back to the earth. I can pick up the faint scents of those who ran last night on the breeze.

I feel the need to run free inside me like claws.

But I keep driving. I let the land work its magic on me. I let the mountains help me remember who I am. I navigate my way around the usual obstructions in the road, from questionable debris made into barricades to suspicious creatures supposedly hawking their goods.

I feel like my head is as close to on straight as it's likely to be by the time I make it to the warehouse that's stood unobtrusively in Phoenix, one of the smaller towns along the river between Medford and Ashland, for as long as I've been alive. And a whole lot of years before that, too.

It's not far from what used to be the Harley-Davidson store, though the actual outlaw biker contingent rarely rode down this way. That would have called attention to what they were doing. In most things, the pack always prefers to keep its business to itself.

I turn into the parking area and drive around back, not at all surprised to see that all three of my brothers' trucks are here.

The fact that I expected them doesn't make me any happier to see that they're here, but I don't run from fights. Especially fights I've had a thousand times before. I take a steadying sort of breath as I climb out of the Explorer. Then I march myself right up to the heavy door that requires a code punched in on the keypad and let myself in.

My brothers are in the office, waiting for me. All three of them are huge. Not as big as Ty, but brawny and gigantic just the same. It was obvious to me growing up that they have a certain effect on females of all species, and I'm sure they still do, not that I ever want to know more about their personal lives than that.

This is not a courtesy that they extend me in return.

They don't even play. They all go silent. Then they glare at me in a heartwarming display of united brotherly condemnation of me, their only sister.

"Good morning to you too," I reply.

As brightly as possible, to be annoying.

"What the fuck, Maddox," the youngest of them, Micah, growls from where he sits at one of the desks, his booted feet propped up before him. "What the hell are you doing?"

"Sooner or later this is all going to have to come to a head," chimes in Asher, the middle brother. He is scowling, looking as if he'd like to bring it all to a head himself, right now. "Who do you think is going to have your back when we've watched you play this game for years?"

Like he thinks Ty and I are going to devolve into fisticuffs. It would be funny if I didn't think that people . . . really do think that. They think Ty hates me. They think I believe I'm better than him.

They don't understand us at all.

But I'm not going to defend us to my brothers, who should know better. I act like I can't hear either of them and take my seat at my desk, where I'm in charge of painstakingly recording every single thing our pack moves, protects, and makes.

Back in the days before the Reveal, the pack pretty much operated on vibes and violence, like every other outlaw biker gang around. These days we're more strategic, in part because we are what keeps most of our part of the world fed, armed, and entertained.

I like to think that's not only because Ty is a visionary but because the things I do support that vision, practically and effectively. I study the patterns in our movements. I pay attention to who attacks our caravans and when. I track the ogres who do a lot of the truck driving, because everyone knows an ogre can't be fully trusted, and I've identified those who tried to cheat us at least ten times this year. I collect and analyze all the things the drivers and bikers riding protection details say about the state of the old interstate and all the other roads they encounter so I can make targeted suggestions on how to avoid trouble spots. All of these things maximize our profits and reach.

And none of these things are under the purview of a pack's queen. If I take up my official duties, return to the den, and focus on only that all day, who will do all these things the way I can? No one, is the answer. I think that makes us weak.

Everyone else thinks I need to mate with Ty and get over myself.

I officiously open up my various notebooks, too aware that Liam hasn't said anything yet. The oldest of my brothers, Liam is the closest thing to a biological father I've ever had, no matter how I try to play like his opinion is the same as that of the other two.

Noise. Easily dismissed.

"Leave her alone," is what Liam says, but I'm not foolish enough to consider that a reprieve. He's the biggest of the three of them. He's also the meanest of them, if he has a mind to be. "We have to get that food shipment up to Vancouver tonight. Get on it."

Asher and Micah obey Liam too, though they make a show of slamming out of the office so they can go make sure the truck is being loaded with the black market foods that are supposed to go on it. And not extra, usually creepy, shit that people are always trying to sneak on board without paying. I respond to that by making a show of acting like I don't notice them banging the door that leads into the warehouse hard enough it makes the whole place shake.

I continue to put on a whole theatrical performance of complete and total serenity despite the fact that I can feel the way my oldest brother is glaring daggers at me.

"Ten years ago, if you'd come to me and said that you thought the prophecy was wrong and this wasn't what you wanted, I would have tried to help you," he growls at me in a low voice.

Low blow. And also bullshit, but I stop pretending that my performative rearrangement of all the documents on my desk is doing anything. "Ten years ago I was fifteen."

"So fucking what?" He belts that out, though he doesn't raise his voice. That means he's not *pissed*, he's somewhere far beyond that. A smarter woman would wince, apologize, and make it right.

Oh well.

"We're not human," Liam is growling at me. "We don't need thirty years to grow the fuck up. You knew what was expected of you long before that. Don't bullshit me."

I look at him and start to say something but think better of it.

He nods. "But it's not ten years ago, Maddox. You've been back from college for three years now. You can't pretend you don't know what's going on here or what the pack needs. What the hell are you doing?"

"It's hard to take you seriously, Liam," I say, and I'm annoyed that it takes an effort to sound calm. "You're older than me and I don't see you finding yourself a mate. Why is it my responsibility?"

"Try again. I'm not the king of anything. I wasn't fated to do a goddamn thing but run free and howl. What the hell happened to you?" He shakes his head, looking at me like I've maybe turned into a swamp demon or some other low-life scum. "I don't know who you are anymore."

"Exactly the same person I've always been."

He's still shaking his head. "I knew it was a mistake for you to go away. I advised Ty against letting you do it."

It isn't that I hadn't suspected that. But he's never said that to me before, flat out. I take the blow. I do my best not to react. "Thanks for that vote of confidence."

"I know you think it's because I have some problem with you educating yourself, or whatever the hell you like to yell at Mom." Liam snorts. "I don't care if you go to class all day every day as long as while you're doing that, you're standing up for this pack and our king. Which, as far as I know, is what we all vow to do every fucking year when the Wolf Moon rises. That's what makes us *pack*." He gives that a moment to sink in like the knife it is. "It's coming up, Maddox. Are you going to promise your undying fealty, once again, to a man you refuse to mate with? Got to say, it makes your loyalty sound like a load of horseshit."

"You have no idea how loyal I am," I tell him. Through gritted teeth.

Liam only stares at me until I find myself looking away again, and hating myself for it.

"You're right," he agrees, in that hard voice of his. "I don't have any idea how loyal you are. *No one does.* And that's a problem that's only getting bigger, little sister. One that if I were you, I'd solve."

He does not slam any doors when he leaves. That makes it worse. I'm sure he knows that.

There's a reason he's Ty's enforcer.

I stay where I am, staring furiously down at all my charts and files before me, and I don't move until I hear them slam their way out of the warehouse some while later, then drive away.

I sit there a long time. Eventually, I shake myself off and get to work.

Because I also have a vision for the things we can do, and that vision is worth fighting for, no matter what anyone else thinks. Including Ty, who could have changed all of this years ago by loudly and publicly agreeing that he didn't need his queen to be as traditional as everyone else wants me to be.

He didn't do that. Here we are.

I can feel guilty about all of this, but that doesn't make it my fault.

I've talked myself into feeling a little more bulletproof by the time I make my way home late that night. I drive into the yard, and the headlights sweep across the dark front of the main house. I miss the days when Winter and her grandmother were in there and all the lights were on.

Maybe I need to stop thinking I'm going to stumble across a home I don't make myself. Maybe that's the lesson here.

I am not my brother Liam, so I take pleasure in slamming my car door shut behind me when I climb out. I head for my cottage, only to stop dead a few feet away from my front step.

Because there's blood all over it. The moment I see it, the wind shifts and I scent it, too. An unpleasant copper that I don't like. It's too acrid.

I take a few steps closer to confirm that at the center of all that dark, ominous red there's another small animal corpse—or what's left of it—arranged like more of an offering than a kill.

But not an offering *to me*.

That's the only part that's clear.

5.

I change into my wolf form and take in the scene before me with my expanded senses. Then I backtrack, loping around the perimeter of the yard and taking in every scent that I can find. I can smell that Winter came back here and then left again. I can follow Briar's confusing scent profile into the woods, seemingly headed down into Jacksonville. By foot.

That's one of her oddities, out here in a place where predators are so thick on the ground that most folks without their own fangs and claws prefer vehicles, but I can't smell any blood on her. Besides, I've decided we're going to be friends.

I can't track the creature on my cottage step. I can track every bird and squirrel within a five-mile radius, but not the critter I want to know about. All I get from it is the same *off* sort of scent that bothered me last night.

If someone is sneaking around, following me and leaving me dead things—and I think it's pretty clear that they are—I should be able to track them. Or at least get a sense of them here, even if they know enough to cover their tracks. There's always *something* to find, especially when there's so much blood and guts involved. And an arrangement that suggests a lot of *handling* of those things.

But aside from that faint *off* vibe, I can't smell anything out of the ordinary.

There's not much that could make me more uneasy.

I don't want to touch the sacrifice, but I don't want to leave it out here, either. I also don't really feel like picking it up with my mouth, my only option in this form. I switch back to my human form and clean up as best I can, burying what's left of the poor creature in the woods.

Once I'm done, I don't really feel like going back and sitting there in my cottage. Not only because someone clearly wants me to know that *they* know I live there. I would say every last member of the Kind, not to mention vast swaths of what remains of the human population, knows I live here on Winter's land.

Knowing where I live in a general sense is no big deal. That's life in a small town. Feeling confident enough to leave whole bloody messes on my doorstep in two separate locations, on the other hand, feels less adorably rural Oregon and more . . . upsetting.

Out in the woods, I stay crouched down over the grave I dug and realize that with all the full moon drama, I never told Ty about that skunk. It's not great that now another grisly little offering has turned up. The very next night, in fact.

Once again, I find myself thinking about those cloaked little horrors who followed Vinča around. I shake my head at the gnarled madrone tree before me, because I know it can't be them. Visions of Briar possibly being a potential target aside, Winter is the one who had the most intense connection to the death goddess. If Vinča was still actually out here kicking around and making noise from her watery prison, Winter would know.

More to the point, she would know *and* she would tell the rest of us.

When lecturing myself on this topic doesn't work, I head back toward the cottages, though I stay inside the boundary of the woods. Keeping myself in the shadows and letting the early December night fall inky and hard around me.

Just in case anyone is hanging around, unscentable for some reason, and watching.

I can't scent Briar in her cottage, which matches the tracks she left on her way down the hill. Everything seems to suggest that Savi *is* in her cottage, though when I knock on the back window, there's no answer. There's not even a hitch in the murmuring I hear from within.

It takes me about two seconds to decide that it's her usual sorcery games at work. Savi is one of the most powerful people around. She's not killing time in a tiny cottage here on a hill in Jacksonville, no matter what she wants Winter to think.

Luckily, I know where she really lives.

And my body is desperate to get out there and *run*, so that feels like a plan.

I start off at a jog, still on two feet. I wait as I pick up speed. I go faster and faster, and when I get to the top of a small gorge, I jump.

I *explode* into my wolf form.

Then I let her run free.

I head up into the mountains, taking the long way over and around them as I make my way toward Ashland. I can sense pack in the distance, but I don't stop. I've had enough pack today, thank you.

The deeper I get into the wilderness, where very few humans have ever ventured, the better I feel. Just me and the places my paws take me, places only paws can go. These mountains have sheltered me most of my life, and I know them like friends. I see the marks of fires over the years, downed trees from winter storms, the shifting map of age and time.

Up high, there's already considerable snow, and it makes everything even better, crisp and clean and cold enough that even I can feel it.

I wish Ty was with me, because I know that he loves the snow. When he can actually enjoy it and even play in it a little bit. Something he'll never do with anyone but me.

Another secret I keep from my family and the pack. Secrets about the man Ty is when he doesn't have to be their king. Secrets that belong to the two of us whether they like it—or me—or not.

It really is easier to miss him when he's not with me—not because I don't love him but because everything about him is so *big*. He fills the space, any space, so intensely that I always feel I have to fight against it. It always *looks* like fighting him, I know, no matter what it is I think I'm trying to do.

Up on this mountain in the starlight, away from everything, I can hear myself think.

And what I think is that I'm really fucking tired of fighting Ty.

I stop moving, finding my way to the top of a large boulder so I can take in the sweeping view of this valley I've never been able to put behind me. Not for long. Certainly not for good. It's dark, but I can see the lights here and there, marking everything from human encampments to Kind parties and what looks like the odd goblin ball. Up above, the stars are heralding the rising of the moon.

It's quiet up here, but not still. The wind picks up, and that feels good too as it ruffles my fur.

The Wolf Moon is coming, and so are the other North American packs. Reality is crashing in on me, but I knew that it would. It always does. Maybe, if the Reveal hadn't happened when it did, I would have had more time to make a case for myself as an independent wolf who *also* happens to be the king's mate.

Maybe, I tell myself, *that will be a lesson you save for your daughter.*

And for a while, I can't tell if what I feel inside of me is grief . . . or hope.

I don't know how long I sit here, making myself a part of the rock beneath me. Or how long I would have stayed here, but something changes.

I feel it, like a tuning fork somewhere deep inside of me, off-key and unpleasant.

I'm not alone.

I scan the area around me, keeping my movements subtle, certain that I would have heard it if someone had approached. Besides, who can? This rock is far, far away from any paths or trails or lost maps.

Still, I can feel another presence, dark and oily. I can smell it on the wind. In my mind, I see lit torches and red cloaks.

I know it's impossible, but the abject horror and slimy feeling that pools in me feels a whole lot like some top-tier death goddess shit.

I want to stay and see for myself. I want to *see* what's either chasing me specifically or is just . . . up here in the most remote part of these mountains for fun.

I want to see what it thinks is *fun*.

But if I stay here, I'm done.

I know this as surely as I know my own paws and the rock I'm on. And one thing about being in my wolf form—I don't overthink.

I run.

I run until I can see the town of Ashland before me. I run and I don't look behind me. I run no matter how it feels inside me, and how dark and thick the night is as it seems to cling to me and tug and me and make as if to drag me back—

I won't go back. I don't.

I skirt the actual town of Ashland and its humans, who exist in another supposedly *mostly* safe area, thanks to the intercession of some very old magical things that like it that way. Green magic. Earth magic.

They spill blood here to grow things, not to cause them pain. But they also don't like monsters that tip the balance, so I keep to the edges until I can make my way up the slope of Mount Ashland, and then around it. I don't slow down until I reach protected land. *Savi's* protected land.

Only then do I let myself breathe, though I still don't look back. I can feel the darkness, a putrid thickness *right there* behind me. But I know I'm safe on the sorceress's land, so I shake myself off. Then I pad away from that warded boundary and head deeper into her woods, which might accept anyone—but don't necessarily let them leave.

With a *go fuck yourself* in every step, I can only hope.

Like everyone, I know that Savi lives up here, with her bird's-eye view of the valley on one side, the high hills of California on the other, and a line of volcanos to the east to keep her company. Also like everyone, I've never actually been here before.

I can feel the power here, swirling around like fog, but there's also a beating heart at the center of it. That's what I aim for as I walk through pristine, untouched snow beneath a canopy of high pines. I don't look back, but if I did, I know I'd see only my paw prints out here.

I walk and walk, because somehow I think *running* would be rude, having already decided to appear uninvited. A docile show of casually wandering into her space, I'm hoping, will be seen less as an invasion and more . . . friendly. Because that's what we are. *Friends.*

I hope.

You never can tell with these big, powerful creatures. They're a lot moodier than you'd think. I know this too well, given I spend a lot of my time sleeping with one of them.

I keep walking, aware that Savi knows I'm here. This is a demonstration on her part. She *wants* me to know that she knows.

I choose to take this as a warm welcome and keep on going, trudging through the snowy forest until I find myself on the edge of a clearing. I pause there on the outskirts.

Sorcery requires drama, so maybe that's why Savi lives in a sprawling, palatial sort of house that makes me think of pictures I've seen of places like Italy. Greece. Or maybe ancient temples—and the moment I think *that*, I'm sure that's what she was going for. Still, it looks airy and open, stone and tile and bright, blooming flowers that should be dead this time of year.

Instead, they're as vibrant against the snow and the night as if they think it's high noon.

The moon is up now and still close to full, so I follow its silvery light as I move toward the house, transforming back to human form as I go. There's a flicker in the moonlight, like its path changes as I walk it, and then I see her there before me. Standing at the entrance to her home.

Savi Wynn, sorceress of old, goes out of her way to make herself look fragile. Pampered, perhaps, but decidedly weak.

I don't think she's any of those things.

Anyone who's spent any time around power can sense the intense punch of hers immediately.

It strikes me as funny that if anyone were watching this, they would see a girl underdressed for the December night—jeans and flip-flops and a T-shirt—walking from deep snow to grass that ought to be frozen, but isn't. Making her way toward a fragile-looking woman in cozy-looking sweatpants and a matching sweatshirt in a lovely rose-gold shade that glows against her dark hair and warm brown eyes and makes her seem almost doll-like.

Real power can be pretty. If it wants.

"How wonderful," she says in that supremely musical voice of hers as I draw closer. "I love when friends drop by."

I try to take her measure the way I would anyone else, but Savi is as unreadable here as she's always been in Winter's kitchen, or in any number of interactions I've witnessed with her before this fall. "I don't think that you do."

"You're the first," she agrees. "But in theory I'm not opposed. Necessarily."

"I should have requested an audience." Now that I've made it all the way here, chased by . . . whatever the hell that was, I realize I definitely should have. It's one thing to run into her organically while she's pretending to be an ordinary renter of cottages. It's something else to ambush her at home. I know Ty would not appreciate something like this. "I realize that's the usual protocol."

"I think we're past protocol, Maddox." I get the impression that's news to her but that she's decided to go with it anyway. She smiles. "But if you encounter a sea of my acolytes, don't tell them. There's a certain amount of bowing and scraping that's necessary to their existence, you understand."

That makes me laugh. Then she turns around and glides into the house, waving her hand for me to follow her. And I might not have been in a sorceress's house before, but I know not to look too closely at the things I see moving in ways they shouldn't in the corners of my eyes.

Hell, no.

If I look straight ahead, I see a simple-enough hallway and courtyards that open up to the night sky. I hear the sound of water fountains gurgling. Or perhaps she has a whole creek running through this place, for all I know. Either way, she leads me to a little table set up in one of the courtyards, thick with those impossible flowers, and when she sits down and motions for me to join her, she looks very much as if she was expecting me the whole time.

It's some creepy-ass sorcery shit, so I pretend not to notice as I lounge in the seat across from her.

"Tea?" Savi asks.

When I look down at the table that was a pretty tile mosaic with nothing on it a moment ago, I find it covered. There are pots of fragrant tea, a selection of plates filled with things I can't identify that smell both delightful and very much not from Southern Oregon. Some sugary, some savory, and I feel my stomach rumble.

Sadly, I was not raised to take food from magical things. Once you know that most fairy tales are more or less documentary renditions of actual unpleasant happenings, you learn to take a dim view of everything from witches in the woods to some fool with magic beans.

Savi laughs, clearly reading my mind. "If I was going to hurt you, I could have done that at any point over the last two months without bothering to feed you first."

"True." I study her for a moment. "But if you'll forgive the implied insult . . . ?"

I tap my nose, and she sighs. Then waves her hand. "Be my guest."

So I shift, then use every bit of werewolf magic I have on my side to determine that she's telling the truth. There's nothing on the table that will harm me, unless you count the carbs.

When I settle back into my chair, human again, she lifts a teacup to her mouth. "Besides," she says before taking a sip, "I have no desire whatsoever to be at war with the werewolf alpha."

"Whyever not?" I smile at her. "It's so much fun that *I* do it all the time."

She laughs at that, a real laugh I'm not sure I've heard before. And she doesn't sit back and watch me eat the delicacies she's laid out for me. She joins in, and that puts me even more at ease.

"I was married once," she says. Then considers. "I suppose, technically, I still am. I can't say I recommend it."

She doesn't elaborate, but she doesn't have to. The fact that she's been here since long before I was born with no sorcerer husband around is eloquent all on its own.

"A mating isn't a marriage," I tell her, sighing happily around a pastry that manages to be savory and sweet at once, but with flavors I'm not sure I've ever tasted before. "It's not a union, and there's no getting out of it. It's total immersion. Pack first, pack forever, you get the picture."

"More than you can possibly imagine," she replies, and I believe her. I can hear it in her voice. I decided I liked her that very first day we all moved into the cottages, and I'm happy to discover that my instinct then was right.

Like all my other instincts are too, no matter what pushback I get.

We drink our tea. The courtyard is sweet and pretty, with the chatter of birds in the trees that grow here—though I decide not to look too closely to see if they're real. Just like I don't breathe in deeply enough to tell if the flowers are, either. Does it matter? This courtyard is a perfect oasis in the middle of a snowy mountaintop. I don't need it to be real to enjoy it.

When Savi sets her cup back down on a small table, I can sense that the niceties have been dispensed with.

I don't wait for her to ask me why I tracked her down here. I tell her about the skunk last night. And what felt like an escalation tonight. I tell her about that weird prickly feeling I got around both of those sacrifices, or whatever they were.

Then I tell her what I felt closing in around me on that rock, and all the way here.

She listens as I speak, interjecting nothing. When I talk about that dark terror that chased me here, she gets that considering sort of look on her face again, this time tilting her head back as if she's interrogating the night sky. I toy with telling her about Winter's dream starring Briar but dismiss it. If Vinča really does have her eye on Briar, that won't matter until and unless the bitch escapes the lake.

That doesn't mean Vinča's not causing trouble all the same. She's a goddess. She can do all kinds of goddess-level shit—like not go away even when put away. For centuries at a time.

"What I have to wonder," I say when Savi doesn't speak, "is if someone down there at the bottom of Crater Lake isn't quite as dormant as we'd like her to be."

I realize that I expect her—or, more accurately, I *want* her—to dismiss my worry out of hand.

Instead, she makes a humming sort of sound. "Funny you should mention that," she says after a moment. "I keep finding small, ritualistically dispatched creatures all over the place, lining the borders of my land."

"Does that mean she's stirring again?" I ask, my voice rougher than I'd like.

That it's not only happening to me is . . . not good.

"She can stir all she likes," Savi says after a moment. "But to transform her tantrums in the deep into dead things on land would require a lot more than stirring. I broke her down significantly. She didn't die, but she's not capable of simply rising as she is. It would be a process."

A bloody and terrible process, I'm sure. "Involving?"

Savi blinks, like she's paging through all the horrible resurrections she's encountered in her time. It takes her a minute. "A vessel, I'd imagine, and some kind of conduit—but that would be getting ahead of things. There would have to be a ceremony, because there's always a ceremony. No doubt a sacrifice would be involved, but I doubt the blood of a handful of hapless rodents would be enough to ensure that a goddess might rise again. Vinča herself would surely scoff at such a downgrade." Savi smiles. "Remember, there is nothing more vain than a god. It comes with the territory."

I think of that horrible blackness rolling behind me, eating the woods as it went. "Define *ceremony* in this context."

She doesn't. She lifts a shoulder. "I keep telling myself that if Vinča was truly attempting to ascend again, the oracle would be the first to know."

"She said her dreams are little muddy lately," I say, and note that I feel oddly protective of Winter when that shouldn't apply here. The oracle's ability to see the future shapes that future. Everyone knows this. She's a public resource, and the state of her abilities matters.

I still want to protect my friend.

"I've actually been finding these gruesome little offerings for a while," Savi offers up after a moment of quiet between us, filled by the birdsong in her thick spring trees despite the snow I walked through to get here. "Not only around the perimeter here. In the woods surrounding our cottages in Jacksonville, too."

I stare at her. "You mean not just the one I found tonight?"

"They are always such tiny, insignificant little creatures. A raccoon at most. It's hard to imagine there's any kind of message there."

"How have I not noticed a rash of butchered animals on our doorsteps? I would scent that immediately. From miles away."

Savi gazes at me. "I scrub them off the scent profile when I find them lying around in public places, like the cottages." When I stare back at her, she laughs. "It didn't seem serious to me. Certainly not serious enough to do anything about it. There are any number of creatures who might take exception to Winter, to Winter and Ariel, to you and me and our mysterious little Briar living there all together. I couldn't tell if the offerings were in protest or warning or just creatures sneaking around being creepy because they can. Besides." Her gaze hardens. "A better question would be why whoever is doing this wanted to make certain you were aware of it this time."

I don't think of much else all the way home.

I don't run through the mountains this time. I take the largely abandoned state road that used to connect the towns in this valley like little jewels strung along the same necklace—Bear Creek, in this case, then veer off onto the old greenway. I used to go jogging here in my human form, not the least bit intimidated by the scary people—mostly human—who lurked about along the wide, pleasant path along the river and liked to set fires, assault the odd passerby, and do as many drugs as possible.

They never bothered me. Back before the Reveal, it was always the marginal people—those who stayed on the edges—who could see me for what I was.

Now it isn't humans who lurk, but they're still more afraid of my wolf than I could ever be of them. I follow the path as it winds its way toward the center of Medford, now in ruins and overrun by vampires. Before I get there, I leave the greenway behind and take Stage Road again, letting it lead me into the foothills, with Jacksonville waiting just beyond.

It's late when I find myself on California Street again, the main drag. The holiday lights tug at me. I feel something like nostalgia for the childhood I never had here. When I pause and think about it, a wolf slinking through the shadows long after the human curfew, I realize it's the same longing I felt then. The yearning for a safe, sweet human life that involved roasted chestnuts, holiday parades, Santa's lap beneath a decorated Christmas tree, and all the things that go with human holidays. Candles. Feasts.

I can't imagine not being a wolf. Not being *me.* But every now and again, on lonely streets in my childhood home, I remember too well what it felt like to wonder. Back when I couldn't quite fathom what fate had in store for me, or what it meant for my future.

I pick up my pace as I lope up the hill, cutting back into the woods, thinking of Ty and these years I've had him in so many ways—if not the way he wants me now.

I would trade a thousand Christmases for a night with him, not that I'd tell him such a thing. He's arrogant enough as it is.

I remember that hope and grief, tangled altogether inside me high up on that rock. So close to the stars before that darkness came for me. That quiet, irrevocable understanding that one way or another, this in-between time of ours is ending.

And I still can't fathom how it will go, this future that fate has already decided for us, whether bitch goddesses rise in a rainstorm of blood or stay lodged down beneath the cold blue water of the lake, halfway to hell where they belong.

When I come barreling out into the yard at the top of the hill, Ty is so much on my mind, and in my nose, that it takes me a second to realize that he is *actually* here, too.

Lounging there against the door of my cottage like he's been there awhile.

I switch forms, because we generally keep our wolves in the woods, as I walk toward him.

His dark eyes glitter in the night, like constellations made of fate and fire, and only for me.

"Thought you were pretty much done with me," I drawl as I approach.

"I'd like to be," he retorts.

That doesn't hurt. We're not in that space—not right now—and anyway, I know he's lying.

"It was pretty dire last night." I shove my hands in the back pockets of my jeans as I take my time walking toward him. "I was pretty sure I was going to get the silent treatment until the new moon."

"I can't stay away from you, asshole," Ty growls at me. "You know that."

I used to think it was just that fated thing of ours. Some power that drew us to each other despite everything. Even all the way across the country, settled deep in all that concrete in New York City, I felt this pull to him. I always feel it.

Like we've been chained to each other from the start.

I'm beginning to wonder if fate has anything to do with it. Maybe it's just us.

"If you could," I say quietly, "that might go a long way toward soothing other people's feelings in the pack. They might not spend so much time worrying about whether or not I'm disrespecting you." I pause and lift my eyebrows at him. *"My liege."*

He smirks at that title that no one calls him, ever, then pushes himself off my front door in another effortless show of grace and offhanded athleticism. Like he does.

"You're definitely disrespecting me," he assures me. "All day and all night, far as I can tell. Good thing you're hot."

I tip my head back as he comes closer and keeps coming, until he's towering over me. "How hot?" I ask. "Exactly? Feel free to give examples."

I smile as he growls at me. Then I laugh as he picks me up, tosses me over his shoulder, and hauls me into my cottage to toss me face down on my very soft bed.

Where he spends a very long time showing me exactly what he means by *hot.*

6.

Cold Moon, Last Quarter Half-Moon

It's a week of more lectures in the same theme from my brothers, snide comments from pack members when I can't avoid them in town, and Ty in one of his moods—which means a whole lot of wild sex and very little talking.

Historically, this sort of mood occurs when he knows that one of us will be unhappy with whatever conversation he's avoiding. Also historically, the upset one is me, so I'm in no rush to push him into saying things I don't really want to hear.

Super healthy as always, that's us.

I focus on work. The trolls demanding tithes on the California border and hiding in the rocks that line Siskiyou Summit, pelting anyone who dares try to pass with debris and the odd explosive. I practice for the upcoming wolf week by keeping my expression neutral—very queenly and demure—when my brothers bitch at me. I allow random pack members to growl at me and only smile sweetly in return. Not because I'm so diplomatic and *good*, as I might like to pretend, but because I know they find it annoying.

By the time Saturday rolls around, I'm ready to step away from all things pack for a minute. So I'm practically gleeful when I catch Winter in the kitchen that night.

"It's like you barely live here anymore," I say, leaning against the counter. There are so many things I want to tell her. Mostly about the dead offerings that still keep popping up. Or the fact that I've had *several* conversations with Briar this week, all . . . pleasant. Friendly, even. Not to mention, Winter is the only person I'd consider talking to about my experience at Savi's house. And the somehow startling news that she's *married*.

This is kind of how I felt about my college friends, except they didn't know what I was hiding from them. Winter knows exactly who I am. Before this fall, I had no idea it was possible to have nonpack friends. *Real* friends. We used to get warned against forming attachments to any humans in school, since nothing could ever come of them.

"Tell me about it," Winter is saying, pulling out the bread she freezes and rations, then prying off a couple of slices with a knife. "I had no idea that my poor grandmother was Dear Abby for every last creature that slithered out of the slime." She remembers who she's talking to, and her mouth curves. "Or from a very nice, upscale den, I'm sure."

"Do you have to serve coffee drinks while providing prophecies?" I ask. "If so, you should charge more."

"I'm basically one-stop shopping." She puts her bread into the old-school toaster and presses the lever down. "Caffeine to get you peppy, cards to make you mopey, and a selection of vampire bodyguards who actually hate everyone and everything to keep us all honest. It's *great*."

"I didn't know you had coffee-stand guards."

"Don't we all have guards?" Winter asks with a laugh.

I realize it's been a long time since I thought of the various patrols that go on around these woods, and around me in particular, as *guards*. But of course they are. None of the powers in this valley mess around with what's theirs.

Though I do wonder how it is that something is running around committing bloody small-mammal murders and taking the time to arrange the corpses like some grisly art project without ever coming to the notice of those guards.

I make a mental note to spend less time on my sweet, unassuming smile that no one believes anyway and more time on a few important questions when I see more of my pack members in the woods around here.

Savi comes sweeping into the back door then, dropping the temperature around her the way she always does. Her scent is like water, crisp and cool, with a hint of something darker and colder beneath. Winter, on the other hand, smells a little bit of that bright humanity, the distinct scent of vampires in general and Ariel Skinner himself in particular, plus something else that I suspect is whatever magic makes her the oracle.

I can pick up all of these things without even trying, here in my human form, but I can't pick up the perpetrator who's only been getting bolder this week. There was a bat crucified and hung on one of Savi's cottage windows last night. I'm pretty sure that what I nearly tripped on two days ago was a raccoon head.

"I've been thinking a lot about what might make Ariel move into a tiny little cottage next to a run-down house in the hills," Winter says, gazing at Savi while the toaster hums behind her. "But he doesn't even really like to stay in the house. Yet you do?"

Maybe she's still coming to terms with how powerful her tenant really is.

"A marvelous thing about containing multitudes," Savi says as she swings open the refrigerator and gazes at her shelf inside, "is that you can always make yourself comfortable wherever you find yourself. That's real magic."

"That and she gets an in with the oracle, obviously," I say, and shrug when Savi lifts a brow at me. "What? It's true. That's exactly why you and I moved in here."

Savi pulls out some of the strange things she claims she loves to eat, all variations on the same sort of theme. Like nuts that become milks, or worse, cheeses. "Meats" that are . . . not. "I hope I never live too long to fully enjoy the beauty of a rustic cottage."

"It's okay," Winter says quietly. "I know how things work now."

I glance at Savi, then touch my shoulder to Winter's. "If that was the only reason we stayed here, we would have left by now."

Winter presses against me for a moment, then busies herself with her toast as it pops back up.

"I'm glad we're all here," Savi says merrily as she arranges her Frankenstein food on a plate and then brings it over to the table. "Winter, we need you to look at your cards."

"You and everyone else," I think I hear Winter mutter. I grab myself a few things from my own refrigerator shelf and head to the table too.

"Maddox and I keep finding dead things around," Savi announces, almost merrily.

Winter fixes herself a sandwich on her toasted bread, then joins us at the table. "What kind of dead things? That's a pretty broad term around here these days. You could mean that the zombies are rooting around in the trash again. They better not be."

"Little dead things," I assure her. "Basically roadkill. Just not, you know, killed on the actual road."

"Are you worried about this roadkill?"

"'Worried' is a strong word." Savi makes a show of drinking whatever it is she has in front her. Essence of something. "We want to see what the cards have to say, that's all. Just to make sure we're not overlooking anything."

"I haven't seen any dead things," Winter says.

"In fairness," I drawl, "you're sleeping with one. That might blur the vision."

Winter laughs. She also gives me the finger. What she does not do is make any move to pull her cards out when we all know she has them on her. They follow her wherever she goes.

"I'm sure it's fine," she says. Dismissively, I think. "It's December. Things die."

"That's true," Savi murmurs. "What they don't normally do is eviscerate themselves and then arrange their mutilated bodies like offerings to a dark lord of one sort or another. So you see the issue."

Winter takes a huge bite of her sandwich and then takes her time chewing. Then even longer, it seems to me, for the swallowing. "The cards and I are having a small break when it comes to any personal questions I might have," she says, when I think she's never going to speak again.

"Maybe that's why your visions are muddy," I suggest.

Winter shrugs, though I'm not sure I believe the nonchalance. "Maybe. I don't think it's anything to worry about. The cards and I just need to get to know each other again, and not in a crisis. But I'll be happy to look into your poor, murdered animals once we're good."

"How can you have a breakup with a pack of cards?" I ask her.

"You say that like they're a pack of playing cards and I'm trying to play 52-card pickup." She sounds a little touchy then, and Savi's lifted brow suggests we both think this. Winter frowns at her sandwich. "You know perfectly well that the cards are a whole thing. Right now they only want to tell me about the overwrought romantic lives of whatever creature shows up in the coffee-stand line."

The three of us sit there in silence. I would not describe the mood around the table as tense, precisely, but it's definitely *something*. Because when Briar comes in through the back door, flinging it open as if she expected that no one would be in the kitchen, she stops dead when she sees us.

I find studying her to be an excellent diversion from an oracle who's at odds with her cards, so I take my time with it. Tonight's punk-girl-goes-slightly-goth-but-lives-in-Oregon-so-is-also-crunchy ensemble involves that same hat tugged down low, her dark hair hanging down out of it and not in braids this time, and a dark flannel thrown over her skirt, ripped leggings, and combat boots.

I decide she's adorable with her nose piercings and quite a few others placed in other strategic places on her lips and tongue and eyebrows, despite what I always thought was true about fae. And fae-adjacent folks. Namely that one or another variety of fae has an aversion to metal. Though I might have gotten that from a book.

Briar blinks at us. "Um. Hi?"

I watch the way she lifts her hand up to her neck, as if she's pressing her fingers into her throat—though she actually rests her fingers a little bit lower.

"Oh, hey," I say, and smile at her. This makes her blink again, and her fingers near her clavicle twitch.

"It's been a minute," Winter chimes in, which seems to confuse Briar more.

Savi looks back and forth between Winter and me like we've started to sprout fungi from our heads. I am forced to conclude that we suck at the whole *attempting to be friends* thing. Winter must look away, because she focuses on her plate again.

Briar shuffles around the now-awkwardly-quiet kitchen. Earlier in the week she asked me about my mother. About Ty, who she called my boyfriend, which is not inaccurate and yet hilarious. Tonight she doesn't ask anything—probably because we made it weird. She slams some pots and pans around, then doesn't use them. She opens and closes the cupboard doors, but doesn't take anything out.

Finally, Briar rushes over to the fourth available seat at the table and sits down with a hunk of bread. Not Winter's bread. This bread looks extremely healthy and brown, with seeds.

I have never seen Briar eat anything that didn't have sugar in it.

We all stare at it. She looks down at it too, and once again, I'm certain I can see some color on her cheeks.

"It's actually my birthday," she belts out into the silence.

For a moment, no one says anything.

Then we all do. At the same time.

"Happy birthday," Savi practically sings, inclining her head as she does. "How wonderful."

Winter shakes her head. "You seem thrilled about that?"

"Kudos," I manage to get out.

We all talk over each other, and Briar looks as if she can't decide whether to be mortified or horrified, but this tracks. This is awkward people doing awkward shit, and it's easy to just roll with that. I can pretend I don't notice awkwardness. That's basically how I survive pack gatherings.

"I don't usually celebrate my birthday," she says when the rest of us have subsided back into the silence. Briar makes a face. "I think birthdays are lame."

"Okay," I hear myself say.

Savi eyes me. Winter keeps her gaze trained on Briar.

Briar glares down at her hunk of bread, then crosses her arms as if it gave her some lip. With that many seeds and a distinct resemblance to bran, I suspect it very well might have.

"You three are the closest thing I have to friends." Briar bites this out without looking at any one of us directly, though her cheeks get even redder. "I'm not saying that I want to be besties or anything weird, but, it being my birthday and all, I thought maybe we could . . ."

No one feeds in the next word for her. I'm not sure any of us can move, and anyway, I know that I have no idea where she's going with this. It could be anywhere at all. Does she want cake and a bit of singing? Is she after a little of that hair-braiding? A few cage matches?

I can believe any of that and none of that when it comes to Briar.

We all stare at her, waiting.

Briar clears her throat. *"Go out,"* she manages to say, as if she's throwing the words from her mouth and really, they're made of marbles. "Maybe we could go out."

"Go out?" Winter echoes, as if she's never heard the term.

"Of the house?" Savi asks, and I suppose it's possible that *she* really hasn't heard the term before.

"Do you want to go out with me?" Briar asks, a little too loudly. A little too bluntly. Almost angrily, really, like this is happening *to* her when she's the one making this offer, and I swear it makes my heart hurt a little. I feel like I *see* her. "To a club. Because it's Saturday. And my birthday. And people do festive shit like this."

There's a beat while we digest this, except I'm already there.

"Honestly?" I say. "I can't think of anything that I would rather do more."

Briar jerks in her chair at that, like she was expecting me to bring the wolf out and eat her for dessert. Like she was expecting to be cruelly rebuffed, and that makes me soften toward her even more.

"Same," Winter says staunchly.

I can feel Savi staring at us, but I grin at my housemate—of a sort—and friend. "We would love to go out with you, Briar. *Clubbing* in Medford on the far side of the Reveal. Whatever that means to you."

This is how the four of us end up milling around a crowd of the Kind in the ruins of what was once an old-age home called the Manor that sat atop its own little hill in the midway point of the valley. These days it houses a collection of various species, all living together instead of off in the usual Kind clans that have been sticking to their own for centuries.

This is the kind of progress I wish werewolves could make too. It's not every day you see a centaur canoodling with a Valkyrie in the middle of a rave, and it might not seem like a revolution, but I know it is. We all got to step out of the shadows that were pushed upon us only for my pack to step back in of their own volition.

There has to be a better way. Maybe it really is dancing.

Maybe I just want it to be this close to the all-pack gathering, where new ideas of any sort are not exactly encouraged, and especially not from females who should be mated by now.

Savi looks around, looks bemused, and disappears. Literally. One moment she's standing beside me, the next she's gone, and a few moments later I think I see her up high on the rooftop of the highest building. Alone.

Briar follows my gaze and looks like she wishes she was up there, too. "This is so great," she says, though she sounds like there's glass in her mouth, and her face is bright red. "I'm going to, uh, go get us drinks or something."

Before I can tell her that she should know better than to drink strange brews made by strange magic in even stranger places, she shoves her way into the crowd. In moments, I can't even track her beanie.

"I don't want to know what happened to all the people who lived here, do I," Winter mutters as she looks around, taking in the crowd around us and the loud music that seems to do its own dancing, lifting and falling and *beckoning* to such an extent that I suspect the DJ must be a siren.

"You already know," I tell her, and I fling an arm over her shoulders as we move deeper into the party.

"Is this really what monsters do every night while all the humans lock themselves up in fear?" she asks, her eyes wide.

I don't know how to tell her that while I understand where she's coming from, I find this *glorious*. Back when I was growing up here, parties like this took place way out in the woods, but very seldomly. *Very* carefully. No one ever wanted to draw too much attention. And even then, there wasn't too much interspecies mingling. We all knew about each other, but it wasn't wise to get together in one place. Better not to be an easy target.

"Not every night," I assure her. Because some nights it rains.

There are mages everywhere, making the sky bleed different colors above this hill. It's better than disco balls and all the flashing neon lights that punctuated the clubs I went to in New York City. The music seems to wind its way into my bones, into everyone's insides from the look of it, and creatures of every description are dancing, laughing.

Free.

There's a lot about the Reveal that I don't love, but then, on the other side, there's this. The Kind out here beneath an open sky without having to worry about being discovered. Without knowing that if we're caught, we'll be the reason our families—or our whole species—will be exterminated.

Exterminated if we're lucky. Experimented on and then exterminated, if not. Humans with their scientific labs and hatred of anything they can't explain have always been *our* boogeymen.

I can't say I miss those days. And though I try to remain sensitive to Winter's mostly human response to this—and what it means that this can happen, here in a place where humans lived—I can't help myself.

For a little while I throw my head back, lift my arms up, and let myself *feel*. I let the beat take me on this journey with everyone else. I let the music do its level best to convince me that just because one world ended, that doesn't mean the next one can't be beautiful.

I want to believe this. I *need* to believe this.

Winter doesn't throw herself into the dancing like I do, but when she does move it's like there's a force field around her. Everyone simply . . . gets out of her way. There's a ring around her wherever she goes, and it's only when she looks at me in confusion that I realize she probably hasn't been in a crowd like this since everything went down between her and Ariel.

"It's his mark," I tell her. "Everyone is here to party, not risk the displeasure of the vampire king. They're giving you space because if they don't, they know they'll have to deal with him. No one wants that."

"I don't know how I feel about that," she says.

I laugh, and dance a little more wildly. "I feel that we should take advantage of having our own dance space wherever we go."

I realize that I have no idea if Winter is the dancing type. I didn't know her very well in high school, we certainly didn't run in the same circles, and the past couple of months haven't lent themselves to a whole lot of levity.

I'm surprised, and kind of thrilled, when she throws her hands up and dances with me.

We dance and we dance. I don't think about pack shit. I don't think about anything. I steer Winter away from any drinks offered by strangers, and I don't let the curious draw too near once they start to get used to the fact she's marked by Ariel. I hope she doesn't see some of the creepier Kind who are here too, swaying on their tentacles and such, but she doesn't seem to notice. Or maybe she's given them all dating advice in the coffee-stand drive-through and no longer finds them all that creepy.

We just dance. We have a few drinks made of alcohol with no magical boosters. Winter and I speculate about where Briar went and conclude that she was overwhelmed by her own invitation and likely had to go decompress somewhere, but the music is too good to chase after her. Besides, she knows where we are.

I haven't felt this light since New York, I realize. And maybe not even then, because there was too much weight on what I was doing, what I was leaving behind while I was doing it, and what my future would hold. And much as I loved my years in New York, I was hiding there.

Not having to hide who I am, it turns out, changes everything.

We keep dancing until the sky starts to lighten in the distance.

The party starts to break up. The music stops, which feels like a small tragedy. Winter and I stagger our way through the crowd and out of the ruins.

And when we do, we come face-to-face with Ty.

He's leaning against what was once a retaining wall, his back to the valley. This reminds me of a thousand other nights across the years. I couldn't go anywhere without someone—usually one of my brothers—reporting my whereabouts back to Ty. He would often show up to take me home, a quiet reminder that I was his to everyone involved.

Maybe especially to me.

I look over my shoulder toward the crowd and think I see Briar's beanie heading in the opposite direction. I can't blame her. Ty's neutral face—the one he's wearing now—makes most people want to cry. And run. I figure I'll catch up with her back at the cottages and see how her birthday went from her perspective.

When I look back, Ariel has appeared.

"Reinforcements?" I ask.

Beside me, Winter laughs, her eyes entirely for her freakishly beautiful lover, all marble slabs of muscle and that cool silver gaze.

"Like I need help hauling your ass home, babe," Ty says, and he sounds growly, but I can hear the laughter in his voice.

"Fantastic," says Savi, floating into view. Possibly descending from the still-bright stars. "We're all together at last. Now maybe we can discuss what's happening around here."

7.

“I didn’t realize we were *all* into clubbing,” I drawl, folding my arms over my chest and smirking at Savi and Ty. And at Ariel too. This is likely foolish, but I’m betting he’s unlikely to kill me in Winter’s presence. Not to mention Ty’s. “We would have had everyone over to pregame.”

Ariel peers at me with those silver eyes of his. He doesn’t say anything.

Ty laughs. “Never more attitude than when you know you’re doing something you shouldn’t. You can’t help yourself, can you.”

Maybe I can’t. Or maybe I’ve never really subscribed to the highly selective accepted wisdom around here that I’m supposed to act as if I’ve been locked away in the den all this time whether I’ve *done my duty* or not.

“Dancing is never wrong, Ty,” I chide him, in a way I would never do if we weren’t in public, and he knows that. His dark gaze gleams, and I can feel my favorite kind of retribution in the air between us.

Savi, who is the one who actually controls the air between us and everywhere else, lets out a long-suffering sigh. “I’ve been doing a lot of research into the consistent sacrifices that have been turning up all over my land, and yours.” She nods at Winter when she says that.

Winter blinks. “Sacrifices?” She considers. “Oh, you mean your little murdered animals. You didn’t mention they were *sacrifices*.”

My gaze is on Ty, who looks equally surprised by the use of that word. Not a big shock, since I haven't told him.

Savi either doesn't care about these undercurrents or doesn't notice them. My money is on the first. "Maddox and I discussed this at length the other night when she came to see me on my mountain."

I can feel Ty's gaze lighting up the side of my face now, so I make sure to keep my attention on Savi instead. I wonder if she's deliberately exposing me like this or if it doesn't occur to her that some things can stay private.

"Combined with her experience of being specifically pursued by what felt like some kind of great darkness," Savi is saying, sedately, which doesn't help me any, "we came to the obvious conclusion. That either our favorite goddess isn't quite as imprisoned as we'd like her to be—an eventuality we knew was possible, though I didn't think it would be this soon—or someone else wants us to think that she's fighting her way free."

Beside me, Winter is shaking her head. "I'm still stuck on *sacrifices*. You said *roadkill*."

"I said *like* roadkill," I remind her.

"It's been small rodents, for the most part." Savi's gaze is cool as she looks from Winter to Ariel, then back again. "The corpses are staged. Eviscerated creatively and presented in the bloodiest possible way. For maximum effect, one assumes. That's initially why I thought it was perhaps a disaffected acolyte, acting in the spirit of overzealous mourning for their lost goddess, as acolytes are known to do."

I am not conversant on acolytes. Still. "A random minion, mourning or otherwise, wouldn't be able to sneak all around Winter's land placing disgusting things on the cottage steps and then disappearing again without leaving any kind of scent trail." I nod at Savi. "I know you've been scent-scrubbing the kills themselves, but they should still have left trails coming to and from the kill sites. There should be hints all over the woods."

"I only do that when I'm in my cottage," Savi says, with a careless wave of her hand. "Who can relax when the air is full of viscera and ill intent?"

Who indeed.

This time, there's no avoiding the narrow way that Ty is glaring at me. But I have to hand it to him. If I wasn't already perfectly aware that he didn't know about any of this, I wouldn't be able to tell that from his expression. It's obvious to me that I'm going to have to answer a whole lot of questions later, but for right now he's letting it ride.

It's one of the many reasons he's the greatest werewolf king in generations. Which is neither here nor there, but something in me warms just the same.

"There is a lot of lore to wade through concerning how and if the death goddess can reemerge," Savi says, nodding in my direction. "Attempting to glean information from magical sources that do not wish to share is always challenging, of course. Scrolls and spells can be very opinionated. They like to keep their secrets to themselves."

She waves her hand as if that is a matter of such obvious fact that it doesn't require any more discussion. It reminds me, not for the first time, that sorcery is a very different kind of magic than mine. Vampirism too. So many stuffy and courtly traditions, ancient hierarchies that aren't always based on obvious merit, and endless intellectual chess matches in and around the things that magic can do, or make someone else do, or be used widely to make whole populations do.

Everything about their kind of magic is a complication layered on a stack of other, deeper, older complications.

Wolves have always taken pride in being different. Simpler. More basic—but also more real, if you ask me. Yet suddenly I wonder if that's part of why we've always been kept on the outskirts of real power. If it weren't for Ty making himself such a force to be reckoned with in this valley, and in the whole of the North American West, would he and I even be standing here right now? Ty—*a* werewolf king, not *the* werewolf king—on equal footing with one of the only remaining known sorcerers and the most legendary vampire around?

If it weren't for Ty, we would have as much say in the magical goings-on in the valley, and the rest of the world, as any random truck-driving and typically larcenous ogre. Which is to say, none.

"There's only one way that Vinča could rise again, according to every source I could locate," Savi continues. "If I could find this, so could someone else. It requires a very old, very powerful ritual called the Three Sisters."

Ariel makes a noise. "The blood of a maiden, a mother, and a crone."

Savi inclines her head. "You're familiar with the ritual."

"I've seen it performed before." That cool, assessing gaze of his sweeps over Savi, then moves to Winter. Then me, and I have to school myself not to shiver. "The obvious conclusion is that someone has cast the three of you in these roles."

Winter makes a face. "I'm literally none of those things. Neither is Maddox." She shrugs in Savi's direction. "Still not entirely sure what you are, if I'm honest."

But I can see it. "It would take some interpretation," I say. I look at Winter. "You're brand-new to being an oracle. A babe in the woods, really. That would make you the maiden. I'm the fated mate of the local werewolf king. The preordained mother to not only his future young but, theoretically, to the whole of the pack. Metaphorically speaking."

I can't help but look at Ty then. He looks . . . not precisely amused. But not furious, either.

"Theoretically," he rumbles.

I move on to Savi. "And you are an extremely wise woman of a great many years. If not whole millennia or two. It's unclear."

"I accept and revere crone energy," Savi says, with one of her mysterious smiles.

"It would make sense," Winter agrees after a moment. "Because it requires interpretation, maybe, but it also requires knowing who we are. Vinča does. She was in my head and all up in our business for a while there. And she certainly knows who fought her at Crater Lake." She blows out a breath. "But I haven't seen any sacrifices."

Ariel moves from over near Ty to Winter's side in one of those tricky vampire flashes, flickering out in one spot and into another. I repress the urge to flinch when he's suddenly *right here*, putting his hand on the nape of Winter's neck. About a foot away from me.

This is something that clearly soothes her when I'm pretty sure all that cold would be the end of me.

"I've seen them. I removed them." When Winter stares at him, Ariel inclines his head slightly. "I assumed these offerings were little more than commentary on my choice of consort. I treated them with the deference such commentary deserves."

I assume that's code for him tossing them in the trash and erasing the evidence, but vampire-style, with tricks and flash.

But he's still looking down at Winter. "I assumed that if they were anything more than that, you would have had a vision."

"Yeah," Winter agrees. "You'd think." She shakes her head. "I can't actually tell if I'm not having visions the way I used to or if they're coming out wrong, somehow. I can read cards for randoms in the coffee-stand line, but my dreams have gone all swampy. I definitely haven't seen anything about anyone getting sacrificed. The last time around, Vinča had no qualms whatsoever about giving me hints of what was to come. Or letting me know how much it would hurt."

"Perhaps she's learned her lesson," Ariel suggests, but his silver gaze is cool. "There is a first time for everything, I am told."

Ty makes a low noise, not quite a growl. "So what you're telling me is that something or someone is getting around Maddox's scenting abilities, a sorceress's wards that have held off hordes of manticores and werespiders without a hitch, and the oracle's visions." He looks around at each of us. "Not to mention all the extra security that's supposedly in place to protect that entire piece of property, including by my own pack. How is that possible? Who has that kind of power?"

Having happily forgotten all about the *werespider* attacks that occurred when I was very small and still give me the odd nightmare, I'm not psyched to think about them now. I also think we all know who *could* have that power, if we hadn't vanquished her. We would also all know if she'd found a way to rise. So even if it involves Vinča, it can't *be* Vinča.

This feels less reassuring than it should, I think.

It's clear the three great powers in this valley agree.

Back behind us, I see the hint of the rising sun above the Cascades. But before it can crest the mountains and spill over into the valley, Savi murmurs something. Even before she's done, the clouds roll in, making the sun nothing more than a suggestion.

"Thank you." Ariel acknowledges Savi and her control of the weather—specifically, the sunlight. It's one of the reasons that vampires are so strong here. The other reason is Ariel himself. "I'll put a closer watch on the house and cottages. I think I'd feel better about all of this if I had a better idea who's lurking around the place."

"No one," Ty says immediately, "or I'd know about it."

Ariel inclines his head. "And yet."

Savi wrinkles her lovely nose and a light mist shivers over us, standing out here on this abandoned hill. "I'll continue my research. Ancient lore predicted what happened at Halloween. It's possible it could point toward what happens next. Meanwhile, I think we should all keep an eye out for indications that Vinča's acolytes are still here. Or gathering here in any kind of force. I personally haven't seen any of the red cloaks, but that doesn't mean that they've gone away. They might simply be biding their time."

"I always thought that if the leader disappears, then their cult falls apart." I smile slightly when Ty looks at me, no doubt wondering why it is I know anything about cults to begin with. Little realizing I took a whole course on the topic in college.

I won't share with him that I was trying to decide if he was simply a charismatic male—or if he was the kind of compelling that could lead to things far more unsavory than simply my own self-immolation.

"You are talking about mortal cult leaders," Savi tells me. "The tragedy with immortal cults, particularly with godheads of any description, is that all that is required is the *belief* that they will rise again. Everybody loves a resurrection story. It can animate whole populations for millennia. No *actual* resurrection required."

She waves her hand. There's a shower of light, and then she's gone.

Winter and I exchange a look. I want to ask her about that vision she had about Briar, however strange and unclear. Maybe she wants to tell me—but we're not alone. I guess we both feel the same strange protectiveness over Briar, though it makes no sense. We both know, I'm sure, that she wouldn't spare a thought for us if the situations were reversed.

Hell, she'd have taken us out already.

"There are wolves in the Rockies," Ariel says to Ty, almost musingly, as if this is what he's actually been thinking about all this time. Yet only now decided to throw it out to the rest of us. Winter and I exchange an amused look. "More than usual."

"I'm sure I mentioned that the all-pack gathering will be taking place here next week," Ty says, with a shit-eating grin that indicates he's sure of no such thing. "Some of them are used to vampires. Others? Not so much. Might want to tell your little subleeches to watch themselves."

"Charming." Ariel eyes Ty for a moment. "Tell your furry friends that we have leash laws in this valley. Or I will."

I expect Ty to react badly to that, but he laughs. And I swear I see the vampire king smile as he disappears in a literal puff of smoke, taking Winter with him.

That means Ty and I are alone at last in this cold, misty morning that Savi has prepared for us. After a long night of dancing, it feels like a soft, cool blessing.

For a long moment, he doesn't say anything. Neither do I. I look around instead, at the remains of the party and the thin, pale morning light. No direct sunlight, just that mist and gray that is at least an improvement over the summer smoke that lasts well into fall. Most of the Kind who were partying have slunk away. Those who live here have crept off to their beds.

There's no one close to where Ty and I are standing at the edge of the hill, like we're the only ones left in this whole valley.

"How long have you been finding these sacrifices?" he asks.

He doesn't look at me while he asks it.

I feel my stomach tremble a little, wondering how this is going to go. Wondering if I've finally had my fill of fighting with him.

"The night of the full moon was the first time," I tell him. "And it wasn't at my cottage that time. It was on the trail on the way to the den. I meant to tell you. But then . . ."

I don't finish that sentence. He knows what happened on the full moon. What always happens on every full moon.

"Pretty sure I saw you every single night between then and now," Ty points out in a low, steady voice I do not trust at all. "Am I missing something?"

I don't answer that either.

He turns then, and takes his time looking at me. It's like he's trying to read things on my face that he doubts I'll say out loud, and I hate that he has every reason to think that.

"And you having conversations with the sorceress because you happen to find yourselves in Winter's kitchen at the same time is one thing. That kind of easy access was one of the reasons I agreed to let you stay there. I'm all for it."

"But," I murmur.

His gaze darkens. "But I'm pretty sure I heard her say that you went to her. All the way down to Ashland and up into those mountains where anything could happen to you. Without letting anyone know. Without giving anyone, even me, a heads-up that you were doing it. Is that what happened?"

I don't bother to argue. "It is."

I expect him to blow up, but he doesn't. He only studies me for what seems like an inordinate amount of time.

Then he makes me feel as if he let out a heavy sigh, though he doesn't actually do it. "If any other member of the pack did something like that, how do you think I would respond? How would you advise me to react?"

In my capacity as his mate, he means. The mate he would trust with all his pack business, he means.

Ouch.

"You're right," I say. "I should have told you. I don't know why I didn't."

"You don't? That's funny, Maddox. Because I do."

He shakes his head at me, and then he starts walking. If he wanted to get the hell away from me—as he has many times in the past—he would do that. He would shift and take off, and while I might be pretty fast, I'm not a werewolf alpha who won his position with his claws, his strength, and the simple fact that no one can catch him.

I walk with him, falling into his rhythm easily, as if his movement compels mine. As if we match. We don't walk a lot of places together, not in our human forms, and there's something about it that gets to me. It amazes me that we can fit so well together as both wolves and humans, but I think better of saying that.

That's not something he's going to want to hear. Not in the strange mood he's in.

We head down the hill, through gnarled trees in the throes of their winter blues. At the bottom, we wander through a haphazard collection of abandoned buildings and old picked-over shops. We keep going until we find ourselves on one of the old roads that winds across the valley floor, crosses what was once the interstate a bit farther south than the center of Medford, and eventually makes its way over to Jacksonville and the hills beyond.

"You know as well as I do that we're coming to the end here," he tells me, quietly, as we pick our way across churned-up asphalt and around downed trees that have likely been left as convenient barricades for those who imagine themselves highwaymen. "I don't have to keep saying it."

The mist is playing hide-and-seek out in the old pear orchards. The clouds scud along the sky, looking like they're trying to collide with the mountains, though they never do. I can almost see the trails etched into the hillsides as we walk, reminding me of hikes I took long ago with human schoolchildren who could never see the creatures who lurked just out of sight.

Now it's the humans who hide.

I take my time answering him, because my heart hurts and I don't want him to hear that. Not now. "Everything ends, Ty. You and me. The world. You're going to have to be more specific. The vague threats wore off a long time ago."

Beside me, he makes a low noise again. Still not really a growl. "I'm not threatening you."

"Aren't you?" I keep my voice quiet too. The air is crisp and soft at once, winter infusing every breath although technically, it's still fall. "You could have put a stop to all of this a long time ago. You could have told every single member of the pack, in no uncertain terms, that you support what I'm doing no matter how long it takes. You—"

"What the fuck do you think I told them?" Ty growls at me.

He stops walking, so I do too. We cover a lot of ground pretty quickly, even on the substandard two feet. We're already up on Bellinger Lane, with its sweet view over pretty Jacksonville, looking like the dreams I can't kick of the normal life I've never had.

Maybe that's been my problem all along.

"Are you kidding me?" Ty demands. "All I do is tell everyone who dares think about you wrong that you have my absolute and complete support in all things. Do you really think this would have gone so far if I didn't?"

"I'm the one they growl at—" I begin.

"If I didn't support you one hundred goddamn percent," Ty belts out, "you would have been mated as a little girl with grown-ass babies of your own by now. That's exactly how it goes down in other packs. In *every* other pack."

My heart is pounding against my ribs. "Do you really want me to thank you for not making sure that I was popping out litters as a thirteen-year-old?"

"You're so full of shit."

He doesn't say that like he's pissed at me. He says it in a kind of exasperation, and again, my heart starts performing acrobatics inside my chest. Like I'm losing something here, right in front of my eyes.

I don't cry, but just now, I feel like maybe a sob is the only thing that might help.

Ty takes his time looking at me. First he looks to the hills. To the woods where we've always been, wolves just like us. Then over toward the town of Jacksonville, a monument to another lost world.

Only when the lump in my throat begins to feel like a possible hazard does he turn to me. He reaches over and wraps those massive hands of his around my shoulders. He even gives me a little shake, to get my attention.

But I like it, because it knocks that sob right out of my throat.

"I like that you're educated, Maddox. It's hot. I like that you're different. I fucking love that you're so hell-bent on proving your worth to the pack. There are a lot of other pack members who should do the same, though they never will, because they think simply existing in the pack is enough. You've been proving yourself for years. Do you think I don't see that? I do."

"Then what does it matter which full moon we choose?" I ask, my voice quiet with all the apprehension and fear, longing and need at war inside me. "Why can't we take our own time?"

"We had time," he tells me. "And we're rapidly approaching a point where I can't protect you anymore. We might be past it."

I blow out a breath. "That point would be where you *decide* not to. Is this about us, Ty? Or is this about your ego?"

I realize once I say it that I *want* him to explode. That I *want* him to storm off or yell or ignite into that flame we only ever douse a little by fucking it out.

What I don't want is the way he looks at me like he knows me, inside and out. Like he can see every thought, dark and light and in between, that scrolls through my head.

Like I might be the book smart one, but I'm the only book he reads—and he knows me by heart.

I don't even know what argument I'm making, especially when he doesn't explode. When he doesn't bring his temper into play, that means I can't either, and I feel . . . entirely too many other things instead. None I want to name.

He grips my shoulders tighter and pulls me toward him. I expect him to growl something in my face. Maybe even bite me.

Instead, he kisses me.

It's a bruising, beautiful kiss. It's somehow all the passion we always have but wrapped up in frustration, longing, and that bittersweet understanding that neither one of us can have exactly what we want.

That we don't get to be Ty and Maddox, following our own road. We don't get to do anything separate from the pack, no matter how much I wish we could. Ty is a king. I'm his queen or I'm no one.

There are no in-betweens. There never have been.

I know full well that if he hadn't carved out these spaces for me, my life would look completely different. Unrecognizably so. If he hadn't supported me, likely with teeth and claws over the years now that I consider it, I never would have had what autonomy I do now.

He might give me a hard time, but he sure as hell doesn't let anyone else do it, not directly. But that's changing too. That's part of why all of this hurts so much, I understand as his mouth teases mine.

Because it's over. It's just a question of when. And how.

Ty kisses me again and again, a dance of tongue and teeth.

It's a kind of mating. It breaks my heart.

Every slide of his mouth on mine breaks my heart and makes it bigger, and if I had ever known how to stop loving this man, this glorious creature, I'd like to think I would have. I would have run off from New York. I would have lost myself, given up my wolf, and lived in cities too large and too packed tight with people for anyone to track me.

I toyed with the idea of those escapes from time to time, but I always came back to this.

To him.

Now there's no pretending that anything's going to change. Now there's just us.

He pulls away and looks down at me, his dark eyes full of realizations that look a lot like the ones in my head. He runs his thumb over my lips and for a moment, out here in an early morning with no one around, he closes his eyes as he rests his forehead against mine.

I know he's feeling all the same things that I am. I know that he's more than the tough-as-nails alpha, the undefeated fighter, the most powerful werewolf in living memory.

For a moment, here with me, he's just Ty.

And I think, maybe this will work out after all. Because beneath pack and fate and noise and full moons, tradition that scares me and traditions that will claim us both, there's this.

Us.

Maybe moments pass. Maybe it's half a day. I can't tell, but when he pulls away he kisses me again, right between my eyes.

"Get some sleep," he tells me. "You know some of the packs will turn up early. They always do, the dickheads. And we're going to have to put on a show, babe. Game faces all around. You ready?"

"I know," I assure him. "I'm ready," I lie.

He gives me that crooked smile I know is only mine. And then he is shifting before me, one moment a beautiful man and the next a stunning, enormous wolf. I smooth my hands over his wide snout, move them up behind his ears, and then I return his kiss. I go up on my toes and I kiss him on his furry forehead.

Ty licks me, then takes off for the hills.

I should do the same, but I walk instead. I walk all the way back to Jacksonville, breathing in the mist that flows and ebbs around the shops. I take my usual path through the woods, a little more aware this time that there should be more pack guards around.

That I should *see* them instead of sensing, vaguely, that there are pack members in the wider vicinity.

When I get to my cottage, I'm delighted to find that there are no bloody sacrifices demanding my attention. I lock the door behind me, crawl into my soft bed, and sleep.

But it feels like four seconds later that I'm woken up again, abruptly.

To the sound of strange wolves howling, right outside.

8.

Cold Moon, waning crescent

Still dazed with sleep and not entirely sure if I'm dreaming or not, I throw open the door to my cottage to find about five wolves—none of them members of my pack—milling around in the front yard.

Another breath, and I recognize them. Scent helps lock it in.

It would be polite to shift into my wolf form. I don't.

I lean against the doorframe instead, cross my arms like I'm bored instead of unpleasantly jolted awake, and wait for the howling to stop.

But they're clearly here to make a point, so that takes a minute.

When it finally dies down—a good five minutes later, which is a long time for them to be making such a ruckus in someone else's territory—the biggest wolf sits there, regarding me cannily. I return the favor. I can see that there's more salt than pepper on his snout these days. His fur is not as lustrously black as it was five years ago.

"Little bit of a brash greeting, McCaffrey," I point out, mildly. Very mildly, so I can't be accused of aggression. "First of all, you're very early for the gathering. Did you not know it starts a week from now?" Of course he knew. He doesn't respond to that, so I keep on. "Second of all, who takes up battle howling in someone else's yard?"

He shifts and then he's there before me in his human form, the stocky, belligerent leader of the New England pack.

Not my biggest fan.

"This is not a den," he says, and then makes a big show of looking all around, as if he expects to see a whole wolf den appear from the forest. "If I had to guess, I'd say that this looks a lot like a place where humans live. Did you sleep here last night, Maddox? With humans?"

Hard to say if he's accusing me of oversympathizing with humans in general, sleeping with one specifically, or just being a shitty wolf. Probably all of the above and more, so I don't give him the satisfaction of reacting.

Another wolf shifts behind him, because of course she does. It's McCaffrey's sanctimonious queen, who I privately refer to not as Deirdre, mother to the New England pack, but Deirdre, the poor, surrendered wife.

She keeps her head piously bowed and remains a full body length behind McCaffrey. She folds her hands demurely in front of her, the very picture of mated submission. That she's beautiful is no surprise. Once female wolves hit about fifty years, they only get better. Deirdre embodies that rangy, lupine glory that all the little wolfing girls aspire to. Ten years ago, I'd aspired to be *exactly* like the gorgeous, elegantly fierce Deirdre.

Then I met her.

These days, fully grown, I can't stand Deirdre. Not because she surrendered, because hey, we all make the choices that make sense to us. It's because she's so deeply snotty about it. In rooms where only women are present, she makes no bones about the fact that the performance of perfect queenly submission is a competition. One she intends to win. In every possible arena.

Weird, I said during a meeting of all the queens and fated queens at the last gathering five years ago. *I thought the role of a queen was to support her pack in a way that brought glory to the pack itself, and particularly her king, but you do you.*

I fear that Deirdre and I were never destined to be friends.

Still, I'm aware that right now, McCaffrey himself is the bigger threat. Going down a rabbit hole of interpersonal queen issues is probably what they want, so I'm not going to let that happen.

I smile at McCaffrey instead. I don't answer his questions.

There are a whole host of things that McCaffrey doesn't like about me. That I look at him directly. That Ty has given me enough rope to hang myself with, or so McCaffrey claims, when what he's really worried about is that I might provide an alternate route for other queens to take. And then what would domineering wolves like McCaffrey do? They like things the way they are. The way they've always been. They see any hint of change as a personal assault.

"Welcome to Oregon," I say. I smile wider. "Have you been here before? If so, it was before my time. I hope you'll enjoy our wild forests. These gorgeous mountains. I don't believe you have their equal back east but I'll admit, I'm biased."

"Where is your king?" McCaffrey asks. He makes a show of taking a deep, heavy, scenting breath. And then a bigger show of blinking around in astonishment, like he's on a stage. "You don't smell appropriately mated, Maddox. Has the king finally tired of your insolence and chosen a more biddable, deserving queen? Is that why you live here like a human, exiled from your people?"

I shake my head like he's being silly. "If you think I'm in exile, why would you take the trouble to hunt me down?"

Then I laugh like *I'm* being silly, because I can't actually get in fights with other pack leaders. Not because I don't want to, and not because Ty would object. He doesn't like McCaffrey either. He would probably egg me on if he was here, but it's a good thing he's not. It's not good politics.

And there's nothing about wolf week that isn't political.

Including what McCaffrey's doing right now. Turning up a week early and flinging accusations around. He almost certainly intends to turn them into rumors he can flood all the other packs with. To create dissension in the ranks. To make the nearly untouchable and invulnerable Ty look like a weak leader.

Textbook, really.

"Our den *is* hard to find," I continue merrily. "I'll be happy to lead you over there. And I hope you'll tell Ty how difficult it was for you to locate it. We do take pride in that."

I congratulate myself on subtly insulting him on his inability to find his way to our den—which I'm sure he could locate easily if he hadn't come here to harass me—while dressing it up like a compliment. Much more deftly handled than him accusing me of being in exile because I'm staying in this cottage. This isn't to say that I've won.

Still, McCaffrey and I look at each other, and we both know what happened.

"Again," he grits out, "what I fail to understand—"

But there are suddenly even more wolves in the yard, with hackles raised and loud cries, as my pack finally makes an appearance. As the so-called patrol that would have heard all that howling the same as I did finally comes to see what's going on.

It doesn't sit right with me.

Even if we hadn't had our little meeting last night—or earlier this morning—about the weird things going on around here, I don't think that I would have appreciated how long it took for my supposed guards to make an appearance. I especially don't like it when I see that one of them is my cousin Beaudry. He bares his teeth at McCaffrey, as well he should.

But he certainly doesn't look like he *rushed* here.

"Took you long enough," I mutter, as the other wolves are busy barking and showing their teeth and doing all the other things wolves do to indicate that they're the toughest of them all. "I guess I'm glad it wasn't a real attack."

Beaudry doesn't shift. He looks at me in a way that I can only describe as disparaging.

"If you were in the den where you belong, it wouldn't matter who showed up, would it?" he asks me in the old language, the language we speak in wolf form. I'm just happy there's too much noise for McCaffrey to hear him. When I only glare at him, he growls. "Sounds like a you problem, Maddox."

"Thanks for your hospitality, Maddox," McCaffrey says as the howls die down, with that sneer of his that I also haven't missed. He didn't like that I was unmated five years ago. He didn't like that Ty made it clear that I had a voice in his decisions then. I suspect he's *really* not going to like hearing how much of a voice I have in our daily pack operations now, so that's something to look forward to.

All I do is smile. Then I wait for Beaudry and the other wolves to escort McCaffrey off the property.

Deirdre hangs back, lifting her bowed head enough that she can peer over her shoulder at me.

"Looking forward to talking with you later," she says, and while I'm sure that's true, I'm also sure that she's not being friendly. "Can't wait to see what you've learned in these past five years. Or how you got the idea to live apart from your pack. Alone and unprotected."

My smile feels a little harder to fake. "I can protect myself, Deirdre, but thanks."

"Goodness. Why should you have to?" She lets out that tinkling laugh of hers that always makes my shoulders try to touch above my head. "I mean, it couldn't be me. I'm much too concerned about my young to risk myself like that."

We both know where she's going with this. I sigh. She leans in.

"But of course, you don't have any young, do you, Maddox?" I only nod, and even roll my eyes, but she's not done sticking that knife in. "Ty is a hundred-year king with no queen, no issue, no legacy. If there aren't already whispers that he's not favored by the moon, there are sure to be some soon. I hope you're proud of yourself."

She lets out a laugh at that—not one that suggests she thinks she's been the least bit silly—then shifts and runs after her shady king.

I wish I could say she didn't get to me, but I'm still feeling the bruises from that conversation I had with Ty before. Her little jab sank in deeper than I'd like to admit. I stay there in the doorway to my cottage, willing my heartbeat to slow down. And for every other part of me to edge back away from the cliff of pure fury that I'd very much like to throw myself right off.

I know that's what they want. It would play right into their hands.

I still feel the urge to explode like an actual wound in me.

I hear a noise and when I look over, I see Briar emerging from her room. In today's gray light she looks somehow younger and older at the same time. But then, fae are ageless. So that's another suggestion that she's got more fae in her than anything else.

I shake that off and scent her, but I still can't get the faintest whiff of anything like power on her—much less fae power. She freezes when she sees me. Her shoulders slump forward, and it's true that I haven't interacted with a whole lot of fae in my life. Growing up, I never saw one here. There were fae in the various places we went every five years to participate in the all-pack gatherings. We do business with a fae enclave down in Eureka.

In New York, there were always representatives of the Kind on the subway. We would all look at each other, nod, and keep ourselves to ourselves. All except the fae, who were always standing about in their full splendor, as if daring the humans to notice them.

They never did, of course. Humans in New York are particularly skilled at paying absolutely no attention to the Kind no matter what they see. At paying no attention to *anything* they see, in fact.

All the fae I'd seen there had an unworldly elegance about them, and a kind of glow. They did not *hunch*. They did not *scuttle*.

They did not fling their palms up to their chests, like they were clutching at their nonexistent pearls. Briar can't seem to help herself.

It makes me want to take over protecting her myself, like I'm her security detail.

"Happy birthday," I say again, and I smile. "I had a great time. I haven't danced like that in ages. I hope you enjoyed yourself?"

"I had to bail," Briar mutters, already blushing and looking like she can't decide if she should smile back at me or run for the trees. "I know you're all, like, dating those . . . that vampire. That fucking wolf. That doesn't mean I want to *hang out*. It's too weird."

"You should see what it's like up close," I say, and laugh.

She huffs out a breath. It takes me a minute to realize that she's actually laughing too.

Those rainstorm eyes of hers actually gleam a little. "Yeah," she says. "I'll pass on that."

Then she scuttles away, off in the general direction of the kitchen. Yes. *Scuttles.*

If being her friend has any benefit at all, I hope that it will teach her to *strut*, not scuttle. Scuttling things get eaten.

I go back inside my cottage and take an overly long shower, mostly because I don't feel like doing what I have to do. I know I have to do it. The packs are showing up at the den, and that means I need to be there as well.

I pack a bag, sigh heavily at the injustice of it all even though there are a whole lot worse things than staying in Ty's personal den, and head out. I've even dressed up a bit, because I know that some packs are fussy. When we're in our wolf forms, we all walk around in fur and that's fine. Yet some packs act like a glimpse of a female shoulder in skin is enough to start the downfall of society as we know it.

As if we don't know how all of the males in those same packs act with the *bitten* women.

I circle around the back of my cottage, thinking I'll take the long way to the den entrance because I'm feeling the need for a little hike to walk off the McCaffrey of it all. I'm dressed in a nice pair of jeans—no tears—an actual pair of hiking boots, and a long-sleeve T-shirt to conceal the sight of my tattoos so that the prissier packs won't get their panties into a twist.

Though it's probably too late. McCaffrey got an eyeful of me in my little shorty pajamas with dachshunds all over them, which I'm sure he'll spin as me attempting to seduce him in full view of his queen and pack.

I really hate wolf week. I'm already exhausted. A nice steep hike will do me a lot of good—

But I stop dead around the back of my cottage, because there's another sacrifice there, waiting for me. Once again, defying everything I know about kills in the woods, I can't smell it until I'm on top of it.

At first I think Savi must have scent-scrubbed it—but she's not here. And if she was, and had, she would have cleaned it up, too.

I also know that it wasn't here when I came home, because I passed right past this spot. That was earlier this morning, and it's not yet noon. That leaves a very small window for someone to come here undetected by my cousin and the other wolves, as well as McCaffrey and his pack. Much less indulge in all this butchery. A very small window and a whole lot of wolves to sneak past, not to mention the clearly defenseless Briar, who could have stumbled on this if she'd come out of her cottage at the wrong time.

I don't like imagining that. I don't like any of this. It doesn't make sense.

I lean into the mess of the creature splayed out before me, scenting it deeply. Looking for anything in there somewhere that will lead me toward whoever—whatever—is doing this.

People can do anything. Sometimes they don't even need a reason.

But I can't find a trace no matter what form I'm in.

I pull back. I try to imagine who or what can keep killing things and leaving no scent behind, with or without an assist from Savi. I bury this latest offering near the others, and only then do I toss my bag over my shoulder and trudge off through the woods.

I walk until I feel less murderous. Then I go to the den.

When I get to the old mine, I nod at the sentries. Today they're a little too busy to give me a hard time. It's almost disappointing. I adjust my bag and walk into the den's dark entry, but I don't go into the grand cavern. I can hear things happening in there, but I take one of the other tunnels that bypasses the cavern and goes deep into the cave system instead.

The tunnel that the men take when they come back to the den and don't want to deal with their mates and their children. The tunnel the men use when they're in the mood to party with the *bitten* in their private rooms as well as up on top of the hill and would rather not explain themselves to anyone.

The tunnel that takes me all the way back to Ty's rooms without parading the fact that I have another place to live in front of assholes like McCaffrey. As I walk down the tunnel, I do my best not to dwell on the unsavory reality that all the males in the pack have their private spaces back here too, some in addition to a space in the family caves. All the males keep their family lives and what they call their *brotherhood* separate. They act like the outlaw bikers they still are, and the expectation is that their women will suck it up. The end.

There's no bargaining. This is how it is.

It's only weird to them when I want to do my own thing too.

I make my way through the tunnels undetected and deposit my bag in Ty's den. And since I'm here, alone, I take the opportunity to take a few breaths in to make sure that murderous rage is still ebbing away. I feel the way his scent wraps all around me. The way it calms me down and sinks into my bones like warmth.

I breathe him in deep.

Only then do I think, *I'm ready*.

Or as ready as I'll ever be to face all these wolves with their traditional pack expectations, so I put on my fated mate face and get to work.

9.

Cold Moon, waning crescent

Wolves keep showing up all week. All of them eager to prove that they'll do exactly what they want, when they want to do it. And more, that they won't be told otherwise by anyone. Especially not by an upstart young king like Ty.

Typical wolf bullshit, in other words.

Still, there's something about wolves simply being *everywhere* in the valley. Assholes aside, I can't help but love it. Wolves howling in the hills. Wolves on two feet, prowling around Jacksonville to poke around in the boutiques, drink coffee, and watch the humans a little too closely.

"This is a safe zone," I tell a cluster of three young wolves from Saskatchewan when they look a little too narrow-eyed and hunt-ready. "You can't eat them."

"We don't have that shit in Canada," one of them says with a laugh. "We claimed the provinces long ago."

"You're not in the provinces," I remind him. "If you want to snack on humans, go into Medford and see what you can find. But I warn you, there are a lot of vampires over there, and they don't take kindly to poaching."

They wander off. Whether to troll the streets of Medford for humans foolish enough to go there, I can't say.

I already knew that things were different here in the Rogue Valley. That was very clear even five years ago, when we were all still in hiding, and all the other pack leaders seemed *astonished* by the way that Ty managed things. Now it's even more clear. Not all of the female wolves are as busy putting on performances as Deirdre, so they're the ones who tell me that while some of the packs live in places where they interact with other Kind clans and with humans the way we do, most of them don't.

Most of them, these females whisper to me in one way or another, are jealous of what appears to be the abundance out west.

"Abundance doesn't fall from the trees like fruit," I tell them all. With a laugh, because I have to seem easy. *Jealousy* of our abundance can easily turn to a run at Ty for having it and hoarding it. "It has to be planned, carried out, and executed perfectly. Ty's been doing this for decades."

One of the older queens, Mariella, was like a mentor to me five years ago. Meaning she protected me from Deirdre. This week we go and have coffee in a corner of the coffeehouse in Jacksonville, and she tells me all the rumblings that people think she's too submissive and well behaved to repeat to anyone else. Especially me.

"Everyone thinks that there must be some magic involved in how Ty was able to transition so quickly once the Reveal hit. Other packs foundered." Her king heads up the Texas pack, and he's significantly less excitable than some I could mention. It's clear she doesn't mean him. "There are some bad feelings too. Some think that if there was magic, why didn't Ty share it with everyone else?"

"This is so funny," I say mildly. "Because I remember Ty attempting to share some of the ways that he was running protection up and down the interstate here in advance of the Reveal, and no one wanted to listen to him then. That's my memory of the last gathering. Why would he think anything changed?"

Mariella nods. "A lot of the packs got a little too excited three years ago when the Reveal changed everything," she says, with an eye roll. "There was no forward thinking, but a lot of time to turn regret into a grudge. They also don't like to collaborate. I don't think McCaffrey is likely to mention this, but word is, they have a significant wraith problem in New England."

I shudder. Wraiths are kind of like banshees in that they seem insubstantial and can float around where you least expect them. Only instead of sticking to their own melodrama, they take it out on everything and everyone around them. They also don't work well with others.

They prefer to feed on them.

"People are hungry," Mariella tells me, her gaze serious over her coffee mug. "And instead of looking to themselves and the situations they could have handled better, they're looking to see what others have. Things they think they should be given."

Every night, after we all sit around the fires, tell stories, and talk like one big, happy family, I relate these things to Ty. We lie together in that big bed of his, tucked away in the farthest reaches of the den. Usually we release a little tension first. Sometimes we take a break in the middle. We always indulge ourselves after, too.

Because nothing is a better counterpoint to endless politics than the way we fuck, so blisteringly hot that we can't think about anything or anyone else until we're done.

The man is like medicine.

Sometimes I forget.

"These old assholes," Ty mutters one night during this endless in-between week. "Always up in my face, telling me that I should learn respect and bend a knee to my betters. Always whining that they don't have what we have here. Mind you, not one of them bothered to listen to me when I told them how to do it themselves."

"The exact point I keep making," I agree.

He runs his hand over my head as I lie there, limp on his chest. His voice is low. Something like proud. "I hope you also tell them that you're a better queen to me without a crown than any of their women could dream of being."

I smile against his skin. "I assume that goes without saying."

Then I crawl my way down the length of him, passing all the delectable ridges in his hard torso. I taste him as I go, lowering myself until I can take that giant cock of his in my hands, lick him until he groans, and then open my mouth wide to take him in deep.

Not that he lets me do that for too long without taking control.

He holds me down until I'm sobbing out his name. Then he makes me scream it.

The next morning, he wakes me up with an arm beneath my belly to tilt my hips up. He gets his teeth on my neck as he pounds into me, making me come hard and long, groaning out the glory of it into his soft mattress and his sleeping furs.

"Happy Thursday, babe," he growls in my ear, his deep voice rich with satisfaction and laughter. "Kick ass today. It's not even wolf week yet."

I think about that when I stop and get coffee in Jacksonville, running into a little party of wolves from the Dakotas. I'm sure they tell me which Dakota, but I don't track it.

"Must be fun," says one of them, a little shit of a male wolf that I vaguely remember as a cub five years ago. "Acting like a human girl. Thinking you're one of them."

"The way you think you're a wolf?" I reply, with a smirk.

He doesn't like that, though some of his friends laugh. I don't have to make nice with assy cublings. Only their kings.

But it's a common theme. After I get my coffee, I walk back outside and find another group of wolves. They're from all over, and they're a little too interested in a couple of human old ladies trying to access one of the shops.

Human old ladies I know.

"Good morning, Mrs. Bloom," I say. I nod at her friend. They were both librarians when I was in school, and I thought they were old back then. Now they practically creak. "Mrs. Schroeder."

"Happy holidays, Maddox," says Mrs. Bloom. "The tourists are already taking over the streets, I guess."

"I didn't think we had tourists these days," says Mrs. Schroeder. "I thought they got eaten." I remember then that she was the one who let me read too much Stephen King at a tender age.

"It's that time of year," I reply merrily.

I turn back to the wolves after the old ladies go inside. "Leave them alone," I say, as softly as I'm able. "Or you can take it up not just with Ty but with the other two powers in this valley. Believe me when I tell you that none of them will be happy."

"Do you mean your sorceress friend?" one of them asks. Another snot-nosed male. "Or do you mean the vampire?"

"You know that you're supposed to go to an oracle, hear what they have to say, and then go back to being a wolf, right?" asks another. Also snot-nosed. Also male. "You're not supposed to act like you're an oracle yourself."

"I'm pretty sure I can tell your future," I say mildly. "If you keep talking."

"Everyone gets it, Maddox," says the lone female in the group, who, in fairness, is likely here to find a mate. I'd be bitter too if fools like these were my options. "You're not like the rest of us. You break tradition whenever you feel like it. Congratulations. Not everybody has that kind of leeway."

What I don't say is not everybody has that kind of guts. I don't say it out of respect for the female, who admittedly doesn't have the choices I do. There's no Ty on her horizon.

But that's what I'm thinking as I walk back to my truck, and then wish that I'd had a fight with both sets of wolves, because Johanna is waiting for me.

She's leaning against the side of my Explorer, looking around at all the wolves and humans and assorted other creatures on Jacksonville's main street as if they're all out here specifically to irritate her.

Though when she sees me, it's pretty clear that I'm the one who irritates her the most.

"Do you have any idea what they're saying behind your back?" she asks me.

"I know what they say to my face," I reply, keeping it cheerful. "I'm betting it's along the same lines."

My mother makes an exasperated noise. "What explanation do you imagine anyone will find acceptable for why it is you're living apart from our alpha?"

"For one thing, that's nobody's business but ours," I say, and practice staying steady while I say it. "I'm pretty sure that's what he would say, if anyone bothered to ask him. But we both know they won't." Her mouth tightens. I keep going. "Anyway, I've been sleeping in the den all week. Exactly where I belong. All nice and proper."

Johanna looks away from me for a moment, down the line of old brick buildings as if she's looking directly into the past. As if she can see ghosts there before us.

"I know you think that I'm needlessly harsh." Her voice is so low that it's as if she's one of the ghosts herself. "But I've lived a hell of a lot longer than you, Maddox. And I'm all too aware of the dangers you seem to think won't apply to you."

"Mom. Come on." I smile winningly, though she doesn't look won. "Nothing is going to happen to me."

"The only reason you think that is because you've been given a false sense of security," Johanna replies, very matter-of-factly. So matter-of-factly that it makes me pause. "Wolves believe in fate, but only to a point. Do you think that you're really the first fated mate who did not wish to take her place?"

"One thing that you refuse to accept is that I *will* take my place. I'll just do it when—"

"Foolish girl," Johanna whispers harshly. "You don't have the time you think you do. The king always has a backup plan he can utilize at will, because there is a way out of fate. For him." She glares at me. "Your death."

Suddenly, I don't feel much like smiling.

"If the king kills his mate himself, fate will provide," she says in the same harsh voice. "You would be amazed how many fated queens meet their end abruptly, usually right around the time they become too inconvenient. Too loud, for example. Too headstrong."

"Ty would never do that." My own voice is a whisper now.

"He would never *want* to do it," my mother corrects me. "That time that you think you have? Maddox. I'm telling you. *You don't.*"

I'm shaken, but by more than what she's telling me. First, it's obvious to me that she cares that I live. I can't quite convince myself that it's *entirely* about her status in the pack.

I don't focus on that part. It might tempt me to get a little maudlin, and that would kill her.

"Ty is not going to kill me," I tell her instead. "You're right. You know a lot more than I do, and you've seen a lot more pack political nonsense than I ever have, but I know him."

"I know him too," my mother says. "And not as a lover. I know him as a leader who will always do the right thing for his pack. The moment that's not you, Maddox? What happens then? If you force that man to choose between his pack and you—which way do you think he'll go? I know the answer, even if you choose to lie to yourself. And if I were you, I'd hurry up and give fate a hand."

And unlike the mother I thought I knew, who usually sticks around and fights to the bitter end and after, she only looks at me for a long moment. There's something stark in her gaze. It settles in me like a real, rough winter.

Then she walks away.

I stay shaken all day long. I go to work, because I can't think of what else to do, and I'm blessedly free of family interference while I'm there. Bigger shipments left the warehouse on their usual trucks earlier than usual this month in anticipation of the gathering that would draw the pack's attention. That means I only have a few creatures to talk to when they come by to drop off the notes I make them keep about their experiences out on their delivery routes.

Maybe because it's quieter than usual, I start to notice that there have been more disruptions along our typical routes lately. Not huge disruptions. Nothing catastrophic. But even though we've consistently varied the times and dates of our runs, we always seem to get caught up on Sexton Summit, above Grants Pass. Admittedly a tricky pass, especially this time of year, but the vampires in Grants Pass rousted out the trolls up that way long ago. There shouldn't be anyone there now to cause problems.

I let that sit.

But something about it keeps poking at me.

Later that night, I drive home, intending to leave my car outside of my cottage and then make my way over to the den for another night of bonfires and storytelling and partying that looks perfectly friendly, and maybe even is.

It's the undercurrents that I'll be paying attention to now. Especially now that I know some people will be in Ty's ear, not just talking shit about me but encouraging him to get rid of me and move on.

I even know when they'll do it, if that's what they're trying to do. Every year, when the Wolf Moon rises, all the wolves in every pack pledge their fealty to their king. It's tradition. It's how we start wolf week proper.

If I wanted to symbolically and dramatically remove a person like me, that's when I'd do it.

That means I have only until Sunday, the rise of the Wolf Moon and the official start to wolf week, before they make their move.

If they make their move.

When I get to Winter's yard and park the Explorer, I think I might go into my cottage and sit in my own space for a moment. A little breather from all the werewolf nonsense. Then I walk up to the front step and know I won't be doing that.

Because there are a line of sacrifices waiting for me, each one of them pinned to my door so that the blood runs down, thick and dark.

There are four. One for every night I've spent in the den.

Yet none at all on the path to the den, I've noticed. Not since the day McCaffrey turned up.

I stand there in the dark, staring at the four separate slaughtered creatures and what's left of their bodies. There's blood everywhere, still pouring down the door from what must be the newest one. It's turning everything a dark and sullen red.

"Maddox," comes a voice.

I must recognize it before I turn, because nothing in my body goes on alert. Sure enough, it's Winter. She comes toward me, frowning when she sees my expression. Then makes a little noise when she looks past me and sees what's on my door.

"It's like a psycho-killer collage," she says. After a moment. "Do *not* put the lotion in thc basket."

"I think it's a little worse than that." Once again, it's hard to tell which animal is which. I'm beginning to think that's the point. It's just senseless ritualistic killing for the sake of it—and the presentation is what matters.

It's supposed to be gross. It's supposed to be unsettling. Yet, all things considered, I have to think that it's down on my list of things to be concerned about right now.

"I had the weirdest dream the other night," Winter tells me. "Not as muddy as they've been lately. And I haven't seen you since. There was a big fire in some kind of clearing with huge rocks all around, but no trees. High up, under the stars."

What she's describing is our gathering place on the hill above the den, and I know there's no possibility she's ever been there. In case I needed proof that her oracle shit was real—and I didn't—she's giving it to me. I don't think she even knows it.

"There are wolves everywhere. They're howling, but it almost seems like they're singing?" She shakes her head. "At some point, I realize that I'm a wolf. But I'm also you."

"I am, in fact, a wolf. So that tracks."

"So I'm *wolf you*, then," Winter says, her indigo eyes bright. "And suddenly, out of nowhere, this other wolf attacks me. It's a boy wolf."

"Male," I correct her. "Unless he's a baby."

"Male," she says, rolling her eyes. "He comes at my back and his claws are everywhere, deep and terrible. I have this feeling that I ought to be able to fight back, but it's such a surprise—such a betrayal—that I don't. I can't."

I let that sit a minute. I try not to let it turn sour. "Can you see the wolf?"

She makes a face. "Not with my eyes. But I know what he looks like."

I think about what my mother told me. And for a moment, I wonder—

But I don't believe it. I don't believe for one second that anyone could convince Ty to hurt me. Still, I'm nothing if not a proponent of *trust, but verify*.

Winter might not be able to tell a whole lot of wolves from one another. But she got to know Ty in a different way, a more personal way, up on Mount McLoughlin two months ago when he helped her get up the trail to the sacrifice that was supposed to kill her. Enough to recognize him, I'm betting.

"Did you recognize the wolf who attacked you?" I ask.

Despite myself, despite my very real trust in Ty, I feel myself tense.

Winter considers. When she shakes her head, I feel a profound sense of relief wash over me. *I knew it.*

"No," she says. "The only wolf I would recognize besides you is Ty, and it wasn't him."

She takes a peek at my face then, and her eyebrows rise. *"Oh.* Did you think . . . ?"

"I didn't." That comes out a little too intensely. "But it's nice to be sure."

"All my oracle stuff has been weird lately," Winter tells me, her gaze steady on mine. "But this was crystal clear."

"Maybe the muddiness is specific," I say, something a little too close to giddy that it wasn't the worst-case scenario. As long as Ty doesn't betray me, I'm okay—and maybe I need to sit with that. I focus on Winter's visions instead. "Maybe there's a reason for it. Like someone or something is deliberately cloudy in your head."

"It isn't you," Winter says. "We know that much. Do you know what the dream means?"

And the thing is, I do.

I lean into my friend, and I stare at the grotesque arrangement on my front door. I'm not sure they're related. I'm not sure they're not.

I think about the images that Winter saw. Clearly a betrayal. Clearly an attack from behind, the way a coward always comes.

I think about the night the darkness chased me all the way to Savi's land. How I ran all that way with that terror thick and heavy on my heels and I didn't sense another wolf around. Not in all the while I was running for the sorceress's sanctuary.

I think about the number of times I've come back to this house, to my cottage, and found these terrible sacrifices. All arranged in such a way that it would have to take someone some time. Time no one should have been here without being discovered by wolf and vampire patrols.

I think about the number of times I've simply made my way through the woods and all the way to the cottage without ever scenting one of my own nearby. Sometimes I've scented members of my pack in the distance, and maybe that's why I didn't really notice that I've never actually encountered the guards that are supposed to be here all the time.

Not for weeks now, and I know that Ty ordered those patrols. That he insists upon them. It's the only reason he allows me to live here. I know that hasn't changed.

It's like all the pieces fall together in my head with a decisive *click*.

I don't like the conclusion I come to. In point of fact, it makes me feel sick, but that doesn't change anything.

Winter's visions are never wrong, but maybe, deep down, I already knew. Maybe I needed her vision to push me toward this conclusion that I would give anything not to draw.

Someone in my pack is a traitor.

And they're gunning for me.

10.

New Wolf Moon

Wolf week proper starts off with its usual bang.

The new moon rises. The Wolf Moon. Our moon. All the packs assemble, crowding in on our own hilltop and spreading out onto surrounding hills. One by one, each pack leader climbs to the highest rock, asks his pack to follow him, and they howl their responses.

It's like a rally. It's always positive. Not least because you wouldn't want to be the lone negative wolf in your pack on the first night of the gathering. You wouldn't want that kind of attention.

I'm a little too aware that there are those who wish me ill, and I can't get Winter's warning out of my head. I make sure that there's no one behind me when it's finally our turn, and I also make sure that my howl can be heard above everyone else's. Just to make sure there's no doubt as to my commitment in the moment.

I'm also aware that a howl can only go so far.

But I make it through with my throat intact.

I'm more relieved than I want to admit.

Ty welcomes all the packs, standing high above us and making the hills shake with our cries. There's never a part of me that isn't proud of him, but I particularly love watching him do this. I love watching him be elevated the way he deserves, his voice loud enough to be heard all throughout these mountains.

And beyond.

There are a lot of kings here tonight, but there's only one Ty.

He's head and shoulders above all the rest without even trying hard, though I know that's a dangerous line of thought. *King of kings,* I think, but I'm going to have to convince him of that.

If he doesn't bite me for daring to say something so forbidden in the first place.

"It is an honor for me to welcome you here," Ty belts out, letting his voice ring in the old language. "I know it's been a tough three years in a lot of ways, but here in Oregon, we think we've cracked the code to the Reveal and figured out how to move forward. How to make certain that wolf-led priorities deliver the best possible outcomes for all of us."

There's a lot of howling at that, too. Whether some of it comes from jealousy, or all of it is purely aspirational as they contemplate becoming as powerful as we are, it doesn't matter. Ty is very difficult to ignore. He's charismatic. He's compelling. He's the alpha among alphas, and female wolves love themselves an alpha.

I can see more than one of them, mated or not, looking longingly in his direction.

I'm not even mad about it.

"We have all week to talk, reconnect, and make our different perspectives heard," Ty continues in that same powerful voice. "But tonight is the first night of our gathering. And it's tradition to invite all unbonded and unmated females to come forward and make themselves known so that any male who thinks himself worthy can fight for their favor."

This gets a cheer even bigger than before. Because this is what *pack first, pack forever*—everyone's favorite slogan—means in practical terms. This is how we keep the bloodlines spicy. This also means that we get to watch the males fight each other, always a good time for the spectators.

It also means that the party is starting.

Assembling the females takes a minute. There are always disputes. Fathers who don't wish for their daughters to present themselves to a gathering like this, usually because they have someone closer to home in mind. Other males who object to a specific female claiming that she is unbonded because he would like it to be otherwise.

In our little corner on the hilltop, my aunts are preparing food. I decide it's better eaten with opposable thumbs, so I shift and sit there by our own cookfire, breathing in the wolves all around me. So wild and, these days, free. We had to be a lot more careful five years ago.

"These females nowadays," tuts one of my aunts. "Taking such pleasure in making the males scrabble in the dirt for their favor."

"That's a strange way to say that no one was particularly interested in your favors, Sigrid," replies another one of my aunts, slyly.

Aunt Sigrid laughs. "Some females know their own mind. I knew who I wanted to win my hand, and so he did. It didn't require a pageant and an after-party."

My mother sniffs. "Bastien snuck in under cover of night and stole me from my family, as is right and proper. All of you are soft, silly girls who needed proof. Bastien didn't need to *prove* himself to me. He saw what he wanted. He acted upon it."

She doesn't say *like a real male*. It's implied.

Both of my aunts become very concerned about the state of our cookfire.

I have to bite back a laugh. I never knew my father, but the man they tell stories about sounds like someone I'd admire. Maybe even love. I like to imagine that if a pack of trolls hadn't gotten the jump on him, he'd be proud of me in return.

Johanna always told me I was stubborn like him. I always took it as a compliment.

I watch the girls as they climb up to one of the lower-level rocks that puts them on a kind of stage. They vary in ages, the only requirement being that each one of them is past her first blood and claimed by no male.

I try to imagine what it must feel like to stand up there, looking down as the horde of males begins to assemble. However those males appear to them at first glance, one of them will be their mate. I've never heard of a mating ritual that ended with an unclaimed female. I wonder if they're excited? Disappointed? If they regret putting themselves forward?

I never had a choice, and these females have a variety of potential mates to choose from. I try to imagine how that would feel. I watch the jostling males for a while, then look up to where Ty is lounging on his rock.

I'm not surprised when his gaze finds mine. Or that I feel it all over me, even from this far.

No, I think, while warmth spreads inside me. *I didn't miss out at all.*

One by one, the females step forward to say their names and announce what pack they hail from. As they do, the males below them jostle some more, making noise and flexing their muscles. Letting the other males around them know that they are contenders.

When the females finish introducing themselves, Ty lets out a loud, long battle cry.

And the males begin.

Tonight's fighting is more of a brawl—and mostly a show. Not exactly friendly, but not deadly either. Just various attempts to show dominance while trying to look good for the women watching above. A few punches. Some grappling.

No one is going for broke on the first night.

I see, with some surprise, that all three of my brothers are out there. They might be pains in *my* ass, but I also like their chances. When I make a sound, my mother looks at me.

I shrug. "It doesn't seem fair to the other wolves that all three of my brothers are out there, making them look bad."

Johanna isn't much for smiling, but I swear I see the corner of her mouth indent.

When Ty determines that the show has gone on long enough—or is possibly worried that the males are beginning to make themselves look bad in front of the females since they're not *really* fighting, not tonight—he calls an end to it.

And then the real party begins.

Just as some packs came early to make a statement, others only arrived tonight for the same reasons. It's all about clamoring for position and consolidating power, but this first day is about fun.

Wolf-style fun means that there are no limits, just the way our males like it most.

After the feasting is finished, the more fragile members of all the packs retreat into the den below or the campsites they've set up in the hills all around. Once they've left us, it's like the night around us changes shape. Ty lets out a howl of command.

There's a pause, and then the *bitten* women come flooding in from their quarters in the next hill. Each and every one of them amped up and ready to get down.

It's chaos. It's dirty. It's the way it always is—a concrete reminder that we are *wolves* and we live the way we want, subject to no one's rules but our own.

Males interpret this through wild, abandoned, excessive fucking. But when don't they think with their dicks? I don't hate that for them. All I want is to extend our moon-given wildness and post-Reveal freedom to everyone else, too.

Not by fucking scrums of *bitten* women—though I'll admit, they always look like they're having fun.

I get up and dutifully make my way toward the group of other queens, and a few fated queens-to-be, like me.

Well, not like me. They're younger. But they all know who I am, and the fated ones stick close—a good call on a night like this, when McCaffrey does as he likes with our new-to-him crop of *bitten* women and Deirdre goes even harder than usual into her *the old ways or no way* crap.

We take over our own rock, up above the madness. Down below, the wolves are having what can only be described as a good old-fashioned outlaw party. The kind bikers were always famous for, but we originated.

Up on the queens' much more sedate rock, we're all very careful not to look as if we've noticed which kings feel that they get to keep right on partying as if they don't have a queen, and which, like Ty, have removed themselves from that part of the free-for-all.

That's between a queen and the king she's bound to. It's all about how he sees his relationship, because his word is always law. If he thinks that he should have access to all the pussy he wants as well as his dutiful mate? That's her problem.

A problem she better not make *his* problem—because if she does, there's no support. Not from anyone. *This is the life,* they'll tell her. Her own father, even. *You better find a way to get right with it.*

One more reason I haven't rushed to take my crown. No matter what Ty promises me now, it could change. People change. And if it does? I'm shit out of luck, the end.

This opening ceremony of the gathering lays it all out, every five years, in case anyone's confused.

Once again, I have to wonder if the *bitten* females have the better deal. They usually come to the life because they like fucking hot, rough, dirty biker types, and when those biker types turn out to actually be wolves, they're here for it. They usually like the wolves even more.

I think it must be fun, the life of the *bitten* females. Once a month, the full moon turns them into wolves and they get to go on their rampages and get carried away by their bloodlust—which usually involves domestic animals. Bloodlust is something the *blooded* are taught to control, or face the consequences. The *bitten* can't turn their prey into werecreatures, though. Only the *blooded* can do that.

So the rest of the time, they fuck. There are far fewer *bitten* men, and a lot of the female wolves find them fun, too. But it's not quite the same.

Mostly because the *blooded* wolves have extremely dirty minds.

And most of them have had a hundred years or more to experiment.

Down below, I see a *bitten* woman between two wolves, one in her mouth and one in her ass. She's shaking and quivering, coming again and again as they thrust.

There's no denying that it looks hot.

This is another thing the unmated wolf girls get to do on the night they declare themselves. Tonight is their chance to get a taste of what's on offer, and very few of them turn down the opportunity. Sometimes, I think I'd love nothing more than to run wild at one of these parties myself and indulge every dirty little fantasy I've ever had.

But every time I tell Ty that, he smiles in that way that makes my toes curl and asks me which wolves I want all over me. And every time, I decide I'm good. My mind might like a fantasy, but my body has only ever wanted him.

"I'm not entirely sure you should be sitting here with us, Maddox," Deirdre says with a titter, breaking into the dark, erotic display going on before me. I jerk my attention back to the gathering of queens. To Deirdre, who looks apologetic. She's full of shit, but then again, that's kind of her thing. Especially tonight. "You could be a queen, but you keep denying the call. I know *I* would never do such thing."

"I'm worried about you, Deirdre," I reply in the same sweet tone. Sweet, with blades. "Don't you have young you should be caring for? Surely a queen as deeply concerned with propriety as you are should excuse herself from questionable parties like this and tend to her babies."

Mariella snickers. When Deirdre glares at her, she shrugs. "I don't care what you do, Deirdre," she says, evenly enough that I'm reminded that she's been queen of her pack a good long while. "I only wish you would do it more quietly. And with less passive-aggressive nonsense, if at all possible."

"I don't know what you mean, Mariella," Deirdre replies. Through her teeth. "My only concern, as ever, is making certain that we all uphold pack traditions, as we are called to do before the moon."

The queens' circle goes quiet at that, because who's going to argue with the moon? Deirdre is probably as aware of the furtive *WTF* glances between some of the queens as I am, though I'm sure she ascribes a different meaning to it. The truth about Deirdre, I suspect, is not that she doesn't grasp that her role requires her to take a back seat to all the actual decision-making. I'm pretty sure what she really feels is that if she has to suffer, then everyone should.

"Too right, Deirdre," I say in my most diplomatic tone. "I apologize. I always get overexcited on the first night of the gathering." I smile at the young, fated mates sitting next to me. "Is this your first?"

But I don't listen too closely to their stories, because I know them already. I know that the younger of the two is fated to old white-haired Janus, who is even now fucking three *bitten* women with abandon below. I know that this girl will be his fifth mate so far, and I can only wonder now if he's been relieving himself of the moon's choices as he grows bored. I'd always thought that they found whatever way they could escape and had taken it.

Everyone says that he's very good at holding on to his territory and keeping the other creatures in that territory in line. I'm sure that's true. I also can't think of a single female who would willingly go to him.

The other fated one is a bit older and promised to Rafael, who is young for an alpha leader and, if I had to guess, strategic enough to know that the longer he waits to mate, the more his queen will be an asset.

I've always liked Rafael.

It's the older kings who refuse to accept that queens can be more than baby factories.

Once Deirdre and I stop going for each other's throats, the conversation flows the way it should. No politics, just a group of women with a very specific role, talking about the things that only we know.

"It's different for you," says Rhiannon, a shy, soft little thing, as she comes and sits down beside me a while later. "You're the one everyone talks about. Maddox went to college. Maddox does what she wants. Maddox tells her king what to do."

I laugh at that. "I sound like an asshole. And I definitely do not tell Ty what to do."

"I can't imagine." She shakes her head. "Gareth is a good king, and a loving man, but he's very traditional. Still, college does sound like fun."

It's these little wins that matter, I tell myself. It's the wolfling girls that Rhiannon will encourage to do the things she couldn't. These things will add up.

The party is still going on when our group finally breaks up, mostly because many of them really do have babies who need them down below.

As I walk down into the den, I feel a kind of longing in both directions. Some part of me wishes that I could hold Ty's babies in my arms tonight, nuzzle them and love on them and raise them to make him proud. The other part of me is fiercely glad that I'm the one who's different from the others. That I'm the one who's carved out my own space, however inadequate it feels to me sometimes.

I'm not in Ty's bed for very long before he appears, and I can tell by the way his eyes gleam that it's going to be a long night.

"What if I'm too tired?" I say, teasing him.

"Then I'd have to figure out how to wake you up," he replies, coming over to me and pinning me to the bed. "I have a few ideas."

There's no chance of us sleeping on the first night of wolf week. Not for a very long time.

Gathering weeks always feel haphazard, but they're not. I think about that over the next couple of days as the men congregate in their important groups and the women remain in the grand cavern, preparing the night's feasts and talking among ourselves.

Also doing the important work of exchanging information we treat like silly gossip but then repeat back to our men later.

I don't even dislike these gathering days surrounded by women, but I know that some of the things Ty will be talking about in roomfuls of males are business related. I also know that nobody knows our business better than me.

Nobody. Not even Ty himself, because I know all the figures.

I don't need anyone to tell me that marching into business meetings is not my place. I swallow my thoughts down and honor my mother by performing my duties flawlessly, because that *is*.

On the third full day of the gathering, Liam comes and finds me while I'm sitting with the old men, listening to them tell tales of our people from long ago.

"You're wanted," he says, expressionless.

"Is it my execution already?" I ask, and laugh.

"Maddox." He doesn't sound angry. His eyes are grave, but not mad. Wary, maybe. "I beg of you. Go easy."

I don't know what that means, but I get it when he leads me back into what's known as church. No gods are required here. It's the place where Ty and his lieutenants gather when they wish to be separate from the rest of the pack. During the gathering, the place is packed full of every pack leader and his highest seconds. It's standing room only—but as a woman, they wouldn't give me a seat even if there was one.

This is the inner sanctum, and it's usually strictly males-only.

I find myself wondering if the traitor is here, watching me. Waiting for his chance. Seething at the fact that I'm once again somewhere I shouldn't be.

Since this place is basically holy ground, I hope he is.

"Unbelievable," McCaffrey sneers, diverting my attention from my own dark thoughts. "Bitches in church? It's blasphemy."

"If you refer to my fated and future queen as a bitch again," Ty says, conversationally, "I'll take out your throat."

It's his tone, I think. It's so light and easy that it doesn't cause the war it could. That I would without even trying.

Instead, there's a little bit of grumbling—hard to say if it's for or against me, or maybe about the potential taking out of throats—and McCaffrey subsides.

"Why don't you fill our brothers in on our shipping lines, the situation with our disruptions lately, and the plan you devised to get around it," Ty says, and I have to admire the way he does that, too. It's not like he's showing me off. It sounds exactly the way it would if he had called any other one of his people in here.

I don't pretend I don't understand this is the opportunity it is.

I nod his way, and then I tell them what I know. Information about the persistent troll issues that are going to be a problem wherever trolls decide to set up camp, and I should know, because they killed my father. What I've come to think are the deliberate sabotage attempts up on Sexton Summit—though whether to cause chaos or toward a specific end, I can't say.

I explain that we've come up with a few different ways to combat those sabotage attempts but that we switch them up on the day of the delivery so no knows in advance and, sure enough, that's made a difference these past few days. I don't tell them what those solutions are.

I tell them all the various items we move, how we move them, and who pays us. It used to be guns, girls, and grass. These days it's basically the same thing, but dirtier to reflect the world we live in, with black market foods that various raiding parties sell to us to distribute after they've raided bunkers and forged their way into lost cities. I talk about the different forms of payment we take and how they've all helped us extend our influence so that despite having no telephones and no internet, we have more access to more parts of our territory than we did when we were all online and connected.

When I'm done, I see some of the pack higher-ups looking at each other in ways that make me think they're on board. Or at least that they see the benefit of what we're doing here and can envision trying some of these things out themselves.

McCaffrey just looks furious. But I was never going to win him over, no matter what I said. I can't count that as a loss.

As I think that, I realize that worrying about winning anyone over is focusing on the wrong thing. I don't need to win anything here. That's the kind of attitude I can't stand when I see it in the likes of Deirdre.

My work speaks for itself. There's no winning involved. There's only stating the facts and letting these men arrive at their own conclusions. Conclusions that I already know will be about politics for some and relationships for others. Only a very few will consider what's best for wolfkind as a whole.

So when I finish with my overview, I wait.

"That's a pretty presentation," drawls Rafael, kicked back in the corner like he's on a throne. He's not actually seated at the table, and I'm certain that the older wolves blocked him out to teach him a lesson about respect. Instead, they now have to crane around to look at him, sitting there exuding alpha leadership without even trying. So maybe someone's winning here after all. "But I have to wonder if it's the presentation that's so slick or the operation as a whole. Can I ask you some questions?"

"Please," I reply.

Rafael shoots a glance Ty's way, but Ty's expression doesn't change. He's sitting at the head of the table—his table, or they'd probably make him sit off against the wall too—and doesn't seem to notice that the person currently standing up and talking to all these pack leaders is his woman.

He might as well outright announce that he sees me as more of a partner than a broodmare.

I guess that in his way, he is.

I'm not sure I've ever wanted to kiss that man more, but that would completely undermine this moment. So I keep my face scrubbed free of any expression too, to honor what he's letting happen here.

When Rafael starts firing smart, interesting questions at me, I answer every one. I walk them through everything we do. I explain the central point again and again, in as many ways as it takes.

It's simple, and it's this: Ty's genius wasn't in reacting to the Reveal. It was in acting as if the Reveal hadn't happened at all.

He didn't let his pack disappear into the revelry. Or not for too long. He sent my brothers to New York to get me, and he otherwise carried on like it was business as usual out here, and because he did, he made it so.

When something blew up, he negotiated with whoever could fix it, no matter who or what they were. No matter if it went against ancient customs, because what the hell, everything was new again. Because of him, there was communication up and down the West Coast. It didn't depend on fancy magic like the kind Savi does, or even the less comprehensive but effective magic that mages do. He circled around using them too, when necessary, but the first thing he did was make sure he let everyone in his network know that shit was still expected to run. Smooth or not smooth, it didn't matter as long as we all kept going.

So we did. We kept going.

A lot of these other packs didn't. They were too busy enjoying the wild bacchanal. Ty always said he didn't find this particularly surprising, since when these same packs were operating only as biker gangs for the world to see, it was the same shit.

I say all of this to them now without actually saying any of it.

And when everyone's asked me everything they want to ask, except possibly McCaffrey—who looks like he'd like to ask me who the hell I think I am—all the men are talking. It sounds more like brainstorming and less like bitching, and I know that has to be an upgrade. I tuck my hands in the pockets of my jeans and sneak a look at Ty.

His expression still doesn't change. He's leaning back in his chair, stroking his beard, but I'm pretty sure the reason he's doing that is to hide his smile.

"As you can see," he says, when the chatter dies down a little bit, "with a little bit of luck, and maybe some bullheaded stubbornness because you know that's the kind of asshole I am, we made it work. I'm glad you got to all hear how, so the next time I come to you with some big idea, you'll see I'm not talking out of my ass."

There's some laughter at that, not all of it good-natured in my opinion, but laughter all the same.

"But, credit where credit is due, what I'm good at is fighting," Ty continues, still lounging there in a way that should look nothing but lazy. His specialty.

I think it makes him look even more powerful. So powerful he doesn't have to sit there like a loaded weapon—he just is one.

"I can make shit happen," he says. "But all of this tracking and analysis crap? Understanding what's happening and watching different patterns develop? That's all Maddox. If I'm successful, it's because Maddox not only has the education but the willingness to take on roles outside her fated place in this pack. That's no small thing. It means we're able to respond quickly and creatively when shit goes wrong. And shit always goes wrong."

One of the old men shakes his head. "I hear you, son," he says, which is already patronizing. I'm sure ancient Alfric knows that Ty is in no way his son and won't like the implication that he could be, so that has to be the point of it. "But I worry about your legacy."

Ty nods as if that's not the same boring old-school crap they always say when they're *concerned*. "We've all heard of females bearing young into their hundred and fiftieth year," he reminds them all. "Maddox is twenty-five."

There's a lot of movement in those chairs now, and I decide it's a virtue after all to keep my eyes respectfully lowered while a roomful of males discuss my fertility.

It occurs to me it's probably not the first time it's come up.

"In the meantime, my legacy is that my people eat well," Ty is saying. "This pack is one of the three big powers in this valley. We stand on equal ground with the vampire king and a full-blood sorcerer from one of the old families." I can see him out of the corner of my eye, looking around the table. "We all know that's not typical for werewolves. There's nothing typical about this pack, and there doesn't have to be anything typical about the rest of our packs, either. There's nothing we're doing that you all can't do."

More muttering from the men, so he sits forward. "I'm not a hundred-year king by accident," he says then, grinning. "I'm not going anywhere, and I got the rest of my legacy covered, Alfric. Believe me."

Everyone laughs again, and even McCaffrey looks slightly less apoplectic than before. The effort to keep my mouth closed is intense. So intense I bite my own tongue, but no one here has to know that.

The men get up and start to file out. They're slapping each other on the back, crashing their shoulders together, and putting on various displays of friendship, brotherhood, and dominance as they go.

The most powerful males in my world and they still behave like cubs.

Ty moves toward the door. He gives me a lift of his chin while he and his loyal VP, the always kind and friendly Connor, pass by me. Then he's gone.

It's Liam who stays behind. I assume it's to make sure that I leave church without looking too closely at anything in here or—worse—defiling it with my femaleness, sacred as this place is to the holy male wolf penis.

I dutifully turn around and head for the door, but he stops me with that same grave look in his eyes. I brace myself, waiting for the takedown. The list of things I did wrong. The ways I've dishonored myself and my family and worst of all, this pack and its leader.

Instead, Liam nods. The corner of his mouth curves.

"Nice job, little sister," he says. "You did good."

I follow him out and down the tunnel, back into the crowded grand cavern with a smile I'm trying to hide on my own face.

Then I let myself begin to wonder if maybe—just maybe—we might be okay after all.

11.

Wolf Moon, waxing crescent

I'm still high on what happened in church when I wake up the next morning. Still so pleased that they listened to me. That they engaged with me. That they didn't dismiss me out of hand as Ty's problematic fated mate.

I snuggle a little deeper beneath the covers in Ty's bed and, for once, don't find myself wishing for windows.

Instead I find myself wondering how many times Ty has defended me like that to them before—or to anyone else in the pack, even—no matter how many times he's gotten in my face in private.

I wake Ty then the way he loves best, even though he threw himself into bed with me only a few hours ago. I crawl down his body and take him in my mouth while he's still soft, getting to experience the rush of blood that fills his cock as I taste him. The way he groans as he wakes and realizes what's happening. The way he wraps his fist in my hair, slowly exerting more control the more awake he gets.

Until he's slamming into me, pumping himself into my mouth, and then emptying himself with a scalding rush down my throat.

He stretches as I crawl back up the bed and flop beside him. He smiles over at me, looking lazy and satisfied, and I feel everything in me shudder—and not just with our typical heat.

It's like my heart doesn't know how to beat anymore unless it's for him.

"Come on," he says after a moment that seems to stretch out too long, his voice rough. And not, I think, from whatever carrying-on he did last night. "Let's run."

We shift and pad out of the den, taking one of the secret entryways that only the top leaders of the pack are meant to know. Once outside, he breaks into a lope. I follow.

We run and run, letting our legs stretch and our breath get hot.

We run through the cold morning in that pretty predawn half-light before Savi sends the fog in again. There's a sprinkling of snow on the ground in the higher elevations. I can feel the cold on my paws, and I like it. Our breath makes its own mist. I can see the heat coming off Ty's huge body and my own, too.

The only sound out here is us, like we're all alone in this ruined world of ours.

When he turns to look at me, we're high on a ridge above the Applegate Valley. Once this offshoot valley was all farms and vineyards, but it long since fell from human control into the hands of various warring bands of ogres, trolls, and anarchist goblins. Among many other unpleasant things.

I can tell by that gleam in his eyes that Ty has other things in mind than a pretty hike.

Turns out, I can feel that same gleam inside me, too. I bare my teeth at him. I start the dance.

I make him chase me, because that's part of the thrill. There's no surrender without a fight. That's not who we are.

Ty is bigger than me and faster than me, but I can corner like lightning. I'm not afraid of a little roughhousing, either.

I give him a good run, but the end is a foregone conclusion.

That's part of why I find it so exhilarating, so all-consuming. It's also one of the reasons I've been so wary of a claiming run. How can I possibly survive it and still be *me* when our normal, everyday runs are like *this*?

Yet as I run, Ty on my heels and his breath rough behind me, it's hard to remember why I care who I am. Not when there's the sheer, elemental glory of *this*.

He swerves, slamming into me. I try to throw myself into the spin, but this time he's on me.

Moon help me, the way he's *on* me.

He pins me down, his teeth on my neck. I feel that huge, gloriously perfect body of his on my back, holding me where he wants me before he slams himself deep inside me.

Wolf fucking is different from human fucking in one very specific way. There is no pretending here. No frills. No experimenting with creative ideas. That's for skin.

Fur is basic.

He holds me down by my neck, I submit, and he fucks me long, hard, and deep until he's done.

Every version of me loves it when Ty takes control, but especially my wolf.

I start coming immediately. With every hard, deep thrust. He takes his time, letting me shake and whine.

He doesn't hurry. He never hurries. He does exactly as he likes.

Because he knows I like it too.

When he's done, we lie there together in the snow with him still too big inside me to pull out. We stay there and we breathe.

His snout on my shoulder. His legs caging mine. We feel each other's hearts beat. First hot and hard. Then gradually, over time, slow and steady.

I try to imagine what this would be like if I was mating with some wolf I didn't even like on a full moon night. When after the actual sex, there was this forced bit of intimacy.

Humans, I think, have no idea how lucky they have it that they can disengage at will.

I'm luckier still because I'll never have to know what it's like not to love simply melting into him. What it's like to *not* let my eyes close, knowing that when he's got me I don't have to do a single thing and he can worry about the rest.

We lie there until the cold seeps in beneath our fur.

"That was a very nice speech you made yesterday," I say as we head back toward the den.

The fog has already rolled in, obscuring any daylight that might try to peek its way through the trees.

"Wasn't a speech," Ty replies, in more of a grunt. "I was delivering facts. Nothing more and nothing less."

But the way he looks at me says otherwise, and I let that warm me all over.

Back at the den, he peels off to confer with scowling males in low tones. I hear one of them say something about *stealing our shit*, but that could mean anything. What's important, I'm well aware, is that after a show of independence and what will be seen as a bid for power unbecoming of a female—because anything they don't like is always considered unbecoming of a female—I need to make a show of putting myself back into the domestic sphere.

It's important to keep the men feeling safe, after all.

The women have gathered up on the open hilltop to lay out food today. Some are cooking over fires, honoring the old ways. Others are hauling in coolers filled with prepared food from elsewhere. The *bitten* women are up on the hill too, helping where and how they can—but always careful in the presence of the *blood* females, who have been known to bite them on occasion.

I move around from one group to another, acting like the hostess my mother keeps telling me I am. It doesn't matter if I'm unofficial. I'm still Ty's, and that means something.

More to the point, it would be taken as meaning something else if I didn't.

I low-key expect everyone to be talking about the fact that I dominated in church yesterday, but they're not, and I know it's not because they haven't heard about it. Few people talk shit more than werewolf males. But instead of sly comments about when I'm planning to ride with the males and what kind of Harley I like—the kind of thing I'm expecting—there's a lot of muttering that doesn't seem pointed at me in particular.

I know better than to ask about it directly.

The thing about female wolf spaces is that everyone gossips, everyone pretends that they don't, and trying to approach these things head-on is the quickest way to learn nothing from anyone. *Direct* is always interpreted as *rude*.

This is why it takes me nearly to the lunch we've been preparing to understand that one of the packs is missing some of their weapons and explosives, which sound like insane things to travel with until you remember that at any moment a person might be called upon to blow up a nest of manticores or a swarm of werebees while moving around the post-Reveal country.

Taking away someone's ability to protect themselves and their pack is going to lead to a bloody fight right here in the middle of the gathering. Everyone is amped for it. The only question is—with who?

Accusations are flying hard and fast.

Some folks think it's the Denver pack, who everyone considers untrustworthy since they separated pretty dishonorably from a greater Midwest pack sixty years ago. Others are certain that it's the New York pack, because everybody lives to hate New Yorkers.

The Denver and New York packs, obviously, vehemently deny the suggestion that they would need shady weapons from a pissant pack that can't keep track of their own shit.

By the time the men roll in, the women have managed to litigate these issues about a hundred different times, winding everyone up in the process.

I don't have to tell Ty any of this. He likely knew before I did, if what I overheard earlier was about this. And besides, he takes one look at the crowd and reads the mood.

"I think it's high time for an update on our mating rituals," he announces from his favorite ledge, shifting everyone's focus immediately.

Not just because it's fun to be a little voyeuristic about other people's romantic lives, though it is. But also because females leave their packs and go to their mates' packs, so the rituals will shift pack dynamics. If all my brothers win mates this week, that's three more females in our pack and more young, swelling our ranks. Some packs will lose their unmated females and have no one to replace them, meaning their future will be dimmer when they leave.

Mating, as I have been told my whole life, has almost nothing at all to do with the individuals involved.

When I think about it that way, it's no wonder that so many wolves have an issue with me.

I don't really want to think about that, so I focus on the unmated women as they take their spots on the staging rock. None of them have dropped out—which doesn't happen very often, but *could*. Fewer males step forward to fight for them, however. Every night, when all the packs gather together to eat and drink and talk about *brotherhood* and *unity* despite their little factions and petty wars, there's been more fighting.

Every night, only the winners stay in.

My brothers, as expected, remain undefeated.

"Worthy females deserve worthy mates," Ty intones, the way he always does as he looks down at the males. "Are any of you worthy?"

The fighting begins anew, and the rest of us sit around and watch it like a sporting event. We wince when some males fall and cheer when others prevail. Up on the staging rock, some of the females murmur to each other. Others are laser-focused on specific fighters.

After a little more brawling, Ty calls a halt. "You can fight some more tonight," he tells them. "Tonight and tomorrow night are all that's left before Saturday."

Saturday is the night before the solstice. The night for mating and celebrating before the darkest night of the year when, usually, there are surprise challenges and political shit to work out—often with claws and teeth.

I study the mating crowd. It looks like there are about two or three males for each female. Everyone else around me is doing the same math, and packs start cheering from their places. Everybody likes it when there's a fight.

Some gatherings, the couples sort themselves out too neatly. They declare feelings and connection, and everyone feels robbed. My aunt Sigrid pretends to be above the shenanigans but would be the first to complain that it was all too boring if there were no battles. *What real woman would accept a man who didn't bleed for her when asking for her favor?* she would sniff.

Now people are talking about the unprecedented midday fight instead of thievery, which was clearly Ty's intention. I don't hear another thing about missing weapons all throughout our lunch.

Afterward, some of the queens want to wander around Jacksonville, which the wolves who don't live here are calling our Human Museum. It reminds them of the days gone by when they used to worry about what humans might do. When we all did. When we had to keep ourselves hidden.

Even if they won't say it out loud, I know they must miss it. Not the hiding part, but the fact that there was a reason for the hiding. There was a reason for everything we did. Our species has always functioned around the idea that our extermination can happen at any time.

Now we're just . . . doing all the same things when none of the same external factors apply.

We walk down into town together. The big group of all the queens has broken up into these smaller and more manageable ones over the past few days, and I don't think I'm the only one who prefers it this way. The older queens, like Deirdre, prefer each other's company, and who can blame them? They've been around a long time and have seen things I probably don't want to imagine.

They also seem to take great pleasure in making the younger queens think that their futures are nothing but dire, no matter who the king in question is.

Mostly, I think the older women revel in this small window where they can be mean without any political consequences. I can understand it. I also don't want to be around it.

The younger queens and I might not be best friends, but we have a lot more in common. It makes the walk into town significantly more pleasant than it would be if Deirdre was with us. I take them along the old trails that wind around the town, trails that used to be cluttered with humans no matter the weather. I show them the view that looks out over the valley, then walk them down into the town itself.

"Rafael is very impressed with you," says his fated mate, with a smile, as we move. "It's too bad there aren't any colleges anymore. I think it would be fun to go to one."

"There are still books," I tell her, not letting myself think too hard about what happened to my school and everyone in it. "You might have to look for them, but I'd read every one you can find."

The way she nods, with a happy light all over her face, makes me think that really, I ought to be grateful that I've had all this time to make a difference. However small.

Maybe it really will be my daughters I have to teach first. Maybe it's these women, who might not accept the lives the older queens do. They might shift things in their own packs. They might be a different kind of inspiration to their own females.

Not to get ahead of myself.

A while later I'm standing outside, enjoying the crisp bite of the weather and letting my queens get themselves coffees and baked goods to their hearts' content, since so many of them live in territories where there's no commerce any longer. An old armored truck pulls up on the street beside me. Loudly.

I don't mean an armored truck like the kinds that used to drive between banks. I mean a truck that's been transformed to withstand monster attacks of all kinds—by hand, I'm pretty sure.

"Do people tell you how much your whole vibe is like Mad Max?" I ask Winter when she swings out of the driver's seat.

She's wearing her usual cargo pants and boots. What looks like a wool sweater beneath the typically Oregon sleek, yet puffy, jacket. Over which, of course, she has that harness she wears, stuffed full of weapons when, surely, she doesn't need them now.

Not when she's the oracle *and* the vampire king's consort.

But we all do what we need to do to feel safe.

"They don't tell me that," Winter is telling me. "Because mostly, they're dressed the same way. They can't let their inner wolf tag in at a moment's notice, you know. They'll need a gun within reach."

"It must be like prison." I try to imagine it. "To be trapped in one body all the time. No matter what your mood is, you stay the same. No matter if it would make more sense to have four legs and some functional teeth, still, you're the *exact* same. It kind of freaks me out."

Winter shakes her head at me. "When you put it that way, it does sound pretty gross. On the other hand, not a whole lot I can do about that, is there?"

I smirk at her. "I could bite you. Your man could bite you. So many doors you could walk through, if only you wanted."

"I'm good, thanks," she says, and doesn't do a good job of not making a face.

She leans back against her truck and looks around the cold, festive streets. There are still people out, because this is Jacksonville and this is where people can be out. So unless it's very early morning, late at night, or literally pouring down rain in buckets, there are always people around. Winter and I both grew up here, so we recognize most of them.

Though they seem a little skittish today.

"Why are the humans so jumpy?" I ask.

Winter slides a look my way. "I don't know, Maddox. It might have something to do with the cacophony of howling wolves, night and day, all week." When I only lift a brow, she sighs. "The last time we heard that much howling, it was right after the Reveal and it was . . . not good." She rolls her eyes. "For us, anyway."

Because many monsters feasted in those days, but the wolves howled about it. And humans can't understand what the different howls mean, so how would they know that what they've heard this week are howls of celebration?

No one at the gathering wants to hear any support for humans. They hunted us for too long. Still, I find myself wondering if there's any long-term way forward if all we're doing is playing musical chairs regarding who's prey and who's predator.

"Is it my imagination, or are people looking at you?" I ask Winter after a moment. "I mean, specifically at you?"

"It's not your imagination." She crosses her arms. "In fairness, I don't know how I would have reacted a few months ago to hearing that someone I knew had taken up with a vampire. Probably not well. They can't decide if I'm a monster myself or if I'm just a collaborator with the enemy. Mind you, that doesn't stop most of them from coming through my coffee line, and not just for coffee."

"It's a shame that so many people got eaten but the hypocrites remain," I murmur.

Winter smiles, though it's a little bit strained. "The funny thing is, I'm not sure what they think the plan is here. Do they think they're going to mount a resistance? Most people are just getting by. It's a grim, thankless world, everyone should find what hope they can, for as long as they can, and . . . I don't know. Seems kind of stupid to act like humans are the only ones around. We should cast a wider net. Maybe figure out how to make friends with the things that want to eat us."

This is so close to what I was just thinking that I wonder, not for the first time, if her oracle deal comes with a side of mind reading.

"It's a solid plan," I tell her. "Nobody likes eating an animal they know."

She wrinkles up her nose. "That's true. Also it's gross."

When I laugh, I draw the attention of some humans passing by—and they don't look any happier to see me than they are to see Winter. Then again, I've known Tim Buckley and Izzy Collins since kindergarten. I never liked them much myself.

"Hey, guys," I say in my cheeriest voice. "Hope you're having a Merry Christmas."

I can tell that Tim, at least, would love nothing more than to curse me out. But he apparently thinks better of that, or is worried about the parameters of the safe zone we're standing in.

"Maddox," he mutters. "Winter."

Winter only stares at him.

Beside him, Izzy looks flustered. "Is it true?" she asks Winter in a low voice. "Have you really—I mean *do* you really—I mean . . . *Ariel Skinner*?"

"He's a vampire," Tim barks at her.

Izzy makes a face at him. "I don't care what he is. Have you *seen* him? My God."

After Tim pulls her away, both Winter and I are a whole lot more smiley.

"He *is* hot," Winter says, very gravely. Getting only slightly red in the face as she speaks. "It's undeniable."

"Facts," I agree.

She sighs a little, then visibly collects herself. "I didn't actually stop to talk about villagers with pitchforks or Ariel's many charms, although I could." She fixes that indigo gaze of hers on me. I know instantly that this is oracle shit. "I had another dream about you."

"Then we have to start thinking critically about the fact that there's only one topic you seem muddy about." I search her face. "Right?"

"We know there's a muddy mess," she returns, evenly. "We might think it's about a certain topic, but maybe it's about a number of topics. I have no way of knowing."

"That sounds very scientific." I shrug. "I'll continue thinking that it's Vinča. Because if she could, she would. With a literal vengeance."

"This dream about you was different," Winter says, clearly not interested in talking about *muddiness*. "When Vinča was planning that ritual on Mount McLoughlin, it was always the same vision, over and over, but grosser and bloodier and scarier each time. I don't know if that's because it was specifically aimed at me or if yours is changing because you're changing things." She looks down for a moment. "I miss Gran. She would know."

Winter's grandmother was a good lady. I reach over and put my hand on Winter's arm. I don't say anything, because there's nothing to say. We were all there. We all watched the old oracle die. We watched her go out like a badass, the way she lived, but that doesn't change the fact that she's gone.

"Anyway," Winter says after a moment, her voice sounding thicker than before. "It wasn't in that same space, those rocks and fires. It was somewhere darker. I want to say a cave?" She's looking in my direction, but she has that faraway look in her eyes. Whatever she's seeing, it's not me. "This time, that same wolf was walking towards you. I thought he shifted, but I couldn't quite see his face. There was a shadow. I can't tell if it was an actual shadow or if that part of the vision was just fuzzy." Her gaze clears. Sharpens. "What I do know is that he hates you."

I feel something cold inch down my spine. I repress a full-body shudder, and it's a lot harder than I want it to be.

"Good news," I say lightly. "I'm used to that."

Winter, I've noticed, doesn't like to argue with people when she knows they're wrong. When I think about the house she grew up in, and what I know of the things that happened there, I assume that this is trauma based, like everything else that makes us all . . . us. In any case, I'm grateful. At the moment I don't particularly feel like being called out, thank you.

"Meanwhile," Winter goes on as if it's not clear to both of us that I'm pretending not to be a little freaked out that her visions are focused on me but nothing else, her voice lowering, "Savi is reporting a serious uptick in the size and number of sacrifices. Ariel says that the ones around the house match hers, but he still won't let me see them."

"He's protecting you." I can't help but smile. "That's so cute."

"I was literally in the middle of a cruel and bloody sacrifice on the side of Mount McLoughlin in October, during which I was supposed to die by the way, and managed not to throw up or cry," Winter reminds me. "I've also lived this long despite the Reveal. I don't think a dead animal is going to kill me."

"Or maybe," I say quietly, "you have enough scary shit in your head. You don't need more."

Winter makes a frustrated sort of noise, but she doesn't argue. "It feels like things are ramping up," she says after moment. "Like it did before Halloween. Except worse this time, because I have no idea what's going on."

I nod. "I hear you."

"I don't even know what's going on with my brother." Her voice is lower, but her gaze is stricken when she turns to me. "Do you? You said he was okay, but *is* he? Have you even seen him since he went into whatever the fuck werewolf detox is?"

I don't take the accusation in her tone personally. It's like the two-body thing. I can't imagine what it must be like to have the power she does and to accept that she has those powers only after a series of upsetting events—only for them to be taken away. Or diminished, anyway. *Muddied.*

Of course hearing howling in the hills and thinking about Halloween is going to have her even more worried about her twin than usual. He's the only family she has left.

"I'll tell you what I'm going to do," I tell her, evenly. "When I go back up to the den, I'm going to go see him myself. You're right, I haven't visited. It's not the kind of place and he's almost certainly not in the kind of state that lends itself to visitors, though. You need to know that."

"I know detox is terrible. Of course I know that."

"This is different," I say. As carefully as I can. "Because it's a blood addiction. It's not the drugs you're thinking about. Drugs are bad enough, I grant you, but there's magic involved with this." I blow out a breath and say the other part. "No one's ever actually done this before."

"What? Ty said that he could do it!" Her eyes are wide, and for a moment she looks the way I remember her from grade school, a long time ago. A little girl. An innocent.

The way we all were, once.

"If anyone can, Ty can," I say loyally, though I also happen to believe it. "He knows how to do it, theoretically. But that doesn't mean that your brother will let him. Okay?"

Winter lets out a breath that sounds more ragged than before, but she doesn't cry. I can't remember ever seeing her cry, not even when we were kids. Then again, I'm not big on crying either. "I'm sorry I asked. But . . . I would like to know how he is."

"I got you," I promise her.

Though I find I'm feeling a lot less pleased with myself when she gets back into her truck and drives away, leaving me there with too many things left to fix. And what feels like very little time to do it.

12.

Wolf Moon, waxing crescent

I keep my word.

I go back up to the den with all my queens in tow that day, and I spend the evening with them. Not only for diplomatic reasons. I like them. We have more in common than we don't. Making these connections is supposed to be the point of these gatherings.

"It never hurts to have sympathetic ears in a number of different packs," my mother murmurs later that night, immediately making me feel . . . gross.

"Not everything is strategy," I mutter.

She whips her head around to spear me with one of those *looks* of hers. The firelight makes her look even more fierce than usual, all those shadows and hollows on her face.

"It should be." Johanna snaps that out like she can't believe I said such a thing. "Why are you incapable of remembering your position, Maddox? Even now?"

I do remember my position. That's why I bite back the response I'd like to make, because we're in public. Nothing instills less confidence in a leader—or a future leader—than watching said leader have a fight with her mom. So I keep it together. I say nothing.

Privately, of course, I seethe—though I let Ty help me work out my tension later when he finds me curled up in his bed.

The next morning I wake up early and sneak out through the private entrance that we used yesterday.

I don't want anyone to see me on this errand. Not that I would care too much if it was my own pack, but I don't want to explain what's happening with Augie Bishop to any of the other packs. They already don't like the fact that I seem to have all these relationships with non-wolves. They have a lot of opinions about what I do and where I live and all the rest of it. It's fine to skulk around human towns like species tourists, apparently—but actually living with them? Getting along with them? They don't like that at all.

They definitely won't like the fact that Ty is trying to help one of them. Especially not when what he's trying to help Augie with is a nasty blood addiction. It's not like the general werewolf population is all that fond of vampires, either.

Once outside, I breathe in the stillness. Everything feels hushed around me as I start off, heading away from the den and going much deeper into the forest—up higher into the mountains. An old mining track that humans used to transport water to the mine runs a ways into the woods, some thirty miles or so, and used to be a fairly popular hike. It's overgrown now, but wolves love that. The wilder the better.

I navigate my way along the old mine ditch trail for a while, enjoying the wet, green morning and the fog that teases its way in and around the trees.

I know where I'm going in a general sense, but I still have to look for the turnoff as I get closer. It's a little mark on the side of a perfectly unexceptional tree in a particularly wily patch of underbrush. It would look like nothing at all to anyone who couldn't also scent our pack in the marking.

I leave the trail and get into even less-traveled woods, the kind of places humans gave up on, reverting to mapping from above. This area is too craggy, too unforgiving, too dangerous for bipeds.

Places like this have the Kind written all over them. My kind in particular.

I keep going until I reach a solid wall of rock. It juts out from the mountainside on an angle, a steep and craggy outcropping. It requires that I shift back and forth between my forms as I climb up it, because neither version of me could do it alone.

At the top, I pause for a moment and look back over the forest, seeing nothing but trees and hills. No hint of habitation in any direction, and there's a part of me—my ferocious wolf heart—that wants only these wild places. The cold wind on my face, out here in these hills that separate the Rogue Valley from the ocean.

Out here where it smells like freedom.

I take a few deep breaths, then I turn around and move toward the rest of the mountain that heaves up even higher than the ledge I'm on. Before I reach the sheer rock face, I stop. And look down.

And down.

There's a dizzying ravine cut deep into the mountainside. It has no other exit or entry except from up here. It's slippery and steep, and only extremely sure-footed wolves can get down there at all. Humans could possibly manage it with rope systems, but they would have to find this place first, and that's unlikely.

We call this *the cell* for a good reason.

Down at the bottom of the ravine, some fifty feet below me, is Augie.

I know they feed him once a day, only easily digestible things that he barely touches because his system is in a revolt against food. Moisture collects on the rocks at the bottom, and he licks them when he needs it. Our sentries come here to slide things down to him, check on his overall health, and otherwise let him be.

He doesn't complain. Mostly, he's delirious. Maybe he doesn't know who he is, much less what to complain about.

Augie has been here a little over a month now, and I know Winter wouldn't like what she saw if she was here. That's why Ty made it clear that there would be no visiting. Not for a long while yet, if at all.

But to my eye, Winter's twin is doing about as well as can be expected. He hasn't died yet, the way so many blood addicts do when they're cut off. Their systems shut down and they can't come back from it, but Augie is still kicking. He also hasn't tried to claw his own face off, as I saw one detoxing creature do once.

This isn't to say he hasn't hurt himself, but we have ways of healing those sorts of minor wounds. That would go under the heading of *more things Winter doesn't need to know about*, unless and until Augie survives.

When thinking these things makes me feel disloyal to my friend, I remind myself that she's not the one who wanted this. She's not the one who asked us to do this. Augie was the one who declared that he wanted to be clean and that he'd do anything to make it happen.

I sit there, looking at his too-skinny frame curled up in a battered lean-to shelter tucked in against the side of the ravine. He's wrapped in blankets, eyes closed, but he's twitching. I remember him way back in school. Growing up, Augie was absurdly beautiful—a blond with those same indigo eyes that have always made Winter so mysterious-looking. He wafted about like some kind of dreamy angel through the notably uncelestial Medford school district, his head forever in the clouds.

It wasn't a huge surprise that he ended up being one of the classmates we lost to drugs. He was always too otherworldly, and if I know anything, it's that it takes a thick skin to survive this world. Before and after the Reveal.

I didn't want to tell Winter that I thought it was highly unlikely that Augie would survive a single week of the harsh cold-turkey detox Ty put him on.

But here he is, still alive more than a month later.

I tell myself it's a sign. That good things are possible even in the darkest circumstances.

I keep thinking this the following night, as I settle in to watch my brothers win the mates of their choosing.

Tonight there are fewer fights, but all of them are more intense. Some females have already chosen a mate, forgoing the pleasure of watching males fight for them. Each of the remaining unmated women have at least two males vying for their attention, and I'll admit it—I wonder what that's like.

I'm sitting on the ledge with Ty, not with my family. I can feel all of his wild heat and leashed power like it's his scent, winding itself all around me. I have to caution myself not to lean into him—not because I don't want to or think he wouldn't welcome it but because this night isn't about us. Sitting up here means too many people are watching us as it is.

Ty has handed over the fighting to Connor, who has the ability to be charming one minute and a scary badass the next. He's doing his drill sergeant impression tonight.

"Let's go, assholes," Connor barks when two males spend too much time circling each other without making a move. "This isn't a tea party."

The males throw themselves at each other, then roll around, snarling.

Beside me, Ty sighs. "Pathetic."

"Must be nice to have males grappling over you," I point out, grinning when he slides a dark look my way. "Personally, I wouldn't know."

"You wouldn't like it." Ty sounds annoyingly sure of himself. Even more than usual, that is.

"I'm betting I would."

"No," he tells me, leaning closer. "You wouldn't. You would be disappointed. Crushed, even."

He wants me to ask why. I refuse to ask why. But he has no intention of telling me unless I do—I can see it in the arrogant tilt of his head—so I cave. I want to know more than I want to hold out, a typical failing on my part.

"Fine," I say. "I'll bite. Why do you think I wouldn't enjoy this rite of passage available to every other female of age? A time-honored tradition beloved by all and sundry?"

There's a new fight below us and it sounds a lot more serious, but Ty's gaze is on me. I have to repress the urge to shiver.

"No one would dare oppose me, babe." He laughs. "And if someone did? I'd kill him. It would take one strike." His dark eyes gleam. "Like I said, you wouldn't like it."

What I do like, though, is how warm and downright *giddy* that makes me. So much so that I almost miss my brothers' turns. Micah goes first. He lets the other male get a few swipes in, but I've seen him fight before, more cat than wolf. He waits until his opponent feels confident, then dominates. It's over fast.

Asher's fight follows a similar trajectory, though he is less strategic. He lets his opponent get too close—or so it seems—and then *explodes*. When he does, he wins easily.

Liam has to fight two opponents, and he does so with the same ease, dispatching one and then the next as if it's all swatting flies to him. It doesn't even look as if he's winded. When he bows to Connor, then the stage full of females, he's grinning.

"Not a bad showing," I murmur to Ty, completely failing at my attempt to *not* sound like I'm gloating at my family's prowess. When I am.

"Not bad at all," he agrees.

I can't help noticing that each of my brothers chose a mate from the three packs with old kings who are no fans of Ty's. It looks like three new sisters for me, which is lovely, but it *feels* like strategy.

The new mated pairs run off together into the remains of Saturday night. The males who failed to secure a mate start drinking away their wounds and grievances. The rest of the men settle in for a night of *bitten* women and other adventures, and I decide it's time to go down into the den when all I can see is creative, athletic fucking in all directions.

I spend the rest of my evening down in the cavern, letting the older women tell me how best to welcome newly mated females into my pack.

"Don't you worry about testing their loyalty," the oldest grandmother there tells me as if that was my first order of business. "You leave that to their men. Because we all know that unless a woman can depend on her man, she's never going to trust his pack."

All the other women around me hum their approval. "I wasn't planning to start any hazing rituals," I assure them with a laugh.

Another one of the old women looks at me, and though her eyes are clouded over with age, I think she sees me just fine. "That's because you're more secure than most," she says, with a nod. "Not worried about your position. That's not true for many. You just remember that."

When my old ladies get tired, they curl up on the couches set all over the grand cavern, because the dens in this cave system are for families or fucking or both, and I head back to Ty's bed.

Yet I'm still awake when he finally comes down to me, smelling of firewood without a single trace of any *bitten* women on him, not that I thought there would be. Still, a man's future queen likes to be sure.

I tell him my theory about my brothers' mates.

"That's not the theory, babe," Ty says gruffly. "That's the whole point."

"I had no idea my brothers were so biddable." I smirk. "I've always considered them to be giant assholes who never do anything anyone asks them to do."

"Maybe not," Ty agrees. "But they do what *I* tell them to do."

"Like everyone else, my liege."

He laughs at that. "Damn right."

He crawls onto the bed with me, still clothed, and stretches out there beside me. I reach over and play with that hair of his that some might call a little too long, but I love it. I thread it through my fingers for a while. Then I let my fingers move over his whole head. Pressing into his skull to release any tension he's carrying.

And he's always carrying tension, along with . . . literally everything else.

"I thought we'd spend the day talking about how to modernize the packs," he tells me, tilting his head back to press into my touch. "Instead I spent all my time appeasing old men and putting out fires because everyone seems to think the packs are stealing from each other, except no one can prove it. Complete bullshit. And a waste of time. Wolves are going to die because of this shit."

"I think that's the point," I say. His eyes snap open and fix on mine, but I don't take it back. "Ty. Maybe I'm crazy. But I think there's a traitor in the pack."

I expect him to immediately shout at me and tell me that can't be true, but he doesn't. His gaze sharpens. "Explain."

So I do. I lay out the sacrifice issue as I see it. And the protection issue—or lack of it. I tell him exactly how long it took for my supposed protection detail to show up after McCaffrey's pack started their howling outside my cottage.

"Too long," he mutters, a look on his face that does not bode well for my cousin Beaudry.

I keep going. "I thought it was aimed at me specifically, but maybe it's not. Maybe this is about the pack. Because if there really is a traitor causing trouble, it makes sense to me that the very day after we literally showed them all a different path forward that instead of working toward it, they'd suddenly be at each other's throats. Over stealing." I roll my eyes. "It's textbook. Every single wolf here could get their own personal arsenal in a heartbeat if they wanted to. There are goblin gun markets all over the place. But they're all territorial assholes, so the very idea that someone might have taken something that's theirs? Instant battle."

"You're not wrong," Ty agrees. He runs a hand over his beard. "I wouldn't be surprised to find out someone was manipulating everything to make sure it goes bad. It just *feels* wrong." He shakes his head. "My gut is always right about that shit."

"Let me tell you what *my* gut wants." I shift on the bed so I can look down at him, full in the face. "But you have to promise to hear me out. Don't rip out my throat until you hear my logic."

"There's only one reason I'll be ripping out your throat, babe," he drawls lazily, though his eyes flash. "But you have just about ten days to get yourself right on that one."

He thinks we're talking about mating. I am definitely not talking about mating.

I must have a serious look on my face, because he shifts his position then too, propping himself up on one elbow. I sit up all the way so I can look directly at him. So he can see how completely serious I am. "It's been obvious for a long time that the packs need unity. And you keep trying to build consensus. You keep trying to get them all to work together, and I just don't think that's ever going to work."

"It will," he says, his voice as serious as mine. "But if I'm honest, I think some of the old guard is going to have to die off first."

That's the way it usually goes. The young wait out the old, but by the time they can do what they want they decide that nothing *really* needs changing. If it did, we wouldn't be living like it's still the Revolutionary War out there.

"Sure," I say. "But in the meantime, you'll get bigger and stronger, they'll all try to challenge you, and we'll all continue living exactly the same way we always have."

He frowns at that, but I don't give him a chance to respond.

"And I don't just mean that in terms of me," I assure him. "I mean all of this. These petty little fiefdoms. Little kings marching around all puffed up because they can dominate a few submissive females and a handful of weak beta males. We were always taught that the original packs were formed the way they were because they all had powerful wolves to run them—but things are different now. There's no one in any pack who could even dream of being as powerful as you are. You know this. They know this."

"I can handle a target on my back," Ty tells me with a laugh.

"You have to," I say. I'm not laughing. "Because tomorrow is the solstice, Ty."

We both know what that means, especially now. Wolf week always ends at the solstice. The darkest night of the year. The one night that any wolf from any pack can challenge any other wolf for any reason. The night hierarchy and common sense don't matter.

On one such solstice night, a hundred years ago, Ty himself challenged the leader of this very pack and won.

"What if," I say, actually whispering because what I'm saying is heresy and I'm suddenly afraid the walls themselves can hear me, "instead of waiting for all of these little kings to challenge you, as they probably will, you issue a challenge yourself?"

He blinks, then looks amused. "Baby. Who am I going to challenge? I can kill all of them. It's not even a question."

"I know that." I lean in and put my hands on his face. His beautiful, impossible face. "What if you crown yourself king of all kings. *The* king. If they won't pledge their fealty to you, they can fight you. Just like back in the old days. Honoring the old ways, as so many of these kings claim they're doing all the time."

I expect him to flip out at this. I expect him to at least shut me down, and hard, whether he thinks I have a point or not. But . . . he doesn't.

We stare at each other. We stare into each other.

And I know, suddenly, that whatever comes next—our lives will always be divided between before this moment and after it.

Ty knows it too. He puts his hands over mine, holding them fast against the planes of his jaw and the rough caress of his beard.

"If we do this," he says, his voice hoarse, "are we doing this together?"

I don't look away from him. I'm not even sure I blink. "We've been doing everything together for a long time, Ty. That's who we are. It doesn't matter what we call ourselves or what they call us. We're still *us*. We're always *us*."

I know full well that it's a vow I'm making. I know that I'm telling him that I'm not fighting anymore. That I'm leaning into him, to this, to the fate we make.

I know that I'm promising him that when the Wolf Moon shines full above us, I'm going to run, he's going to catch me, and he's going to stake that claim at last.

I'm promising him that I trust him more than I fear what lies ahead for us.

"Us," he says, his dark eyes bright and hot. His own kind of vow.

Then he pulls me closer.

He kisses me in that same bruising sort of way he did after that impromptu rave. He pulls me down with him, he gets his hands in my hair, and he keeps kissing me.

He kisses me like there's no beginning, no end, just this.

And I can feel that fire dance inside of us, but he doesn't crank up the heat. This is different. This is sacred.

This time, maybe for the first time, we don't *fuck*. That's not the right word.

Because this is true love. This is the real fate that's held us in its grip all this time. This is the two of us, coming together. Becoming one.

This is the only way we can get our souls entwined.

Ty explores every part of my body. He pulls me over him so I can straddle him, and so I can see him worship me. With his hands. With that look on his face.

Over again we turn and I hold him inside me, doing my best to lock my legs around him, though he's so broad and his muscles are so hard—

It's as if I can't take him deep enough.

Still, we fit. Whatever we do, we fit.

I stop pretending that there's any possibility of me feeling whole without this man. My mate. My king.

My destiny.

When we come, we do it together, and it feels like pure joy.

We hold each other for a very long time. So long it begins to feel like a different kind of communion. But eventually, I turn over and I look at him.

"I miss the stars," I confess. "That's one of the reasons I like the cottage so much. I can see them from my window."

"Baby," Ty rumbles. "I can give you the goddamn stars."

He pulls me with him out into the tunnel and then outside. We sneak back up to that hilltop, but we don't join the party that's still going on around the fires. We skirt around it and head for the next hill, where Ty and I avoid the sleeping packs from the Southwest and climb halfway up a very tall pine tree.

We keep going until we make it to an old lookout spot with a still-sturdy platform.

He sits with his back against the tree trunk and wraps me up in his arms. I lean back into him, my back to his chest, and we don't say a word.

Maybe we're beyond words.

I tilt my head up to look at all the stars high above me on the second-to-darkest night, bright and beautiful as if to whisper the truth—dawn is coming.

Dawn is always coming.

I feel no death goddess darkness encroaching tonight. There are nothing but constellations up above us and the whole, complicated, magical galaxies that Ty and I have made between us.

For a moment I can pretend that the solstice isn't coming. That we can always feel exactly like this with no test, no fight.

That it can be only the two of us, with the world like the far-off Milky Way, something to look at and marvel at that doesn't affect us in the least.

Just for a moment, I lean into him and let myself believe it could.

13.

I wake up on the morning of the solstice to the sound of raised male voices in the tunnel outside the den. But whatever alarms that might set off in me subside when I hear Ty's deep rumble of command threaded through those voices. I bury my face in the soft pillows that smell like him. And me. And us.

I feel shaky, but it feels like leftover joy. As if I took the stars to bed with me when Ty and I finally made our way back and wound ourselves around each other in what was left of the dark. The voices outside get louder, like a wave, and I can't exactly advocate for an equal partnership with my whole chest and also pretend to sleep through things that sound unduly dramatic for a Sunday solstice morning.

I roll out of bed. Grumpily. I pull on some clothes and then make my way out of Ty's bedroom and into his living room, where I sat with him as a young girl so long ago. I can see the ghost of her if I squint—that girl who had been told she was a woman that night. A girl who'd believed what she was told, had been determined to do the right thing, and was so relieved, eventually, when she realized that Ty had protected her from herself that night as well as everything else the pack would have accepted as no more than his due.

Lucky little ghost, I think, and let her go.

I move over to the door, but I don't open it. The men are still loud out there. And there's no need to insert myself into situations that don't involve me directly. Not when I can gather information without drawing fire instead.

I can only catch snippets from the other side of the thick door, but I get the gist of it. Actual fights have broken out over the stealing accusations now, and all I can think is that this is exactly what I was telling Ty last night. Territorial wolves are too easily manipulated—and I'm more certain by the moment that the same someone, or *someones*, is behind it.

I just can't figure out who.

"I don't care what day it is," one of the wolves in the hall is snarling. "If I think you're messing around with my ability to protect what's mine? I'm ripping your fucking head off."

"I know you don't mean my head," I hear Ty drawl.

In that dark, dangerous way of his that I'm sure sets many necks to prickling.

"Let's take this into church," I hear Connor say, always the voice of reason. "Instead of shrieking in the halls like a bunch of fucking banshee bitches."

That characterization draws an immediate unfavorable response, obviously, but it also gets them moving.

I wait until I hear the voices fade off, presumably back into the tunnel that leads to church, because I don't want to deal with any pack drama just yet. Not when Ty and I have so much more than mere *drama* lined up for later. When I can't hear them, or sense them in any way, I slip out of Ty's den, head for that secret entrance, and treat myself to a chilly morning run.

I loop around Jacksonville a few times, aware of other wolves taking similar solitary runs in the hills. I'm not the only one getting the energy out before a long solstice night. I scent each of them, but nothing stands out. An unmated female from the British Columbia pack. A pair of young males, still mostly cubs. An older mated male and his young.

I give them all a wide, respectful berth so we can all enjoy a little time away from the gathering. Then I make my own path through the freshly fallen snow in the forest that surrounds Winter's house. As I go, I keep my eye out for any other tracks. Any hint that there's someone else out here. Whether guard or enemy, I'm not picky.

But I could be the only creature alive on Winter's land this morning. The woods are still. Not even the rustling of trees or other animals to disturb the early-morning peace.

It doesn't feel like peace to me, I'll admit. It feels a lot more like *waiting*. Like a hushed, caught breath.

I head to my cottage and make a trip around its perimeter. I don't find any new carcasses, though I'm not sure that means they weren't left here. I can smell the faint hint of blood, not old enough to be the sacrifices I saw myself. I suspect that what new mutilated creatures were left here were cleared away by Ariel's minions, or even Savi herself.

There's nothing I can do about that, so I lock myself inside the cottage and sit for a minute on the edge of my bed. I'm going to miss my windows. I'm going to miss the skylight above that lets the stars in. I'm even going to miss my tiny shower that Ty always referred to as a torture device. I'm *really* going to miss my wall of books, because there are no bookshelves in Ty's den. The walls are too craggy, having been dug out by the claws of kings long past who all had better things to do than read.

I'm going to miss my little transitional life here. These few, strange months.

"It's okay," I assure myself, once and then again. "What's coming is better."

What's coming is going to be the best yet. Or it will be the end of us. Either way, my time here is coming to an end.

I soak in the hot water in my narrow shower, wrap my hair in a towel when I get out, and dress in an outfit that I think best expresses my commitment to Ty and the new order I feel certain he'll be ushering in tonight. That means a shirt with a low V-neck that shows off my tattoos. Spells and incantations wound around my arms. Ty's paw print between my breasts that's marked me for years now.

On New Year's Eve I'll get another one, like a hand around my throat. Indicating my claim and my crown at a glance.

I find the very idea makes me feel shivery again.

I pull on my favorite pair of festive jeans, which is to say, kick-ass black. I sink my feet into some motorcycle boots that I think once belonged to my mother and have definitely done some kicking in their day. I throw some shit into my hair to make it wave even more dramatically, and then I study myself in the mirror. He's going to be the king of everything, and I'm going to be the queen that stands by his side.

Not behind him. Not beneath him.

Not unless I'm naked, anyway.

I shrug on the leather biker jacket that I know Ty likes best. I study myself in my mirror, and I look like a grade-A biker bitch, hot and tattooed and exactly who Ty deserves.

Will I also infuriate a lot of the old guard who like their mates to look soft? Damn right I will. That makes it even better.

Will I irritate a lot of the women, too? So many of them are encouraged to stay home with the babies and let the biker side of things get taken care of by the *bitten* women who are more than happy to ride bitch and suck dick all day long.

Yes, I think. Yes, I will irritate them. But maybe, when Ty—and, hell, my own brothers—begin to show these packs a better way to live, I'll inspire them, too.

In the meantime, my looking like a biker fantasy is only going to help Ty's case. Because a biker fantasy is exactly the kind of independent woman wolves like to chase and then don't know what to do with. So, being males, they put her in a cage and convince her that she should be embarrassed that she's exactly who she always was. That being: exactly who they wanted.

My mother, for example. A female less suited to motherhood and nurturing, I can't imagine. Johanna was made to be powerful, so she took her power where she could find it, forever having to listen to lectures on her femininity from men who were just pissed she wouldn't mate with them.

If everything goes according to plan, I think as I look at myself and the little illustration I've created for tonight, we might get to work dismantling those cages too.

Since I'm here at Winter's place, I head to the kitchen and let myself in. I nod at Winter over by her coffee machine and Briar sitting at the table. With, as usual, a gigantic bowl of sugary cereal.

"Where do you get that?" I ask her, looking at the bright red box with a frog on it. "That's some next-level black-market shit. I haven't seen any cereal for sale anywhere since before the Reveal, and you know no one's actually *making it* anymore."

"I have a dealer," Briar says, and then she smiles at me. "First thing I did after the Reveal was secure the sugar cereal."

I laugh at that, while also being pretty sure that's the longest sentence she's ever said to me. Certainly the longest pleasant one, anyway. There's still not the slightest whiff of magic or power around her, though I do notice the silver chain of a necklace peeking out of her typical black band T-shirt. I eye it out of curiosity because I'm sure I've seen it before . . . but it's not like I know jewelry. A chain is a chain.

"I hear that," Winter is saying, bringing me back to black-market cereal. And dealers. "We didn't have any coffee for at least the first three months after the Reveal. It was brutal. I vowed, once things eased a little bit and it was possible to get supplies, that I would never be without coffee again. No matter what it took." She inhales the scent of the coffee she's making herself. "And I have kept that promise."

Briar smiles even wider at that, and I realize this is the most smiling I've seen her do, too. I like it. It makes me feel like this friendship deal is on the right track, and that means that if Vinča is coming for her, we'll be right here and ready to give the death bitch something else to worry about. I like that even more.

Also I just like this girl in her beanie and her goth clothes and a smile over contraband necessities in these dark times.

"You get it," Briar says to Winter. She doesn't even sound awkward.

Everyone goes back to not speaking, and when my pulse kicks at me a little, I'm sure I'm having solstice nerves. And, you know, major wolf-pack revolution nerves.

Or maybe missing-all-this-in-advance nerves, too.

We're all together in the quiet, and I know I'm going to miss the comfort of this, too. In the den, someone's always speaking. There are arguments in the tunnels. There are always couples getting frisky in the alcoves. Someone's always talking, someone's probably singing, cubs are always roughhousing. There's no avoiding interaction. Even in the grand cavern, which has a huge kitchen at the back where we can all go and prepare food as we like if we're not sharing a meal, you can never avoid someone else's presence. Which almost always comes with some noise.

Wolves are not shy and retiring.

Once again, I tell myself that the things I'm giving up are worth losing, because Ty is the major benefit on the other end. Especially *this* Ty, who has grown as much as I have over the years, since he's now clearly as sick of the systems we live in as I am. I'm not sure he was ten years ago. Five years ago.

But he is now.

I can handle a cave if it means I can make my life what I want it to be. If I can make *our* life what it ought to be. It seems like a fair trade.

Winter goes over and sits at the table with her coffee. I busy myself flash-frying up one of my classic breakfasts, but by the time I transfer my pile of meat to the table, Briar is already storming out.

Winter and I sit there a moment or so, long after the echo of that slammed door has faded.

"She was *smiling*," Winter whispers, in a wondering sort of tone, but pitched low like she thinks Briar might be lurking outside the door. I can scent that she's not. "How sweet was that?"

"No pun intended," I reply.

She shakes her head at me. I grin.

I'm really going to miss this, but maybe that's a good thing. You don't miss the things that don't matter.

Winter sips at her coffee. I eat.

"I went and saw Augie," I tell her after a few bites. I glance at her just long enough to see something that looks like brightness in her eyes. That emotion I see so little of in her—and try so hard to hide in me. "He really is okay."

Winter sits with that for a breath. Then another. "Do I want to know what *okay* means in this situation?"

I wonder if she already knows. If she sees things she doesn't want to see and wants me to confirm or deny them. I wouldn't blame her.

"It means he's alive," I tell her. Steadily. "He's alive, and while I would not describe him as *well*, it could be worse. He has a long road ahead of him and a whole lot of battles to fight. No one else can fight them for him."

"Meaning he needs to suffer through it," Winter finishes. "When I can't help thinking that he's already suffered enough."

"We don't get to decide *what* we suffer," I say quietly. "Only *how* we suffer." I spear a bit of sausage and egg. "My grandmother used to say that."

What I don't tell her is that I didn't like it when she said it to me, either.

"I hope he stays strong, of course." Winter blows out a breath and slumps a little in her chair. "But if he *could* stay strong, he would have. Years ago. If he *could* stay strong, he wouldn't be in this position in the first place." She shakes her head. "Does that make me sound like a monster?"

I shrug. "Wolves drink a lot. And party a lot with anything else they can get their paws on, if I'm being honest. Packs put up with a whole lot of bad behavior in the name of a good time, because that's our due as wolves, you understand. We howl where we like, wolves forever, all that bullshit." I make a face, but I also make it clear I'm not kidding. "But what we don't tolerate is addiction. Strong wolves have it a lot worse.

They get locked up underground and are left to waste away, down to skin and bones. They won't die. They might wish they did. But when they make it through, they're clean. The weak ones don't make it that far, and some think that's a gift."

Winter makes a small noise. "Is Augie locked underground? He was in a vampire holding cell for who knows how long. I really don't think—"

I reach across the table and put my hand on hers. "You didn't choose this for him, Winter. He chose it for himself. This is what *he* wanted, and I'm pretty sure he had a much better idea of what he was in for than you do. That's a good thing."

She sighs and closes her eyes, rubbing her forehead with her free hand. "It was so nice to have him back. If only for a little while. I'm just afraid that he won't make it back from this. And then I'll wish the rest of my life that he stuck around, blood addicted or not."

"You don't mean that." I shake my head at her when she looks at me. "That would mean he didn't claim his life at all. That he was drawn along on the tide of his addictions forever. If he didn't try this, he'd be nothing but an addict. Forever."

"I know. I know that if I was a good person, a good sister, I wouldn't think this was any kind of a gray area."

"His addiction makes him a target," I say, evenly. I know she knows this, but it bears repeating. "Especially now. It made him the bargaining chip that he was when Ariel used him against you. It makes him a pawn, forever, for anyone who can get him his fix. Maybe he wants to live whatever life he has left on his terms. I have to respect that."

It takes her a moment to give me a smile, but eventually I manage it. "Thank you," she says, and her eyes are still bright, but I don't think they might spill over anymore. "I appreciate you updating me. I'll try not to have too many more breakdowns."

I wave my fork magnanimously. "Have as many breakdowns as you like," I tell her. "If I can help you, I will."

Winter chugs her remaining coffee and then goes over to her coffee machine to start making herself another huge mugful. "You're the one with the scheduled breakdown, I think. Don't you have your solstice tonight?"

"It's not *my* solstice." I laugh. "It's yours too. The darkest night of the year comes for us all. I wouldn't be surprised if the vampires throw a little shindig themselves, given a long-ass night is their time to shine."

Winter looks taken back. "Ariel did say that there was something at the MMA school tonight, now that you mention it. Is there usually a solstice party?"

"I don't know that I would call it a party in the classic sense," I say carefully, because I assume if it's a vampire thing it will involve a lot of blood. I've made some guesses, but I don't really know where she is in her journey from decidedly anti-vampire to taking and giving blood with one. And that's not getting into all the rest of the creepy shit vampires can do. "Most creatures like to mark the turn of the year tonight, yes."

She looks at me for a moment. "What a careful and completely unsatisfactory answer."

I grin. "Hey, all I know are rumors. This might shock you, but Ariel Skinner has never invited *me* to any vampire parties. On any night of the year, much less tonight."

Winter lifts her mug at me in a kind of toast. "I'll be sure to let you know if you're missing out."

I should tell her, I think. I should let her know what Ty is going to attempt tonight and what it could mean if he succeeds.

Yet if I tell her all that, I'll also have to tell her what will happen if he doesn't—and that's something I don't particularly want to think about myself. It won't only be Ty who is killed if he can't fight off all challengers. It will be all his lieutenants, and their families.

It will almost certainly be me, too.

Unless the winner thinks it would make more sense to humble me instead, and force me to mate with someone else and take a silent, servile role for the rest of my life. Wolf justice is brutal. They'd kill me straight off too, but wolves don't like to waste a fertile female.

Especially not when decades of humiliation could be dished out instead.

These are not scenarios Ty and I discussed, because we both know all the possibilities. I find I can't bring myself to talk them out with Winter, because I don't really want to explain it all to her. It would make those possibilities far too real.

What I do instead is hug her, hard, as I go to leave.

"Oh," she says, clearly surprised. Her gaze narrows on me. "Are you . . . ? You're fine, right?"

"Happy solstice," I tell her, and slip out the back door.

I walk back to the den, taking a different route through the snowy forest. I'm thinking about celebrations, bloody vampire parties versus the usual werewolf bacchanals. I feel a surge of those nerves again and remind myself that I'm going to get to watch Ty fight, which always thrills me.

He fights the way he fucks.

Lyrical. Creative. Wildly athletic.

Better yet, he always wins.

"He always fucking wins," I whisper to myself, fiercely, as I scan the trees above me for any lurking banshees. Kind of wishing one might come at me so I could *do* something with all the sharp, jangly energy inside me.

I'm daydreaming a little bit at this point, thinking of banshees and Ty and fighting and *winning*—

Maybe this is why it takes me a moment or two to recognize the way the hair on the back of my neck is prickling. Another alarm, and this one for a much closer danger.

Not banshees this time.

I don't change my pace. I don't look around. But I am positive just the same. I can *feel* it, everywhere.

Something is watching me, malevolent and *focused*.

As I move, I can feel it move, too.

I keep walking, and I decide that it doesn't feel like that darkness that chased me to Savi's house. This feels smaller, but still deadly. Less catastrophic weather shift and more stalker.

It feels the way Winter's vision sounded. I inhale, but all I smell are wolves. Lots of wolves. This is the main path to the den, and we're at the end of a gathering week. Every wolf here has left scent behind.

Traitor, I think.

Not a death goddess, but a wolf. A wolf I know, or I would find an odd scent in the mix. Maybe after I make it through the solstice, I'll have to unpack all the levels of what it means that one of my own people could do these things—but I have to live through today first.

Right now, I'm out here in the woods with no one around and a traitor on my heels. A traitor who's a little overly interested in me. I see Winter's vision in my head as if it's mine, and I don't like it.

On the other hand, I do like my chances with most wolves. With every wolf except Ty, as a matter of fact. I'm not fated to be his queen because I'm weak and slow.

Sure, if this was a wide-open field, I might worry. But it's a forest. Nothing chasing me is going to corner as well as I do, and it's unlikely that another wolf has as much riding on tonight as I do. There's no possible way.

I don't shift forms. I keep sauntering along, and as I go, I feel the presence get closer. I can feel the hatred like mist all over me. It moves closer still.

I keep myself from tensing up. I tell myself to keep my breathing even. I don't want whoever is tracking me to have the slightest idea that I'm aware of them or that I think I'm anything but alone.

I know this old trail as well as if I cleared it myself. I'm approaching a narrow turn that I know leads down beneath an old felled tree trunk propped up across the path against a big rock. It creates a kind of natural tunnel, and if I were going to jump someone, that's where I'd do it.

I make myself keep walking, seemingly oblivious. I can feel the tension in the air. I can almost scent the stalker behind me. It's *almost* there. I can almost pull in a deep-enough sample of the scent signature that I should be able to identify the wolf in question—

But not quite. *Not quite.*

I start to take the turn, and I hear footsteps quicken behind me—

Let's fucking go, I think, and I get ready to shift—

At the same moment, two of the younger wolf queens with their cubs in tow come barreling out of the tunnel from the other direction.

We all come *this close* to a full collision. I avoid mowing them over with sheer force of will.

The little cublings squeal with joy at the near miss, bounding around and barking at everything. Rocks. Beetles. Me.

"So sorry." Rhiannon laughs, trying to corral her little wild ones, seemingly oblivious to how dazed I must look, because I sure feel it. My heart is pounding so hard it hurts. "We're on a mission to get these wiggles out."

"They're absolute monsters," confides the other young queen, shaking her head. "Devils, every one of them."

By the time they corral all the children and get them heading off along the path again, whatever was on my heels—about to attack—is gone.

Taking any chance I had to finally figure out their identity with them.

But it takes me much, much longer to settle.

14.

When I finally get to the den, the vibes are excessively off. It's a whole loud, temper-fueled uproar in place of the usual celebratory situation.

It's certainly not the way a solstice is supposed to feel.

Different packs are shouting at each other in the great cavern, and it's not just the males I hear going at it this morning. The women have gotten involved too, and the accusations are flying—many of them attached to decades of gossip, because why use claws when rumors land the harder punch?

I pick my way through the threats and occasional scuffles until I make it to the set of couches where a lot of my family are already sitting. Watching the show, not participating in it.

Yet.

"Has this been going on all morning?" I ask, watching an Ohio wolf hurl himself through the air to land on the neck of a South Carolina wolf, who does not take being tackled with anything like grace.

They're encouraged to deal with themselves by the bucket of water tossed over them by a dour-looking old granny from Missouri.

"You're acting like you need housetraining," she tells them in disgust. "For shame."

"This shit has been going on since last night," my brother Micah tells me.

He's sitting on one of the couches, an arm casually extended along the back and his new mate at his side. She doesn't lift her gaze, but that doesn't necessarily mean anything about her personality. It's considered good manners to keep a downcast eye in the presence of higher-ranked wolves, and a newly mated female of a younger son in a new family is considered the lowest status there is.

Micah continues, "We offered to replace anything that's missing, just to shut everyone the fuck up, but it didn't help."

"In my day," Aunt Sigrid says with a sniff, "no one would *dream* of behaving like this in another wolf's den. Much less on the solstice during a gathering. It's embarrassing."

For a change, the rest of my aunts appear to agree with her.

My mother is standing with her arms crossed, peering out at all the bad tempers around her. After a while, she turns back to me, her cool eyes assessing.

"To the casual observer—" she begins.

"Since when are you casual?" I ask.

"When have you ever been casual?" Micah agrees, and we both laugh.

I realize, with a jolt, that this is the first time I've been around this many members of my family in quite a while without one of them jumping down my throat about my *intentions* and my *destiny*. It feels like a sea change, but I don't want to call attention to it.

My mother shoots a quelling look at both Micah and me. "This is manufactured," she states in her unvarnished way. "Someone is clearly invested in a bloody solstice tonight. I won't be the only one who thinks so, either."

Micah lets out a grunt, a noise that neither confirms nor denies what my mother said. But something in the way he does it tells me that this is probably something that was already discussed in private. Between Ty and his lieutenants.

That means there are fail-safes in place.

It also means that Ty is really going to do it.

That sizzles in me like gasoline, and there's nothing to do but let it burn.

"If there's blood," I say with perhaps a little too much intensity of my own, because I'm only made of flesh and blood myself and this is getting to me too, "I hope Ty spills it. And may the inevitable deaths of those who challenge him serve as a warning to others."

For the first time in a very long while—maybe ever—Johanna nods at me, her cool eyes actually . . . approving?

"How bloodthirsty," one of my softer aunts tuts. "Must we always take the lowest, most animalistic road? Are we truly no better than a pack of rabid street dogs?"

But everyone else is grinning.

"A blood call requires a blood answer, Gretchen," my mother says crisply, and now I can *hear* that approval too. I'm tempted to get a little silly over it, but that would reverse any approval in a hurry, so I suck it up. "We're wolves, not lapdogs."

Her gaze, however, suggests that maybe poor Gretchen should check herself. Or maybe be a bit more embarrassed that *her* mate hasn't hunted so much as a squirrel in recent memory. I'm pretty sure I hear Johanna go on to mutter something like *Pacifists and vegans deserve to get eaten*, just loud enough to make Gretchen's chin wobble.

The rest of the day feels interminable. Inside me there's a kind of ticking clock with every last part of me attuned to every single second between now and the coming sunset. It will happen just before 5:00 p.m. I will *feel* when it sets—I don't need a watch, I'm a freaking werewolf—but I feel as if I'm counting every second all the same.

Meanwhile, this is still the last official day of the gathering. I can't pace around, counting down the hours, the way I'd like to do. I can't indicate I'm overly concerned about what the night might bring. I watch the entrance to the cavern for a while at first, thinking I'll be able to tell who the traitorous stalker is by who comes in after me, but I give up. There are more ways into the den than the entrance to the communal caverns, as I know very well. I have no way of telling who's come in from where.

Besides, despite all the muttering and squabbling in the cavern, I have to act as if this is any normal solstice and everyone is getting along. People are watching me whether or not they *also* want to kill me. I make a point of talking to the females in all the currently furious packs, acting as if I don't notice the simmering tensions. I'm also taking advantage of my status here, because the packs I wander into have no choice but to talk to me. Politely.

Brawling with other males is one thing. Baring teeth at a king's fated mate in his own den? That's the kind of disrespect that leads to the sort of vicious pack justice that wolves swear by—when it's not being visited upon us personally.

My brothers all congregate in our part of the cavern around midday and I take that as a small break from dispensing my razor-edged version of hospitality. Liam and Asher bring their mates with them, and that means it's time for formal introductions all around.

Micah's mate is Leah, a pretty brown wolf from crochety old Janus's pack. When her eyes aren't politely downcast, I think I see a little more fire in there, and that makes me happy. Asher's mate is from the always problematic Deep South pack, and I can't get a read on her at all. She's unfailingly polite and makes the most of her gray-and-silver loveliness, but she's clearly holding her cards close. I can't really blame her.

"You can call me Magnolia," she tells my mother and me, her drawl as exquisite as her manners.

When she moves on to the aunts, Johanna lifts a brow. "I wonder if Magnolia is actually her name," she murmurs, for my ears only. "Or if she prefers to keep her real name to herself. If so, it really does beg the question—what else does she not intend to share?"

"You really do see plots within plots, don't you?" I ask her.

"I certainly hope that you do, too," my mother retorts. Sharply. "Or the first plot that comes along will be the end of you. I don't think the pack can afford it."

"The pack," I tell her with a little more temper than I usually deliver in her presence, "will be fine. More than fine. No matter what I have to do to make sure of it."

Johanna nods as if I didn't take a tone with her at all. "I approve of this newfound sense of civic duty, daughter."

"There's nothing new about it." I don't modify my tone any when I say that. "If you can see everything, I wonder why you never saw that."

When she only lifts a brow at me, it makes me wonder. Did she really never see it? Or has Johanna always believed that her role is to play the most vicious sort of devil's advocate and critic to help me—to help all of us—stand strong in our positions?

I'm not sure I want that answer, either. It feels more complicated than I need in the middle of an already too-complicated day.

Liam's new mate I already know. It's Kendra McCaffrey—old, horrible McCaffrey's youngest daughter. Also Deirdre's youngest daughter. A sleek black wolf with Arctic eyes, who has always seemed clever enough to survive any male. Even a male like Liam.

Whether she can *handle* him or not remains to be seen.

Still, the thought of how furious her parents must be that Kendra has been claimed by a member of our pack makes me smile even more brightly than I might have otherwise.

"Welcome to the family," I say, inclining my head, because I outrank everyone else—including my brothers—and the honor of welcoming new members into our family falls to me when we're all being formal.

"It's an honor and a privilege," Kendra replies in the old language. She delivers a deep bow.

Her manners are glorious, as expected, but I think I see the kind of canniness in her gaze that reminds me exactly who her mother is. When she's swept into a conversation with some of my aunts, I look up at Liam. "It's just as likely that she's a spy," I say softly. "I'd be prepared for that."

"I sure hope so," says my brother, with a particularly *aware* gleam in his gaze that I'm not sure I need to see from the closest thing I have to a father figure. "We're going to have some fun, Kendra and me. Figuring out who reports to who and what they have to say will definitely be a part of it."

The hours drag by, even with those unsolicited visuals.

I look around the cavern to see the newly mated females doing the same thing in all their new family groups. Doing their best to integrate themselves into their new packs smartly. Politely. In ways that will set up the life they'll have to live with the strangers who claimed them and make it something they can tolerate. Hopefully even *like.*

This is how it's always been done. *Females are the threads that bind the whole,* my grandmother used to say, usually when she was mad at me for my "selfishness." Selfishness aside, she was right. Females hold the packs together with their bodies and the babies they produce. Conventional wolf wisdom holds that a male is less likely to go to war against an enemy pack if his daughter is one of them.

That sounds like a lot to ask of a daughter, I think—and not for the first time. It's also one more thing I haven't had to experience. All these newly mated female wolves will have to do that mending, that binding, whether they like the male who claimed them or not. Whether they like his family and his pack or not. Just as their aunts and their mothers, and mine, did before them.

They are swept into a new pack overnight, subject to new pack hierarchies and dynamics, and mated to a man it's possible they neither like that much nor even know particularly well. No matter what they feel, they're expected to get on with it. And they usually do, because the quickest way to rise in importance in the family and in the pack as a whole is to start producing the next generation.

Maybe it's because I'm finally ready to be claimed myself that I'm paying closer attention to what all these women around me go through. Not what it *means* in the broader sense, but what it's *like.* The bargains they must make. The relationships that they are expected to form, then support.

It seems brutal to me. Head off to a gathering, watch males fight for your favor, then accept the victor because that's the done thing. No one changes their mind when the fighting's done. Females are raised to understand that their job is to bring wolves together, not tear them apart. We are all raised to believe it's our sacred duty.

Deep down, I still believe it is.

While I might go about it a different way myself, I find myself honoring my sisters today. My mother, my aunts. The newly mated females I see everywhere. All these brave women who understand their duties and have put their very bodies on the line to perform them.

It makes me wonder why all the songs we sing are about the deeds of men.

I know the answer, I decide later. The afternoon wears on, and some of those songs are being sung. Less in the usual celebration of the solstice and the end of our gathering today and more in an obvious bid to do something about the mood in the cavern.

Males need the songs, I decide. They need their bravery to be celebrated. Females celebrate their children instead and raise their babies to be better. We play the long game while the men sing and fight, fuck and die.

I have to hope it's a game we can all stop playing one day, no matter who sings the loudest.

Either way, I'm pretty sure I'm not the only one who's relieved when it's finally time to leave the cavern and head up to the hilltop to watch the sunset. To bear witness to this long, dark night that must be survived before the light comes back.

It's supposed to be about hope.

I believe it is—it's just a different flavor, this time around.

As the sun begins to set, Ty climbs high up on his rock. He doesn't have to quiet the crowd because they all subside as he stands for all to see. I can't help but think that he looks like a god up there—a proud, strong werewolf male, seemingly chiseled from the very stone he stands upon.

That he's beautiful as well as powerful is part of the reason he's so dazzling. So compelling. I can't pretend otherwise.

I know I chose my outfit right when people look from him to me and I don't see too many curled lips or rolled eyes that might indicate they don't get why he's mine.

Or maybe they're as intimidated by me—and Ty—as I feel they should have been all along, the assholes.

"My people," Ty belts out in greeting, and there are answering howls all around. "Tonight is the last night of our gathering. I've spent these days getting time with all of you. Some I already knew. Some strangers I'm now proud to know. But one question has been with me throughout this week."

He looks around, his dark gaze moving through the crowd until I feel it land on me. I stand a little straighter and put my shoulders back, in case he needs the support.

The way he lifts his chin a little higher, I think maybe he does.

I got you, I think, and maybe he even feels that, too.

It's a huge crowd, but everyone's quiet. Everyone's hanging on Ty's every word.

He keeps going. "I keep wondering why, when the world is completely different than it was three years ago, we're all clinging to antiquated, old-ass notions of what a werewolf is. What a werewolf can be. What we *are*."

There's rumbling at that. Good or bad, I can't tell—and I'm in the middle of it.

Ty seems wholly unconcerned. "The vampires in this valley have bargained to keep the sun away. They walk in daylight. That's only one example. The Kind have renegotiated their own legacies in the wake of the Reveal, their most sacred myths, and made something new. Even the humans, nothing but prey at the best of times, have managed to carve out their own safe zone here in Jacksonville. In places like Jacksonville all over the country." He lets that sit for a moment. Then he hits them. "Why is it that wolves think we must live in the exact same way we always have?"

There are shouts from various directions now, but Ty pays no attention to those, either.

"I know that tonight is usually a night for petty challenges," he says. "But I want to throw out a bigger challenge to all of you. Your packs are struggling. Your packs need direction, and they aren't finding it in these same old ways that we were forced to follow for ages." He holds up a hand when the shouts get louder. "It's not my intention to dishonor the paths that our ancestors took. But I can't be the only one here who thinks it's time we modernize."

He holds out his hands on either side of him then. He looks all around, from hilltop to hilltop. "I put myself forward. Not only as *a* king of my pack, but as *the* king of all the packs."

There are howls now. Loud barks, support and horror at once.

"I'm not a power-hungry asshole," Ty tells the crowd of wolves. "You might think I am, but that's because I get results and you probably don't. I can't fix that for you. What I can do is fix it for *all* of us. I think it's time for us to rise. I know—and you know—that I'm the one who can lead us where we need to go. But, my brothers and sisters, you sure as hell don't have to take my word for it."

He leaves his hands stretched out to both sides. And I swear, the way he sweeps his gaze over the crowd, he sees each and every wolf here.

"You don't like it? You think I'm full of shit?" Ty laughs then, loud. Long. Enough to get the attention of every last pack member, friend and foe alike. "Then fight me. I dare you."

15.

For a moment, it seems like every wolf in the Jacksonville hills is frozen into place. I tense, sure that I can *hear* all those minds whirling. *Did he say that? Does he mean that?*

Is this happening?

Something electric, some kind of communal understanding, shimmers through the packs. It's like a wave. It builds as it goes—

And then, with battle-ready roars from all sides, wolves launch themselves into action.

All the males of fighting age and stature hurl themselves toward the center of our hilltop, pouring in from all the surrounding hills. The family groups they leave behind at the gathering fires huddle together, protecting the young and the fragile.

For a moment I wonder if we misread this moment. If the wolves are assembling to take Ty down together—the only slight chance they would have to best him.

But it becomes clear very quickly that there are already chosen sides in this battle. That Ty has support.

A lot of support, I see, as they arrange themselves behind him, and a wildfire emotion too militant to be a simple sob gets trapped in my throat.

It's Ty and his men, of course, but it's also the rest of the younger, newer kings. The ones who can clearly imagine a different path and a different way to live. The ones who looked at Ty's success and didn't begrudge it—or at least, not as much as they wished they could replicate it.

On the other side, with McCaffrey at the forefront, it's exactly what I expected it would be, though it's clarifying to see them clumped together tonight as if they're the ones on a stage. Janus. Alfric. That crusty-looking grandpa wolf from Utah. All the old, bitter, angry wolves who prefer the world we lived in before. The world where they lorded it about in their dens and their territories as they saw fit while their packs were too cowed by the humans and their weapons to argue.

They still want to control things the way they always have, even though we're three years into a completely different world.

No matter what happens here tonight, I'll remember who stood for the archaic old ways that—big surprise—favor males like these scared old men. I'll remember these little kings who are so desperate to keep what little power they have that they'd sandbag their own packs' prospects to do it.

"Fantastic," Ty drawls as he eyes the battle lines from above. "Looks like a party."

At first everyone adheres to the old rules of protocol. When one of McCaffrey's lieutenants steps forward, my brother Liam laughs out loud.

"I can't accept this insult to my king," he declares. "I will fight in his stead." He doesn't look at Ty as he says it. He keeps his gaze squarely on McCaffrey's man. "And may the moon guide me as I teach this lesson."

Ty inclines his head.

Then we all get to watch as my brother spanks McCaffrey's man. It only occurs to me to look at my new sisters toward the end of the fight, when it's still unclear if these will be fights to the death or simply to surrender. Leah and Magnolia are both sitting down. Leah is covering her face. Magnolia is in what looks like an intense conversation with pacifist Aunt Gretchen.

Kendra, by contrast, is standing with her head high and a look I can't read on her face. When she catches me looking, she swallows. "I know who my father is," she says quietly.

"That's something that could have any number of meanings," I point out. Then I shrug to show that I don't mean that aggressively myself. "It's all right to acknowledge that this is complicated."

Kendra blinks, then looks back toward the fight. "Your brother is currently fighting the mate my father handpicked for me and intended for me to choose. I was ordered not to put myself forward here with the rest of the unmated females. There were consequences when I did anyway." She shoots a look at me out of the corner of her eye. "I am . . . not displeased with the shift in my circumstances."

Giving in to an urge, I reach over to grip her hand. I squeeze it. "There has to be a better way. I intend to find it."

Kendra nods, hard. She squeezes my hand in return, and the look she gives me is fierce. It makes me wonder if this sister thing will be more like having friends than I imagined. "I will help you," she vows.

Liam wins decisively, though he does not rip out the older man's throat. He makes it clear he could, his teeth holding his opponent fast until McCaffrey's man has no choice but to whimper, thereby announcing his surrender.

Though Ty's dark eyes gleam, he otherwise doesn't acknowledge it. This is strategic. If he were to start crowing about this victory, it could look like he cares too much about winning and therefore, some will argue, it will prove this is about his ego after all.

I can tell that he wants to fight himself, but he can't. Not while the kings who oppose him only send out their lower-ranked men.

On the solstice, any wolf can challenge any other wolf for any reason, but this is different. It's obvious that the older kings are sending in their seconds to show they don't respect Ty enough to fight themselves.

If Ty fights them anyway, it will make him look weak.

This is exactly the kind of shit Ty hates and wants to be done with. I'm betting the older kings know that. They likely expect Ty to crack and jump in.

I know he won't.

The fighting goes on, rising slowly through the ranks of different packs' lieutenants on our side—each of them jostling to take a turn and demonstrate their support of Ty—until it finally reaches Connor. Kind, reasonable, extremely tough Connor, who has always stood at Ty's back.

As Connor stands in the ring, I think about the fact that he's an older wolf too. He was the VP for the king that Ty deposed, and rumor has it that Ty kept him on to soothe those who thought Ty was too much of an upstart and too hotheaded to handle the changes he created with his challenge.

He's doing it again tonight.

Connor eyes the line of older kings and their many bruised, bitten, and bleeding underlings, then throws back his head to howl. Announcing to anyone who can hear him that he can still fight.

That's what he does, taking down high-ranking wolves in several opposing packs until Janus surrenders. It's the first chink in the old kings' armor.

I think it's a game changer.

The old white-faced wolf backs away with his nose toward the ground, muttering about fealty. All the males in his pack do the same.

Beside me, Kendra makes a low noise. When I look at her, she looks triumphant. The way I feel myself—but can't show. Not out in public like this, when too many people can see me.

One by one, the old kings fall.

Until it's only McCaffrey's pack that remains standing against Ty.

"This has gone on long enough," Ty says impatiently. "Do you imagine that you can stand against not just me but all the wolves in North America? Surely even you aren't that delusional, McCaffrey."

"I've never liked you," the old man sneers. "It's time somebody taught you some manners."

That reverberates through the hills like the slap it is.

Ty laughs. Then he leaps down from the rock above, landing nimbly and easily—and directly in front of McCaffrey. "By all means, motherfucker. Teach me."

But McCaffrey is not the king Ty is. He has minions to do his dirty work, and he sends in another one of his lieutenants. This means Liam goes back in, and when more of McCaffrey's men join the fray, more of Ty's supporters do too.

I can't take it anymore. I move away from my family, winding through the crowd until I reach what feels like my proper place. I stand behind Ty, studying McCaffrey's pack on the other side of the makeshift fighting ring.

Maybe it's unsurprising that it's Deirdre who catches my attention. She looks pinched up tight with temper—and is aiming it at me, if I'm not mistaken.

Somehow, this tracks. Ty is trying something no other wolf has dared to try. Packs are fighting and drawing blood. Her mate is sending other males to get beat on in his name.

But sure, Deirdre is pissed at *me*.

As the men shout insults at each other and then lunge in—shifting into blurs of claw and fang—the older woman eases around the outside of the ring to close the distance between us. "Stop this," she hisses at me. "You have to *stop* this."

I don't actually laugh, though I come close. "Why in the name of the Wolf Moon herself would I do that?"

She presses her lips together so hard I'm shocked they don't shatter. "You young people are always so eager to move on from the old ways," she bites out, a blank sort of fury in her gaze. Or maybe it's something else. Something like grief. "You have no idea what you're doing. Or what you're wrecking with your carelessness."

"I think that some of the old ways make perfect sense to carry forward." I lean in, and it's a measure of how distraught she is that she doesn't recoil the way she usually does when I get too close. This tells me that tic of hers was always performative, but I knew that. "Particularly the old law that states that should a king leave behind a queen with a dependent son, it is her choice of successor that will oversee the pack."

Deirdre pales. Her gaze flickers, and I can't tell where her eyes dart in that moment. To Kendra? To the son in question, a little boy of maybe five who should be back around her pack's gathering fire?

"If I were you," I say in a low voice, "I would think about that."

"What does it matter if there is only one king and he's out here on the West Coast, a million miles away from me and mine?" She spits that out at me, but she's also looking across the ring, and this time I can see exactly what has her attention.

McCaffrey, her mate. The king who claimed her long ago and has made a great sport of fucking *bitten* women *at* her. The man who wanted to marry off her daughter to one of his seconds, who was soundly defeated in the very first fight tonight.

I reach over to grab her wrist. I'm not gentle. "Deirdre," I say, with great deliberateness, "you have never been kind to me."

Her eyes widen, but I push on.

"I don't need to sink to your level, however. So hear me when I tell you this, because it is a kindness whether you want to believe it or not." I angle myself closer to her to make sure no one around us can hear me. "If I were you, I would pick a replacement. I would make sure that he's biddable. And I would encourage him, *strongly*, to make himself indispensable as one of Ty's resources. He'll need one in every pack. If you play your cards right, your role won't change at all."

For a moment, when she stiffens and looks down her nose at me as if I've lost my mind, I think I've misjudged her. Or this moment. One fight ends and another begins in the center of the ring, and she clears her throat. Then looks around.

"Point taken," she says quietly. She glances at me swiftly, then says, even more quietly, "Take care of my girl."

Then she sweeps away, looking regal and untouchable, as if she came over here to give me a talking-to. And delivered it.

I turn my attention back to the fight. McCaffrey's men, with help from a couple of the Canadian packs who seem to be internally divided, keep throwing themselves in and getting smacked back. Ty simply stands there, his arms crossed, looking forward.

Straight at the old man who's the only one still standing against him.

Until, finally, McCaffrey throws back his head and roars into the night.

"Finally," Ty growls.

He leaps up, shifting in midair, before landing once again—this time with his teeth bared and hackles raised.

Then the real fight begins at last.

It's vicious and fast. It's loud. It's high octane, two alpha wolves clashing together and tearing out chunks of each other as best they can.

McCaffrey gets a good swipe in, raking his claws down Ty's side. Ty howls, but he doesn't retreat.

If anything, taking a hit makes him go harder.

And in the end, there's no real contest.

It becomes clear almost immediately—to me, anyway—that Ty *let* McCaffrey swipe at him. That what he's doing is toying with McCaffrey and exhausting him.

Stalking him. Luring him in and tearing him down.

Until, in the end, Ty has McCaffrey on his back, by the throat.

Ty shakes the old man like he's nothing more than a fractious cub.

"Give me your fealty," Ty growls. "Or I'll rip your throat out here and now."

McCaffrey growls back at him. "Go fuck yourself."

There's shuffling all over the hills. Low rumbles, but it's hard to tell if it's unease or excitement.

Maybe it's both.

Ty shakes McCaffrey again. Harder. "Don't be a fool, man. This is how you want to die? Going out like a bitch?"

"Fuck you," McCaffrey barks at him. "And your ego."

The fighting ring is smaller now. Too many wolves are pressing in, watching. Growling.

"One pack," a familiar voice cries out. I glance back and see Rafael, nursing the wounds he sustained fighting one of Janus's men. "One king."

All around us, wolves take up the chant. "One pack, one king. *One pack, one king.*"

"Last chance," Ty tells McCaffrey, pitilessly.

"You will never be my king," McCaffrey growls at him. "*Never.* I would rather die."

"Then die, asshole," Ty replies, and then—in one harsh, smooth motion—ends it.

A flash of teeth, then McCaffrey's throat is gone.

Ty moves back, but leaves the old man to bleed out there in the circle.

It only takes moments. We all know when he's dead.

For a moment, the hills all around us are silent. Hundreds of wolves hushed, quiet, in this moment that's changed everything.

Then, all around, the howling begins.

It goes on and on. It's a song, a very old song we all know well, but it's not usually sung in unison like this. Not by so many wolves from all over North America. Not on the night of the solstice with the packs drawn near.

"The king is dead, long live the king."

Then slowly, even that shifts and becomes the same chant as before.

"One pack, one king."

By the time Ty climbs back up to his rock, everyone is cheering.

My heart is beating so hard I think it would knock people off this hilltop if they could hear it. I don't lie to myself. I don't pretend that everything is magically solved or that old tensions aren't still bubbling along. There will be those who never forgive Ty for this, but from the sounds of things, they'll be outnumbered. That's what matters.

Anyway, that's what diplomacy is for. And failing that, the fact that Ty's just proved that he really can fight anyone without much effort.

The critical part—the amazing part—is that Ty has changed the world.

Right here, right now.

Everything that wolves have taken for granted for as long as anyone can remember is different now, and when that sun comes up in the morning, it truly will be a new day.

There's a wild, sobbing thing inside of me that I don't think I've ever felt before.

It takes me a lot longer than it should to realize that I'm happy.

I'm just *happy*, full stop. So happy and so filled with hope that I can see, with a kind of upsetting clarity, how very much *not* happy I've been. For a long, long time.

The contrast makes my head feel like it's spinning, so I keep my gaze trained on Ty until I feel solid again. Until I feel like me.

He shifts into his human form and stretches so we can all see that the gashes McCaffrey left behind are already mostly healed.

No need to announce that he's better than the old guard he literally just trounced. We can all see it. We all have the same rapid healing powers, mostly available in the magic that lets us change forms.

But the moon favors Ty. That much is clear.

It's always been clear to me.

"I am honored," Ty belts out, and everyone cheers. There are a few more verses of the song, in both its old and new versions. "On this longest night of the year, we get to celebrate the dawn of a new age. The age of wolves."

Everyone goes wild. Even I find myself howling like a *bitten* girl. That's how this feels. Like the moon is *mine.*

Better still, the king is.

Ty quiets us, then continues. "We are wolves, and wolves do not hide. Wolves do not cower in the face of old fears. Wolves do not let our history dictate our future."

The howling seems to echo back from the dark sky, it's so loud, but Ty is looking down at me. His mouth curves, and he beckons for me to come to him.

I don't think twice. I leap up and go to stand with him.

He takes my hand, lacing my fingers with his, making it clear that I belong *beside* him. A subtlety I know will not be lost on anyone. Especially the females.

"My pledge to you is that I'm yours," he tells the crowd, and I can hear the cheering from the farthest hills. "I belong to the pack, and as long as I draw breath, I will fight for all of us. There will be no success in one quarter unless it is shared in all."

There is even more wild, jubilant cheering at that.

"None of what I'm going to do is possible without my fated mate," he tells them when the cheering subsides a little.

He looks down at me, and there's nothing but pride on his face. In his dark eyes. And he's not showing this only to me. He's letting every wolf here see it—here and now, while his new throne is brand-new.

My throat hurts so much I think I might actually cry. I don't know how I hold it back, but I do, because the queen to a king like this has to be as strong as he is. She has to complement him. This is what I always said I wanted.

I refuse to let him down now that he's giving it to me.

"While I was busy building what I have every intention of making our werewolf empire, shared among us equally, Maddox was studying the things we need to know to move nimbly through anything this world throws at us. She's the one who planted the seed. *We should live like wolves,* she told me once. *But we should dream like humans.*"

This time when they roar, they're roaring for me.

Ty doesn't let go of my hand as he waits for that clamor to die down. "That means we treat obstacles as opportunities. We think big and worry about it later. We do not molder away in our caves, dreaming of full moons. We rise. We fight. We *build.*"

He lifts my hand and presses his mouth to our linked fingers. "We dream, my brothers and sisters. And we dream best together."

There are so many kings who have always made their women crawl and scrape, stand behind them, present themselves as little more than available possessions at all times. This is an odd, courtly sort of gesture as a counterpoint, and I know Ty is aware of it. That this is one more strike against the old ways.

To me, it feels like healing.

"We could have officially mated at any point," he tells the crowd. "Instead we created a partnership and, together, we will usher this pack—this one, glorious pack—into its bright new future. By the end of this year, she will accept my claim. But the new age of wolves has already begun."

He lifts his other hand high in the air. "It's the solstice. Tomorrow isn't just a new day, it's *our* day. I invite you to celebrate with me."

Then he shifts in such a rush that I shift with him, helpless to resist in the blast of all that energy. When he throws his head back to howl out the glory of this, of us, of *pack* into the night, I join in.

So does everyone else.

I do spare a thought for Winter and the other humans no doubt shuddering in their homes at all this howling, but all I can think about is this bright new kingdom we've made here tonight.

And better yet, what we'll do with it.

16.

The longest night of the year is still ahead of us, but first, there are practicalities to consider. Like the burning of McCaffrey's body—werewolves never leave bodies behind for anyone to study, and a new dawn isn't likely to change that—and the application of first aid for those who need it.

There are also new pack dynamics. Ty and I sit there on that high rock as, one by one, each of the packs come before him and pledge themselves to him. Some with more enthusiasm than others. Some through the wounds they've sustained. Some with huge grins.

This is how we create the first unified kingdom of North American werewolves in memory.

"You were right," Ty tells me in a low voice at one point. "It's more powerful that I haven't claimed you yet. A queen will always follow her king. Even an independent female like you was expected to fall in line eventually. Everyone expected the claiming would sort you out. But you made it clear you follow no one unless you want to, and yet here you are at my side."

There was a time he would not have said these things with all that admiration in his voice. I remember all of those times, so I bask in it now. I bask pretty hard.

"Maybe you shouldn't have given me such a hard time," I suggest. When he swivels his head to look at me, all that arrogant astonishment and *high king* energy, I shrug. "I'm just saying, in the future, maybe react less and listen more."

He laughs at that, and I feel that same connection of ours sizzle between us, powerful enough to supercharge the dark. "I'll remember you said that, babe," he assures me.

Though really, it's a threat. One I can't wait for him to make good on.

Except first there are all of these conversations to get through. These negotiations, because that's really what they are. The remaining pack leaders acknowledge Ty as their king, but they also give him all of their problems.

Problems that, in some cases, he's already solved.

Like when he announces that he's sending my brothers to the various packs their mates came from for a season or two, in defiance of tradition, just to make sure that things run smoothly. Not to mention handle whatever sore feelings might remain.

During a lull, I eye him. "It almost seems like you were planning this all along."

"I might not have taken the jump to declaring myself king." He runs a hand through his hair, and I wonder if I'm the only one who can tell he's tired. Not that he'll show it. Not for hours and hours, and not until he's in private. "But I was real clear on the fact that I needed my men in other packs. Just to help steer the ship in our direction."

"Did you really think McCaffrey would accept it? That doesn't sound like the asshole I knew."

"Your brother seemed to think that it wouldn't be a problem." He looks at me, his mouth twitching. "I think maybe you don't know how persuasive Liam can be."

"Maybe I don't want to," I retort, and it takes an effort not to look around and find Liam—and Kendra, most likely—out there in the crowd.

The hour gets later. Slowly, the families trickle away, packing up their things and retreating to dens below or their campsites on distant hills. As they do, inevitably, the wildness begins to creep back in.

The *bitten* girls dance. The males' laughter gets lower, rougher. The central fire is high—just high enough that it's easy to make out writhing bodies, wolf and human forms in various combinations of spectacular positions.

Sex is thick in the air, and finally—*finally*—this long solstice night feels like a celebration.

Up on the rock, Ty pulls me over his lap. I can feel him, hot and hard, that enormous cock already huge between us.

"I don't believe I've sworn my fealty to you yet, my liege," I whisper, looping my arms around his neck.

"You know you haven't," Ty says, in that low rumble that I can feel everywhere. "And until you properly swear yourself to me as all my subjects must do this night? I'm not going to let you come."

I laugh at that. At him. At us, maybe. I tilt my head back, and he sinks a hand into my hair and wraps the wavy mess of it around his fist so he can keep my throat bared to him.

Then his mouth is there, that terrible heat, a magic fire that rages in all directions.

He moves so he can reach between us, unzipping my jeans and pushing them off my hips. He palms my ass for a moment, then grunts and lifts me off him so he can tear them farther down my legs, cursing a little when they get caught on my boots.

But he's not particularly fussy. He leaves my twisted jeans like manacles and pulls me back over him, tearing my panties off with a careless tug.

It makes everything in me *light up* like the stars high above us.

He releases himself from his own jeans and shifts me up and over him. I kneel up and let him guide me as I settle back into that straddle so we can both watch me as I take all of him. That slow, thick slide down the length of him.

Always too big. Always just right. Always a moment of *too much* that quickly turns itself over into all of that glorious heat.

I love every single part of it.

"I'll need that pledge now," he tells me when he's seated almost all the way inside me, impaling me, his mouth on my neck. "I need to be entirely certain of you, baby. After all, only a fool trusts faith."

But he's laughing while he says this.

"Trust, but verify," I manage to get out as I finally take that last, impossible inch. My head droops forward with the effort but he pulls it back again, that hand in my hair its own directive.

"You get me." His voice is a velvet order. His cock is like steel. His free hand is on my hip and he grips me, harder. "I need you moving. I want to see you work. And I need the words."

I don't dare disobey him, and anyway, there's not one part of me that wants to.

"Yes, my liege," I murmur. "My king."

It takes a wild effort to open my eyes and look at him. To hold that intense, dark gaze of his.

It takes more effort still to shift my hips and then start rocking myself against him. Creating that friction. Lifting myself up and then sliding back down. Feeling that stretch, that mad fire, that connection that pours into every part of me. My nipples ache. My ears feel flushed. I can feel that cock of his in my toes.

I do this over and over and over.

"I pledge myself to you, Ty Ceridwen," I tell him. I punctuate these words by lifting myself up and then letting myself fall again. "Once *Rix* of the Western Wolves, now Ty of North America, high king of the werewolf packs. I'm yours."

I prove it by creating the push and the pull, and he's letting me. Insisting upon it, even.

I brace one of my hands against his chest, all that ridged, hot glory in a black T-shirt. This helps. It helps me rise higher and slam myself down harder.

"I swear to you my loyalty," I pant at him as I move. "King of all kings, king of my heart, king of the wolves, and king of me, I give to you everything I am and anything you desire."

"So prettily said," he says against my mouth, nipping me. "I wouldn't have thought that vows could come so easily to a woman who's avoided them for most of her life."

I bite his jaw and he laughs. "I gave myself to you a long time ago, Ty," I remind him. "You're the one who wanted to fight about how."

"Baby." He shifts beneath me, wrapping his arms around me and that easily, that smoothly, taking complete control. So that now it's like he's the one using my body to fuck himself. So hard and deep and hot that I can feel the orgasm barreling toward me. "We're always going to fight. And we're always going to win."

Then neither one of us speaks for a long while. He plays with me, almost taking me there and then backing off, repeating this irritating pattern until I'm writhing against him, out of my mind.

"Ty," I whisper. *"Please."*

He laughs, his beard in the crook of my neck, then he growls out an order. "Come," he finally grits out. "Now."

When I do, I throw my head back and I scream loud enough to be heard all over this valley, and truly, I hope that everyone, everywhere, hears it.

If that's not fealty, I don't know what is.

Ty lets me buck and shake all over him, but he's not finished. He leans back, shifting the angle, and he keeps rocking into me so I brace myself above him for more.

I let the storm take us both.

Down below us, all around that fire, I can hear the rest of our people celebrating in the way we do, earthy and gritty. Dirty. I realize that this is the first time I've taken part in this so directly. Normally, Ty takes me off somewhere, because it's tradition to treat the queen differently. To keep her hidden, even though there is no other female in the pack who doesn't enjoy the freedom she finds on these fires at least once in her life.

None of us are hiding any longer.

I start coming again, harder this time, because he's given me this, too. Without even discussing it, he's making it clear that I'm more free with him than without him. And when he finally releases deep inside of me, I can feel the heat of him everywhere.

I can hear the laughter from below. I can hear the fire crackle and dance. I tip my head back up, kiss him on his beautiful face, and smile.

"I hope the grand high king isn't too tired," I say. "Because I think I may have to do that again."

"Your wish is my command," he tells me.

Then he shows me, again and again.

Ty and I spend the whole night up on the hilltop. Not always on the ledge, though I think that I'll remember our time there for the rest of my life. We sit and drink a few beers here and there. We talk with the other wolves, tell stories and share laughter, and as the longest night takes its sweet time heading toward daylight, we work together to build connections.

To make it clear that Ty has no intention of being any kind of tyrant. To prove that he meant it when he said that he's for wolves. *All* wolves.

And at sunrise we are there to howl at the sun and welcome back the light.

But then, for a moment, I think I can feel the whole earth shake beneath me.

"Did you feel that?" I ask him as the sunlight pours in all around us. I know it won't last. I can already see the fog developing at the base of the trees. I should bask in the light while I can. But that shaking unnerved me. "It seemed like some kind of . . ."

I don't know where I'm going with that. I've greeted the morning after the darkest night of the year before, but it never felt quite like this. Like an explosion, and not inside me—but we don't get earthquakes around here.

"It's been a long night," Ty says, and if he feels that strange uneasiness the way I do, he doesn't show it. "And we're not getting any sleep anytime soon, babe. Suck it up."

He throws his arm over my shoulders and we walk down into the grand cavern, where he spends the rest of the morning engaged in more diplomatic wrangling, going over all the rest of the things that have to happen in the wake of such a huge change for wolfkind.

His first official act is to hand out weapons, ammunition, and explosives to the packs that are leaving at first light rather than letting them all continue to fight about stolen property.

"Consider it the kingdom's property," he growls at everyone. "Take my shit and shut the fuck up, because it's all *our* shit." He pauses for a moment, then grins at the wolves in question, all of them taken back. "Safe travels."

By late afternoon, most of our visitors have headed out. It's down to pretty much the usual Rogue Valley pack again, so the den feels both empty and cozy around me as we set it back to rights. I don't go and sit with my family the way I would have done before last night. I'm over with Ty now, on the raised rock shelf where I first slept in his furs as a girl.

It's another indication that everything between us has changed. That everything is different.

I would know that anyway, though, because no one is talking to me like they're disappointed in me today. Females who only looked at me sideways before make a point of coming to ask my advice on small, insignificant things. What do I think the weather will be for the full moon? What are my thoughts on the mysterious elk herds that seem to choose new and random seasons all winter long, making it harder all the time to hunt them?

These are all olive branches. I accept them.

"I underestimated you," my mother tells me when she comes and climbs up onto the ledge where the king spends his leisure time in this cavern. She waits for me to notice her. She waits to be invited to approach. She even waits for me to invite her to sit, acknowledging my rank.

I thought that I would celebrate when this day came. Instead, I find that it feels nothing at all the way I thought it would. I didn't expect that I'd feel nostalgia for what's gone, because at least I knew it.

Everything ahead of me is unknown.

"Of course you underestimated me," I reply to her as she sits. "But don't worry, Mother. Everyone else did too."

"It's actually brilliant," Johanna says, and if she heard the undercurrent of something like hurt in my voice, she brushes it aside. "You've quietly upended generations of tradition. Now, no matter what your intentions were, everything you've done your whole life will be viewed as strategy."

I grin at her. "Maybe it has been."

She sits next to me on the low-slung couch and looks out into the great cavern. I follow her gaze, tracking the electric lights that hang from cords attached to the rock walls by thick metal staples. According to the stories I've heard, even that was a fight. Old-school wolves thought electric lights were too human and would make wolves too soft.

Johanna isn't only looking at light fixtures, of course. She's looking around at the different family groups. Some of them are sitting together, talking quietly. Others are still rearranging their areas in the wake of so much shared space this past week. I see a few older females engaged in what looks like deep-cleaning, no doubt to get unwanted scents out.

"I've been pushing for so long, and it all happened so quickly, in the end," Johanna says softly. Almost wistfully, I think, but that doesn't sound like my mother at all. "Your brothers are off playing royal emissaries in far-off packs. They might as well be kings themselves, as close as they are to Ty. The packs will have to treat them as leaders. Meanwhile, you've managed to be accepted as our queen without lowering yourself to go through the mating ritual like everyone else."

"Not all of us can fall in love the way you did," I point out, mildly enough. "Besides, no one kidnaps their mates any longer. It's pretty much frowned upon in polite pack circles."

"I was not raised to expect *love*," my mother says with a short laugh. I think that she's not going to look at me, but then she does. Her gaze is steady, and something about the resignation I see there makes my heart ache. "Your father was a fine, storied male. It was an honor to be chosen by him, and so I dedicated myself to making certain that his choice was never questioned." She nods as if that's nothing more than common sense. "Still, it took us time to trust each other. And more time still to build some kind of friendship. I always thought your brothers understood this better than you. Now I wonder."

"All of you had to go out and find mates or accept them when they turned up," I remind her. "I have always known my mate. It has never been a question of *who*. Only *when*."

"I am trying to compliment you, Maddox," my mother says after a moment, and again I think she sounds something like *wistful*. "You know that's not something that comes easily to me." Again, her gaze finds mine. "I apologize for assuming you didn't know your own business. And for thinking that you would embarrass the family when, on the contrary, you have now elevated us beyond my wildest dreams. I would have said that no wolf could rule us all, but I believe Ty can. Particularly with you at his side."

I reach down and pinch myself on my own inner thigh, hard. I'm sure that will wake me up, but it doesn't. Johanna really said those things. Directly to me.

I'm not dreaming. I also have no idea how to respond to something so . . . completely out of character.

Luckily, I don't have to. It's almost as if she hits a wall. As if she said too many supportive, even *loving* things and has completely drained that battery. She stands up abruptly. I watch her visibly remember that there are no gray areas any longer when it comes to pack hierarchy and me. She blinks, then offers a bow.

I have the urge to tell her that bowing isn't necessary, but I hold it back. The truth is, pomp and circumstance might not be necessary for *me*. What it does, though, is remind everyone else who I am.

Wolves like to push boundaries. They like to play games. If I allow them to do it with me, sooner or later, I'll regret it.

I'm thinking about that when Connor approaches, and instead of jumping onto the ledge, he only leans against it to look up at me.

"You've all been hidden away for a while now," I say, meaning the remaining high-ranking males in the pack. Off in their church,

I assume, coming up with their world domination plans. "There's no need to worry. I have things handled out here."

"He knew you would," Connor says.

I find myself looking at the leather cut he wears, giving epic biker chic. It's also covered in badges that spell out his long service to this pack. His kills and his conquests. It's not lost on me that he's seen queens come and go. I'm lucky that he's always seemed supportive of me—even when my own brothers and mother were not.

Today he gives me an approving nod. "He sent me to get you. Thinks you've been babysitting long enough."

I laugh at that, though I don't dispute it. I get up and jump off the ledge to stand beside him, still basically in last night's clothes. And feeling it. I stole one of Ty's T-shirts at some point and, as far as I know, left my jacket on the hilltop. Someone will scent me on it and return it, I'm sure. What I keep being shocked by is how hungover I feel when I had very little alcohol last night.

Everyone knows that hitting the cocktails hard is for after regime changes, not *during*.

I follow Connor as he leads me through the cavern and then into the tunnels. This muddled, thick feeling reminds me of my party girl days, back in my first year in New York. I took Ty seriously when he told me to do my thing. I got out there and I did it. There wasn't a club I didn't hit. There wasn't a bar I didn't pour myself out of at some egregious hour. I danced and I drank and I indulged myself. I slept with hot girls, I kissed pretty boys, and I fucked dangerous men with the careless abandon of a girl who knew *she* was always safe because she carried a wolf around with her.

I kept waiting for something—someone—to erase that imprint Ty had left inside me, but nothing did. Nothing and no one ever came close.

Nothing ever could, I came to realize that year.

That was why, when I came home that summer, I decided it was high time I saw what I was missing.

I'm so busy thinking about all that—about the way I walked into the den the night I got home and hurled myself straight into Ty's arms—that it takes a moment to realize that Connor is taking an unusual turn. He's walking away from the regular tunnels and getting into the deeper part of the den where most of the pack never comes at all.

Something in me whispers a warning, but I dismiss it. This is *Connor*. He's been Ty's right-hand man since before I was born. There's no possible way that he could wish me harm—and even if he had some kind of personality transplant and did wish me harm, he certainly wouldn't do something about it *here*. He'd be scented in an instant.

Still, I slow my pace a little and keep myself behind him, just in case. He'll have to turn around to attack me, and that will give me critical moments to shift and fight—

We turn a corner and I feel like a paranoid fool. We're suddenly in a tunnel that has bright lights blazing. I can hear Ty's voice in the distance.

I have to force myself to unclench my fists and can only hope that Connor didn't notice.

Connor leads me into a big, wide room that has a large table in the middle, where Ty and his lieutenants are standing. It feels weird that none of my brothers are here, I think, but I keep that to myself. When I venture closer, I see that they're looking at a big, blank map of North America.

"I don't want to make a big fucking thing out of this," Ty is saying. "Meaning, I don't want anyone asking questions about it. But I don't see any reason why we can't make sure we know what everything looks like these days instead of relying on outside takes on that."

"Consider it done," one of his lieutenants says, and the others nod their agreement.

"Initial reports by the full moon." Ty waits for them to nod to that, too, then continues. "We like how it's looking, we'll spread this out farther."

There are a lot of fist bumps and chin raises at that, and then they all roll out—though not without giving me some kind of acknowledgment on the way. Some incline their heads. A couple murmur a verbal indication that they know things have altered. Beaudry even swats me on the shoulder.

"Like that you two are solid," he tells me as he swaggers off, and I can't decide if I'm moved or weirded out that I have his part of the cousin vote.

Ty waves me over, so I go and look down at the map too.

"We're going to use this as a command center," he tells me. "I don't need the rest of the pack trickling in and out of here, so it will be guarded. But I will need to know the actual territory that all the different packs occupy. Especially the more remote packs who haven't had any oversight in a long time."

"Smart," I tell him.

He straightens, running his hands over his hair to shove it back. Then he looks at me with a kind of wonder in his gaze. It makes me feel . . . breathless.

Then again, so does the way he reaches over and fits his palm over the nape of my neck to tug me closer. Everything in me hums, even though I can tell that this isn't about sex.

This is about the vows I made to him. This is about *us*.

"Come on," he says, low and rumbly. "I need to get out of here."

We ride into Jacksonville. It's cold and gloomy outside, a December afternoon tipping over into a foggy evening and that first quarter half-moon set to rise. Yet when I wrap my arms around Ty and hold him close as he navigates the roaring, muscular bike through the hills and down into town, everything feels like sunshine and blue skies to me.

Jacksonville's main street is more crowded than I expect it to be, but then again, it's a winter evening toward the end of the year. The sun might be creeping back, but that won't be obvious to the naked eye—especially the human naked eye—for a while now. What they have instead are these festivals of light.

I can't pretend I don't like them too.

He parks his bike and I swing off. Then he takes my hand and we walk together, all the lights from the shop windows and strung up around the buildings gleaming on us. Making everything shine.

There are carolers dressed like they wandered out from some old movie. There's an actual Christmas tree, with decorations and everything, blazing with light like the Reveal never happened. The people all around us seem happy, almost giddy, and they don't get too uptight when they recognize Ty and me.

Not always the reception here in the human safe zone, I know.

Ty shifts from holding my hand to slinging an arm over my shoulders, and everything feels . . . good. That's why it feels so weird at the same time. I'm not used to *good*. I'm used to varying degrees of trouble.

I'm sure that we'll have more than enough of that. Yet in this moment, on this street, it's all pretty songs, crisp air, spiced cider, and Christmas cookies that the old librarians I kept safe from random wolves are handing out to the passersby.

"Because it felt like high time to start baking again," I hear one of them telling a happy customer.

I feel a lot like singing carols myself. Especially with cookies.

Then, suddenly, I see the swirl of red out of the corner of my eye. *A flowing cloak,* my brain tells me, and my whole body goes cold.

I whip my head around, but it's just a caroler. A human with a pretty voice singing soprano, not some creep brandishing horrible knives from behind a nasty plague-doctor mask.

Ty looks down at me, his gaze assessing. "You okay?"

"Never better." I'm sure he can hear that my heart is pounding. I feel almost queasy.

I don't want to admit that I saw a red cloak and my first thought was that it had to be one of the death goddess's asshole minions right here on California Street. I can remember them much too vividly, dancing around a clearing high on Mount McLoughlin, blood everywhere, those nasty masks on their faces and that same feverish true believer shit making their eyes blank.

No matter what species they were.

It was worse up at Crater Lake on Halloween.

Ty doesn't believe me. "Kind of looks like you've seen a ghost, babe."

"I don't believe in ghosts," I tell him loftily. "Not really. It's a way for people to talk about shit they regret, that's all, and I don't regret anything."

"Not yet," Ty drawls, and pulls me in closer to him. "It's hard to remember, but you're still pretty young. You have hundreds of years left to fuck shit up."

"I was under the impression that fucking shit up was our pack motto," I tease him. "Isn't that right? *Fight me* and all?"

He laughs, and I can see the half-moon in the sky. It feels like a blessing.

By the time we get back to his bike, I've almost completely forgotten that I thought I saw some of Vinča's faithful in the crowd around us. I've also almost forgotten that there was ever any friction between this man and me. Everything today feels so smooth. So easy.

Like fate finally stopped pushing so hard and we finally fell into place.

He swings onto his bike and starts it up. I slide into place behind him. I tuck my fingers in the back of his jeans and like the burn of his hot skin against my knuckles. I'm thinking that this unofficial but accepted queen thing kind of rocks as he takes off.

Ty shoots back up the hill and then loops around so he can take the road out of town, like we're chasing down that half-moon. I feel the same thing he does, I'm sure of it. A restlessness. A longing. The call of the open road, because being on a motorcycle feels like flying.

I'm thinking we might ride on through the night just to see where we end up, but as we pass the old towns that were built along Bear Creek, the river that runs down the center of the valley, a flash of blinding light almost knocks us over.

Ty manages to pull the bike over to one side without injuring either one of us, though it's a close call and it kicks up clouds of dust. I hold on to him, hard, and when the light subsides, Savi is standing there.

Though she's not *really* standing there.

"Winter's house," she says, in a disembodied voice that I only realize after a moment is *inside* of me.

"Fucking sorcery," Ty barks at her. "Stupid fucking smoke-and-mirrors bullshit that's going to get someone killed, and it was almost me, asshole."

"Winter's house," intones the apparition again. "Now."

Then the light disappears as abruptly as it came.

Ty and I stay where we are, holding on to each other there on the side of the road, while we wait for our eyesight to return to normal. For the dust to subside.

For Ty's temper to creep back down from the red zone, not that I blame him. I'm not delighted with what just happened myself.

"I don't like being summoned by some spooky bitch with a goddamn fetish for the theatrical," Ty rumbles, sounding more pissed than usual. Probably because he was less in control of that bike than he likes, especially with me on it.

He's always the most furious when he's being protective.

"She doesn't usually do that," I remind him. "I think it must be bad."

Ty blows out a breath. Then he looks over his shoulder at me, and his mouth crooks up in one corner. "It's always bad, baby. That's why it's fun."

He spins us around so fast it's dizzying, then aims us back toward Jacksonville. We race into town, cut away from the main street before we hit the crowd, then blaze our way up the hill and into the woods to Winter's house. When we pull up in the yard, Winter and Ariel are already there on the front porch. Savi is off to the side, looking like a piece of polished ivory that happens to be propped up by no particular visible means.

Ty growls at them all. "I don't appreciate hologram shit in my head."

"How about this shit?" Savi asks. "You'll like this even more."

She hums something, then lifts her hands up until another bright light appears between her palms. As she murmurs something else in a language far too old for me to understand, the light grows and grows.

Until, still murmuring her ancient spell words, she throws it.

It seems to go everywhere. It ricochets all around without actually hitting anything and then spears its way deep inside of me. At the same time, it sinks deep into Ariel. Into Winter. I can hear it when it hits Ty, because he roars out his displeasure.

He doesn't like it at all. Neither do I, but that doesn't matter.

Nothing matters, because images are cascading through my head. A vision of Vinča with her wormy face and her rotten mouth, clawing her way out of what looks like a birdcage.

But it's ribs, I realize with a sickening lurch in my belly. She's creeping her way out of someone's *ribs*.

I see Vinča's temple, which is supposed to be securely at the bottom of Crater Lake, laid to waste. It's nothing but rubble and ash, and there's no creepy death goddess to be seen.

What I do see is an empty lake bed, cracked and parched, and I almost think that this is some random Eastern Oregon shit—but then, in the vision, I look up.

And realize that I'm standing at the bottom of Crater Lake. An *empty* Crater Lake.

There's a loud, terrible sound, like laughter in the sky, and then I'm back in my body with another horrible *lurch*. I'm standing next to Ty's bike. I'm in Winter's yard.

I'm also gasping for air.

I reach out and am wildly grateful to find Ty's steady, rock-hard body beside me. Though when I look at him, his gaze looks as dark as mine feels.

But he looks furious, not sick.

"To catch you up," comes Savi's cool voice, like an icy wind, "Winter's visions are back. That's one of them. I'm sure you get its meaning."

On the porch, Winter looks hollow-eyed. Ariel has his hand on the back of her neck, and I get the impression he's holding her up.

"Vinča is back," Winter says, in case we missed the slithering out from *ribs.* "I don't understand how. But she's back. And if I'm not mistaken, she's already walking among us." She swallows, and I'm guessing she feels as sick as I do. "Walking *inside* someone."

"Well," I make myself say, because it's that or scream. "We all saw the ribs. She won't stay there."

17.

First Quarter Half Wolf Moon

"Something happened last night," Winter tells me, looking pale. "Something changed."

The two of us are sitting inside her house in what was once a cozy den—in the human sense of that word—with a television that still sits there on the wall, useless. Nothing but a dark mirror these days.

Savi left with Ariel and Ty. I would have gone with them, but it was clear to me that Winter shouldn't. Not in her more fragile state. I'm pretty sure I got the vampire king's version of an almost-smile when I announced I'd stay. Ty only scowled, but he didn't insult me by telling me to be careful.

He didn't have to tell me. One thing about the oracle's house is that it's impenetrable. Winter kept it pretty tightly locked down, but I can smell the vampire all over it now. Not to mention sorceress warding and the werewolf patrols that I could scent myself on the way here.

I also checked the bars and steel plates over the windows when Winter let me venture deeper into the house than the communal kitchen. Something she saves for special occasions.

"Last night was the solstice," I say, trying to keep my voice light. I've seen her with a Vinča-shaped headache before. She hasn't said that her head hurts now, but I'm betting it does. "Things always happen on the solstice. That's the point of celebrating it."

"I don't mean that kind of stuff." She rubs at her temples, but smiles. "The vampires do throw a solstice party, it turns out. And it's true that a great many things happened there, but that's not what I'm talking about."

I file that away as something to ask about later, since I have a not-so-small fascination with what vampires get up to in private. Not coffins and bats, I'm guessing, though I'm holding out hope that Winter will confess to both.

Though maybe not while we're waiting to hear if our favorite death goddess is on a new rampage. One involving tearing her way out of someone's rib cage. "The creepy-ass vision," I say, because of course that's what she's talking about. "I'm sorry you have that shit in your head. I didn't like it in mine. I know we weren't sure about it right after, but the magic we used on Halloween was solid. Vinča should be locked up tight for at least another millennium."

"I don't think she is," Winter says. In that voice that isn't quite hers.

It reminds me of her grandmother. A regular little old lady most of the time, but when the oracle came out to play, Gran was different. Like the thing that makes them see makes its presence known in their voices, too.

Winter reaches into a low pocket on her cargo pants and pulls her cards out. As little as I want to know what's coming for us, I have to take it as a good sign that she is apparently communicating with her cards again. That the breakup didn't take.

She taps the deck, then flips the top card over. When she makes a humming sort of sound, it seems to connect to some kind of tuning fork in me. I don't like it.

Her eyes shift to something far brighter than mere indigo. "It's something in the stars," she tells me, as if she's looking at those stars herself. From inside this little room with covered windows. "A doorway. A window, maybe. And it's closing, fast. But it's not closed yet."

"I don't remember there being any windows in that temple," I mutter. Not that I investigated it closely, but we all saw it hovering around in mid-air, practically *singing* with all its bad energy.

Even remembering it makes my stomach clench.

Winter shifts on the couch beside me. She's sitting with her legs crossed, frowning down at the cards in her hands as she shuffles and then flips over another. "You have a target on your back," she tells me. "You know that. It just got bigger."

"I have a number of extremely cool tattoos on my back," I contradict her. "Not a single target among them, thank you." She lifts her head and blinks at me. "When don't I have a target on my back, Winter? People are either going to come for me or they won't. I'm not going to lose sleep about it."

"I might," Winter retorts. "I have."

We hear the back door creak open, and then the telltale signs of Briar moving around in the kitchen. The sound of the cereal cabinet opening and shutting. The sound of cutlery in a ceramic bowl. The refrigerator door. But neither one of us calls out. Or makes any move to go into the kitchen.

We sit there in silence, watching each other, until the back door creaks shut.

It's quiet again. I can hear Briar's footsteps outside, and it sounds like she's muttering to herself as she heads back in the direction of her cottage. Possibly she's muttering about the cold out there. Or maybe she likes to move about with a mantra on her lips. Hard to say.

Winter makes a sound when I look back at her. "I don't want to scare her."

"Yeah."

When we get quiet once more, I wonder if we're both imagining what that would be like. To be ignorant of all the things going on in this valley, all the time. To be able to carve out some kind of life in these strange days that feels relatively normal.

I daydream about it a little. I think Winter does too.

We're still sitting there when Ariel and Ty return. I notice that Ariel is now capable of simply appearing inside Winter's house, meaning he has that full-access invitation. More interesting in this moment is that he did that puff-of-smoke thing he does *with* Ty, who looks both disgusted and faintly outraged to have been transported in this manner.

Savi is nowhere to be seen.

"The lake looks the same but feels wrong," Ariel tells us. Ty only glares. "The sorceress has retired to her lair to see if she can find the right spells to determine what's wrong."

"She's freaking out," Ty grunts.

"We'll run patrols," Ariel says, exchanging a look with Ty, indicating they've come to some kind of agreement between them on that. "But until the sorceress can ascertain what has happened, we can otherwise only wait."

Ty shakes his head. "It's not right up there," he says. He and Ariel exchange another look. "Something's up, and it's not good."

I think of that early-morning *shaking* I felt and hold back a shiver.

There's nothing else to be done, so Ty and I go back to the den. I think we might forget about our troubles in one of our preferred fashions, but instead he's called away immediately to consult on matters that I know he'll tell me about later. Yet protocol demands I pretend I don't know what's happening while it's actually happening.

Maybe this is as close as I get to my fantasy about what Briar's life must be like. All that blissful ignorance—but if it is, I hate it.

I lie in Ty's bed and stare at the carved rock ceiling. I remind myself that you can't change everything in one day. Not even on the solstice.

In the morning, what's wrong about Crater Lake is clear, and we don't need Savi's spells to figure it out.

It's flooding. And fast.

The water from the lake is draining, pouring out, and rolling downhill.

And pretty much everything is downhill from Crater Lake.

This time, the tense meeting of the valley's three powers takes place at Ariel's mixed martial arts school in downtown Medford.

We take the bike again. Ty navigates his way through piles of debris and shuffling zombies—both actual zombies and the crowds of drug addicts who haunt what's left of the city center. The same vacant eyes and imperviousness to the condition of their bodies, the weather, the danger they're in at any given moment, and everything else.

It's a dark, overcast day. Maybe this is why I can see that there are more lights on in the buildings downtown than I've seen in years. Things are changing around here, and it's not the sporadic gentrification projects that I remember coming in fits and starts while I was growing up. For one thing, I doubt very much that this is human driven.

I'm not human, however. I might miss the ones I befriended in New York and quite like the one I know here who also happens to be the new oracle and maybe not entirely human any longer, but I also like the idea of us monsters taking back the cities we had to hide in for centuries.

I peer into the lit-up windows as we pass. The little old houses that still stand. The apartment buildings that were built closer to the center. There are far fewer bars and steel plates over the windows here than in Jacksonville. Even more proof that it's not humans venturing out of their few safe zones.

I'm pretty sure the slimy dens, dark caves, swamp mud, and other traditional monster-type dwellings have lost their appeal all around. I might be a revolutionary in the werewolf pack, but I'm certainly not the only one in this valley to ask an ancient Kind clan why it is that the whole world got to change except us.

If I didn't have fate and responsibilities and the big man in front of me to consider, I'd probably think it sounded like fun to go live up at the Manor and rave my face off. Or move into one of the abandoned buildings down here, where the streets aren't likely to scare me. I'm not the kind of prey that's hunted here. Quite the opposite.

Besides, I saw *Les Misérables* on Broadway while I was in New York. There's a part of me that wants nothing more than to build a barricade, wave a flag, and sing a song. Preferably without the second act to make it all less fun.

I choose not to tell Ty any of that as we make our way around a few songless barrier piles set up on Main Street. Somehow I know that no matter how indulgent he might be feeling about me right now, musicals are not likely to be his thing.

Still, I can hear the people sing as Ty rolls his bike up to the front door of Archangel MMA and leaves it there as we walk inside.

Everybody knows who rides big, kick-ass Harleys like that around here. Not to mention who controls the gas to run them. Even the most blood-addled, gutter-dwelling addict wouldn't dare touch a werewolf's bike. And all the other, less addled but more full of themselves monsters who hunt down here know exactly which werewolf's bike that is.

Ty could leave it running. It won't move an inch.

Inside, I'm disappointed to find that vampire headquarters are still, for all intents and purposes, a big old martial arts studio. I don't know why I thought Ariel would have switched it all over to dark velvet and capes.

Wishful thinking.

No one sits down in the rows of bleachers against one wall. Ariel and Savi are already there, and Ty rolls right up to them in the center of the polished wood floor. I trail after him, smiling at Winter when I come to stand next to her. She looks better than last night. I hope that means the death goddess headache is gone.

"What I don't understand," Savi says, her voice less serene than usual, "is why the patrols that were already supposed to be occurring at Crater Lake were stopped."

By the time she gets to the end of that sentence, it's clear that she's not *serene* at all. I've never heard her anything but calm before. She even *looks* a little less perfect than usual. Like she might actually have been up all night doing whatever it is sorcerers do when they're looking for spells. Usually she looks like she's spent a month in a spa.

"Then you're not very observant, sorceress," Ty is replying, but he often sounds this grouchy. That he's probably also tired has nothing to do with it. "I made it perfectly clear that the wolves had shit to do last week. That did not include babysitting a body of water."

"There were patrols," Ariel interjects coolly. "There have been vampires up there every night and every day, as always. Suggesting that whatever occurred was meant to occur outside of our notice. Planned, even."

Savi shakes her head. I don't think I've ever seen her this close to what I would call upset—and it doesn't make my stomach feel great. That or my sense of impending doom.

"They took out the tunnels," she says, and she sounds almost . . . shrill? Scared? Neither one is good. "The lava tunnels. Tubes. They've been blocked for centuries, but they blew them up and the water is draining out of the lake. I can't think of any good reason for that to be happening. I knew I felt something just before dawn on the night of the solstice. I couldn't figure out what it was."

I remember that uneasiness as the sun rose. That *shake*. I feel my whole body tense.

"What did you feel?" Winter asks Savi.

The sorceress looks around our little circle. "What I don't understand is why none of you felt anything."

"We had some stuff going on," I say, and I don't know why I don't tell her the truth. That I felt something all right but was more concerned with all the other things that happened before and since.

"What can possibly be as important as a death goddess on the rise?" Savi demands, and she has definitely lost her trademark chill. It's disturbing.

I accept that I don't want to say I felt a thing because I'm already not in love with the fact that the ice queen sorceress is losing her shit.

"The solstice, as I believe you are aware," Ariel says coolly, either unaware that Savi is unraveling or choosing not to care, "is when my community holds a blood ball."

"Blood balls are archaic," she snaps at him.

"That is not how you have always felt," Ariel replies, and I watch, possibly holding my breath, as Savi's expression . . . shifts.

For a moment, she looks something like . . . young. Vulnerable.

This is both more and less disturbing.

But then, so are blood balls. They are what they sound like. Vampires bring their dates, dress up, do courtly vampire things, and feed while they do it. I believe they have blood addicts cavorting about in the place of the *bitten*, but that could be a rumor.

What's always been clear is that it's a sex thing.

I deliberately do not look at Winter.

"What about you?" Savi demands, her gaze shifting to Ty—to get the attention off her, I have to think. "Do werewolves also have a blood ball?"

"We party and we fuck a lot," Ty drawls. "If that's what you mean."

"I want to clarify this for my own understanding," Savi belts out, and she's actually getting louder. Blood balls or no blood balls, she's not doing okay. I feel like we should all be paying closer attention to this. "All this time, Vinča's minions have clearly been assembling up there. Yet no one thought that it was worth paying attention to, even in the face of our theories about the potential Three Sisters sacrifice. About the potential for exactly something like this to happen?"

"I guess the entire world is on your shoulders, babe," Ty tells her in a drawl that sounds friendly but is not. "What a burden. If only you had magical powers at your fingertips and the ability to do whatever the fuck you want so you could watch the goddamn lake yourself."

Savi looks pale. And furious. "I apologize that I thought my efforts to comb through treacherous archives from forgotten civilizations was where I should focus my attention. I assumed we were all playing to our strengths."

That's skating perilously close to her suggesting that she's the brains and Ty's the brawn, and nothing about that can end well.

"Ty was also involved in a small revolution on solstice night," I tell her before everyone loses their shit. "Just to put things into perspective." When they all look at me—including Ty, who scowls—I smile. "You're looking at the king of the werewolves. Not *a* king. *The* king. The high king, if you will."

Ariel studies Ty for a moment, and I feel like I can *see* strategies whirl around him like a vampire's cloud of smoke. Then he inclines his head. "I will confess that I have always considered you *the* king. The others ceased to matter too long ago."

Ty might not like hearing that, I can see, but it also confirms his decision.

"I'm happy for your promotion," Savi bites out. She does not look happy, but I'm sure she will be once she has time to reflect. That time is clearly not now. "I think we have to assume that the minions did a little more than simply blow things up at Crater Lake. We should operate as if Winter's visions are inviolable facts until proven otherwise."

Winter nods her head. "It's what we talked about before. There's clearly a vessel. But who?"

"The *who* will be very important," Ariel says then. "Generally speaking, vessels are meant to be temporary. If Vinča is clever, and I am afraid she is, she will have found one who cannot be broken. Or found until it is too late."

"We have to watch the lake closely," Savi says in a rush, almost as if she's having a different conversation in her head. "Everything will depend on what we find when the temple is revealed."

"I just want to point out that we still haven't figured out the leaving of sacrifices," I say. "Were there any last night?"

Savi and Ariel exchange a look then. The good news is that Savi looks more like herself. "They're getting more elaborate," she tells me. "And therefore significantly more revolting."

Ariel nods. "Whatever happened on the night of the solstice, it did not end the sacrifices. If anything, it has emboldened whoever's leaving them."

"I think we should assume that we're talking about Vinča's acolytes until we can prove otherwise," Winter says. "After all, what we know about Vinča is that she really likes dead things. It tracks."

I would very much prefer not to be one of Vinča's dead things. I think better of saying that.

The meeting breaks up, and Ty and I walk outside. As expected, his bike is right where he left it. Without a fingerprint on it.

For a moment we stand there, on Main Street, with the river moving below the bridge. I can scent the Kind in the air all around us, friend and foe alike. I'm aware of the dark clouds and the cold.

My head, though, is stuck on that vision of Winter's that I can't seem to shake. I'm pretty sure I dreamed it all last night. Or maybe I've been running a greatest hits reel. The vision Savi put in all our heads mixed with Winter's other dire predictions. The wolf who wants me dead and is stalking me. That plus the gristly rib-cage situation equals . . . nothing I want to have stuck in my head.

Oh well.

"I don't want to believe she's really back," I say quietly.

"Not really looking forward to it myself," Ty agrees. He looks down at me. "But we'll deal. Won't be the first bitch that needs to be slapped down twice. Probably won't be the last."

I know he means the gender-nonspecific bitch there, and I move closer to him. I reach over to put my hands on the wall of his abdomen. I want his heat. His strength.

"I keep thinking it would help if we were stronger. And it's my fault we're not." That hurts a little to say, but I say it anyway. "I should have mated you already. Years ago."

"I would normally agree with you," he tells me, and it looks like there's something tender there in that dark gaze of his. Something that's only mine. "But, turns out, the move was to not be mated for the solstice. It wouldn't have had the same effect if I'd claimed you years ago, and I don't like saying that any more than you liked saying what you just did." I flush, and he reaches over to smooth his thumb over my cheekbone. "Don't lose sight of the endgame now, baby. You can't rule the world if you're not ready for the bullshit that comes with it. And I can promise you, there's always going to be bullshit. Might as well start with a death goddess who can't seem to die already. Not to mention the traitor in our pack we haven't found yet."

"Yet," I say, because a whole lot of shit has happened, but I haven't forgotten my stalker. And won't.

And it's not until we're halfway home, up Bellinger Lane with a view over the gleaming lights of Jacksonville, that what he said just then really hits.

Finally, the two of us are completely on the same page. He even admitted that I was right. Retroactively, he would still do it all this way.

We're really, truly the partners I always dreamed we could be. The partners everyone told me no werewolf male would ever allow.

Of course we are, I think then, staring up at the moon that's slightly more than a half, and always seems more potent when it's visible in the day. *Just in time for Vinča to rise up and fuck us over.*

18.

Ty takes us back to the den and starts shaking shit up.

The bulk of his lieutenants are off on mapping missions, in new mating arrangements with the newly kingless packs, or focusing on our delivery commitments up and down the treacherous I-5 corridor. Though it is more a suggestion of a corridor these days.

What this means is that every other male in the pack—including some of our guests who stayed behind for pack-unity reasons when their actual packs left the gathering—has to step up and level up. After the wolf week we just had, every male in the pack is more than here for it. They all want to prove themselves worthy. They all want to make it clear that while all the packs might be one pack now, *this* part of that one big pack is the best.

"I think they're showing off for their high king," I murmur to him as all the males in the den charge toward the stairs from the grand cavern to the hilltop after Ty makes an announcement that it's time to get to work.

He doesn't crack a smile—not when he's in his commander-of-everything mode—but I can see the way his dark eyes gleam. "Damn right," he rumbles at me. "We got shit to do and a death bitch to handle, among other things. Kissing my ass is the icing on that cake, babe."

I get caught on the *other things* part, since there's not much I can personally do about whatever shenanigans Vinča is planning. What I *can* do is keep up my vigilance where our traitor is concerned.

Once all the males in the pack have been summoned to the hill, filing past me where I pretend I'm not sniffing them to see if they smell wrong to me in some way—they don't, sadly—Ty creates new teams. Patrols around the forests close to home as well as in the flooded mountains up by Crater Lake. Then he decides that he and Connor need to give them all a crash course in training maneuvers.

That lasts the rest of the day and well into the next.

When Ty heads off to coordinate the finer details of his Crater Lake patrols with the vampire king, I decide to take a page out of his book. It's high time that I turn over the domestic side of den life into my mother's capable claws. Officially.

"You've waited my whole life to whip this place into shape," I say when I find her, quietly and efficiently analyzing the supply situation in the big den kitchen now that all the other packs aren't ours to feed. "I mean the whole den, not just the kitchen."

Johanna allows her lips to curve. "Longer than that."

"You have my full support," I tell her, and I mean this with every part of me. "I've never wanted this part of being Ty's mate. I trust you."

I do trust her, because I know her. She keeps things moving the way they should. She already knows all the undercurrents and dramas here. She also knows how to shape those things. Besides, she was always on Ty's side, and now that I am too—and so publicly—there's no tension between us.

The part of me that's her daughter might find that tough, but Ty's future queen is all for it.

And I don't have it in me to play den mother. Especially not after a week with Deirdre and all the young fated ones and newer queens.

I duck out of the den and head over to Winter's, keeping my awareness high since I know the wolves are preoccupied and we still don't know who our traitor is—but I don't scent anything worrying. Given that scenting hasn't been as reliable as it should be—and not only because of Savi's scent-scrubbing around the cottages, I think, remembering how I couldn't scent my stalker either when Savi was nowhere around—I also take note that I don't stumble over any torn-up bodies.

I find Winter in the woods behind her house, which is absolutely not where she should be, and especially not alone. "You were there when they were discussing how bad the sacrifices are at the moment," I say when I roll up to her without her glancing even once in my direction. The very opposite of safety-first behavior, and *she* can't shift into a wolf.

"Can confirm." Winter is still not looking at me. She's staring up at the trees around her, scowling.

"Do you think it's coincidental that I wandered upon you out here in the woods?" I ask her, shoving my hands in the jacket I threw on because I wanted to feel cozy. The cold is turning Winter's cheeks red, but it doesn't bother me. "It's not. I could scent you pretty much from the moment I stepped out of the den." When she doesn't respond to that the way I think she should, meaning at all, I bump her with my shoulder. "Winter. If I can track you, anyone can. Including people significantly less marvelous than I am."

Winter waves a hand. "I think there are new and improved wards. Savi was here very late last night, muttering around the way she does."

"You know she's not *muttering*, right? Those are spells."

"Why doesn't that make her a witch?" Winter looks at me then. "I feel like it's been too long now and everyone assumes I know all the things they do, so I can't ask. But I do wonder."

"Witches are supposed to be in balance with nature, so they have to pay the price for any imbalances that come up with the magic they do." I lean against the nearest tree and smell the smoke of woodburning stoves in the distance, spicing the cold air. "They're more like wolves that way. In tune with the seasons, very concerned with the moon, and all of their magic is a conversation with the natural world. Sorcerers, on the other hand, are born magical and can manipulate the natural world, and everything else, to their own ends. It's a completely different kind of magic system." I consider. "A person can become a witch, but only sorcerers are sorcerers."

Winter considers that. "Why is some magic genetic and other magic something you can get through a bite or a course of study or whatever?"

"Because magic does what it wants," I tell her, something that is as obvious to me as the location of the sky. I have to remind myself that Winter's only known about magic for three years, and only understood her own magic for a couple of months. "When it wants, how it wants. That's just the way it is."

Winter makes a low noise at that, as if she wants to argue but can't quite think of what to say.

"But you haven't answered my question," I say. She looks at me again, and I let my eyes widen. "Hello. Wandering around in the woods like a too-stupid-to-live heroine begging to be axed right out of a horror movie?"

"It's Christmas Eve," she says blankly.

I count days from the solstice in my head and think, *Oh, yeah.*

Winter glares at me when I have no other reaction. "I need a Christmas tree, Maddox. The world might be a hellscape on a downward spiral at the best of times—"

"In fairness, that's always been one of Medford's selling points, no?"

She looks like she can't decide if she wants to scowl or laugh. "That's no reason not to decorate a goddamn evergreen tree."

I blink and peer up at the great many evergreen trees stretching above us. "Do you really do that? Chop down an innocent tree and festoon it with trinkets?"

"Please don't pretend that you don't know that just because you've been howling with the wolves for the past week."

"I . . . am a wolf. So."

"You grew up here. I saw you eyeing the Christmas tree in Jacksonville last week which, yes, was also chopped down and is now covered in ornaments. Welcome to the world you've lived in for the past quarter century."

"Werewolves really aren't Christmas tree–type people." I shrug. "I think they're pretty, sure. I like a lot of lights this time of year, but that's not a religious thing. The only rituals I'm into involve the moon."

Her face changes then, and she looks softer. Wistful, almost. "Gran always made sure there was some kind of Christmas situation in the house each year. No matter what state my parents were in. No matter what was going on with Augie. Even when my grandfather was sick, she decked a hall or two to mark the occasion. And, despite everything, she pulled something off the last three years, too."

"I didn't know she was . . ." I don't know what word to use for the old oracle.

"She liked a Christmas tree," Winter says quietly. "It's not a tradition that I intend to let die."

Her voice rings out a little and echoes back from the trees. It's late morning, and the mist is still pulling here and there beneath the sullen sky. Christmas trees don't mean anything to me, but I understand grief. And loss.

"Let's get you a tree, then," I say, trying to sound festive, though when I do I'm suddenly reminded of that swirling red cloak in Jacksonville. I try not to make it obvious when I look around, certain I can feel eyes on me. "Luckily enough, this is the Pacific Northwest. One thing we still have is trees."

Too many trees to count, in fact.

Finding the right one is not the quick and easy process I expect, however. It turns out that any old tree won't do. Winter has very intense and specific criteria for the Christmas tree that she intends to take back into her grandmother's house, though it is not the kind of criteria that can be shared. Or explained.

"I'll know it when I see it," she tells me.

It's afternoon and edging toward dark when I finally reach over and wrench the axe out of her hands, whack down the tree she's chosen at last, and then carry it back to the house. In fairness, Winter helps. But to preserve her dignity, I don't point out that I'm the one who's carrying most of the weight.

Inside the house, the real work begins. It takes several trips down into the basement and back up the rickety old stairs to pull out every box with *Christmas* written on the side in old, spindly handwriting that I know is her grandmother's without having to ask.

Winter makes us mugs of hot chocolate from her secret stash that she only pulls out every now and again. And only, I'm pretty sure, with me.

That's how Ty finds us later, sitting cross-legged on the floor in the dining room in front of a bright and happy Christmas tree straight out of a holiday movie. It's covered in lights and decorations, most of them handmade. All of them with stories that Winter has spent time telling me. First haltingly, as if she was embarrassed. Then, laughing.

I don't tell her that this is a kind of spell work too.

"What the hell," Ty growls when I open the door to the pissed-off-sounding knock that I knew immediately was his. He sounds grumpy, but his hand moves to find my face and his fingers track the line of my jaw. It's a while before his gaze moves past me to take in Winter and her tree. "Where the hell did that come from?"

"We've been decking the halls," I tell him, smirking. "Obviously. Thinking of making it a den thing."

Ty doesn't dignify that with a response. "Your fae friend was walking alone," he says.

"Briar?" Winter asks, like we have numerous fae wandering around the property. "She does that."

I squint at the boarded-up windows but, of course, don't see anything. "She walks everywhere. Always has."

Ty looks incredulous. "How is that safe?"

I think about that night I know that *something* nearly got me. That someone was *right there*. "I don't think anyone thinks it's safe. It also hasn't been a topic of conversation. She's not a human." I shrug apologetically at Winter. "She doesn't smell like a snack."

"Besides," Winter says, not looking as taken aback by the *snack* comment as I think she would have been even a month ago, "she's our friend. She lives here. She should be as protected as we are."

"Did you ask her to come in?" I glare at him.

He glares back. "No, I fucking did not. I told her to get her pointy-eared ass inside her cottage before I had to clean up her entrails, and she took off running. Which, hate to say, would only make a predator with less self-control than I have chase her to the ground."

Winter and I gaze at him with what I think are twin looks of dismay.

Ty folds his arms over his chest. "What?"

"I think she's lonely," Winter suggests.

"Everybody's fucking lonely," Ty retorts. "Not everybody prances around in the dark, begging something to eat them like an asshole."

"Briar isn't an asshole, she's just a little awkward." I shake my head at him. "I'm surprised you even recognized her. Have you ever actually *met* her? *Talked* to her?"

I don't share that hanging out with Briar is pretty new on my end too.

"You probably terrified her," Winter says, frowning. "I don't think I'd like it if a giant werewolf reared up out of the dark woods and started barking at me."

"A fae is a fae is a fae," Ty says in that stubborn voice of his that is a lot like his *high king* voice, now that I'm thinking about it. "Note that I'm saying *fae*, not *defenseless kitten*. There was no rearing and no barking. I told her what was up and she took off. The end. Why are we still talking about this?"

"Maybe we have to approach this differently," I say after a moment. "Maybe we need to get us all in one room."

"Us all who?" Ty growls.

"She lives here," I tell him, patiently. A little too patiently, even, and his eyes narrow on cue. "She's one of us whether you approve of her or not."

"Do you like sugary cereal?" Winter asks, then laughs at Ty's expression. "I just thought maybe you two could bond over that if you do."

"Christmas dinner," I blurt out.

Both Ty and Winter frown at me.

The more I think about it, though, the more I like it. "We should invite her to Christmas dinner. That's a thing, right? Savi and me too. And you and Ariel," I assure Ty when he looks like he's about to object. "We can have a little *found family time*. The holiday version. Like people do when they all share spaces and lives, like it or not."

No one breaks into cheers after this suggestion, though I think it's genius. The more friends Briar has, the better, as far as warding off Vinča goes. And it sure won't hurt her to have friends who are also the three great powers in this valley. I have to think that's likely to keep the death goddess from messing with her—or at least make it harder for Vinča to try.

"In this holiday version am I . . . *cooking*?" Winter asks skeptically. "Like in the sense of a *dinner party* in which I prepare and serve food to guests?"

"I could cook," I tell her. "I cook all the time. It's actually a life skill? But you've made it clear that you think my cooking is not actually cooking."

"If your meat is raw *after* you cook it, you didn't cook it, Maddox. By definition."

"I like a feast," Ty says after a moment. "And it wouldn't hurt any to have a sit-down with the vampire and the sorceress that's not based on an immediate crisis, for a change."

That had also occurred to me, thanks to wolf week. Sure, wolves fight a lot. But first there's a lot of attempts to bond better—especially among the males who call each other *brother*. None of which would hurt here in the Rogue Valley.

"I like this in theory," Winter says, frowning, though the way she says it makes me wonder if she has some thoughts about the relationship between our big powers here. "It's the part where I prepare a whole Christmas dinner that I'm having trouble getting my head around."

"Your boy can get you whatever you want," Ty tells her, probably just so he can be a dick and call Ariel, immortal vampire who was once an actual Spartan, *your boy*. "Or what's the point of being a vampire king?"

"Something to keep in mind is that none of us will know what a Christmas dinner is supposed to look like," I tell her. "You're talking two werewolves, a vampire, a sorceress, and a dark fae. Not your extended human family, gathering to grade you on how well you made your grandmother's pie."

"Gran was not a pie person, though she sometimes pretended otherwise to be polite," Winter says quietly. "Deep down, she was always suspicious of hot fruit."

I don't know why that makes my chest feel tight.

"We'll assume it's on unless we hear otherwise," Ty says then, like it's a done deal with invitations. "And to be clear, I also love a pie."

He steers me out of the house, leaving Winter gazing up at the sparkling tree with that wistful expression I saw earlier. Out in the dark, he propels me along with his hard hand heavy on my neck. I snuggle into it.

We both pause in the yard, looking for movement in the shadows, but there's nothing.

"I like the idea of this Christmas dinner," I say when we start moving again. "It's not like the solstice was all fun and games. Maybe it's not the worst thing in the world to take a time-out and get to do a little community building outside the den."

"You think that's how this works? Time-outs and celebrations for shit that has to happen whether we celebrate it or not?" He's not starting a fight. I can hear the difference in his voice. It's a quiet question and not undeserved, either.

I stop walking. "I think that we're going to have to figure out how to create space." I think about the week I spent in the den and how *close* it all is. I think about the grand cavern and how so much of wolf society is how we perform in public, because everything is so public. More importantly, I think about how little I've really seen of Ty since the solstice, and when I have, if I want to really talk to him, we've had to leave the den. "Things are different now. In the den, you can't take a step without everyone all over you for every little thing. Maybe it's time that we made it a little harder to access you."

"I grew up with that kind of king," Ty says flatly. "It's not going to be me."

"I'm not talking about random hierarchies to keep people at a distance," I say patiently. I haven't thought about this with everything else that's been going on, but now that I am, it makes sense. "You already have that with your lieutenants and all your biker roles, by the way. I'm talking about space. You actually don't need to know who's being mean to who in the kitchen. That's not information you need to have as it happens. People shouldn't be able to simply run into you in a tunnel and unload on you."

I can feel his resistance all over him, but he doesn't shut me down. "It's worked fine so far."

"We're not the same pack that we've been all this time," I tell him. "That's a good thing. This is a time of transition. There's a lot going on, and if you can't figure out how to take some time away from it, you're going to burn out. Then what use are you to anyone?"

Ty looks like he wants to say something then, but he doesn't. He starts walking instead, still guiding me with that hand on my neck, so I walk with him. The moment we leave Winter's yard and let the woods swallow us up, I notice that I can scent wolves—pack—as we go.

Those protection details I've been certain were canceled.

"Funny how there are people watching out for us now that you're here." I laugh as I say it. "There weren't earlier, though there were the other night. The ass-kissing is on point."

He gives me a sharp look. "What do you mean?"

We've made it to the path that snakes down and around to the den now, heading toward that same little tunnel that's even spookier in the dark.

"I thought you canceled—" I begin.

But I don't finish.

Because the scent hits us both at the same time, like a blow to the face.

Blood.

Ty snarls and crouches down, looking around like he expects an actual attack to follow. I shift in a rush, certain that if I can smell *that much* blood, it's safer to be in wolf form. Where I have much bigger teeth and sharper claws.

I move forward along the path, and the smells are *loud*.

They hit at me, bold and hot, and it takes me a moment to parse them. To do more than simply *react* to them.

I keep moving until I'm inside the tunnel, and that's when I see them. Two bodies. Two bodies slashed and hacked beyond all recognition. There's so much blood I can't immediately tell what kind of bodies these are, even though the carcasses are much bigger than anything I've seen left for us before.

This time there are little treats left behind. The severed heads of the creatures in question. One a stag, the other a doe.

They sit there, lifeless eyes and matted fur, in the center of piles of guts all tangled up with each other so it's impossible to see which is which.

"Feels like a threat," Ty says from behind me. He moves closer, and I can see the muscle in his jaw working as he stares down at the scene before us. "Never did like being threatened."

He looks back over at me and nods. I take that as the command it is. I throw back my head and let out a howl, alerting the nearby sentries. As well as the rest of the pack.

They all come running, in human and wolf forms.

Connor is the first one there, muttering curses when his boots slip in the mess.

The other, recently promoted men push in close to look at the slaughtered deer, and I comfort myself with the knowledge that none of the lieutenants who've left to carry out different tasks for Ty could be our resident psycho.

Not that I really thought my brothers would betray me, not like this. But it's good to have confirmation all the same.

The scene is studied and discussed. My mother herds the horrified mothers and curious young back into the den. A few of the young men are tasked with cleaning the kill from the path, and the rest of the crowd disperses back to their duties and the dark.

That's when it occurs to me that there is still no scent signature on the bodies themselves.

Not only that, but every male wolf who could have done it came to the scene, so they'll all smell like it. Meaning it could be anyone.

"I know," Ty says when I say this to him inside the den, keeping my voice low so no one can hear. "I wanted to see how fast everyone showed up."

"Did anyone make you suspicious?"

"I don't know." He shakes his head. A sign, I think, that he's wearier than he likes to let on. "I don't like this shit. I was on that path maybe twenty minutes before and it was clean. You could sense the pack all around you on the way back the same as I could. How could someone get in there, kill two reasonably sized deer, and then disappear without a trace?"

I don't think he's actually asking me that question. He already knows what I think.

Ty doesn't look at me as we make our way into the grand cavern. He's too busy letting that dark gaze of his move over everyone gathered inside. He doesn't say the word, but I feel it echo inside both of us.

Traitor.

It leaves a sour taste in my mouth for the rest of the evening.

Ty's already gone when I wake up—probably busy trying to sniff out the traitor here in the den, if I have to guess. Though he'll have to do it carefully. If he starts making accusations without uncontestable proof it could lead to muttering about crowns not fitting the ego beneath and so on, and it's too soon into this new role of his for that.

I lie in bed, fretting up at the lack of skylight above me. I think about Winter's two warning dreams about me. More specifically, about the wolf who wants to kill me. With the noise and anxiety of wolf week gone now, I let myself think over everything that's happened since the last full moon.

Dead things left everywhere. Someone stalking me. A traitor in this pack who not only got *this close* to me in the woods but almost certainly had everything to do with stoking the tensions during the gathering that pushed everything to a boiling point.

Just because it worked out in Ty's favor doesn't mean it wasn't treacherous.

And the more I lie there, thinking about treachery, the more I start to connect the dots. Or ask myself why I hadn't connected the dots before.

The first sacrifice I saw was on the path outside the den. Not far from where whoever was stalking me almost got me. The same place where we found that mess of guts and heads last night.

In my head, I realize, I've been dividing those ripped-up creatures from the ones I've found all around the cottage and the ones Savi's seen at the borders of her property. I've unconsciously divided them. One seemed like the work of Vinča, possibly, or some minion of hers. The other seemed liked pack shit.

But what if they're not separate at all?

Once I think that, I start thinking about all the other things that have felt like the sacrifices over the last few months or so, even if they weren't actually sacrifices—and I sit up then, my head spinning.

Because I can think of another consistent, annoying issue that we've been having for a while now—and I'm suddenly *certain* that I have to get to the office to look through all my meticulous notes to see if I'm onto something.

I hike down from the den and pick up my trusty old Explorer from where I left it in the parking area at an old trailhead that no one uses anymore. Then I drive through the hushed, quiet valley morning down to the warehouse in Phoenix. I nod at the wolves I find there, a couple of younger guys just back from a run down south.

"The summit is a death trap," one of them tells me, scowling south like he can see over the mountains that rise up at the California border. "And I don't mean the snow up there, though it's from hell."

"It's always bad this time of year," his companion says. "But this was real bad."

"There were also too many trolls," the first wolf tells me. "It's like they knew we were coming."

This is the same thing that a lot of the wolves have told me lately. Even some of the ogres have made it clear that there's been an uptick in attacks on our people out there. No matter how much secrecy we try to impose over what we're doing and when, someone always knows.

Today I have to wonder if that means the traitor has his fingers in our business as well as our community. That actually makes me feel a little sick, but I don't want the wolves here today to see that.

"Did it affect our shipments?" I ask, stone-faced.

My brothers would scoff at me and ask me who the fuck I thought I was talking to—*of course* they got their shit done. These young males are a little more in awe of their king's chosen mate. When they finish falling all over themselves to assure me that they *walked* their deliveries through a troll-infested blizzard *both ways* and would welcome the opportunity to do it again, I let them go.

Then I walk into the office and start sorting through more than a week's worth of paperwork, filing away the notes and receipts that the drivers and riders leave for me. Plus the various forms of payment that come in and are stacked in the warehouse until the pack can allocate them where needed, or need to be recorded and written out so the higher-level members of the pack know who owes us a debt.

It feels even more important now, after the solstice and Ty's new role, to not only keep my records pristine but to make sure that the pattern recognition that Ty bragged about in church that day remains so on point that it almost feels predictive—

Hard to do if I missed someone systematically sabotaging us, though.

Really hard to do if all the great things Ty said to all those men about me were bullshit because I missed the most crucial part of it all.

No one's here in this warehouse now. No one can see me when I stop what I'm doing, sink down to the cold floor, and put my head in my hands. Then breathe a little heavily as the emotions I've been keeping at arm's length for days come for me. Hard.

Feelings plus the idea of a traitor sit on me like a boot on my throat. What's ending. What's beginning. What we won on the solstice but all the things we've lost, too.

It makes me think for a moment that it might be my time to cry after all.

But I don't. I breathe my way through it, raggedly. Loudly.

I slowly get my shit together, here in this warehouse where I carved out my independence when I first came home from school. Traitor or no traitor, sabotage or not, I know my time here in this office is coming to an end. Or it will change like everything else, anyway, because everything all around me is different now. And will get even more different once I'm fully claimed.

This isn't a someday thing anymore.

It's *soon*. It's pretty much right now.

I knew when my brothers fetched me home from New York after the Reveal that I needed to have a good reason not to mate with Ty immediately. Vibes and my feelings wouldn't cut it.

I picked the one thing no one could argue too much about—pack business. The thing that made our pack more solid than all the others and better off than most of the other Kind in this valley. I threw myself into an aspect of the business that no one else had touched and made myself indispensable.

I organized everything in this office, created systems to keep things running smoothly, and started tracking everything we did.

It means, I explained to an unreadable Ty a few months after I came back from New York, *that you can expand without worrying about whether or not you're losing that personal touch. It means there's no limit to what you can do.*

You think I want to expand? Our territory is our territory, babe.

Right now it is. I didn't back down. *But look how the world's changed already. Who knows what it will look like in a year. Three years. Ten years.*

He'd let me keep going, even though I was sure he knew that because this kind of thing wasn't something queens did, what he was doing was giving me another excuse not to run with him beneath the full moon.

Maybe he did it because he believed in me. Maybe he did it because he liked the idea of keeping his hand on what was happening all over the territory. Maybe he always saw himself getting bigger than the territory he'd won all those years ago.

Either way, he's let me do this for three years. Now we're going to do the other, bigger thing. It's neither good nor bad.

But it's different.

My college graduation felt a lot like this. I didn't need anyone to come and celebrate an accomplishment most of my pack didn't consider worth my time in the first place. Graduation was for me—but that was the trouble. It was the last thing that was mine.

I knew as it was happening that it was very unlikely I would have anything else that was all mine like college had been.

Taking off my cap and gown felt like stripping off my skin. When I felt that same shift all around me, the way every last monster across the world did that night, at first I wondered if I was imagining it. If I was transmitting my feelings, somehow.

It took longer than it should have for me to understand that the confusion and chaos was widespread and not personal at all.

I wondered, as I hunkered down in the apartment my friends never returned to, if it was possible I was as self-centered as everyone in my pack always told me I was. Imagining that something so catastrophic was about *me*.

Peak Maddox, I was sure they would say—if I ever saw them again.

That first night, I didn't think I would. Some of the Kind danced in the streets. There was celebrating everywhere. The type of celebrations that came with the crunching of bones and the screams of the innocent.

The wolf in me approved, but the human college student I'd been playing for four years cried. A lot.

By the time my brothers got there a week later, I'd managed to hide that part away.

Yet here it is again, that same heavy feeling of loss no matter how much I'm also looking forward to the future.

Except this time around it comes with a heavy, sick sense of violation.

Because maybe this wasn't mine the way I thought it was. Maybe someone has been using my patterns and predictions to hurt the pack I've been so sure I was helping. Maybe this has been going on for years, this desecration of the thing I've made so much a part of me.

I pull out all my old notes and start flipping through them, trying to see what I missed.

Trying to see a deliberate, traitorous saboteur looking back at me from all the careful notations I made. About what the packs in what was left of Seattle wanted in their area. About the black markets down south and how different it was in the wastelands of Eastern Oregon, and even more different out where there never was much but desert.

But if there are treacherous paw prints all over my notes, showing me how someone got into our business like this, I can't find them.

And the thought of confessing this to Ty—that I'm not at all what I've been pretending to be, what he *believed* me to be all this time—makes me want to curl into a ball like the wolf I've never been and fade away into the concrete floor.

I don't, much as I wish I could.

Besides, Ty would come find me anyway.

"I have to train other people to track our business," I tell him when I find him in the map room back at the den, because I decided on the drive back to Jacksonville that more eyes on my work can only be a good thing. Maybe someone else can find the traitor's trail in my notes—or figure, like I do, that said traitor was certainly using all my work to their advantage.

I join Ty at the big table, staring down at the map. It's beginning to take shape. As each lieutenant comes back having tracked the territory he was given, it will fill in more. Until, when we're done, we will know every last inch of North America, fully scented and fully ours. More systems in place. More ways to expand and maintain the things that make us who we are.

Assuming someone doesn't sabotage that, too. "It should never be dependent on one person," I say. "Me or anyone else."

"I'm all about diversifying," Ty agrees, frowning down at the map. "It's not accidental that I made sure I have a man in each of the three packs I trust least. If this is nothing but a cult of personality, it will die when I do. That's no good for wolves."

I want to melt into him. I want to climb him. I want to lose myself in him when I know what I *should* do is tell him that I'm a fraud.

I can't bring myself to do anything but stand there.

"You can appoint the people you want," he tells me, because *he* doesn't know that I must have missed something. *He* doesn't know that he essentially lied to the whole of wolfkind about me the other night. "Make them fight for it. Or at least, interview." He laughs at that. "Whatever you do, I want to make it clear that these are positions that command the same level of respect as any other upper rank in the pack. Running a business is the way we run our territory. The end."

I know it's more than that. Letting me pick high-rank positions is an explicit indication of that partnership we already displayed to everyone at the solstice. He's not telling them I'm an equal. He's showing them—and we're still not official.

And I know I don't deserve it.

"Think about it," he tells me, studying my face too intently as he looks down at me. "But not now. We have to go play grab ass around a Christmas table. Whatever the fuck that is."

Maybe I'm more of a coward than I ever imagined, because I smile at him. I take the out.

"Come on," I say. "It will be fun."

And I'm determined it will be. Even if it kills us.

Because I'm more than a little worried that this might be the end of us, too.

19.

Winter is in the kitchen when we get there, slamming pots and pans around. I leave Ty with the rest of our awkward and wildly dangerous party, spread out through the dining room and the starkly furnished living room.

"I'm here to help," I tell her.

"Oh, don't be deceived," Winter says to me beneath her breath. "I'm hiding in here. Savi waved her hands around and said that a feast would appear *upon requirement*."

"Is that like . . . dystopian DoorDash?"

Winter shrugs, but her indigo eyes are dancing. "I guess? Except more vegan? Also, I don't think we have to tip."

"I know I'm a terrible person," I confess, happily, "but I really can't wait to watch Ty Ceridwen contend with a vegan meal. I don't actually know what he'll do. Combust?"

Winter grins at that and leans back against the counter. She folds her arms and nods toward the rooms on the other side of the steel-reinforced kitchen door.

"I don't think Briar wanted to come."

"But she did." I saw her when Ty and I came in, all of us using the front door now, according to the scents I picked up on the way in. Not because Winter is any less wary of the Kind being in her space but because she has a terrifying lover to keep that space safe for her.

Briar is out there now, having made a nod toward the festivities in the form of a red flannel shirt thrown over her usual black. She is standing ramrod straight at one end of the dining room table, her hand at her neck. Or slightly below it, as if she's testing her own heartbeat. Or maybe the necklace she was wearing that time.

I assume she's standing on her own because she's dying of awkwardness, standing out there with Ariel and Savi. A chilly convention if ever there was one—though Savi still looks . . . not quite like her smooth, pulled-together self.

"She's here now, but she was reluctant." Winter sighs. "I had to pound on her cottage door for a long time before she opened it. She looked horrified at the invitation, but then she just . . . smiled like it hurt her a little and said she would love nothing more than to join us."

"I mean, that sounds a lot like Ty's reaction, really."

But Winter doesn't laugh. "I had a pretty epically disgusting dream last night," she continues, and I frown when she reaches up to rub at her temple. "It was . . . blood. So much blood, and wolves in the night." Her voice takes on that singsong quality it often does when she's translating the things she sees in her head. "A moon, not full. A trail in the dark. I was running and I was terrified, and then it was on me—" She swallows, making a face. "I think I *was* a sacrifice. I could feel the knives. I could smell my own . . ." Winter laughs, and her hand is shaky as she drops it from her face. "Then she was there."

I don't need to name her, but I do. "Vinča."

"It was very gross," Winter assures me. "There was a worm situation, but in me, and I was choking and she was laughing—" She blows out a breath. "Ariel said I was screaming in my sleep. He was not happy."

"Did you see who was stabbing you?" I ask her quietly.

She sighs. "I couldn't see. What's the point of seeing all that and not getting to see the thing that matters?"

We stand there with that. Then I straighten my shoulders, thinking about the traitor in our pack and how they clearly got the packs to fight all the way up to the solstice. "Maybe it's so you'll suspect *everyone*. Like . . . all of us."

"That's what Savi thinks," Winter says. "She said I should assume I'm being deliberately led astray."

"Have you noticed that she's . . . ?" I don't really want to say it, but Winter nods.

"I've noticed."

I tell myself that's something.

I go back out into the dining room then, with a couple of beers in my hand and a smile on my face. Ariel and Ty are deep in conversation when I walk up to them.

"There's no way that a goblin could beat a vampire," Ariel is saying.

"Anyone can beat a vampire if they stand close enough to a window and can raise the shade," Ty argues.

"Are we talking about actual combat or cheap tricks?"

"It's all combat," Ty says with a laugh. "You're either fighting to survive or you're playing a game. Me? I don't play a lot of games."

I hand him a beer. "Wow," I drawl. "Apparently Reddit survived the Reveal after all."

They both frown at me—neither one of them big on social media back in the day, I'm sure—then get back to their critical debate.

I look over at Savi, who is sitting in a wing chair that's been shoved back against the wall, giving an excellent impression of a grand empress who appears to have wandered into the wrong empire. Not exactly in social mode, I see. When I move past her, thinking I might explore the house, she shakes her head.

"I wouldn't," she murmurs. "Everything except this area is fiercely and aggressively warded." She cuts her gaze to the vampire king, who somehow looks deeply relaxed. For him, anyway. He's standing in a wide stance with his hands behind his back that suggests leashed violence to me but I know is chilled out for him.

"He oversaw the warding," Savi tells me. "With some intensity."

I like it, and I can't pretend I don't. "You can't blame the man for taking his consort seriously."

"Indeed not. Yet I do have to wonder why it is that we are taking these measures rather than the more reasonable approach." She glares in the general direction of the woods outside, beyond the boarded-up windows. "Which would be setting a trap for our favorite ritualistic fox rather than waiting to see what it does next."

"This isn't the sort of fox who's going to skip into a trap." I lift a brow. "Or any one of us would have caught said slasher fox. Or at least gotten some kind of clue as to who it is and what it wants."

I think of the escalation of entrails that I've seen around my cottage and it's connected, now, to the bloody messes closer to the den, too. I don't like how that sits in me. Slashers and sabotage and we still have no answers—

But this is supposed to be a social evening. Community, not catastrophe.

The moon knows there will be more than enough of that. And likely soon.

As if she can read my mind—and I don't know that she can't—Savi sighs, then waves her hand. A goblet of something sparkling appears in her grasp, and she takes a long pull.

She's making me itchy. "What's going on with you?" I ask her.

Across the room, Winter comes in from the kitchen. She looks around and raises her brows at the sight of the supernatural bro situation in the corner, where Ty is currently extolling the virtues and comparative martial prowess of the average bridge troll. Ariel is shaking his head as if he is actually in pain.

This, I like. The two of them friendly can only make things better in the valley. And in my personal life, given how tight Winter and I are.

She and I exchange a look, then Winter smiles and makes her way over to Briar, who's still looking like she might actually be facing a firing squad.

I turn back to Savi. She is draining her goblet and when she's aware of me watching her, she waves her hand to fill it again.

"You're acting strange," I tell her. "You seem . . . frantic. I've never seen you look anything but smooth and controlled before. Are you really that afraid of a death goddess you already neutralized once before?"

Savi laughs, but there's an edge to it. "No."

"Then what?"

She looks away, as if she can see through the boarded-up and steel-plated windows. "In order to get the information we need, I had to . . . access some places that are less secure than I like." Savi glances at me. "Imagine libraries, of a sort. Some are open to the public. Others are closely monitored. I had to dig around in a few that I think might have set off a few alarms."

I'm picturing the sorcery police. Flashing lights and inclement weather? Disembodied roadside holograms? It seems silly to me—but then, you can never really know someone until you know what they fear.

"I'm sure all is well," she says, tipping her chin up. "But there is a *slight* chance that all the digging I had to do has exposed me to my enemies."

I want to laugh at that, but Savi is not an overdramatic New York City college girl. She's an ancient being of tremendous power. If she says she has enemies, she's probably not being hyperbolic.

"Your enemies?" I ask. "Barbarian hordes? Ancient evil things I wouldn't know how to name?"

"In a manner of a speaking." Savi downs the contents of her goblet again and aims a tight smile at me. "My husband."

There's a flash of something in her gaze that lands funny in me. It hurts. It makes me wonder if *she* hurts, but it's gone in an instant.

Then she's rising and murmuring as she goes, waving a hand in front of her. As I watch, the table arranges itself. Place settings appear. There's a centerpiece made of fragrant evergreen and what look like holly berries. Another wave of her hand and the food arrives. There are platters of things I'm not sure I can identify. Meats, both real and clearly

. . . not real. I see Ty scowl at the vegan platter like it's blasphemous. There are pastries. Breaded items that smell divinely yeasty. Vegetables that smell like the earth and butter, two of my favorite scents.

I think I understand the Christmas thing as we all sit and then pass dishes around the table. We're all here. We're sitting down at a pretty table making pleasant conversation, and there's a Christmas tree beaming at us from the corner of the room.

It's actually . . . nice.

The world is a shithole and everything seems to get worse no matter how many times you think it's going to get better, but for a moment here, it's just *nice*.

Everybody eats, or pretends to eat. Savi fills her plate with mashed potatoes and acts as if she's never tried them before. Then she and Briar dig into the vegan platter that Ty keeps looking at from the corner of his eye, like he thinks it might attack him.

Everyone might be awkward, I think, but the more we sit around the table, the less awkward it feels. Or maybe it's so awkward that it circles right back around to okay.

Maybe it's the drinks.

We don't talk about anything important. No discussion of death goddesses or Crater Lake floods or slasher rituals, because Briar is here. No talk of doom in front of a civilian no matter how much fae blood she might or might not have. No pack politics for those who don't need to know our business.

Especially when someone already knows too much about our business.

"Don't you get bored up there on your mountain?" I ask Savi, to distract myself from the things I'd rather not think about. "It seems lonely."

"I am never lonely," Savi replies airily. She lifts a brow. "I have entirely too many minions for boredom, Maddox."

Ty and Ariel are talking about combat and sparring styles, digging deep into what sounds like archaic forms and systems that, of course, they both seem to have studied. Extensively.

Winter and I talk about high school.

"Remember junior year?" I ask her. "When there was all that curious so-called flooding that closed the school down that spring, even though it was a dry year?" She nods. "Succubus infestation."

Winter makes a face. "What about that ridiculous blizzard in May when we were in sixth grade?"

"Dragons," Savi interjects blandly, clearly not inspired by the combat chat. "Not the inspiring kind. Salamanders with delusions of grandeur. They needed to be frozen out."

"What about you?" Winter asks Briar. "Where did you grow up?"

It almost seems to me that she *flickers*, as if she's here and then not here, like old TV static—but maybe that's the wind outside that we can hear buffet the house every now and again. Or the introvert in her dying a little because she was both perceived and addressed.

"When I was small we had to work," she says, quietly, but sounding less awkward than usual. "But I liked it."

"Where did you say you grew up?" Savi asks. "The place where I was born no longer has a name in any language you would understand."

Briar blinks, and then reaches up to tug her usual beanie down more securely over her ears. "We moved around a lot."

"Military family?" Winter asks. She knows perfectly well Briar isn't from a *military* family. But it's probably genius, because it gives Briar a way to talk about things it's clear she doesn't want to talk about.

"Yes," she says, sounding . . . more careful than unsure. "Every time we were . . . relocated, it was challenging."

We all gaze at each other.

"What was your favorite place you ever lived?" I'm afraid this is feeling like an interrogation, so I lean in and smile, because the reality is I'm just nosy. "I lived in New York for a while. I loved it."

"I like it here," Briar says, simply, and there's something about the way she says it. It makes my skin feel tight. It makes my throat constrict.

I realize that she makes me want to cry, and I couldn't even say why.

"In fact," Briar says, but stops and clears her throat.

She looks down. Once again she reaches up and rubs at that space below her throat, and I realize that she has some kind of talisman there. It must be what's on that necklace, and I wonder what kind of talisman a funny, private creature who doesn't smell like anything gravitated toward. A protective rune? A knife?

"In fact," she starts again, looking up with her gray gaze something like *resolved*, "I like it so much that I'm going to throw my own party. You did Christmas," Briar says, and smiles at Winter. "I—uh—I want to do New Year's. It will be great. We can wish in the new year together. Like I said, you're all the closest I have to friends." She commits to a scowl then. "If you want, I mean. It's fine if you don't. So."

I find that I can breathe easier when she returns to the abruptness I associate with her. That I feel less like I might cry. Like her awkwardness is somehow as endearing as it is off-putting, though I bet she would try to swing on me if I said that to her.

"That sounds *amazing*," I say.

"Yes," Winter murmurs. "So amazing. Love New Year's. Love counting down to another year while hiding in the house and keeping the zombies away. Can only improve that with friends."

"Good," Briar says. She looks down at her mostly untouched plate and seems to crumple a little. *"Good."*

Now as I look at her, I don't see a surly goth girl. I see the bones in her face, suggesting she isn't eating even when she's not having an uncomfortable holiday meal with people she barely knows. I see her anxiety and her helplessness, socially anyway.

She still makes my chest hurt. I still can't fathom why. I just know she makes me want to protect her. Even from herself.

After dinner, we sit around some more. Savi lazily waves a few fingers, and that's the entire cleanup operation. Briar mutters things, chews on her fingernails, and then disappears—but not without smiling pretty big before she goes. A while after that, Savi, Ty, and Ariel end up in the den, talking in low voices but not as if they care if they're overheard.

Winter and I sit in the chairs in the dining room, staring at the tree we put up the night before.

"It really is pretty," I tell her. "I might be a convert."

"Consider my Christmas tree your Christmas tree," Winter says, and smiles at me. Then, after a moment, the smile fades from her mouth. "I hope he's okay tonight."

It's snowing outside. It blew in when Briar left, rushing out the front door and letting it bang behind her. I think of Augie, huddled in his prison.

"I think that he's better off where he is now than where he was before," I say. Carefully. Kindly.

Winter nods. "That's not a small thing. I know that. I . . . It will have to be enough."

We sit there for a moment. There's a fire in the fireplace. My belly is full. I can hear the rumble of Ty's voice, and it soothes me. Everything is changing, but I'm not unhappy with that. I'm not anything close to unhappy with the *changes*.

It's the traitor who's been sandbagging us, the traitor I never saw despite all the complaints about disruption along our routes—but I shove that away.

"I miss so many people," Winter tells me in a hushed voice. "But I'm also okay with this. With us. With this night, no matter why we did it. It felt . . ."

"Like family," I murmur.

We look at each other, then away. We don't hug or anything too sappy, but when I feel myself smiling, I know she is too.

Much later, Ty and I go outside and stand there in the snow, letting it swirl around us. I set my hands on his hips and I hold my head back so I can catch snowflakes on my tongue.

I should tell him, but I don't. I rationalize it. I tell myself that he has so few nights like this, where he doesn't have to be the king of everything. Where he can just be himself. Why should I let some asshole traitor take that too?

"I told them I'd be coming back tonight, but they know where I am," Ty says, looking down at me with that light in his eyes that I love the most. "Do you want to spend the night in your cottage?"

I smile at him. "I love my cottage."

He looks more serious than I think he should. "I know you do."

I don't want him serious, not now. Not when I know what a gift it is to have time with him away from the den. Away from the pack.

I take his hands in mine and draw him backward, then turn so I can lead him across the yard toward my cottage. The snow keeps coming, and it's cold. Refreshing. It's in my hair and on my eyelashes, and I can feel the cold wet of it in the places we touch.

As we get near my cottage, I'm not sure if I see something fluttering at the corner of my eye or if it's just more snow—

"Stop," Ty growls out, yanking me back flush against him.

Not in a cute way. It's an order.

I freeze there where he holds me. All I can feel is his heart in his chest, and mine keeping time. But I don't protest.

In the next moment, I see it, mostly hidden by branches laden with snow until we stop. Until we look.

A figure in the trees, and all around him, steaming entrails melting the snow.

His back is toward us. I don't understand how he doesn't know we're here, this figure in black crouched over his work.

I quickly realize it's because he's making noise. He's chopping with an axe, again and again, and a quick scan makes it clear that there have to be the remains of at least five animals in front of him.

Something else is clear too.

I've been thinking *he* since I saw him. Now I can study the figure, and that confirms it. He's big. Wide.

Ty is growling, low and long. I'm pressed against him, but my entire body is wired and ready. I can feel my fingertips splitting open to let the claws out.

The figure leaps to its feet in a fluid, athletic, *smooth* motion—

And both Ty and I know him immediately.

I feel Ty's body go stiff. I think I might whimper. *How . . . ?*

But it's like we're frozen.

In utter disbelief. Maybe something closer to despair.

We watch him tilt his head, clearly scenting the air, and then he turns around. His eyes are gold against the dark, announcing that he's a wolf—

But we already know that.

"Connor," Ty grits out, sounding as winded and sucker-punched as I feel. If a whole lot more furious. "What the fuck?"

20.

"Fuck you," Connor snarls back at Ty.

"What the hell is this?" Ty belts at him. "All this bullshit is *you*? Why would you betray the pack—and *me*—like this?"

I can't make sense of this. I can't *believe* this.

Too many things are whirling around in my head, like a kaleidoscope shifting pieces into patterns that never resolve into a single, comprehensible image. All those sacrifices. All that *blood*.

Ty isn't the only one who can't get a grip on this. On everything it means, and everything I now have to look back on and wonder about. This means that it was Connor stalking me. More than once. That his are the eyes I've felt on me, making my neck prickle, making me jumpy. That he has been coming for me—all while showing me nothing but his trademark kindness and support to my face.

That he's been the one sabotaging our runs.

It makes my stomach twist.

I think about a few days ago, when he walked me through the dark tunnels of the den and I had the strangest inkling that he was a threat—but I'd been sure I was just being paranoid. He'd done nothing. I hadn't even mentioned it to Ty, because I'd thought I was being silly.

I think, here in the snow with the woods and the blood and Connor with an axe, that this is a lesson. I'm known for all kinds of things, but being *silly* isn't one of them. Maybe next time I'll listen to my instincts.

Right now I want to know how Ty's trusted and beloved VP turned into a traitor.

"She's coming, you asshole," Connor bellows at Ty. I watch his fist clench around the axe he holds. "The goddess of filth and misery is coming. The princess of pestilence *will arise*, and all of this will mean shit. *You* will mean shit."

Vinča.

Somehow this is about fucking Vinča.

I can't decide if this is better or worse.

I feel Ty's powerful body quake with the same impossible realization that careens through me. In a way, I suppose it makes more sense. The fact that there were sacrifices at Savi's place too. The idea that this is about the three of us, Savi, Winter, and me. None of that really tracks if this was all a traitor to the pack focused on wolf shit.

Not that Connor being a fucking death clan minion is something I can get my head around.

"You fought against her on Halloween," Ty growls at him. "You personally rid the world of more of her creepy little minions than I can count on one paw. How the hell do you go from calling red cloaks candy to chopping up furry animals in the winter woods and pledging your fucked-up allegiance to a goddess who doesn't give a shit if you live or die?"

Connor's gaze is a dark hole. It makes my spine feel like it's slicked in ice.

"One of her faithful found me afterward and led me to the truth," he tells us, his hand seeming to convulse on the handle of the axe. "She showed me. The destroyer of worlds rests, but is not finished. The prophecy did not fail. She will rise again and this time, there will be no stopping her. Her oaths are stained in blood."

Always with the blood, I think.

"She's not here now, motherfucker," Ty throws back at him. "The only bloodstains are the ones you keep making."

Connor sneers and lurches forward. Ty swings me around so I'm behind him, his big frame between us. I hold on to him, my arms around his waist, and keep my eyes on the threat.

The threat I'm still having trouble believing is really a threat. Then again, that's a whole lot of blood on the ground.

"It's just you and me and a few carcasses tonight," Ty goes on. "And I'm going to need you to explain how you go from being my second since the day I won my crown to this bullshit. Chopping up animals and leaving them all over the place like a deranged psycho. Sneaking around and fucking up protection details." He shakes his head. "I was so sure it couldn't be you. Even though no one else would have the authority to call back any protection I set out, I was convinced it couldn't be you. I told myself it was impossible. I came up with a hundred theories about how someone was working around you because *no fucking way* could it be you."

They stare at each other as the snow drives all around them. They're both breathing hard. I can see their breath against the dark. I can see Connor's chest move. I can feel Ty's.

I'm breathing hard myself.

My head is less of a kaleidoscope, but I don't like the conclusions I'm drawing. I don't like any of this.

"Yet here you are," Ty growls, his voice shaking with temper. Betrayal. Fury. "Making like a serial killer and much too close to Maddox's cottage."

That electrifies Connor. It almost seems to me like he's on something, careening from one emotional high to another and still with that axe in his hand. Not to mention that grim pile of mutilation behind him.

"You think you're smart," Connor snarls at him. "You swagger around, calling yourself some kind of high king when all you are is a pussy-whipped upstart who's never known his goddamn place."

I feel Ty stiffen, and I like that Connor is landing blows even less than the rest of this.

"You're a traitor," I tell him, my voice calm and clear in the snowy night. Despite the blood and how I still feel like I'm reeling, I pull it together. "You can call me anything you want. You can claim you found *truth*. You betrayed your king, and you're a traitor to the pack. In the end, that's all you are. No one will ever sing about you. No one will remember you—they'll only remember what you did."

I can feel the growl in Ty, though I'm not sure it's audible. It's like he's simmering and it's beginning to boil. The heat of his fury should be enough to melt the snow.

"And what they'll remember," I continue in the same steady way, my eyes on Connor, "is that you're a two-faced bastard who sold out everyone who loved you. What a legacy."

"I've heard more than enough from you, Maddox," Connor growls at me, and he starts tossing that bloody axe from palm to palm. This is not exactly comforting. "I should have killed you when I had the chance. And do you know how many times I had the chance? A thousand times when you were a girl. When it became clear again and again that your role in this life is to pervert everything this pack stands for."

"I think that's you, friend," I tell him.

"Hey asshole, news flash," Ty barks out. "This pack stands for what I say it stands for. If you have a problem with that, take it up with me. Don't sneak around like a fucking coward, trying to scare females."

"Another legacy right there," I can't help but drawl. "Did you really think you were going to scare a fucking sorceress? Or get anywhere near the vampire king's consort?"

"I watched you sleep," Connor growls. "I was as close to you as a breath, and you didn't even notice."

Ty laughs at that. Loud. Long. It makes the trees seem to cower, but that's better than imagining Connor—drenched in blood and entrails—staring into my windows. "That works for me, because I'm going to watch you die."

"You still don't know what this is about," Connor shouts at him. "I don't give a shit about you. I don't give a shit about your mouthy, unworthy bitch. Neither one of you will survive the night when she comes. *She will make you pay in blood*."

That echoes back too, a distorted roar against the canopy of trees laden with blankets of snow.

It's a very pretty place to find out someone you trusted is a monster. A real monster.

"How does a werewolf become the blank-eyed minion of a death goddess he helped put back into her place?" I ask him. "That's what this is about for me. One of her *faithful* showed you the way? Does that mean she fucked you until you crashed out and started massacring woodland creatures?"

Connor has clearly had enough talking. Or maybe he really has had enough of *me* talking. Either way he throws back his head and howls.

Then he glares our way and throws his axe.

It flies through the air, spinning end over end in a shower of blood until Ty smacks it out of its flight path.

One swipe of his arm and it ends up embedded in a nearby tree.

Connor only laughs. It's a madman sort of a laugh, which suits this grisly moment, but I still can't really believe this is happening. He throws out his arms, there's a flash of familiar energy, and then he's a wolf.

And he doesn't waste a moment.

He catapults himself straight at us.

But Connor doesn't make it to a full landing, because Ty leaps up, shifts midair, and swats him out of the air too.

Then everything gets even more deadly.

It's teeth and claws, and it's vicious. It's frenzied.

I might not be able to believe this is happening, but reality doesn't seem to give one shit what I *believe*. Two enormous wolves clash again and again, rending and tearing at each other, no *belief* necessary. The two of them fight in front of me with all those animal bodies in a wet pile behind them as they grapple in the bloodstained snow.

I do the only thing I can. The thing I must do. I shift. Then I throw back my head and I howl down the goddamn mountain.

I start howling out our version of a 911 call and I don't stop.

Everyone comes running. The pack pours out of the woods and the hills. Winter and Ariel and a set of vampires I assume must have been on watch appear. Briar stumbles out from inside her cottage, wearing what looks like pajamas—but still with that beanie.

Even Savi appears, bathed in her usual golden light, though she frowns when she sees the piles of guts and gore in the trees. Not because it's nauseating, I think, though it certainly is. She almost looks as if the way Connor arranged the bodies means something to her.

I can't concentrate on that.

The fight doesn't stop just because there are spectators. The only thing that stops is my howl, now that everyone is here. Now that everyone can see what's happening and who the traitor is.

The wolves can scent it. The vampires too—they certainly know their blood.

Everyone else can draw reasonable conclusions about why Ty would be fighting his VP within five feet of my cottage with an abattoir at the ready.

Connor keeps coming at Ty. Ty swats him back again and again. Then, as the fight goes on, Ty lets the other wolf get close. Yet every time it looks as if Connor's about to sink his teeth in deep, Ty somehow rolls away.

This happens again and again, until it becomes clear to me—and possibly everyone else watching—that Ty is actually toying with his former VP.

Batting him around like a toy, exhausting him, making him work harder than Ty has to in order to keep him at bay.

Ty isn't exactly *resting*, but he's making it clear that he's not fighting at full capacity, either—and he's a lot younger and stronger than Connor, which would be an advantage even if he wasn't a better fighter.

Which he is.

I remember him telling me that he could take down all the kings, too. He really, truly is more powerful than any werewolf in memory—and I don't think it's occurred to Connor that he's giving everyone gathered here a demonstration of *exactly* why Ty is the first and only high king of the werewolves.

Thanks, asshole, I think.

Connor keeps coming for Ty, like he's not tracking the fact that Ty's toying with him. He attacks again and again, and it starts to seem as if he's not feeling the swipe of Ty's claws, or the size of his teeth.

"Why?" Ty demands. "Why would you do this? And how long have you been working against me?"

Once he says that, things begin to come together in my head. The uptick in bullshit along our delivery routes that I knew about but attributed to chance and asshole, shit-stirring, lower-dwelling members of the Kind. Routes that we kept switching, that no one outside the pack could know. It grew in intensity until right before Halloween, then stopped for a while, before returning—until I started telling only the men who were making the deliveries which routes to take, right before they left.

Something I didn't do during wolf week, because I was busy. And that's why the bullshit was rising again.

I'm glad I didn't tell Ty any of this earlier. Because fuck Connor. There's no way I could have avoided what he did. There was no way I could have figured it out from looking in my notes, either. Connor is the VP of the pack. The wolves I told to tell no one wouldn't have thought that applied to Connor. Ever.

I think about how Connor heard me talk about disruptions in church that day. He knew that we were onto him—but by then he'd also gotten on the Vinča train. Whoever got to him after Halloween turned his existing grudges into a little holy war of carcasses and intimidation instead of messing around with our shipments up and down the West Coast.

But it started a long time before then. I know the inciting incident as well as I know my own name.

"It started not long after I came home from New York," I call out. "If I had to guess, right about the time you sanctioned me working in the office instead of submitting to my fate like a good little wolfgirl."

There's a lot of grumbling at that, I hear. From wolves who probably felt the same way back then, if we're being honest. But everything's different now.

Besides, no one else took to a little bit of bloody stalking and fell in with a death goddess. The grumbles of moral superiority aren't entirely unearned.

Connor is crouched low, facing Ty, his tail moving back and forth in warning. He hears me, though. I know this when he bares his teeth in my direction.

"Fucking cunt," he growls, which is hard to say in the old language, but he makes it happen. That takes commitment. "Filled with demands and no sense of duty. Making a mockery of this pack."

"Great, so you hate me," I say, as if he bores me. "Join the club."

In truth, I'm surprised at how much that actually gets to me. He was always kind. Tough and rough around the edges like most of our males, but supportive where it counted. I knew that a lot of members of the pack weren't exactly thrilled with my decisions over the years, obviously. They let me know it all the time. My own mother was one of them.

But to go to these lengths? And let me trust him all along? That hurts.

"You think I'm bad for the pack, but you've been sandbagging us for the past three years?" I shake my head at him. "How does that make sense? Where's *your* sense of duty?"

He flinches like I landed a blow. He moves like he's going to come for me, but Ty angles his huge body between us.

"You're the weakness in this pack," Connor growls at me. "He's too blind to see it, but no one else is."

There's more growling from the pack now, and it's not at me.

Ty bares his teeth in a terrible growl. His golden eyes find mine, then go back to Connor, but when he speaks he's talking to all of us. "He started this years ago. Figured he could weaken the pack's standing before the gathering. If we were weak, he assumed that someone would challenge me and take me out. Put the pack back on the right foot." He barks out a laugh. "With a little psycho-bitch death cult conversion in the middle to make it that much creepier to be a liar and a backstabber and a traitor to us all."

The wolves press in, many of them low in battle-ready positions. All of them, I'm happy to note, focused on Connor as their target. Not Ty.

Not a single one focused on Ty—telling me that whoever Connor has been working with, it's not another wolf.

It's a little hit of relief in the middle of all this ugliness.

"Too bad it went the other way, I guess," Ty is saying to Connor, shaking his head as if he's disappointed when it's clear he's not. "Such a fucking shame that you were wrong not only about Maddox but about me."

He looks around at all the wolves who've come tonight, then. He doesn't seem to spare any of them. "You think I don't know all the shit you've been muttering all these years? Do I really strike you as someone who's led anywhere by anyone? Much less my dick?"

This time the growls have a different tenor. A little more rueful, maybe.

"If I want to follow Maddox's advice it's because it's good advice," Ty snarls. "If some of you would start listening to something besides your own testicles, maybe we could take this pack out of the Dark Ages."

This time there are barks of support, and the volume starts to rise. What's clear is that Ty is done. He doesn't look at the pack again.

He delivers his full and furious attention directly to Connor. "But you're not going to have to worry about that, old man. You should have stayed in the Dark Ages."

"The one I serve is coming," Connor snarls back at him. "And she will have her vengeance. Just you wait."

"If you mean that worm-faced death bitch, bring it," Ty throws back at him. "Last time I was bored out of my mind with her douchebag priests. As far as I can tell, she has pathetic taste in minions. You're not changing my mind on that, *brother*."

The way he says *brother* is an insult. It's deliberate. It makes most of the pack howl, because it's as good as a death knell.

Connor knows it. He throws himself into the air, claws outstretched, going straight for Ty's head.

What it looks like is that Ty simply . . . moves aside.

That's all.

It's simple and elegant, and it doesn't look like he does anything at all.

When Connor crashes to the ground, everything is quiet. Breath held in all directions—until we all realize that Connor isn't moving.

It only takes a second before I can see that there's fresh blood everywhere.

A lot like someone ripped the better part of his stomach out.

Ty circles back around Connor's fallen body, then lets out a long battle cry. The wolves all around echo it, me included.

"Say hello to your bitch goddess for me," Ty taunts Connor, leaning down close so he can growl into his treacherous second's face.

Yet Connor, even though he's gurgling blood, laughs. "She's already here, asshole. Do you really not get it yet? It doesn't matter what you do. You're all marked for death. *She's here.*"

Ty snarls and rips out Connor's throat, and it's done.

The snow continues to spiral down from above. The wind is cold, sweeping down from the mountains. I see the glimmer of Savi's usual golden light, but it doesn't seem to make a dent in the darkness.

The pack is restless on their feet, but no one makes a sound.

I don't think I'm the only one who feels Connor's last words lingering.

Like the pool of blood on the snow at our feet and all around, they seem to stain everything.

21.

The cleanup is grim and quiet, with only the snow on the breeze as any kind of commentary.

I see more than one wolf spit at Connor's corpse. I refrain, though it's a battle. Ty is sitting on his haunches, growling slightly, making certain that every wolf in the pack knows what happened here.

Making sure the fate of the traitor is clear.

I make my way around the crowd to the pile of bodies Connor was busy chopping to pieces. More deer, I think, when I get closer. Possibly even horses. Many of the once-domesticated horses have gone a little wild now, out in the hills for years after their people died. Or were eaten.

Savi is standing next to the pile of awful and slick remains when I get there, frowning down at the mess of it as she mutters things beneath her breath.

Though I'm beginning to think that if any of her spells could help us, they would have already.

I do not voice this uncharitable thought.

Winter trudges up to us, wrapped in a parka, with Ariel close behind her. The vampire king's cool gaze moves from the mound of sacrifices to Savi, then to the agitated wolves moving around the place where Connor's body still lies. Paying tribute to Ty and making their contempt for the betrayer known.

Ariel takes in the sight of Savi, Winter, and me standing there and shakes his head. "Perhaps the three of you should endeavor to present less of a target? I'm not sure there's any need for you to gather in one place. Not without appropriate safeguards. The goddess never has only one minion."

"Yes," Savi says, and it seems to me that I can hear cracks in the smoothness of her voice, which is not encouraging. "I often like to wander about a dark wood, helpless and alone. Thank you for reminding me that it's not wise."

"It's not you I'm worried about, sorceress," Ariel shoots back.

Ty is still in his huge wolf form. He makes no move to shift back. Instead, he howls.

The pack responds immediately, sounding close enough to thrilled that they have something to *do*. Though I suspect Ty did it just so he could watch his vampire and sorceress counterparts attempt to repress their unease as the pack leaps into action to do his bidding. They drag Connor's body away. Others come over to handle the slaughtered remains as well.

"Merry Christmas," I murmur to Winter, and then I shift too.

I can read that look in Ty's still-flashing gaze, bright with the gold of wolves and battle, and I run with him back to the den.

The death of a wolf is always treated like a tragedy. McCaffrey was treated with respect, and I don't have to like the man to agree that he deserved it. The death of a traitor, of *one of us* turned against everything we are, leaves us all reeling.

They take Connor's body up to the hilltop and begin building the funeral pyre. I stay with Ty, tending to his minor wounds in the grand cavern, where everyone can see both of us and assure themselves that we're okay. That Ty, specifically, is fine. That Connor did not manage to do much of anything out there.

Eventually we all move up to the hilltop to keep our usual vigil next to the funeral pyre. The pack gathers as it always does while the fire claims one of us, but notably without the howls of lamentation, stories, and songs that another werewolf death would require.

With any other werewolf death, those things would be natural.

It's not until my mother seeks me out that I pay attention to what's happening outside the tight inner circle of Ty and his trusted few. Far fewer than there were before tonight.

"You knew him as well as anyone." I study Johanna in the flickering light. "You ran with him many times. And often went off with him around the fires."

"I would have run with him no matter what," my mother says flatly. "He was second to the king. For an extremely old-school male, he was shockingly interested in female pleasure. This is no small thing, daughter." She holds her head high, and I suspect that she came over here to tell me these things openly. To make sure no one thought she was hiding them. "I never had any cause to regret sharing his bed, on a run or not. But I will tell you this. I do not think he ever fully integrated into the pack that Ty was building, for all the lip service he gave it." She sighs. "Looking back at it now, I really think he went off the rails when you were born."

"He was always so nice to me," I mutter. "That should have been a clue. People either love me or hate me. They're not *nice* to me. I'm too polarizing for that."

I know it's serious when my mother does not take the opportunity to lecture me about my big head or tell me I am only polarized in my own mind because I refuse to accept fate, or my place, or whatever else.

If you'd told me I would miss those little talks, I would have laughed. I never would have believed it.

She is very serious when she keeps talking. About Connor, not my ego. "Before you came along, I think he fooled himself into imagining that Ty would never come to the attention of fate. Seventy-five years on the throne and no hint of a mate? He wasn't the only one who began to murmur that maybe the moon didn't wish to involve herself because Ty wasn't a real king."

I roll my eyes. "You can't be serious."

Johanna, who never jokes, only gazes at me. "Your appearance, while a delight for me, did not exactly create jubilation in all quarters. I thought Connor got over it in time. Apparently I was wrong."

I think about that as the fire dwindles and the pack, seemingly chastened in all directions, heads back to their own private dens.

Down in Ty's den, I'm not surprised when he hauls me to him the moment we cross the threshold. I wrap my legs around his waist as he slams me against the nearest wall, and then everything is a blistering rush of heat and need.

His mouth is on mine, a kiss of fury and fear, need and wild passion. Between us, he frees his cock and pushes in deep. He waits for my body to adjust around him, then he pulls me back away from the wall and holds me in place with his feet spread wide and a hard palm on each of my ass cheeks.

Then he does what he wants.

He makes me come again and again. My head is thrown back and my arms are looped around his neck, and I completely surrender myself to this vivid display of the emotions I know he doesn't want to show any other way.

The emotions I know he won't admit are eating him alive.

When he finally comes, it's scalding hot and goes on forever.

He carries me into the bedroom and we tumble down onto the bed together, a tangle of not entirely removed clothing and quivering limbs. We are little more than sweat and panting, holding on to each other for dear life.

The specter of Connor's betrayal is wrapped all around us. It's like a smell that tells us both entirely too much and can't be banished, no matter how many breaths we take.

I don't say anything. I hold him and listen to him breathe as his big body presses me into his soft bed. Eventually, he flips over and lies there beside me, staring up at the uneven curve of his ceiling.

"It's not your fault," I tell him.

"It is," he replies immediately. "He was my VP for one hundred years, Maddox. Who's fault is it if not mine?"

"His. It is entirely and only his fault."

"But here's the thing," Ty says quietly, here in this cocoon of ours in the dark. Here where no one can hear us. Where no one but me will listen. "How can I trust my judgment after this? Why should I ask anyone else to trust it? I had no idea. What kind of king am I if I had no idea that the man I trusted the most was sharpening knives to stick in my back all the while?"

He doesn't speak again, though eventually exhaustion takes him down and he sleeps. I don't. I lie there in the dark, wondering why this part feels like a bigger betrayal than I think it would have if it had been directed only at me.

I was creeped out by someone stalking me, targeting me. I was sick over the idea that someone was using my work to hurt the pack. But the fact that Connor made Ty doubt himself? It makes me feel incandescent with sheer fury. It makes me wish we could bring the old man back from the ashpit so I could take a turn at his throat.

When the next day dawns, my eyes are gritty and I still don't know how to handle it.

I move around the den. I go into the kitchen and make myself breakfast in the hopes that protein might make that burning fury inside me ebb a little bit.

When I hear people muttering about last night, about how they never liked Connor anyway and blah blah blah, I can't help myself. I turn on them, staring them down across a wide countertop in the den kitchen.

"How fascinating," I say, with a certain scathing politeness. "Did you know?"

It's a mated pair I've never thought about one way or the other. Now I'm fairly sure that I will root against them until the end of time. They both flinch a little, as if having all of my attention on them like this is alarming. *Polarizing*, even.

I sure hope it is.

"Um," says the male.

"Because if you did know that Connor was a traitor to this pack all this time and you kept that information to yourself, what does that make you?" I ask in a voice that would make a razor feel dull by comparison.

The male looks as if I've struck him. The female bursts into tears.

I feel . . . not as bad about that as I probably should. I make myself a huge plate of food and eat it standing there at the counter with a face that could make children cry. Or so I assume. No one comes near enough to me to find out.

I can hear Ty barking out orders as he puts wolves through their paces up above. He sounds as friendly as I feel.

I decide that no good can possibly come of me sitting around and snapping at everyone, so I go and take an extremely long bath in the hot pool tucked away in the very back of Ty's den. It's a natural pool fed by the hot spring that the rest of the pack can access from the outside and downstream a bit.

Here it's private. It's only Ty's. That makes it mine too and I float there, trying to get that stomach-hollowing feeling of betrayal to ease its grip on me. Trying not to hear the stunned fury in Ty's voice.

Trying not to go over every single interaction I ever had with Connor in my life, looking for hints that he hated me *this much* the whole time.

Only when I'm wrinkly and pruned and significantly happier—or anyway, notably less feral—do I pull myself together and hike my way down to Jacksonville.

The walk is good. It's cold outside and there's snow everywhere. I suspect that Savi, who pretends not to pay attention to what she calls *the solicitations of the damned*—that being the wishes of humans—actually likes delivering them all the white Christmas she knows they like.

I can tell they like it because today is the day after Christmas and Jacksonville's main street is hopping. The humans do indeed look as if sugarplums danced in the vicinity last night. There are impromptu snowball fights in the streets. Good cheer seems excessive and overabundant, and I can't tell if I'm drawn to all that foolish, pointless joy or wish I could steal some of it for myself.

I duck into the coffeehouse to order something sugary and regrettable and possibly tasting of gingerbread, but I'm surprised when I see Briar there.

It never occurred to me that she . . . goes to the same places that anyone else would. It seems so unlike her. *Like you have any idea who she is,* I remind myself.

Like I have any idea who anyone is. Isn't that last night's takeaway?

I walk over to her when I get my drink and tilt my head at the empty chair opposite her. For a moment, she looks alarmed. Then she smiles, so I smile back. I sit down across from her and for a moment it's just us, the old brick wall beside us, and the clamor of coffee patrons.

"I didn't think you drank coffee," I say after a few moments drag by. "Although I guess if you put enough sugar in it, you might like it."

"Yes." She shakes her head, like she's having some kind of internal discussion. "I like sugar. I am very fond of it."

"I'm sorry about last night," I say. I turn in my chair so I can put my back against the wall and look around at the other people here. But they're too human when I still have all that blood and betrayal in my head. I look back at Briar. "That was pretty gross."

"The world is pretty gross," Briar says quietly. "The Reveal didn't make anything worse. Just more visible."

That lands with a wallop. I redirect my attention to the mug in front of me.

"You're lucky you didn't grow up here," I tell her, taking a sip of my drink, which tastes like gingerbread houses and makes me want to cry or maybe throw up, though not because it doesn't taste good. "I did, and what that means mostly is that everywhere I go, I see memories. Ghosts when I don't even believe in ghosts. All these people who think they know me because they've known me all my life." I look at her. "These are not the same thing, despite what some people might think."

"I'm fascinated by species that crave connection," Briar says in that same quiet way, though she doesn't seem awkward any longer. "I might think that it's good for me. Or that it's something that I should allow, or force myself to seek out. But I don't *crave* it."

I have the strangest feeling that this is a real moment, somehow. That the hint of something like vulnerability I can see in her now isn't a game. She's not putting anything on.

I'm not going to be like Ty and stop trusting my instincts. The story of Connor for me, I decide, is that I should trust them *more*.

"Who would crave connection?" I ask her. I let my mouth curve. "It's a pain in the ass. It's not like you can connect only one way. You let someone in and then they're in. They're all over you. They could smother you, fuck you up, leave you in shambles, and what can you do about it? You're the one that gave them the tools to do it in the first place."

She makes a sound that's kind of a laugh and kind of a gasp, then shakes her head. "Yes," she says. "That. It's not comfortable."

"Maybe that's the point." I think of Ty. I think of having to walk around today, knowing he's hurting. And not, for a change, because of me. He's hurting and there's nothing I can do about it. Yet I hurt for him as if it happened to me. I shake my head. "Maybe we're supposed to hurt. Maybe that's how you know it's working."

Briar surprises me with her other smile. The genuine one. "Then I am significantly more connected that I imagine, I guess."

I don't know why that's funny, but it is. I laugh. She smiles some more.

When I leave, I still don't want to go back to the den, so I trudge up the hill toward Winter's instead. Today, just like last night, I can sense pack everywhere. I should have been able to do this the whole time.

I blame myself for this, too. I should have been more vocal. Maybe if I hadn't been so busy trying to justify my own choices, I would have called more attention to the protection detail part of things. Or the *disruption* factor.

Maybe if I had, I could have . . . changed the outcome of this. Or made it better, anyway.

No one is at Winter's house when I get there. I let myself into the kitchen and sit at the table, basking in the quiet. When I feel consoled and a little less likely to explode, I wander over to my cottage. I find myself checking for sacrifices out of habit, but there's nothing. Not even a trace of last night to be found, which I know is down to Savi and her removal of scents and stains.

I wonder if she'd smite me herself if I suggested she open a cleaning business.

I go into my cottage and curl up in my little chair, though every time I tell myself I'm going to sink into a book, I find myself staring off into space instead. It's like I'm looking at that kaleidoscope again, waiting for the images to form into something I can understand.

In the meantime, I find that I'm not as comfortable here as I used to be. Maybe it's because Connor told me he watched me sleep. I stare at my windows balefully, imagining that while trying my best *not* to imagine that.

Maybe it's that I'm not hiding from anything anymore, and much as I loved it here, it was a place to hide.

I don't love that revelation.

It's a relief when I hear a vehicle coming up the drive.

When I throw open my door I see that Savi is in the yard, standing with her back against the driver's door of her pristine SUV. A vehicle I thought gave her away from the get-go. Only a sorcerer could drive around this valley, through wildfires, mud, and snow, and still have a car that looks that shiny.

"There you are," she says as if I'm late for an appointment. "Get in."

"If I want to live?" I reply dryly.

"If I thought you didn't want to live, I wouldn't bother with you." She frowns at me as I walk toward her through the gray light. "Life is complicated enough when you're not flattened by a death wish, don't you think?"

"I wouldn't know. I've never found death all that appealing."

"My understanding is that it's a great void if you're lucky and torture if you're not," Savi tells me coolly. "I've never felt the need to experiment, myself."

I climb into her passenger seat and sit there, feeling raggedy on her pristine white leather.

She doesn't seem to notice. "This has always been my issue with Vinča. I don't understand the lure of a death goddess. First of all, obviously, a god doesn't care about anyone or anything but itself. How many times must history teach us this lesson? At best, a godhead is a capricious narcissist who can be appeased by a few rituals and a little self-abasement. Like a man, in other words."

"Preach," I murmur.

Savi drives at what I consider a reckless speed out of Winter's yard and onto the bumpy, bottomed-out dirt road that leads down into town, but naturally her enchanted vehicle does not seem to encounter anything but smoothness. Everything she touches is always smooth.

But not her. Not today. She is *vibrating* with tension. Her hair looks like she hasn't brushed it, or said the right spell for it to brush itself. If I didn't feel so feral myself, I'd probably mention it.

"A *death* goddess makes even less sense." Savi makes a derisive noise. "Especially *this* death goddess. They're all the same, of course. They just want destruction for destruction's sake. They think it's *art* to rip things apart and never build anything, never create anything. It's all misery and pain, forever and ever, amen."

The hills are slick with snow, but she takes them as if they're dry. I've ridden on the back of many a Harley and have always felt perfectly safe, but I find myself grabbing for the bitch handle in her passenger seat.

She's still ranting. "It's all so boring. Every minion seems to think that if she rises, they will too. The sad truth is that if she bothers with them at all, it will only be to destroy them. As painfully as possible. In all her rituals and dark little ceremonies, it says as much. *She is come to destroy, she is the end of all things, she is the mouth that will suck on the bones of the world and chew through the gristle.*" Savi heaves a sigh. "She *says* she will kill everyone and everything, and still her acolytes dance for her. Your wolf last night died for her when she would never do the same for him. I cannot understand it."

Your wolf. I repress a shudder at that.

"I agree with everything you're saying. But I doubt one of her cult members will. I think they believe that death is part of the fun."

"I hate cults," Savi mutters darkly. "If I was a god I would be much more interested in clear-eyed followers, not this blank, mindless thing that hers have going on."

"Are you considering elevating yourself?" I ask brightly. "A little ascension in between death goddess risings?"

"You joke." Savi drives a little bit too fast through Jacksonville, seeming not to notice when a set of humans dive out of her way as she plows through an intersection. No hint of brakes. Or any apparent awareness when they shout after her. "But in certain periods of history, sorcerers were worshipped as gods."

"Who wasn't?" I reply airily. "According to my grandmother before she died, there was a time when the world cowered in an appropriate fear of werewolves. The glory days, she called it, though she could never pinpoint *when*, exactly, this was. She was not a fan of wolves having to diminish themselves in the world."

"Sometimes," Savi tells me as she takes the hill out of town, her voice dark and arid at once, "diminishment is survival."

I don't ask about that. Something about her forbidding tone keeps me from it. I lounge in the passenger seat as she drives down to Winter's coffee stand and pulls into the line. We inch up toward the front, watching truckloads of various creatures get themselves coffee and a little card reading. Some shout at her. A few throw their coffees.

Some cry, and I see Winter reach out and hold their hand the way a doctor might.

I wonder if she knows how completely she's become the oracle by now.

When Savi pulls up, she stares up at Winter and frowns when the cards are offered. "Your shift must be over," she says.

"It was over two hours ago." Winter cracks her neck on one side, then the other. "But I figure as long as I still have stamina and no headache, why not keep going?"

"Because you're exhausted and the cards are getting cranky," says her coworker, a girl I remember from school. She laughs at Winter, then looks my way and, oddly, turns red. "Go on. Get out of here."

Winter walks out the back of the coffee stand, nods at the vampires who lurk menacingly and glower at every car that pulls up. With them around, she doesn't have to carry her guns or dive into her car like an action hero.

Instead, she climbs into the back seat of Savi's SUV like a normal person back in perfectly normal times, and we drive down into Ashland, past the snowy fields, the whitecapped mountains leading the way. Once we get to Ashland, we drive through Lithia Park—which is always green these days, thanks to magic best left to its own devices—and then out into the mountains until we're bumping along unmarked roads again.

We wind around and around, catching stunning glimpses of Mount Shasta in the distance, all the way up to Savi's estate.

I don't think Winter has been here either, but she does a great job of not looking particularly overawed as we pull up to the sprawling house. It looks even more like a temple an old god might fancy to me now. Maybe the sort of temple sorcerers enjoyed during their divine eras, but something keeps me from asking.

Savi flows her way out of the car once she parks it near one of the doors, beckons us to follow her, and sweeps into the house.

Once again, I keep my eyes on her and try not to look at the things happening in my peripheral vision. When Winter starts to drag, her attention clearly getting caught and wrecked, I loop my arm through hers and drag her with me.

"Never look directly at anything in a sorcerer's house," I tell her in a low voice.

She blinks, her eyes wide. It takes her a moment to focus on me. "Is that a thing you tell little wolflings?"

"It's common sense. Do you know magic? If not, don't mess with it. Even if it's trying to mess with you. Especially then."

"Wise words indeed," Savi says, suddenly beside us. Instead of leading us to one of her courtyards, she turns into a room that smells so deeply of magic that I feel my hackles rise before I even enter.

Winter stops on the threshold too, her head jerking back. "What is this place?"

"My dungeon," Savi says, then laughs when we both stare at her. "I'm kidding. It's a place where I cast a spell or two as needed. I thought it was high time that I warded the three of us. Instead of places I think we might go."

"That seems smart enough," Winter says, carefully, her pulse rocketing in her throat as she looks around the room. I can hear it.

I look too, my attention going immediately to the windows that look out at different views. The night sky. A wild, cold ocean. The Milky Way. The valley. A desert made of shifting sands and a sun so bright it hurts. It's dizzying.

I clear my throat. "I wasn't aware that you could actually ward people."

"Nothing can or can't be done," Savi says, though it sounds to me like she's talking to herself. "It's really more a question of . . . what can the magic do? What can you make it do?" She shoots a look in our direction. "Most of the time it's about harnessing creativity, that's all."

She beckons us in. Winter and I look at each other, but we go. Savi seats us around what looks like an ornate basin, though I know, somehow, that it isn't plain water in the round bowl in the center. She shows us how to sit with our knees touching and tells us to lift our hands and hold them over the bowl, the same way she does with hers.

"This is a very intense spell," she says. "It's also very effective. It can take a moment or two to settle into the bones."

"Like arthritis," I say.

Savi sends me a dark look and frowns until I get my hands in the right position.

Then she begins to chant.

I've heard her chant too many times to count. That low muttering that Winter talks about, that spell work she weaves into everything. It's like a song. It's like a dance of sound and shape, and I've heard it over and over again.

I've never been a part of it before.

I can feel the magic wind its way around and then sink into me, and it occurs to me that I shouldn't be so comfortable with this. That I shouldn't throw myself into magic when I know better than to *look* at it.

Yet nothing about this feels like a threat. Nothing about Savi ever has to me, not since I met her at Winter's door and actually talked to her myself. I might be wrong about her too, the same way I was wrong about Connor. I know that's a possibility.

Still, my body isn't reacting the way it usually does to threats. My wolf side is happy and at ease.

You either listen to your intuition or you don't, I tell myself.

I decide to listen. I let go.

Savi is speaking in a language I don't understand. Her mouth moves around words I can hardly fathom, in a cadence that's unlike anything I've ever heard before. As she speaks, it's almost as if I can feel each word attach itself to my skin.

Then they sink in deep. They winnow their way down to the bone, where they glow.

This goes on and on, and soon enough, it's as if we're somewhere else.

Everything is light. I can see shapes move all around me and not just in my peripheral vision. It's as if we're floating. I'm aware of the three of us, individually and together.

Like we are a rune all our own.

Everything is golden. Everything is bright.

Everything feels carbonated, and I begin to feel giddy.

Soon enough, it's as if everything is spinning. I can feel Savi's words deep in my bones like an ache, but it's like we're dancing anyway. Even though I'm fully aware that somewhere back on a mountain in Ashland, we're sitting still.

The more we move—or don't move—the more everything spins and folds in on itself, collapsing deeper into that aching glow of spells on bone.

Until, at last, everything goes beautifully dark.

22.

Wolf Moon, waxing gibbous

I wake up on some kind of fancy chaise, feeling more well rested and content than I have in . . . maybe ever. Who knew sorcery agreed with me like this?

I sit up and see we're still in the same spell room. Winter is on a similar-looking chaise across from me, rubbing at her eyes like she's a bit less awake than I am.

"That was quick," I say to Savi, who is standing by one of her windows, frowning out at something I can't see from my chaise. "I don't know why I feel so . . ."

"Refreshed," Winter contributes, around a yawn. "I don't think I dreamed a single thing. It was glorious."

"The good news is that the wards I created took hold, and they did it fairly quickly," Savi tells us. She turns back from her window, and I'm briefly distracted by all the *flowing things* she's wearing that make her look like a sorceress of old in some video game. "The bad news, I'm afraid, is that *quickly* in spell terms was still longer than expected."

I stretch my arms up over my head. "How long?"

"We started the spell work on Friday afternoon," Savi says, managing to sound both apologetic and matter-of-fact at once. "It is now Sunday afternoon."

"Oh shit," Winter says, jumping up from her chaise. "Two days? Ariel is going to—"

"*Ty,*" I breathe, my heart kicking in. He'll freak. He must already be—

"About that," Savi says. She waves at the window she's standing at, then indicates that the two of us should come closer.

Winter and I crowd in, staring at the scene unfolding before us.

It takes me a minute, but I recognize those woods.

"This is here," I say. "This is your land."

Half the pack is assembled outside Savi's wards. They keep throwing themselves at the wards, checking for weaknesses. There is also a selection of terrified-looking mages with them, clearly doing their best to use magic to break in.

There is also what appears to be a whole battalion of vampires. They keep shifting in and out of their various smoky forms, fangs out, also testing the wards.

"How long have they been out there?" Winter asks, her eyes wide as she stares out.

"Oh, you know." Savi sounds airy. "A minute." She shrugs when I lift a brow at her. "Anyway, you're both awake now. Might as well face your personal armies before they wreck the wards I have *painstakingly* erected over the course of *many* years."

"This is not the time to play disappearing games," is all I say, in a low voice, hoping Savi can see how serious I am. "Vinča is no joke, and she's all anyone's thinking about right now."

I remember the Connor of it all as I say that, but then, he turned out to be a minion too, didn't he? So it's all the same dance around the same death goddess that I grew up hearing about—the way humans tell ghost stories about Bloody Mary while looking in mirrors.

No one thought those prophecies would actually come true. That a mess of planets would align to bring on the Reveal and put Vinča back into play. That she would do her very best to rise on Halloween.

That she's apparently not imprisoned in the watery deep, as planned. That there are ribs involved and she's currently lurking inside someone, waiting to bust out again.

Vinča Vinča Vinča. I'm fucking tired of Vinča.

"Vinča is exactly who I was thinking about when I crafted this spell," Savi retorts, looking like I slapped her. Once again, I can see the cracks in her unbothered, smooth exterior. She even scowls at me. "Do you think I have any desire to go head-to-head with that putrescent psychopath again? I can assure you that I do not. If the wards we now wear on our bones keep her away from us, all the better." She tilts her chin up in a manner any wolf would read as instantly belligerent. "I will tell your men this myself, not that I, a sorceress of old and mistress of the fate I choose, need to make myself palatable to males."

Winter and I exchange a look and don't point out that this is not a power issue for us. I don't think I'd react well if Ty disappeared for a couple of days with no explanation. I'm more than happy for Savi to do the explaining on this one.

She is muttering again. Suddenly there's a swirling sensation again, everything is golden and bright, and then we're all standing in the snow some ways down the mountain from Savi's house.

For a moment, there's a kind of startled, intense pause.

Then the shouting kicks in.

Wolves are everywhere, baying and barking. Ty bounds toward me and knocks me down, then stands over me, all of his fur standing on end. I let him. When he's clear there's no threat, he starts licking me roughly, letting me know he was scared and he's furious and he needs to make sure I'm okay.

"I am," I tell him. I can see the indigo rings of his eyes, starker than usual today. "I'm okay."

I say this a few more times, and then he shifts in a blur and hauls me up to my feet. His gaze moves over me, dark and assessing, and then it goes murderous when he turns it on Savi. He doesn't let go of me while he does it.

"What the fuck were you doing in there?" he demands.

I can see that Ariel and Winter are standing pretty close together, with Ariel's hand at her neck and a look on his face that I would not like aimed at me. Though Winter seems fine.

Savi doesn't appear to be the vampire king's favorite person right now either.

"I haven't done that spell in a long time," Savi is saying, very casually, as if she doesn't notice the bared teeth aimed at her from two different species. "I haven't done it like *this* ever, actually. I knew it would take a minute." She smiles, fully serene, and by now I can read that smile. It means she's actually not the least bit sorry. "I didn't realize there would be quite so much of a time lapse."

When there is nothing but the sound of the wind in the trees and glowering from all sides, Savi lets out an elegant sort of tinkling laugh that she must surely know can only fan the flames. Maybe she's tired of this winter already and looking for a little fire.

"We thought you were all dead," Ty growls at her.

Ariel looks as if he's been turned to stone. "That can still be arranged."

"Don't be silly," Savi says, as if that is something the vampire king is renowned for. His giggly *silliness*. "If I was dead, all my wards would drop immediately and you could have strolled right in." She looks at Ariel. "Surely you know that, vampire. You've seen enough wards in your time."

"What I know," Ariel says coldly, "is that sorceresses are inherently untrustworthy. As you have proven."

"I don't really know what happened," Winter says then. She has her hand on Ariel's chest, and it sounds like she's going off on a tangent, but there's a certain gleam in her gaze that suggests to me she knows exactly what she's doing. "I personally feel more rested than I have since sometime in junior high school. I have to take that as a win. I didn't know I *could* sleep that deeply."

She looks at me then, raising her brows, and something else occurs to me, too. This valley succeeds the way that it does because these three intense and powerful beings get along. Wasn't that what Christmas dinner was about? The vampire king has a consort now. I'm about to accept Ty's claim to make me his queen. Savi is a wild card, but whatever spell she did just bound Winter and me to her. That makes all of us responsible for maintaining this peace.

No matter how many times Vinča tries to mess it all up.

"Look at us," I say. Soothingly. "We're all fine. Crisis averted."

When Ty gets me back to the den, however, he's clearly not convinced. He insists on examining every part of me, scenting me on such an intimate level that if he wasn't so furious, it would be hot.

"Two days," he thunders at me, over and over again. "I thought you were dead, Maddox."

"I would be able to feel if you were dead," I remind him, after repeatedly assuring him that—as he could tell—I was alive and breathing and *fine*. "You should have been able to feel if I was."

"That's how we found you at Savi's place, asshole," he growls. But he's all over me, his face in mine, and this isn't our usual flash fire. He's *raw*. "We couldn't get to you, Maddox. I can't be in a situation where I can't get to you."

I want to fight with him, but I know that if the situations were reversed, I'd be as ripped up about this as he is. It was a blink of an eye to me. For him it was two interminable days when there have already been too many terrible things this fall. This happened literally within hours of his finding out that his own VP, friend, and confidant betrayed him. Everything he thinks he knows is inside out, and on top of that, I disappear?

I'd be a little bit feral myself if I were him.

I let him scent me all he likes. Until he's satisfied that Savi didn't plant any sorcerer's land mines inside me, somehow.

"You don't know what she did," he growls at me.

I can feel it, though. "Savi is not our enemy," I tell him.

Then I wrap myself around him and hold on while he rages a little bit. While he gets his panic out of his system. While he gets my scent all over him and can relax.

Eventually he pulls away and moves back on the bed, raking his hands over his face. Through his hair that is falling everywhere today, making him look like a wolf gone Viking.

"The full moon is three days from now," he says when he speaks again. "We need to talk about that."

"There's nothing to talk about," I assure him. "It's a winter moon. It's going to rise late and sullen and take its sweet time getting up there, too. And no matter when it does, I'll be right there beside you, ready to go."

The words I think he's been waiting for all this time, not very patiently.

Today he frowns at me. "I don't want you to do that."

Something in me stutters at that. I realize that I'm holding my breath, but I can't bring myself to let it go. Not yet.

"Maddox." Ty reaches over and pulls my hands into his. "I'm releasing you from this. You deserve a king who knows his own people. Who can see it when someone's got a knife to his back, and that's clearly not me. After all the ways you stood up for this pack, and for me, when neither they nor I thanked you for it . . ." He shakes his head. "I think you deserve better."

That stuttering thing in me shifts. This I can deal with. This is not . . . him not wanting me.

I would rather face Vinča all by myself than face Ty not wanting me.

The truth of that feels like a new sort of ache, everywhere.

I wrap my fingers around his. "I do deserve better," I agree, and his dark eyes blaze at that. *Good,* I think. *Dick.* "What is this noble bullshit? This isn't the king who is supposed to claim me at last beneath the full Wolf Moon. This sounds like some whiny bitch."

"Hey. Watch yourself."

I hold his gaze and keep it steady. "I don't need your self-pity, Ty."

The funny part is that my heart actually hurts for him. It feels like a weight in my chest, but I also know that the worst thing I could do right now is cry. Try to hold him. Make this soft. That's the last thing he needs.

At the end of the day, Ty is a warrior king. One of the most sacred jobs I have is to make sure he can fight. That's what he needs, so that's what I do. "Connor betrayed you. That sucks. I'm sure that others will betray you, in time, because no matter what else is happening in this world we can be sure that people who suck will find new ways to keep on sucking. But it won't be me."

I say that last part a little more intensely than the rest. And I keep going. "What I need is for you not to betray me, either."

He scowls. "I'm trying to do you a favor."

"I don't want it," I shoot back at him in the same intense tone. "And anyway, you can't release me. Don't you know? There's only one way out. If you want a different mate, you're going to have to kill me. My mother told me that. It's the only way you can clear the slate and let fate sort you out."

He growls at that, which I guess tells me how he feels about murdering me.

Still, a girl likes to be sure. I let go of his hands and lean closer, tilting my head back to expose my neck to him. "Go on. Rip my throat out. End it now."

"You little shit," he growls at me.

I tilt my head back even farther. "One bite and it will all be over. I'm sure that will solve all your problems."

He leans forward and puts his mouth on my neck. He bites down, too—but it's not to hurt me.

Quite the opposite.

Ty licks my pulse, laughing when it picks up. His hand wraps around the back of my neck, and he tugs my head around so he can look at me.

"Never say I didn't give you a way out, babe," he tells me, his voice serious. "And you better always remember you didn't want it."

"Oh no," I murmur. "I guess we're stuck with each other. You're going to have to meet me when the full moon rises after all, and get ready to run when it hits that zenith."

It's a lot later, and I'm a lot limper and giddier, when we both hear some barking from outside that indicates he's needed. He bites me on the throat again, a little warning nip, and rolls away.

"Don't disappear again," he throws over his wide, beautiful shoulder. "I won't like it as much the next time."

I take a very long, hot shower and wonder why I'm not more concerned about losing a day or two. Because . . . I'm not. At all. It's not the loss of days that feels odd to me, only my reaction to it. Surely that should be the sort of thing that a normal person would find . . . troubling, at the very least.

Yet try as I might, when I draw up the laundry list of troubling things that have happened recently, feeling loopy and giddy and *rested* from some spell Savi cast doesn't make the list.

When I leave Ty's den, I'm thinking that I'll head into the grand cavern, but I stop, still deep in the tunnels. Do I really want to explain myself and my impromptu vacation on the heels of the Connor thing? I don't. That's the easy answer.

A more complicated answer is that if I feel anything about my loss of days, it's that I'm running out of time. Vinča is already in a vessel, waiting for her moment. Moments around here are usually moons. That means it's three days to another bloody battle that's not even my top emotional concern regarding the night in question.

Maybe I feel like there are loose threads that need addressing before the next potential apocalypse.

I told Winter on Christmas that I thought Augie was in a better place. Today there's something kicking in me that tells me I need to go see if that's true. I turn away from the communal caverns and head out the back entrance. Then I run out into the woods instead, following that mining trail as it winds deeper into the Siskiyous.

I don't know what I expect to see when I make the climb to the top of the crevice and peer down into it. I would have heard if something had happened to Augie. I expect him to be alive. It's just . . . what kind of alive?

Maybe it's because I had an enchanted sleep, or because a creepy stalker I thought was a friend *watched me sleep* without me any the wiser, but *quality of life* seems important to me today.

When I look down, I can see Augie huddled in his lean-to. He has all of his blankets wrapped around him, but he doesn't look like he's shivering. Or twitching like he was the last time. He's sitting up. And when his eyes lift and meet mine, I can see that he's lucid.

I don't say anything. I don't know what to say. I don't even know if he can recognize me in my wolf form.

Either way, all he does is nod. Then he returns his attention to contemplating whatever it is that's in front of him. Something inside him, I figure, because from my vantage point there's nothing down there but him.

Him and whatever demons he brought with him.

Still, deep in my gut, I know that whatever happens and however it looks on the other side, Augie is going to make it. I'm sure of it.

I can tell Winter that the next time she asks.

When I get back to the den, Ty meets me in the tunnel outside his rooms.

I can see immediately from the look on his face that something's wrong. I wait, and whine a little, shifting from paw to paw.

"More sacrifices," he tells me. He doesn't point out that if there are more, it means Connor wasn't our only problem. I get there all by myself. "Looks like three goblin females, crucified—literally fucking *crucified*—and hung up behind Savi's house."

"Behind it?" I try to take that in. "But Ariel's men and the pack were all over the place up there."

"Exactly," he says. "Now there are idiots in cloaks all over the place."

"Great," I mutter. "That sounds like a party."

"No way is Vinča out there fighting in some minion parade," Ty says. He rubs his hand over my furry head, and I lean into it. "All things considered, maybe you should be over with the oracle tonight. The vampires are already down there fighting, and I'm feeling like I need to jump in too. The fewer minions, the better."

I think about the implications of that as we head out. Ty has all of our patrols on high alert, especially in the wake of the one-two punch that was Connor and my little weekend spell break. He handpicks a selection of the lieutenants he has here, the most promising of the younger males, and orders half of them to patrol the woods around Winter's house. He takes the rest with him as he streaks off into the hills on the way to Ashland.

It doesn't occur to me until I walk in the front door and sit down in a chair in the living room—where Winter is already sitting, gazing up with a curious look on her face as if the Christmas tree that's sparkling at her holds the mysteries of the universe—that I was able to walk right in. She's clearly not bothering to lock anything up any longer.

A few months ago this would have been a straight-up death wish. Tonight, however, I'm pretty sure it's because our tough little human is starting to realize the place she occupies in this valley. That, and it probably means there are more of Ariel's vampire warriors in the woods. Not to mention whatever spell Savi put on us, to ward us—though I doubt Winter trusts that any more than I do at the moment, since we have no idea if it works.

Then again, maybe she's finally crashing out. No one could blame her.

"I take it you heard," she says, without looking at me as I settle in my chair. "I saw it."

"You saw . . . the three of them? Goblin females, Ty said?"

"It wasn't immediately clear that they weren't the three of us." Winter is sitting with her legs crossed in the armchair, and she's playing with the cards between her hands, though her gaze is unfocused and still aimed at the tree. This is how I know that she's not done with her oracle shit.

"You thought it was us?" I blink. "You, me, and Savi?"

I don't like how spooky I find that.

She looks down at the cards and shuffles them absently. "I wanted to see if the cards had anything to say about the days we lost at Savi's. Ariel had a lot to say about that."

When she looks at me, her mouth curves at whatever expression I must be wearing on my face. "Ty was unimpressed," I say.

"I received a history lesson on the kind of spells that can knock a person out for days and have them acting perfectly fine until, guess what, their entire body explodes or something equally exciting. Apparently there is no shortage of such spells."

"Sure," I say, with a shrug. "But why would Savi cast a spell like that on herself?"

"There were several challenges to my intelligence, which I found rude," Winter says with that same curve to her mouth. "The major gist of which was that I, insensate for days, have no idea what Savi did or did not cast on herself."

"I hear you," I say. "Or I hear him, I guess. But that wasn't really the vibe."

"Ariel Skinner, ancient and immortal king of the vampires, does not find *vibes* a persuasive argument," Winter tells me. "Ask me how I know."

"Did the cards tell you what she actually did to us, then?"

"When I asked them what she did, I saw us bathed in light, protected, and stronger, somehow." When I start to say something, probably something like, *Maybe the men could calm down, then*, she holds up a finger. "But when I asked them if we were safe now, I saw the three females instead. Hung up on crosses and flayed wide open."

"Those are not the vibes we like at all."

"No," Winter agrees.

We sit there for a while, staring at the tree and the lights. I don't have the images that Winter does in her head—I don't want them—but it's not like I can pretty up three crucifixions into anything palatable.

"The full moon is going to be pretty busy for you," she says after a minute. "I have to figure that's going to be her move."

Fucking Vinča. "That's my assumption. Everyone loves a full moon."

"Do you think things will change a lot, Ty being the new high king and all that? And with everything that happened with his friend?"

"I think," I say slowly—carefully, like I'm sounding it out as I go, because that's what it feels like—"that everything has already changed. Connor was trying to hold on to a world that ceased to exist. Vinča is basically the same. The Reveal didn't just send the Kind out of hiding. It made us ask ourselves why, on some level, we preferred to hide all along."

We sit with that awhile, then decide that what we need tonight is hot cocoa. We move to the kitchen, and she's making us thick mugs of the contraband chocolate when the back door flies open.

Briar, of course. With her usual delicate entry.

She looks typically surly and only nods at us as she comes in, then starts rummaging around in the refrigerator.

"Do you want hot cocoa?" Winter asks her.

Next to her at the counter, I look at her and widen my eyes.

I feel sorry for her, Winter mouths at me.

Briar takes her time straightening up from the fridge. "What?"

"Hot cocoa," Winter says. "Literally chocolate in a mug that's drinkable."

"It's tooth-ruiningly sweet," I add. "You'll love it."

"I know what hot cocoa is." Briar looks from Winter to me and back. "Why are you guys so weird all the time?"

Pot, kettle, but I just smile. "I'm a werewolf. Not entirely house-trained."

Briar looks like she's trying not to smile.

"I lived through the Reveal as a human," Winter replies. "Now I'm the oracle. I don't think there's much weirder than that."

Except whatever Briar is, which, yes, dark fae. But there are a lot of different kinds of dark fae. In my experience, small as it is, they are never alone. Why is she?

I've got a lot of questions for Briar, actually. It just never seems like the right time to ask them.

We all sit down around the kitchen table, and Briar takes a sip of the thick, creamy concoction that Winter puts before her. "That is good," she says, sounding surprised. "I've only ever had the instant stuff."

"That's actual heresy in this house," Winter tells her. "Just so you're aware."

I would describe the silence that descends after that as companionable. Sweet, even.

That feels like progress, so I jump in. "What exactly do you do all the time?" I ask Briar. "Winter has a job. So do I."

"You do?" Winter interjects, looking shocked.

"I do." I shake my head at her. "Did you think I was a lady of leisure? Biker bitch–style?"

"Yes," they both say, at the same time.

"I will take that up with Ty immediately. I should have been treated better this entire time."

When they both continue to stare at me, I relent. "I do office stuff. The pack has certain business ventures, and I oversee them."

Briar looks bored by that, which is how I like it. Winter doesn't look convinced, but then, she knows me better.

"Why do you keep working at the coffee place if you're the whole big-deal oracle now?" Briar asks Winter. "If people don't want to pay for you to see their future, you don't have to tell them, do you? Is it like . . . a calling?"

"It is a calling." Winter wrinkles up her nose. "Not one you can choose not to take, either. And it pays as well as I want it to pay. But I like coffee."

She says that so adamantly that I don't have the heart to point out that I think what she really likes is something that makes her feel like whoever the fuck she was before the Reveal. I'm betting she probably knows that already. Or is choosing not to know it. Either way, who am I to force a confrontation with oneself?

"I have a knitting shop," Briar says.

I do not look at Winter. I do everything in my power not to look at Winter, but I can feel her stiffen beside me with the same astonishment.

Briar looks from her to me, then smirks. "Of course I don't have a fucking knitting shop." She takes a swig of her hot chocolate. "There's a bar down by the old factories. On the railroad tracks, pretty much. I'm a bartender."

"Gold Rush," I say. "Is that still around? Didn't it used to be called something else?"

"I always thought that was a weird place to have a bar," Winter says. "Maybe if they hadn't taken so long building all those apartments there it would have made more sense. Instead it's all factories and logging paraphernalia and that weird McAndrews overpass and then—oh. A bar."

"It's still a bar," Briar tells us. "The menus are a little bit different. Caters to the Kind. And that's how I have rent money."

"I'm always looking for a good watering hole." I laugh when they both look at me. "I am. All the ones I know of are overrun with wolves."

Winter frowns at me. "Surely a feature, not a bug."

"I love my pack. I love being a wolf and everything wolf-related." I lift my mug and mock-toast them with it. "And sometimes, I like to keep my skin on and stop thinking about pack dynamics for five seconds."

"There's a strict no-bullshit rule," Briar tells us. "The owner, Mac, is part river snake. He takes that shit seriously."

"Nobody likes to go to a bar and end up dead," I say. "It ruins the vibe."

Winter's eyes gleam as she drinks from her cup.

Briar looks at me seriously. "There's no point worrying about death. You have to think about the fact that it's part of life. Whether you're immortal and therefore exist in opposition to death, or mortal and are therefore dying from the moment you're born, none of us escape it."

When we both stare back at her, she shrugs and looks down at her mug. "I don't know. I find that soothing."

After Briar's gone off somewhere—presumably to her bartending gig—Winter and I lie on the living room floor, staring up into the branches of the tree, as if we can take on all that sparkle by osmosis.

Strangely enough, I find Briar's take on death soothing too.

Though not enough to take away the very real sense that everything around us is getting worse.

That Vinča is getting closer than she should.

That those goblin females who Winter thought were us are only the beginning, and far more terrible things are coming.

That there are worse things than death—and one of them is, almost certainly, dying horribly at the hands of a vengeful goddess.

23.

Wolf Moon, waxing gibbous

It's late the night after next when a vampire messenger appears to the sentries outside the den—because like hell would any vampire ever be invited in—and instructs them to inform Ty that his presence is needed down at one of the old timber yards in Medford.

In force.

I go with him because that sounds a lot more interesting than sitting in the grand cavern, watching my mother mete out justice and introduce consequences as she sees fit. It's not that I think she's doing a bad job, it's just the childhood trauma. It does rear its head.

We run out of Jacksonville in pack formation, barreling along the overgrown roads. We cross what was once a farm until it became a sports complex of some kind and is now little more than a ruined old building with pools where various creatures who prefer to stay wet and sleek like to congregate.

We skirt that whole mess, then make it down to the old railway tracks and the log yards there. There are vampire warriors guarding the entrance, and they nod at Ty. One of them puts his hand up to me.

Ty growls. "I wouldn't touch her if I were you."

The vampire manages to look both arrogant and disgusted with Ty at the same time. "He won't want her in there. His orders are very clear."

I have never liked it when people assume that you should *just know* who they're talking about. Even if I do know who they're talking about.

That maybe colors my tone when I respond. "He can tell me that himself," I say, then push my way past him.

I then instantly regret it because the interior of what was once a factory floor or warehouse, and is now a repository for nothing good, is overrun with the death cult minions.

All I see are red cloaks, swirling in every direction. Those terrible masks that make them all look uniform despite their differing shapes and scents. It makes everything in me go cold, same as always.

But the real mind fuck is the fact that there are so many of them.

Just in case I thought—hoped—that maybe all this stuff is nothing more than Vinča reaching out from her temple and playing games with magic, that notion takes a hit.

This time there are even more than I remember being up on McLoughlin that night. A whole lot more than there ought to be, given how many were killed on Halloween.

"What the hell do they want?" Ty growls.

"I'm going to go out on a limb, given the whole death goddess they worship and whatnot," I drawl. I look at him. *"Death?"*

Ty rumbles some more, glaring at all the minions. "You want to sacrifice yourself for some goddess who wouldn't take a piss on you, go right ahead. What I don't get is why *I* have to die because *you* believe in a goddess that I think is an asshole."

Then he hurls himself into the battle.

I follow, and I'll admit, I'm more than ready. The last time I got to well and truly mix it up was up on McLoughlin that night. It's all been protective detail over Savi on Halloween and wolf week duties since then.

I've always liked a good scrap, and once I get past my distaste of my opponents tonight, I let loose.

I try to keep track of the minions I take down. As I lunge in at them I avoid their wicked knives that we can all smell are drenched in something vile. Likely some kind of poison to make death at their hands even more unpleasant.

It's the vampires who take most of the enemy fire. Their preferred game is to go in hard, then turn to smoke as the minion attempts to strike. They usually become corporeal again a split second later when their enemy is overextended and they can easily slip a knife or a fang in deep.

That they have practiced fighting like this for more lifetimes than I will live is obvious. And impressive.

When we've beaten them all down, leaving only a few who managed to slip away and escape into the night, we all stand around and it's clear that we feel the same . . . oddness. The vampires begin to move the cloaked carcasses out toward the old rail yards where boxcars still sit.

"Three humans, a couple of goblins, two gnomes, a few actual trolls, and one of those beak-faced things," I list off. "That's a whole lot of cultish unity amongst Kind clans who usually avoid each other."

"Vinča herself often appears beaked and winged," Ariel says quietly, doing something magical to the blade he carries to rid it of blood. "Perhaps she has a special draw for others similarly equipped."

"We don't know why they were here," Ty points out, looking around the warehouse. "They don't seem to be protecting anything. Feels a lot like this was a decoy. Question is, for what?"

"For what, indeed," Ariel mutters.

We all move back outside. Ty and I scent the air, but there are no answers. The fact that we're near the logging yards reminds me.

"Want to grab a drink?" I ask.

When all the wolves look at me, Ty barks out a laugh. "Not you, assholes. You can be sure that my queen is not talking to your mangy asses."

"Briar is a bartender at a bar down here," I tell him. "It's right down this road."

I can feel Ariel and Ty look at each other over the top of my head. When neither one of them argues, I turn toward the road in question, assuming they'll follow along. Yet while I can scent Ty easily enough, Ariel seems to be nowhere.

Then suddenly, he's back and Winter is with him.

"Are we really going to a bar?" Winter asks me.

"It's like a double date," I say, because that's probably the most horrifying thing I can think of to say in that moment. Ty only sighs. Ariel doesn't dignify that with a response.

Next to me, Winter laughs.

It's foggy again tonight, and there is still snow on the ground. We pick our way down the road, heading toward the lights we can see beaming in the distance. There's movement on the railway, and Winter squints in that direction.

"Why are they all running?" she asks.

"Um." I think of all the death cult dead that the vampires loaded into the boxcars. "I think there's a buffet?"

It's a testament to how the last few months have gone that Winter doesn't ask any follow-up questions to that. But I'm betting she won't curl up with an old copy of *The Boxcar Children* anytime soon, either.

We get closer to the bar and find the building short, flat-topped, and still painted white, the way I remember it. There are lights strewn all over it and hanging over a patio that even hardcore monsters aren't sitting on when it's this cold. From inside, I can hear the thumping of the music.

It almost feels like any Saturday night in Medford before the Reveal.

I'm the one who swings the heavy door open. As I do, I look back at my companions and smirk. "This is like the beginning of a joke. A vampire, two werewolves, and an oracle walk into a bar—"

"And immediately get eaten for telling stupid jokes," Ty mutters, and moves past me to stalk inside.

The rest of us follow behind him.

To say that the sudden appearance of two of the kings of this valley causes a ripple effect is to vastly underestimate what happens inside Gold Rush.

There's no scratch of a record. Mostly because there are no records. The music keeps blaring, a powerful woman's voice that makes me think of flower children and whiskey. And possibly also early deaths from too much heroin.

Heroin sounds quaint to me these days.

Ty and Ariel act as if they don't notice anything. As if they can't see the way that every creature in the bar is frozen into place and staring at them.

They stride up to the bar, where a hedgehog shifter loses control of himself at the sight of them and has quills poking out, ripping holes in his flannel shirt and his trucker hat.

Briar, by contrast, stands behind the bar as if she might be meditating. Her arms are folded, and her trademark scowl looks welded to her face.

"Way to make an entrance," she mutters.

"Only kind I know how to make," Ty tells her, shifting so he can survey the whole packed establishment behind us.

Ariel sweeps a cold sort of glare from one end of the bar to the next. "A pint of O positive and a shot of AB negative. Body temperature, please."

Briar doesn't react to this. She turns and starts making drinks—which involve what I believe are blood bags hung on hooks at the back of the bar. I watch Winter's mouth drop open.

"You go to bars?" I hear her ask her lover.

"Little seer," he says, in an indulgent tone that I know by now he only uses for her, "there are very few things I have not done. Surely you know this."

"How did I not know that there were . . . *blood bars*?" Winter asks.

Ariel orders her a drink. No blood involved. Ty and I order beers, because wolves aren't fancy.

Then we all stand there, elbows on the bar, pretending that we're not keeping an eye on the crowd. Though we are. I watch quite a few creatures look from the group of us to the back of the bar, once or twice in rapid succession, and figure they're checking Ariel's reflection. Or maybe they're confirming that the oracle still hasn't become a vampire herself.

After a while, conversations kick in again. No one in the bar is unaware of the fact that two kings of the valley are here, but the music keeps playing. The pool game resumes in the corner.

The four of us simply . . . hang out. And talk about things that don't end in blood or death or horror.

I'm not pretending that we didn't fight a battle before this. Or that there aren't battles yet to be fought later. There's just something remarkably sweet about standing between Ty's outstretched legs in an actual bar, having a good time with the oracle and the vampire who have become our friends over the course of this life-altering season.

Real friends.

I know that if I were to say that to Ty, he would immediately dispute it. In all the history of werewolves I've ever been told, I've heard of alliances made with all kinds of other monsters—human and Kind. But never *friends*.

I think maybe I need to put that on my list of things to change, too. When I'm fully a queen and ready to start making the pack around me the one I want to live in, like you do.

I'm on my third beer and all is right with the world—or at least the little sliver of it that I'm involved in right now—when a golden light appears. One moment it's appropriately dive bar dim, the next there's a shimmering golden spotlight.

Once again, everyone in Gold Rush goes quiet. This time, there is a man in the background singing about a black-hole sun, which feels oddly appropriate.

"Are you all . . . in a bar?" asks Savi from her little hologram. The sorcery version of a text message.

"Come have a drink," Winter orders her, sounding as cheerful as a person should on her own third drink. "I can promise you that *we* won't knock you out for two days."

I'm still laughing about that one when Savi appears in a humming, extra-golden bit of a light show that has all the creatures in the bar flinching and covering their eyes.

"Is that really necessary?" Ariel asks Savi as she alights before us and aims a beatific smile around at the patrons of the bar.

"How can I say if it's necessary or not?" she asks mildly. "I do not habitually present myself in establishments of this caliber. For all I know, I was as likely to be greeted by pitchforks as not."

Ty rolls his eyes. Savi ignores all of us and glides closer to the bar to aim a smile at a glowering Briar. "Surprise me," she says.

When Briar hands her a drink that smokes and appears to have sharp-toothed guppies in it, all Savi does is thank her. Then she murmurs a few words over the concoction so that the next time I look, it greatly resembles what I've always imagined mead might look like.

She sips at her reconstituted drink and then gazes at each one of us over the rim. "I'm fascinated by the fact that you decided to be so *public*. Now, of all times."

"This is called spontaneity," I tell her. "You might give it a try."

Savi runs a finger around the rim of her drink and whispers something. Then she takes her finger, dips it in the drink, and puts it in her mouth. When she pulls it back out from between her lips, something shifts.

Winter and I shiver. Ty growls.

Ariel sighs. "We could simply have stepped outside, sorceress."

"No need," Savi says with a laugh. She looks at the rest of us. "We can speak freely. No one here will be able to hear us. To them, it will simply seem as if we're having an unexciting conversation about whatever it is they think we would be talking about." When neither Ariel nor Tyler look at all impressed, she lifts a shoulder. "I don't trust anyone. That's why I'm still alive, despite the fact that I've had enemies hunting me for longer than I care to admit. You would do well to think about these things."

"I rarely think about anything else," Ariel retorts.

"I don't have to think about it," Ty says. He smirks. "I'm hard to sneak up on."

"Anyway," Savi says with a roll of her luminous eyes, "tomorrow is the full moon. Another reason I find it remarkable that you're all out carousing tonight."

"We took a pit stop to fight off some of Vinča's minions," I tell her. "So not really as relaxing as a night of pure carousing would have been."

"I do not carouse," Ariel says icily.

"Of course not," Winter murmurs. "I'm sure it all gets boring after the first few empires fall." She smiles at the look he gives her.

"We're pretty sure that all the red cloaks were a distraction," Ty tells Savi. "But we don't know from what."

She considers this. "Maybe the point is that we won't know. Maybe they're just making noise. I think we have to be ready for her to make her move tomorrow."

"We need to assume that it's battle stations the moment the sun goes down," Ty says. "And we keep you three as far away from each other as possible. If you think she's going to make this happen on the back of a sacrifice that involves all of you, the simple workaround is to keep you separated."

"One of the things I did with the spell I cast," Savi says quietly, "is to bind the three of us together in such a way that we cannot be tracked. Not when we're all together."

Ty stares at her. I watch the muscle in his jaw jump. "That's a risky decision to make all by your fucking self."

"I thought it was strategic," she replies coolly. "The three of us are not exactly helpless. Rather than secluding ourselves in little bolt holes of questionable security all over the valley, we can stay somewhere together that allows us to use *all* of our power."

"I don't hate it," Ariel says after a moment. "I also think it's unexpected enough that it might take Vinča and her followers by surprise as well."

"The good news is that we all told Briar we'd have a New Year's party with her," I remind everyone. When they all stare at me blankly, I widen my eyes. "New Year's Eve is also tomorrow, friends. It's a real big night all around."

"I forgot," Winter says. "I was so focused on my first Christmas without Gran that I forgot it was New Year's too."

I look over at Briar, storming around behind the bar like she has half a mind to start beating on it with her fists. Energy I can appreciate, honestly.

"None of us can seem to scent or scan anything on her that feels the least bit dangerous," I point out. "Why not hang out with her on a big night like tomorrow? It doesn't sound like she wants to come here. When she invited us, she said we should *hang out*, not that we should *go out*. Maybe we should make it seem like we want to stay home. It's already warded. Protected. There are patrols."

Ty is quiet. If he's not automatically telling me no, I'm pretty sure that means he can see what I'm saying.

Winter nods. "I think the three of us need to stick together."

"Did you have a vision?" Savi asks, looking intrigued.

"No." Winter shakes her head. "But I've seen a million horror movies. The minute you split up, you die. Everyone knows this."

There's a little more discussion, but not much. It's clear that we all agree. Savi does that thing with her drink again, it seems like something shimmers in the corners of my eyes, and then it's obvious that we're back in tune with everyone else again.

Ty and Savi head out to go get a last look at Crater Lake before the day of the full moon dawns. Ariel tells them that he'll meet them up there, on the other side of the towns that were flooded when the lava tubes were blown open, with what sounds like only a few hardy—and pissed-off—survivors. The lake itself might be empty now, but there's still no sign of Vinča or her temple. No one thinks this is a good sign.

While the three great powers of the valley make their travel arrangements, Winter and I get Briar's attention at the bar.

"Thanks for telling us about this place," I say. "I used to come here in the summers when I came home from college."

"I always *meant* to come here," Winter says.

Briar looks a lot like she wishes we hadn't. I smile broadly. "And tomorrow night? Are we still on?"

Now Briar looks horrified. Then embarrassed. "Do you not . . . ? I mean, I'm totally cool to do nothing."

"No, we want to hang out," Winter assures her. "Obviously."

"Are you a party in the New Year sort of person?" I ask, leaning into the bar. "I went to the ball drop in Times Square once and it was hideous. I kind of vowed that I'd never do a New Year's party again."

"I can do whatever," Winter says, so casually that I almost believe her. But she keeps going. "If I'm honest, though, the way everything's been the past couple months? I wouldn't mind being low-key."

"I hate bars and parties and people," Briar says flatly. "I am one hundred percent up for low-key. Like, to the point that if we all fell asleep and forgot about it, that would be fine too."

I laugh. "We won't forget about it. Mind you, that doesn't mean I won't be asleep by nine."

Then we throw some money on the bar and follow the waiting vampire king out into the cold night so he can whisk us back home.

Like the most magical and deadly Uber around.

24.

Full Wolf Moon

Ty wakes me on the morning of the full moon by surging deep inside of me, rolling me over him on the bed and then clamping his arms around my back so he's controlling the angle and his own depth even though I'm on top.

He makes me turn bright and hot. He makes me come, crying out his name.

Then he does it again, just for good measure.

The third time, he flips us over and takes it slow. So slow that I'm writhing beneath him, actually sobbing. And interspersing that with the most creative curses I can come up with, because I know that he's torturing me on purpose.

"Good girl," he murmurs when I come again, falling completely apart beneath his hands. "Happy claiming day, Maddox."

I want to bite him but instead, I melt. I wrap myself around him and hold on tight when he rolls us up and carries me like that into the shower.

Unlike every full moon that I can think of in recent memory, I wish that we could get to the moon's full height immediately. I don't like that this one features the death goddess's potential rise in the middle of it all, when on Halloween I was delighted to divert attention from Ty and me.

This is how I know that if Vinča does show up, I'll figure out a way to take her down.

Because nothing is going to keep me from running tonight.

Ty insists that we grab breakfast in the grand cavern, and I know why he's doing it. He wants us to come out together exactly like this, both of us smelling scrubbed clean and clearly not just intimate with each other, but united. Connected despite the Connor thing, and my weekend at Savi's, and our entire tortured history.

He's not going to make an announcement, but he's still letting everyone know how things stand. I have to respect it.

My mother finds me as we're eating and performs her little bow to both of us. Then she sits, her head lower than mine, because nobody knows protocol better than Johanna.

I listen with half an ear as she fills me in on all the gossip of the den and makes sure that I know the implications in every possible direction.

"Do you ever think," I ask her, holding a piece of bacon, "that a lot of these interpersonal issues would cease to be a factor if we didn't all live on top of each other?"

Johanna laughs. "All the time. But what wolf do you know who allows his pack to live beneath the sky instead of in a cave?"

Beside us, Ty grunts, though whether in support of skies or caves is unclear. I open my mouth to tell him and my mother that I would like to start thinking that way. That I think a little privacy would do wonders for pack relations.

Not today, I caution myself. Not when there are so many other things that need to happen between now and morning.

Living arrangements can wait.

Meanwhile, I can't help but think that it would be smart, and awfully helpful, if Ty and I were already fully mated for Vinča's new resurrection tonight. It would only make us stronger, especially when we have a bond that's already so intense outside of the claim. It would allow us to communicate better, because I can already sense him. He can already sense me. My understanding is that once we're truly mated, that connection will be even more intense and reliable.

All useful tools to have in the fight against a powerful, horrible being like Vinča.

But that's not the day we have ahead of us. So I try to enjoy the day that we do have.

After we give our quiet breakfast performance, Ty assembles all of his returned lieutenants in the mapping room and I sit in, taking notes about the things they saw. I'm particularly interested in those things as they relate to the lines of supply and demand Ty intends for us to open and monitor.

I might have gotten a little lost in the Vinča stuff and the claiming that will finally happen later tonight—because I refuse to let anything *but* that happen—but as the men talk about what they saw out there I find myself thinking about the kingdom Ty is building. About how different everything will be, so different from how it's always been. Wolves striving, not hiding. Wolves controlling their environments instead of reacting to them.

I like this future. I like it a lot.

I will do everything I possibly can to live through this night so I can see it for myself.

After that meeting wraps up, I head down to the warehouse in Phoenix. I tell myself I'm fired up after hearing all the talk about the future, but when I get there I find myself getting all of my affairs in order.

As if I think that there is some possibility that Vinča could rise tonight and there might be something left after that. I doubt there will be much of a world left, much less someone to come along and pick up where I left off. That's not really my impression of what happens when a death goddess razes the world. That's certainly not what she claimed she'd do the last time.

It was definitely sold to us as the kind of apocalypse that left no room for plucky bands of rebels to eke out an existence against the cruel background of her nonsense, the way they do in all the books and movies and television shows that imagine these things.

Still, I don't stop. I leave detailed notes describing everything it is that I do, and I tell myself it's not because I think I'm going to die but because I *want* to live. I want to make sure that these systems I've built can stretch out and hold the kingdom Ty's building as securely as possible.

On the drive back from the warehouse I can already see the shadows getting long and that winter sun draping itself above the western hills. My plan is to go back to the den and see Ty one more time before meeting him to run the full moon—and before all the rest of the things that may or may not happen between now and then—but as I look at the swiftly darkening sky, I don't think I should. I remember what Savi said about the three of us together. There's no doubt that's the smarter play.

Yet I really don't feel smart as I drive up the old Highway 99 that pokes around to the west of the big interstate as the local route up from Ashland. The sun is setting on this last day of the year in reds and oranges, and maybe it's the usual New Year's thing that gets me thinking about this life I've led. These years of being fated, then unofficially mated to Ty. My escape from this valley. My return. All of our fights. All of our tempests and tempers.

I remember all of our years with perfect clarity. These last few as notable for our partnership as our passion, though both have grown so much that we're almost unrecognizable from where we started.

"I can't lose him," I whisper, as if the sunset is listening. As if this last bit of the year can intervene. "I want *all of him*. Tonight."

I feel those words settling in me. They feel different. Bigger, maybe. More intense. Like spells I'm pressing into my own bones.

I understand, then, that this is how it's *supposed* to feel. This is what a claim is supposed to be about. This deep determination to be *with* him in all the ways I can. This conviction that all the things that have always worried me about claims and mating from a distance don't matter, because this is us.

This understanding that Ty and I can make the world what we want it to be, so we can certainly make *us* what we need to be too.

I feel silly for ever imagining otherwise.

It makes me sad for all the females like me who weren't allowed to wait until they felt like putting themselves forward at a gathering. All the females who weren't allowed to find this iron conviction deep inside themselves.

I feel it now. He is mine. I am his. And I want everything that goes along with that.

I decide there's no point in beating myself up for not getting here sooner. It took all of those moves I made to get me to this one. It took everything I did, everything we were, to be sitting in this rattling old vehicle on New Year's Eve, finally completely certain that there is nothing I would rather do than run with him, submit to him like a wolf and partner with him like a human, and have him call me his forever.

That I have to deal with Vinča's beak-faced, wormy bullshit in the middle of this makes me highly motivated to do whatever is necessary to get rid of that bitch once and for all.

I'm actually gritting my teeth a little as I drive up Winter's bumpy driveway. Everything feels like déjà vu tonight, or maybe it's just a hint of that "Auld Lang Syne." I remember the first time I drove up here like this. How I had an irritated pack of bodyguards who all warned me that trying to rent one of the cottages here would piss Ty off. They were right. It did.

Though he still let me do it.

I remember meeting Savi and Briar for the first time. I knew who Savi was on sight, of course. I knew Briar was one of the Kind at a glance. Made of magic, if not, apparently, able to access any.

I never thought I'd be friendly with either one of them.

I knew Winter best—though, back then, I barely knew her at all.

Now look at us, I think as I swing out of the Explorer and let my boots hit the cold, icy ground. We were all hanging out in a bar last night like regular old twentysomethings on a sitcom somewhere. Practically idyllic, if you squint and tell yourself that there weren't three gorgons and a whole drunk-ass manticore at Gold Rush last night.

The sun is behind the hills now. The dark night falls like a curtain. Savi, apparently not wishing to bother with her fancy vehicle, appears in the door of her cottage. On my other side, I hear the front door to the house open, and a glance tells me that Winter's there.

She starts toward us, over the yard that still shows patches of green grass beneath the thinner patches of snow.

"So are we immediately invisible to all trackers?" I ask. "Or do we have to be holding hands and braiding each other's hair?"

"If you touch my hair," Savi tells me with a smile, "I will use your intestines as macramé."

"I can tell how much I've changed in the past couple of months," Winter says. "Because honestly? That sounds like arts and crafts, not a murderous, psychotic threat."

"Welcome to the Reveal," I say grandly. "The true reckoning is never with the monsters without, but rather with those within."

Winter keeps walking over and Savi comes forward, and then we're all sort of standing there by the side of my car.

"Are you able to monitor what's happening?" Winter asks Savi. "Assuming something is happening?"

I figure that's the nervous energy talking. We all know what's happening. We have to sit right here. We have party time with Briar to attend to tonight. At least this keeps us tucked away and hidden from any rising death goddess attacks. Or her gnarly minions who might have a hard-on to murder all three of us in what I assume will be the most revolting sacrifice yet.

Meanwhile, with Crater Lake parched and desiccated and Vinča's temple nowhere to be found, the rest of the powers in this valley are spread out. The wolves are patrolling the hills, waiting for moonrise in a couple of hours or so. The vampires have the valley floor, and they've stretched out their patrols to cover halfway to Roseburg. Savi's minions are less weaponized, maybe, but they're everywhere.

"Let's hope that this time it takes." Winter smiles, but it's forced. Her eyes are shadowy. "I don't have another grandmother to lose."

"The magic on Halloween was sound and should have held for another thousand years," Savi says, fiercely enough that it sounds like she's been arguing about that. With herself, with others, I can't tell. "The only thing I didn't factor in was the particular celestial situation we're in right now. A conjunction of—"

Clearly Winter and I are looking at her with the same expression, because she stops. She blinks. "All we have to do is get through tonight, and that's done. No more celestial interference. When she goes tonight, she'll stay gone."

She crosses her arms, and I notice yet again that she's a far cry from that smooth, perfectly polished Savi who moved into her cottage here with a series of gleaming white roller-bag suitcases, not a hair out of place. Tonight she looks significantly wilder. Her flowy clothes look like they annoy her. Her eyes are flashing. Even her dark hair seems to be doing as it wishes, tumbling this way and that and even flirting with a wave when I've never seen it anything but straight.

I don't want to tell her that I notice. That feels like a calamitous course of action on a night that needs no extra calamities.

Winter is not studying the sorceress for clues to her mental state. She looks rough. "Even if we manage to beat her back again, I want to know how we can keep this from happening again. If the stars align down the road, what's keeping another set of acolytes from trying this all over again when that happens?" She looks from Savi to me, then back again. "Is there really any way to fully defeat a god?"

"Of course," Savi says, matter-of-factly. "If no one believes in them, what power can they have? Gods, especially gods who have been shunted off into the deep and no longer affect people in any meaningful way, are ideas more than anything else. Tomorrow morning, I believe a little judicious pruning of her red-cloaked followers is in order, and we'll nip her next attempt to rise in the bud."

"What I like," I say then, "is that we all seem pretty certain that we're going to make it through the night." They both frown at me. "I know that *I* am. I have shit to do."

Winter laughs at that. Savi only frowns more. Still, we all turn when we hear the noise of Briar's cottage door slamming open.

She's standing there, her head tilted slightly to one side as if she's listening intently. The music from her cottage is so loud that I can't imagine she's listening to us. Or anything.

Savi draws herself up and sweeps toward her. "Do you really wear that beanie inside your own house? Are you cold-blooded?"

Briar laughs a little bit. "No, I'm not cold-blooded. I'm not even cold. I just . . ." She lifts her hands up and puts them on either side of her head, where her ears ought to be if they weren't concealed in the beanie. "The way I was raised, you never *prove* anything. You let others draw their own conclusions, because they will anyway."

"If you want to keep your pointed ears hidden away forever, you should," I tell her. I even reach out and put my hand on one of her tattooed wrists. "Though, Kind woman to Kind woman, I'll tell you that not hiding yourself away, for any reason, is always it. I had to hide who I was for a long time, obviously. We all did. I didn't realize that it felt like amputation until I didn't have to do it anymore. I didn't know that I could be all of me. Using all of my limbs however I want."

"I'm not hiding," Briar snaps back at me, yanking her wrist back. By then we're all gathered at her front step, and as she looks wildly between us, I feel like there are emotions behind her eyes. *Right there,* and yet I can't quite grasp them.

I can *almost* see them. I can *almost* comprehend her.

Though I think, very distinctly, *She doesn't want you to comprehend her.*

Another blink, and she smiles. "Okay, New Year, new me, right?" Then she tugs that beanie off her head at last.

I remember the fae I saw in New York. Tall and lithe, gleaming a terrifyingly compelling gold that we all pretended not to see. Just as we all pretended not to see their obviously fae ears pointing up high, announcing who and what they were to anyone and everyone who might have some doubt.

Briar does not gleam. She's not golden. But something about her seems to shift as she stands before us and pushes her black hair back so we can fully comprehend the high points of those ears of hers. That she, naturally, has pierced in multiple places.

Apparently fae *can* wear metal.

"There aren't a lot of your people in this valley," Savi says. "Or are there? Normally dark fae make themselves known."

"It's like I told you," Briar says. She runs her hand through her hair as she turns, then leads us into her cottage. "I move around a lot."

I look over my shoulder and I take a deep breath, pleased that I can scent pack—and not too distant. I'm also pleased that as far as I know, there were no sacrifices found today.

From what Ty said, the goblin clans—usually violently opposed to unifying with each other and certainly not with anyone else—have all volunteered to help in whatever way they can tonight in response to the sacrifice of three of their females. Once the goblins were in, word got out to many of the other Kind clans. They're all banding together, and I have to think that means only good things.

I want it to mean only good things.

I can't see the moon yet, but I can feel her. I can feel the tug inside of me, even more insistent than usual. I know that the *bitten* will be getting restless now, already pacing. Already feeling that change coming in, hard and relentless.

I pull in another breath, then follow my friends inside.

"Did you really go to Times Square for New Year's?" Winter asks me as I come in. When I nod, she makes a face. "Was it horrible?"

"Hideous. Packed in like sardines for hours in the cold." I shake my head in remembered outrage. "And if you bite someone it's a felony."

I laugh at the expression on her face, then I look around at the inside of this cottage that I never expected to see once Briar moved in. I'm expecting some kind of junkie's nest, not that she has exhibited the faintest sign of addiction. It's just that she doesn't come off as a person who prizes order or neatness.

So I'm deeply surprised to find that the place is sparkling. Clean as a whistle. Shockingly spartan, even. Her music is kicking, the expected punk rock shouting and posturing. There are no particular decorations, only black curtains over her windows, which is also . . . not entirely unexpected, but done in a much nicer way than I'd imagined from the outside.

I watch as Savi looks around, expressionless, though I somehow know she's as shocked as I am.

"I was expecting a little more black sabbath," Savi murmurs.

Winter nods. "The band?"

Savi blinks. "There's a band?"

"Anyway," Winter says brightly, and lifts up the bottle that she's been holding at her side, "I brought wine. Not sparkling, sadly. Ariel claimed he could get me some if I really wanted, but it sounded very dramatic, and possibly dangerous. So plain old wine it is."

Not to be outdone, Savi waves a hand and a plentiful charcuterie plate appears, piled high with cheeses, fruits, chocolates, and more. I can feel my mouth watering.

"Happy New Year," she intones. "May this odd Gregorian calendar moment be meaningful for us all."

"I didn't bring anything," I tell the group. "Save, of course, my boundless enthusiasm that is a centerpiece of any decent party."

"I can't decide if you three are the closest thing to friends that I have," Briar says after a moment. Her rainstorm gaze touches all of us in turn. "Or if I actually hate you."

"Fair," I say.

Then she turns the music up, and we get festive. There's eating. Lots of eating, because Savi can conjure up pretty much anything and we take advantage. We drink. At a certain point, I realize that Savi is probably doing something to that wine bottle too, because it never seems to be empty. There's nothing in this cottage but a twin bed on one wall and pillows on the floor, so that's where we sit. I'm lounging there, thinking how odd it seems that somebody with Briar's bare-house aesthetic also has a mandala-patterned area rug in the center of her floor.

I tell myself this is why people are interesting. This is why it's important to try to get to know them. You never really know who anybody is.

Except, I think, Ty. He is the person I know best, aside from myself. That makes me feel warm.

Not only that, but he's not hard to know. Hard to know well, yes. But Ty is always Ty to everyone he meets. It's part of what makes him so powerful.

It's part of why I love him the way I do.

The music changes from punk rock classics to something else. Something I've never heard before. It teases and beguiles. It's like a seduction of sound and suddenly, I don't feel like lounging around.

All I want to do is dance.

Stranger still, everyone else is dancing too.

If asked, I would have sworn up and down that this was a non-dancing kind of a group. But here we all are, dancing around and around in the center of that throw rug on Briar's floor. I'm spinning and spinning, except at some point I realize that *I'm* not spinning, it's like the room is.

Holy hangover, I think, but it doesn't feel drunk and sickening. I don't either. It's wilder than any drink I might have had.

It's *in* me, and I can't stop.

I think, *Stop dancing*, but I don't. I can't. My body is moving. My hands are in the air. My feet are going this way and that like I could do this forever.

I wonder if I ought to be frightened, but I'm not. Not yet. More than anything else, I'm trying to figure out what on earth is happening.

But everything is spinning and spinning, and I try as hard as I can, but I can't seem to focus.

The only thing I can manage to focus on is Briar. She has her head thrown back, her arms spread wide, and she's only wearing a tank top tonight. I can see that the place where she likes to put her hands on her chest isn't an empty, normal span of skin. There's a medallion hanging there.

That flash I saw of its chain comes back to me now, because it's a medallion I recognize.

Winter used to wear it. Augie gave it to her. If I'm not mistaken, the purpose of that medallion is to keep the wearer's power under wraps.

It's why Winter not only thought she wasn't an oracle but didn't believe that her grandmother was either.

As I stare at Briar, still caught in the dance, her eyes open and she looks straight at me.

But it's not Briar anymore.

I know this the same as I know Ty. As I know myself.

It's not Briar anymore.

Other things poke at me that feel random, but can't be. Like all those minions in the lumberyard last night. It seemed like such a funny coincidence that the skirmish was just down the road from Briar's bar, but was it? And how effective was Savi's privacy bubble while we were talking about tonight, anyway?

It makes me wonder about Savi's ward on the three of us.

I try to shout. I try to warn the others. I try to *do* something, but the snare of this dance and this spin is too tight all around us.

I have the feeling that whatever protection spell Savi did on us no longer applies.

I can't look away from Briar. I think she knows it. When she smiles, everything in me goes cold and dark. She rips the necklace off her neck and throws it.

Yet I don't hear it fall.

Because we're not in Briar's cottage anymore. We're not dancing, either.

We're somewhere cold and dark, and everything around us feels harsh and frigid.

And when the spinning stops, my heart does too, for a second.

Because it's clear to me immediately that wherever we are, wherever we've landed, we're stuck here.

25.

The dark is oppressive and deep, seeming to actually shove against me like it wants to fight me, but I can feel the moon somewhere in the distance. I can feel her song in me despite the darkness, despite the pressure.

I look up, and there she is, high above me and yet low in the sky. I know that she's low. I always know exactly where the moon is—the werewolf promise—so I don't know why it also seems like she's so high as well.

Though this is only one of a number of things that don't make sense right now. At least I can think again.

When I pull my gaze away from the moon, Briar has her arms up and she murmurs something.

Just like that, there's light.

It pours into Briar's hands from some unseen source, like she's holding her palms beneath a faucet of white light that only she can see. She cups her hands and then she throws it up into the harsh, hanging darkness.

The light expands and then surrounds us, like a kind of cone.

It's so bright that my eyes water. It's so bright that it takes me a moment to see that it's not just us in the cone.

I feel Winter press against me from the side. I can hear her pulse, too, rapid and wild. Scared. I don't blame her.

On all sides, surrounding us, there is a sea of red-cloaked acolytes and priests in their darker robes. Savi is pressed in with us, but she looks less taken aback. Or maybe it's just that she's looking around already, taking stock.

"We're in the crater," she says flatly. "We're at the very bottom of Crater Lake."

The dried-out crater where a temple should be, but isn't. The place no one thought Vinča could be if she had a vessel to take her away.

"Very good," Briar says, but it doesn't sound like Briar at all.

As I look at her, no longer wearing that necklace, I can feel that dark, seething black energy pour out of her. I see the vision Winter shared, that cage that turned out to be ribs, and I know exactly what happened to Briar. Why she's acted the way she has—particularly since the solstice.

It all makes a horrible kind of sense. She was right there all along. She must have used one spell to hide her power when she first moved into Winter's cottage. Then swiped that necklace to make it easier.

Meanwhile, we felt sorry for her. We wanted to *be friends* with her.

Winter is staring at Briar, her eyes wide and not quite focused. "I know you," she whispers.

"I warned you I'd be back, you crushable, contemptible human slime." She laughs then, tossing back her head and letting out a scream that I think would level buildings, if there were any left up in these mountains.

Vinča. Inside Briar's body.

But not for long, I think, and want to throw up.

Savi mutters something, but all that does is bring Vinča's attention straight to her. "I detest sorcerers," she snarls with Briar's mouth. "Nothing but tawdry want-to-be gods for hire."

"I have never met a god that wasn't for hire," Savi replies, and somehow, here, kidnapped by dark fae magic out of a cottage in Jacksonville and delivered to the bottom of a dried-out, desiccated Crater Lake, Savi is herself again. Smooth and impenetrable. "Your tedious, bloody sacrifices? Your tithes and demands?"

"You can call it whatever you want," Vinča tells her, with the voices of the dead in her vowels. "As your bloody sacrifice will be next."

She waves her hand and her priests surge forward. I can see them coming for me, but I'm still not prepared to be tackled and slammed down into the earth so hard it knocks the breath out of me.

They expect me to shift, so they wrestle my hands behind me and bind them with thick silver chains. They do this first. Then my ankles, too. I can feel the silver, heavy and dull. The priests are very pleased with themselves, but they've mixed up their lore. Silver only kills *bitten* werewolves.

It won't kill *me*, but it does make me less effective. It won't prevent me from shifting, either, but what it will do is slow my shift down so much that they'll likely see it and interrupt it. I'm betting they have silver bullets. Those also won't kill me simply because they're silver—unless, of course, that bullet hits me straight through my heart. Or any other killshot.

They even manacle me in just the right way so if I do manage to shift, I won't be able to get my limbs free.

To one side I can hear Savi murmuring curses, but the priests only laugh. I try to look around, but it's clear they only slammed me into the ground.

"Gag her," Vinča orders her priests. "I'm tired of her spell casting."

I don't hear Winter. I want to sit up and look for her, but I don't want to call more attention to myself. If I twist my body I can see the full moon above me, so I tilt my head, and I focus on her with all my might.

Then, very carefully, I shift. But only a little. Tiny, incremental amounts and focused only on my head.

It's excruciating. The silver makes it worse.

I feel my bones slide and snap. I feel my face change. I shift *just enough* and then I stop, even though it's agonizing. It's like a thousand knives stuck . . . everywhere.

I pull in a deep breath and I hold it for a moment while the priests are busy subduing Savi.

Then I let out one long, loud, endless howl.

I hear it pierce through the dark, but more importantly, through that bubble of light Vinča has arranged around us.

The noise of a wolf call like this shocks everyone, and I know this because no one moves. For one beat, then another. *Fuck it,* I think, and I howl even louder—

And then they're on me. They kick and they strike and I pull the shift back, snapping my human features back where they belong. This hurts a lot more than whatever blows they think they're landing.

The next thing I know, they're taping up my mouth as well.

This also feels better than partially shifting, a thing we are always lectured to never, ever do, lest we get stuck that way.

It's not until they prop me up in a heap with the others that I see Winter is perfectly fine, considering. She looks a little glinty of eye, which suggests to me that she didn't like being manhandled and tied up any more than I did.

Of the three of us, she's the only one who isn't wearing a gag.

"Don't feel left out, my little fortune teller," Vinča croons. She's still in Briar's body, but she doesn't even move like Briar now. She's sinuous, somehow. Long and slithery and terrifying. Where Briar stooped and hunched and hid, Vinča expands.

It's one of the more horrible things I've ever witnessed, and that's saying something.

She comes over and pats Winter's cheek. This is not less horrible.

"I wanted to eat you alive," she confesses, lowering Briar's face with its piercings to gaze straight at Winter. This means she's also too close to me, and the urge to bite her nearly makes me lightheaded. "I wanted to feast on your entrails and wear your collarbone as a hat. This would be small-enough recompense for your defiance."

She makes a clucking sort of sound, and then, for a moment, I am certain that I can see worms crawling beneath her skin. Burrowing this way and that, making tunnels in Briar's cheek. Her chin. Her brow.

I feel my gorge rise and my throat tighten.

But Vinča isn't done. She gets closer and snaps her teeth a scant hair from Winter's nose. "And I still might, when you have been bled out and harvested and offered up. I hope that gives you pleasant nightmares."

"Nightmares used to be more unpleasant," Winter tells her. Conversationally. Like she doesn't have a death goddess in someone else's corporeal body *in her face*. "I used to get those horrible headaches, but they've gone away. I thought that was because your power was gone."

And then she smiles, in a manner I can only describe as shit-eating and provocative, directly into the goddess's face. Briar's face, but there's no Briar behind it.

The slap Vinča delivers, with a screech, sends Winter's head spinning back and, if I had to guess, probably hurts her neck, too.

When the goddess storms away again, Winter runs her tongue over her teeth. She tries to crack her neck on both sides, winces, and then eyes Savi and me. "Worth it," she says, her mouth full of blood.

The priests began to chant, which is never a good sign. The three of us are slumped together haphazardly, a little heap. I find my head is ringing, but I can't tell if it's the chanting, or the fact they took me down so hard, or the way that I howled like that without being fully shifted into wolf form.

I have to hope that it was loud enough. That I let it go on long enough.

That they heard me all the way down in the valley.

Even if they didn't, I tell myself, it's okay. Deep down, no matter what magic hides me from Ty, I know that he'll come. I know it.

He can sense me the same way I can sense him. That has nothing to do with tracking. Not the kind Savi warded us against.

If it did, he wouldn't have found us at her house.

After a while, the priests come back for us. There's more chanting and carrying-on, and this time they have small bowls filled with foul-smelling pastes that they rub on our foreheads. Then, shoving the tape away, on our mouths. With brusque and relentless hands, they rip my shirt and smooth the rest of the paste between my breasts, right over Ty's paw print. Like they're rubbing the vile-smelling stuff over my heart.

There's not anything even remotely sexual about it. I find that's actually scarier.

I can taste the paste where they slathered it on my lips, and it makes me heave. I don't want to think about what it *is*. I want to think even less about what they expect it to *do*.

I can hear similar sounds of revulsion on either side of me. I wouldn't say I feel *comforted*, but at least I'm not alone.

Then they're manhandling us again, picking us up and half carrying, half dragging us a little ways across the crater floor to a large flat-topped rock.

"It's always a fucking rock," Winter mutters.

On my other side, Savi is whispering with her head tilted down, the better to hide what she's doing, I think. She glances toward me, the tape they used to gag her around her chin, and her eyes a fury.

Rain, she mouths.

I think that's an excellent idea. I try to shift again, to let out another howl, but something isn't right. My body won't do it—and I wonder if it's that paste.

They toss us up onto the rock and climb up to arrange the three of us with our backs touching, like we're witches awaiting trial. Crone, mother, and maiden, and we all know how those trials went for the accused.

I look out at the acolytes who press in toward this rock. All of them are chanting now. All of those red cloaks are flowing as they move. Their plague-doctor masks are as unsettling as ever.

I would very much like to join Savi in some pruning. I would like fewer of these minions around if there's a next time. If we live long enough to worry about such things.

I force myself to look beyond all that red-cloaked chanting. I have my perfect werewolf vision no matter what form I'm in, so I look past the cone of light all around us, too. When I concentrate, I can look farther. Up those steep sides of the crater, which explains why I thought the moon was in the wrong place.

Up on the crater's rim, I see something flicker. It looks like smoke.

Vampire, I think. I've never been so happy to see one.

If the vampires know we're here, the wolves do too.

I don't allow myself to think about how scared I am until now. Until I know that Ty is on his way. That it's possible he's already here.

That it won't be only me making sure I run with that moon tonight.

I make myself breathe. I make myself relax the muscles in my body when what they really want to do is tense themselves to failure. All I need to do is keep this moment going until reinforcements arrive.

No sacrifices until then.

"So wait a minute," I say, when Vinča dances back toward us, making her borrowed body move in ways that would probably make me feel sick if I thought about them too closely. "Was that you all along? Butchering all those poor animals? Hiding in plain sight? Eating boxes upon boxes of tooth-decaying cereal?"

Vinča is at the edge of the rock they've arranged us on, and for all that she is an ancient goddess with death in her eyes and nightmares skittering beneath her skin, I can see that what she really wants to do is stand here and brag.

Like every other narcissist douchebag I've ever encountered.

"This vessel cannot contain *my enormity* for any length of time," she tells me haughtily. "It is already woefully insufficient. Yet it was the only one available. All of the rest of these creatures are soft. Too easily reduced to useless sludge when pushed beyond their tiny capacities." She sniffs and looks down at Briar's arms with all their tattoos. "At least the fae have *some* connection to the ancient magic. The sugar helped. Or she would be little more than a viscous puddle by now."

"That is . . . disgustingly specific," Winter mutters.

"So it wasn't you," I say, as if this is a perfectly cordial conversation. As if no one's tied up and bleeding. As if no one is planning to use our bodies to bring nothing but death and suffering to what's left of the world. "It was just a sacrifice free-for-all, then."

"Many of those who worship me let me know the ways they revere me," Vinča tells me, looking smug. "For millennia, I have received such devotion. I do not expect a mangy werewolf cur to comprehend my might or my power."

"They are vast indeed," I say, soothingly, the same way I would tell a wolf like Deirdre that yes, yes, she was *absolutely* independent and *so* powerful. "You had Briar specifically kill all those things all around the places that we live. They had to be hand delivered."

I refuse to say Connor's name, but I know it had to be him too. The ones near the den, certainly. Maybe more. I also get the feeling I know exactly which acolyte of the Goddess of Filth turned him.

"One of the reasons this vessel was chosen was that she was so specifically and strategically placed," Vinča is saying, and she's losing control of Briar's body. Or maybe she's experimenting. Her tongue darts out of slack lips. Her eyes roll back and stay that way, all white, with veins pulsing. "I did not think that she would be required. I did not imagine that I would not rise. Yet all things happen as they should. Now I can fully inhabit this putrid little world, harness the power of the moon and the stars, and take my rightful place at last. Your unwilling sacrifice makes it that much sweeter."

"I'm often known as something of a sugary treat," I agree. "But I do wonder—"

"Silence," Vinča orders. "It is come."

That doesn't sound good.

Then I feel it. There are *things* slithering over my body. Things I do not want to identify. Things that I am deeply concerned match the horrible, wormy things I can see working beneath her skin.

As I stare at her, she still half-wears Briar's face. But every now and again, like a flicker of static, I see that beaked, terrible other face of hers. The one I've heard Winter describe.

I could have lived the hundreds of years of my life without ever seeing it myself.

It makes me want to vomit. The things I can feel crawling all over me—

I can't think about that.

I can hear Savi and Winter breathing harder on either side of me, and I know it's not happening to only me. That doesn't make it better. But it's not worse, either, and that feels like . . . something.

Vinča lifts herself up. She rises from the bottom of the crater, levitating herself high above the three of us. In another effort to pretend I can't feel anything crawling on me, I tilt my head back, look up, and there she is. Hanging in the air, her chest pointed toward the moon.

My moon, I think, in something darker than fury. *Not hers.*

I can feel the creepy-crawly, horrible things moving on me, and I have a flash of insight then that I don't want at all. It's that paste. That's where they're heading.

I have to assume that when they get there, this will all get a whole lot worse.

Vinča stretches out, framed perfectly by her dome of light. All around us, the red cloaks sway. The priests call out their chants and the acolytes repeat them. Over and over again.

I can hear Savi muttering out her spell. Winter is shuddering and makes a low, miserable sound.

"This would be an excellent time to be saved by that vampire king who supposedly will kill anyone and anything that touches me," she grits out. "As I've been repeatedly assured the past few months."

"I don't need Ty to save me," I growl. "I just want him to hurry up and free me so I can start collecting heads."

Up above us, Vinča is starting to . . . expand.

At first I think it's a figment of my imagination. An unhappy hallucination.

I stare up at her and I see her bones stretch, breaking to stretch more. I know what that looks like. I can feel it in myself every time I switch forms.

Another shot of pure ice washes over me.

I think about what I know for a fact. Vinča is *in* Briar, but she wasn't fully inhabiting Briar. Not until tonight.

Whatever she plans now, she clearly has to use Briar's body to achieve it. Whether she will be bursting free of it and creating her own with the pieces that are left or fully taking over the body of the dark fae, I can't say.

But it's clear that every word that's chanted makes another gristly, hideous break or stretch happen. I can hear the joints pop, the bones crunch, and that awful cracking sound. Vinča whips around and around as if she's writhing on the floor, though she's hanging in midair.

My only comfort is knowing it must be extraordinarily painful. I love that for her.

Come on, Ty, I think, reaching down deep inside of me and trying to find that link. Trying to pull on it as hard as I can, telling myself that it won't matter that we're not mated yet. That I'm not fully claimed.

What we have is bigger than any of that.

Ty, I think and feel and scream from deep inside of me, *I need you.*

Then I do it again, so hard it feels like something rips deep inside me, but I don't care. *Now.*

26.

I measure time by the beat of my heart. I focus on it and try to block out everything else. One beat. Breath. Another beat.

I tell myself sensation is a lie. Perception is what I make it. It's not an eleventh-hour attempt to achieve enlightenment, it's a defense mechanism. The less I feel what's happening to me—crawling all over me—the better.

Another beat of my heart. Another breath. Something like a sob rolling up from deep inside—

But then, in the distance, I hear it. Maybe what I mean is that I *feel* it.

It's possible I *scent* it in the air. It's all of these things at once.

Pack.

They're here. They came. They found us.

I tilt my head back so that I'm closer to Winter and Savi and can make sure Vinča—still writhing in the air above us—isn't paying attention to me. Much less to what I'm saying.

"They're here," I tell them, low and fierce. *"They're here."*

Winter doesn't answer, but I can feel her vibrating. With tension, horror, fury—maybe all of the above. She blows out a breath and mutters something. It takes me a moment, beneath the clamor of the goddess's snapping bones and stretching sinew up above, to make sense of it.

"The tunnels," she says.

I remember those maps in the den. Not only maps of our expanded North American territory but the ones on the walls that showcase all sorts of geographic points of interest around here. Including the lava tubes that were blocked for centuries, then opened on the solstice. Then were used to empty out Crater Lake, washing away structures and lands and flooding the old reservoir at Lost Creek Lake.

Rumor is, it flooded most of the Klamath Basin, too.

Savi murmurs something and, suddenly, it's like I can see with a different part of my head. I know that my eyes are showing me what's right in front of me—the dancing acolytes, the red, flowing robes. Now there's another screen inside my head.

I can see them coming. My heart kicks up a gear. I can see vampires and werewolves, an army of goblins, and shockingly, representatives of almost every other clan of the Kind I can think of. All the denizens of the Rogue Valley. Marching together.

Something that never would have happened before the Reveal.

Almost as if I'm not the only one who would prefer to make this new world we have into something that's really *ours* rather than descend into something darker and grimmer. I tell myself it's worth the creeping horde of nightmares crawling up the length of my body. *It's worth it.*

If we make this work. If we end up somewhere brighter.

The moon above knows that *everything* is brighter than what Vinča has planned. It's right there in her title. *Death goddess* doesn't exactly conjure up a relaxing beach vacation of a future for anyone.

Though really, I think as I watch the swaying red cloaks in front of me and the approaching Kind army inside my head, what I'm most interested in right now is any future at all.

Savi and Winter tense beside me. Winter is muttering what sounds like *come on come on come on.*

Deep inside me, I can feel that link I have to Ty begin to hum.

Then they're here, charging out of the lava tubes with a loud roar. They're barreling across the parched floor of the crater, heading straight for the cone of light.

And us.

The roaring gets the acolytes' attention. They turn to look in waves, and they all start shouting themselves. Then they all begin running—straight toward the approaching wave of the Kind.

Here on our rocky altar, we three remained bound, with Vinča's little pets wriggling and crawling and pinching as they climb higher and higher.

Vinča herself is still up above in Briar's poor body, deep in the throes of some macabre dance.

Run, I think at the Kind as they come. *Run as fast as you can.*

Then I think I'm having an understandable mental break when I feel water splash on my head. I ignore it the first time. I tell myself it's probably something disgusting. Another insect coming for the horrible paste on me or Vinča's blood or—

It's really a choose-your-own horror show at this point.

Another drop lands. Then another. Then a few at a time, and I can see when they hit my legs that it's nothing upsetting. In fact, it looks like—

She's doing it, I realize. Savi is making it rain.

"Rain," is all I can manage to say. I sound reverent. I *feel* reverent.

"This is a decent start," she says. "That should grow. And continue. And in time, refill this crater." She sits up straighter. "Hopefully it will soon be as if Vinča was never here in the first place."

"It's also washing this disgusting shit off of me," I grit out as the rain picks up. "Which is all I care about right now, Savi."

"Hard agree," Winter pants.

The rain is a game changer. As the paste washes off, the things on me stop all their creeping and crawling. I may have to tear all the skin they touched off my body later, but that's a privilege of survival.

We're not there yet.

On the screen in my head, I can see the battle is engaged, and already hideously bloody—though the red cloaks confuse the issue.

"What is . . . ?" I shake my head, but I'm still seeing the same thing. "Where did these fucking *giants* come from?"

As I ask the question, however, I see the answer. Two acolytes run toward each other, chanting wildly. When they collide, there's a sickening *sucking* sound. Then everything is gristle and sinew, a rough and wet explosion of viscera and blood.

When it's done, there's one larger, scarier acolyte in the place of two.

Vinča is making giants.

These oversize fighters roar at the moon up above, just peeking over the lip of the crater, sending its light cascading down the still-damp sides. They roar and then they attack, and their weapons involve picking up their foes and crushing them in their hands, mashing them up like fruit.

Everywhere I look, it's a bloodbath.

I can't see Ty—but I can hear him.

I can hear him barking out orders. I hear him letting out howls that distract the enemy and direct his own fighters. My people. My pack. They move like the wind. They work in pairs, tearing out throats and bellies, then rolling on to the next.

The vampires are all deadly precision, taking their smoke shifting to even more lethal extremes. Ariel is in the middle of things, moving so fast that it looks like he's not moving at all.

Yet wherever he casts his gaze, enemies fall.

As long as I can hear Ty's unmistakable voice, I feel safe.

Or *safer*, anyway.

With Ty near, the Kind fighting, and those awful *things* no longer torturing me, I can think again. The rain keeps coming down, and I turn my attention to the way they've bound us.

"Can't you get out of your ties?" I ask Savi.

"They appear to have enchanted my bindings," she says coldly. So coldly that I figure she's been working on them awhile. "Spells do not seem to work."

I wiggle my hands until I find Winter's. Then I concentrate and practice my half-shifting again. This time I push the shifting energy into my hands, easing them into claws—and it makes me sweat, it hurts so much—so that I can tear through the ropes they used on her.

It's another searing agony, but I manage it.

Then I slam myself back into my full human form and am glad that Winter takes a moment to untie her own legs. I need that moment. The silver might not be poisoning me, but it burns all the same. It feels like I swallowed fire.

Winter moves behind me, and when I glance that way I see her working on Savi's enchanted bindings. I'm still sweating, ready to half-shift again and use my claws if Winter can't get them off—but I hear both of them let out a breath and I take one too, because they're both untied now.

I check all around us once again. All of the acolytes and priests are busy fighting, save for a small clump of them off toward the back side of the crater. Vinča is still above us, contorting wildly, though I don't think she can be the one casting the spell to keep her there.

I nod, and it takes Savi only a quick spell to remove my manacles. I feel the silver fall away like a rush of light all over my body. I feel it inside and out.

The three of us turn toward each other, carefully. We examine each other.

I brush a few worms and something gross-looking I don't want to identify off Winter's arm. Savi picks something out of my hair that makes her grimace.

We don't talk about it.

I hope we never will.

"The three of us must put distance between our bodies," Savi tells us. "The more distance, the better. The wards I placed on us must have fallen in the cottage, and I suspect what remains is an inability to *find* us while we're together. Not ideal in a battle."

Winter understands immediately. "Put me in a tunnel. The moment you do, Ariel will find me. My mark will lead him right to me."

Savi looks at me, and I nod.

"Right," Savi says. She looks up toward Vinča, then away, and I see a wash of gold move over her skin. "Now, Maddox."

I jump off the rock.

I shift in midair, hit the ground hard, and run.

I run like every wolf in the world is at my heels and it's time to prove I'm the queen I should be. I run like I think I can outrun Ty, the swiftest wolf of all.

I run—and I head away from the main part of the battle toward the back of the crater. I'm sure I saw a set of priests in that direction, and every instinct I have is telling me that they're the ones keeping Vinča high up in the air, twisting and turning and coming much too close to taking form.

A death goddess walking in a body again is the end of everything.

I don't need anyone who knew Vinča back when to confirm that to me. I feel it like I feel my own blood in my veins, pumping hard and letting me fly across the crater floor like I'm my own damn Harley.

As I run, I see a burst of gold in the sky. In my head, I confirm that Savi has removed Winter, and herself, from that altar. It also looks like she's taken out most of that dome up above Vinča.

But that golden light shooting all around has alerted the acolytes that all is not well on the sacrificial rock. Some of them start to turn back, and the fight begins to change shape.

I keep running. I can see a gnarled trio of priests in front of me, chanting as they march around what looks like a rune burned into the earth.

I don't have to know what it means to know it's not good.

I pick up speed, and when I get closer, I launch.

I leap straight into the air, claws and teeth ready. I take down the first priest, ripping out his throat, and then I throw myself at the next.

He tries to fight me but I tear him apart, using his body to climb until I can get to his throat, too.

The last one breaks and starts to run, but I catch him in two quick strides and make short work of him as well.

I realize as I wheel around that whatever wormy bullshit Vinča cursed me with is gone. They settled down when the paste washed away, but I knew they were still there. My full shift cleared them off me. I hope Savi and Winter can do something similar, stuck in their bodies the way they are.

I run back and forth across the rune, tearing it apart and flinging the pieces in different directions. I dig my claws into it. I wreck it, because Savi's rain is still pouring down, and the last thing I want is some evil rune lurking beneath the water when the crater fills again.

Seems like what's happening now is an object lesson in letting evil things lie where they shouldn't.

Only when I've destroyed it do I start running back toward that figure I can still see up above the rock in the distance.

The moon is moving over the crater, and she's calling for me. She's reminding me what day this is, and that only makes me angrier. I shouldn't be here. I should be on the hilltop above the den, listening to the drums, getting ready to run with Ty.

I run harder over the crater floor. I make myself run faster. On the screen in my head I can see myself, a blur of speed on the far side of the main fight, zipping across the crater like a comet.

When I get to the rock, I jump. I bound up, rebound off the rock, and yank Vinča right out of the sky.

In the distance I hear a wolf howl of loss and I freeze.

I can't move again until I hear Ty's voice joining in the chorus.

There are too many Kind down. Wolves and vampires are lost. This crater is awash in blood.

But the scene Winter shows me makes it clear that our losses are nothing compared to theirs, and that's what I hold on to. The moon is fully above the crater now and I understand, somewhere deep in my bones, that this is Vinča's moment. This is why she's here.

Sure enough, even though I knocked her to the ground—because she's so fond of sucker-punch tackles—she is laboriously climbing to her feet in the janky, messed-up body that she stole.

"You are a pestilence," she screeches at me. "You are nothing but a vile little dog—"

I shift as I throw myself toward her for the pure joy of rearing back with one arm, then punching her in the face.

"I don't want to talk to you," I tell her as she sprawls out on the ground at my feet. "I want to talk to the girl whose body you took."

The goddess is flat on the crater floor. She looks up at me, touching her face as if she's never felt pain before. She looks . . .

Horrified. Shaken.

I kick her again, so she can truly experience it. So she can marinate in mortality and the delights of a mortal form.

"Where's Briar?" I demand.

The goddess shoves Briar's dark hair back from her face. I see that flicker of static, and I can tell when it's Briar looking back at me. Her eyes are wide and solemn. The way she holds her face is completely different.

She gazes up at me, looking something like woozy.

"Why are you doing this?" I grit out at her. "And why are you doing it *to us*? We were friends with you."

"Were you?" Briar touches her spilt lip and winces. "That's not how I remember it, Maddox. You thought I was a freak."

"Look where you are," I shoot back. "You *are* a fucking freak. So what?"

"You wouldn't understand." She coughs, then looks bewildered and a little bit scared. I wonder what sort of rearrangements have happened inside of her, organs and bones, muscle and fascia. "I made a promise lifetimes ago."

"Some promises are not meant to be kept."

"You would know about that, wouldn't you." She snarls as she says that. "Behold the queen of the hundred-year king who will not take her crown. Who are you to talk about vows?"

"Actually, asshole," I retort, "that's what I have planned for after this. After I take you, and that wormy, disgusting death goddess bitch, and stomp you out of existence. Crowns all around, Briar. I wish you could see it."

"You should worry about what you're going to see," Briar shoots back. "The darkness will come alive. Death will sing."

"But I'm the one with the pretty voice," I say. "Didn't you hear me howl?"

I don't wait for Vinča to come back, to flicker into control of this body. I don't have to consult with anyone to know that what she's trying to do here is take over Briar so she can have a corporeal form at last. Vessels are temporary, Ariel said. What little I know about them is that a being like Vinča can make hers near invincible. If she wants.

Long enough to channel all her rage and fury into a world she wants to cast into darkness, anyway.

The presence of all the priests in this crater suggests to me that they all want exactly this.

The moon is high above us. We are situated in the center of the crater. I doubt very much that they put this altar here by chance.

This is the moment. It's now or never.

No one else is close enough to do this. It's on me.

I see every moment I had with Briar since I met her at the end of September. It all flashes through my head. Surly mornings in the kitchen. Her strange, halting invitations. That moment earlier tonight when she looked almost as if I'd actually shown her how to free herself when she took that beanie off her head.

I think about all the things I don't know about her. The story of hers I wanted to learn. I want to know it even more now. How did she end up promising anything to a death goddess? Why would any fae—who live such long lives and can move in and out of worlds so easily—bother to give a promise when they're far better at extracting them?

The moon beams down on us. I see the dislocated, discordant body in front of me ripple, nauseatingly. Then stretch in directions that should be impossible, especially all at once.

Time's up.

I'll tell the story of Briar, the dark fae who I should have gotten to know better, the way I want to, I suppose. I have to live to do it, however, and there's only one way that's going to happen.

I shift as I lunge, and I don't go for the throat. Instead, I take one clawed paw and punch it into her chest. I go deep. I follow it with my snout, digging deep.

Things are jumbled around and not where they should be, but I know what I'm looking for, and I find it. I sniff. I open my mouth.

Then I rip her heart straight out of her chest.

I know it's not right by taste alone, clear to me though I'm doing nothing but holding it in my snout. I can see it from Winter's oracle perspective in my head. Smoking black. A piece of charred meat.

For a moment, everything seems to shake with indecision. Briar is Vinča again, and the goddess opens her mouth to scream, or maybe devour the world—

But then she drops, like a puppet with its strings cut, straight onto the ground.

And everything stops.

27.

Everything is quiet.

Too quiet.

The moon above us is the only thing that moves, something I can feel in increments inside of me more than see. Still, she reminds me the way she always does. Not just of who I am, but that my work isn't done here.

This needs to be the end. I'm the one who will end it.

That's the full Wolf Moon up there. I have a claim to honor tonight.

This shit is personal.

I have the heart that Vinča burned to a charcoaled crisp in my mouth. The taste is worse than that disgusting paste her priests slathered all over me. I spit it out into the air and then shift as it falls back toward me so I can catch it in my hand.

Then I stare down at what's left on the ground. Briar's body, ruined Vinča.

As I do, I can feel that damned heart in my hand *beat.*

Right there against my palm.

More than once, in case I think it's a fluke, until I have to accept that it's finding its own rhythm.

In the distance, the acolytes—who dropped when Vinča did—begin to stir. They heave themselves to their feet and they run, knives pointed directly at me.

But the Wolf Moon is on my side tonight.

She is headed toward the other side of the crater. I can feel the way she moves, and when she gets there, there will be no moonlight left in this dried-out pit that should be a lake. It should take even less time for her to no longer beam down on this altar rock area.

At my feet, what's left of Briar slithers.

I turn toward the altar and explode into action.

One step, another, then I jump.

I land hard on the rock, and as I do, I hear a terrible scream.

It's coming from Briar's heartless corpse. It's coming from the heart in my hand. It's everywhere, filling up the crater, sick and terrible.

I take the burned-up heart in my hand and throw it high, toward the moon—

Where it explodes.

Something in me does, too.

I feel myself toppling through space, blown backward by the strength of my throw and the exploding heart, and I know that I'm going to hit the ground hard—

But Ty is there.

He catches me before I hit the ground.

I feel limp and strange, but his arms are around me. I can smell him. He's *here*. I open up my eyes and I gaze at him.

"You caught me," I say.

He looks like he's taken some heat tonight. There's an ugly slash down the side of his face. There are scrapes and dark bruises all across his wide tattooed chest. I'm thankful for the rain that helps wash away the blood and grime.

Ty looks down at me and shakes his head, as if scolding me. Always scolding me. I don't know why I like it. Why it makes all the noise inside of me . . . quiet down.

"I always catch you," he rumbles at me.

He sets me down on my feet, but everything feels like jelly. Ty peers down at me, then he takes his thumb and rubs at my mouth, making me wonder which particular revolting thing is on me.

Whatever it is, it doesn't keep him from leaning down and kissing me on my forehead. It doesn't keep me from sagging against him. I close my eyes, breathe him in, and watch the screen in my head.

Savi is flowing her way through the battlefield that seems to part before her, and it's hard not to make Red Sea comparisons. She slides like an inevitability through all of those red cloaks, smiting them with golden bursts of sorcery as she goes.

She murmurs as she moves, locating the wounded Kind in every pile of the fallen.

With a few words and a wave of her fingers, she moves hurt vampires and wounded wolves out of her way. I watch her for some time before I realize that she's gathering up all of the acolytes and removing anyone who is not one of Vinča's faithful.

Then she piles them all together in a heap, ignores the falling rain, and sets them on fire.

I open my eyes again when Ariel appears in his typical whirl of smoke. Winter is holding on to him, her arm looped around his neck. She looks pale and sickly, I think, but the vampire king is way ahead of me. He barely spares her a glance as he tears open his own wrist and then puts it to her mouth.

She grips him with her free hand, and drinks.

It's another level of intimacy, then. Me sagging against Ty because I can't stand of my own volition when I would normally hurt myself so as not to appear weak. Winter taking her lover's blood that we all know will heal her and keep her human body strong and something a little better than merely human, which is something I doubt very much she shares with anyone but him.

Meanwhile, Ty and Ariel discuss the battle we just won in their low voices. They sound dark, I think—but less urgent.

Eventually, Savi makes her way across the crater to us. She looks polished to a smooth shine again, not a hint of a hair out of place despite the enduring rainfall. Her gaze is assessing as she sweeps it over

Winter, less so when she looks at me, and she nods slightly. Apparently pleased with what she sees.

Or what she doesn't see, I think, that paste and those *things* rolling back over me for a moment. I shove them away.

Winter smiles up at Ariel, kisses his wrist, then wipes her own mouth as he pulls his wrist back, shakes it once, and heals.

I straighten, but not before I press a kiss to that sweet spot between Ty's pectorals.

Then we all, finally, turn and look down at Briar's body.

"We will burn her twice," Savi pronounces in a voice that reminds me that she is made of old laws, from ancient cities no one alive now will ever see.

"And then flood this crater all over again," Ariel agrees, sounding even more ageless and stern. "Just in case."

I think someone should say a few words for Briar. I think that someone should probably be me, but I also remember the way she looked at me before she died. Before I killed her.

Maybe I'll keep my oddly conflicting feelings to myself.

Savi builds a bonfire around the sacrificial rock. All the Kind clans gather around, some nursing injuries, others looking around furtively—not used to interacting with other Kind species if it's not violent, if I have to guess.

The priests go on the fire first. All the rest of the minions are burning in that pile on the crater floor, but Vinča's priests get special, personal attention. Their bodies are covered in their runes and their symbols, all of them carved deep into their skin, and though the priests are already dead we can hear each rune and symbol moan as the fire reaches them.

"Black magic fears the light," Savi says with satisfaction.

When we finally lay Briar's ruined body on the pyre, we throw in all the charred bits of heart we gathered up, too. Then we all flinch, because the flames scream. And they counter the charred black darkness in her that we can see swell and then shrink as the relentless fire burns and burns.

I find that my urge to say a few words is truly gone. I really take in what Vinča did to Briar, the horrific tangle of her limbs, with half of her seeming to be inside out. Not to mention what I did to her.

I stare into the flames for a long while, Ty's arm over my shoulders and the heat of him rivaling the blast from the fire.

The hour grows later. The moon is getting higher in the sky.

The wolves are getting restless.

Most of the pack's females are back in the den, too far away for a mating run tonight.

But I'm not.

The wolves start howling. They circle the fire, doing a decent impression of the ritual the way it's supposed to go—even without the drums.

All around us, I'm aware of the other members of the Kind who might understand what's happening here but have certainly never witnessed it before. I see Savi and Winter exchange a glance, both of them looking various degrees of wide-eyed or fascinated. Maybe both.

It makes sense to me that this is how this happens. Nothing typical for Ty and me. Nothing run-of-the-mill. Only the death pyre of a death goddess beneath the Wolf Moon for the first high king and his famously reluctant queen.

If I'd planned it this way deliberately, it couldn't suit us more.

I stand straight, feeling like myself again—and a little bit more. A little more kick, courtesy of the moon. I can feel her pull. I can feel everything.

Longing. Yearning—if, of course, he's male enough to catch me.

I push away from Ty and grin up at him.

"My liege," I say, and I let everyone hear me, because the run will be ours—but the pack has earned the right to hear me claim Ty, too. To acknowledge the moon, and Ty. To signal that I am finally embracing my fate. "There's a full moon tonight. You might have noticed."

I feel everything in Ty still. His dark eyes are so intense I can feel them inside and out. They gleam—but he doesn't smile.

We're years past that.

"If I were you, baby, I would run," he warns me. "Take a head start. See if it helps you."

That's all the warning he's going to give me. I know that in every humming inch of my body.

I shift like lightning, and then I run.

And as I run, I hear the wolves howling my name. I head for the sleek, steep sides of the crater and I barrel my way up.

The moon is almost there. I can feel her everywhere, urging me on.

I run.

I feel it—we all feel it—when the Wolf Moon hits her greatest height. It's that loud, wild song that heats my blood and spurs me on, and this time, for the first time since I was very young, I let it carry me.

I let the howls of my pack light me up and make me faster.

And everything changes because I'm part of it. It sings in me and I am the song, and Ty is already behind me. He's *right there.*

We streak out of the crater and I cut to the left and race along the rim, scenting him not three paces behind me.

He and I are one. Together, we make a glorious harmony.

I want to do this song of ours justice. I take to the mountains and he chases me there. He loses ground when I cut beneath a fallen tree. He catches up again when I lose my grip on some rocks, but I make my fall an attack—taking him out at the knees and then switching direction while he's still on his back.

I've never run this hard or this fast.

It's like running to the moon herself. *For* her.

I can feel him at my heels. I can hear the way he sounds out the glory of this, so loud that every wolf, all over Southern Oregon, can hear.

I howl back.

Somewhere in between Crater Lake and Mount McLoughlin, I try to turn a tight little corner in the Sky Lakes Wilderness, then slip.

That's the end of it.

And the beginning of everything else.

I discover, as he takes me down at last, that what I always thought of as a submission is anything but.

I do my part. He does his. Together we make one bright and burning song beneath the moon.

We sing out, into the trees. Ty surges deep inside of me. I take him in deep.

We fuck ourselves free and we come and come and come.

This goes on so long that I can't tell the difference between the two of us.

When I know myself again, when I'm conscious that there's some separation between him and me however little I want it, he's deep inside me. I can still feel his cock, thick and engorged, and we wait there for it to subside.

Tonight, he takes his snout and he pushes my head back, exposing my throat. He rolls us so we're both lying with our bellies toward the sky. Then he lets a howl out to the moon that seems to shake every part of me.

I feel a wild heat on my throat, like his hard human hand wrapped tight, though I know he's still a wolf and still rooted deep within me.

I howl myself when it hurts, and when it's done, Ty licks my tears away and hums as if they're precious.

I know that when I look at myself again, I'll see a patch of darker fur in my wolf form. In my human form, I'll have a new tattoo.

My crown at last.

I feel shivery and shaky. I feel *great*.

And we've lain like this before, too many times to count. But tonight, everything is changed. Everything is new.

"My queen," Ty says in the old language, his snout at my ear.

I already feel different, but those words are like runes. It's like he's carving them into my flesh, my bones. I feel myself shimmer into someone new. I wonder if the fire will hear me moan when I go. If it will be Ty's name.

"Your queen," I say in the same old way, formal and forever.

Then, together, we howl out the true name of the moon that only werewolves know, and it's done.

It's like a different source of light is in me now. As if there is the sun now, the moon always. And now this. Us.

Burning bright forever. Connected in ways that I can *feel.* I can't feel that link that I knew was fate, drawing us together.

Instead it's like I'm inside of him too. As if we will never be apart, no matter what our bodies do. It's beautiful. It's hot. It's our song, and we get to sing it for the rest of our lives.

"Did you know?" I ask him, in wonder.

He nips at me, gently. "I hoped."

Eventually, we separate, but when we sit up we press against each other. Feeling ourselves separate takes some adjusting. I feel almost like a new cub again, unsure how to operate my own body.

We sit there for a long while, all alone. Away from the noise in the pack, the burning bodies of our enemies, and the future unfolding before us.

As soon as we see the first hint of the coming morning, we break into an easy kind of trot and head back down, out of the mountains, and into the brand-new year.

I am claimed now. We are mated. All of our struggles with fate are over.

Vinča is gone, and the world is new.

And if I have anything to say about it, ours.

28.

Wolf Moon, Last Quarter Half-Moon

It's almost a week later when we gather at Winter's house for a battle post-mortem, which seems to be the go-to place after potentially apocalyptic run-ins with death bitches. Crater Lake is full. The lava tubes are blocked once more.

Almost like it never happened. Unless you were there.

"Winter and I scoured Briar's cottage," Savi says. "There's a whole dark fae rune situation under that throw rug."

"I knew that rug was weird," I mutter, slumping in my favorite chair. Over by the boarded-up window, Ty smiles. He smiles a lot more these days, but then, so do I.

"I found the necklace my brother gave me," Winter says. "Tossed in the corner of the cottage."

I realize I remember that—and that I forgot to tell them about it, what with one thing and another, a battle and a claiming and all the rest. I recount everything that happened to me in that crater when they weren't with me.

"She was wearing that necklace for a while," I tell them when I'm done. "That's why we couldn't scent any power in her. She was deliberately hiding it." I think about how her scent was always confusing. Maybe that should have been a clue when the scents of the sacrifices were equally confusing, but I can't turn back time. I frown at Winter. "When did you lose that necklace?"

"Around Halloween." She shakes her head. "I don't know."

"I keep trying to tell myself that she sort of accidentally fell into her role in all this," I say, turning it over in my head. "But I don't think she did. I think it was all planned. Up to and including the fact that she was nowhere to be seen over Halloween. She played us."

"One of her priests told me as much," Savi says then. Everything about her is moneyed and smooth, like her short period of dishevelment was a figment of my imagination—but I don't think it was. "Vinča apparently suspected that we would bind ourselves in exactly that way. She was banking on it. I handed her the ammunition she needed to get us exactly where she wanted us—and she placed Briar here to make sure it happened."

"And it didn't work out that well for her, did it," Winter says. She shrugs. "Fuck Vinča. Fuck Briar, too."

I don't consider myself particularly sentimental, but I'm finding it hard to dismiss Briar completely. Likely because I'm the one who killed her in the end, and it doesn't matter that Vinča would have done it anyway. Taking a life isn't something a person with a soul should just . . . move on from.

I tuck her away inside me and keep it to myself.

"We found this, too," Winter says, digging something big and gold from her pocket. She flips it through the air in my direction and I catch it.

I know exactly what it is. An old-school biker ring with 1% emblazoned on it, useful in fistfights and to announce a person's outlaw status to the world. I also know who this one belonged to, and not only because I can scent him on it.

"I guess Briar was Vinča's faithful minion who showed Connor the truth," I say, as I suspected in the crater. I toss the ring to Ty.

He scowls at it, then grunts. "That dumb fuck. Wouldn't be the first man I know to confuse pussy for truth."

I feel the last remaining puzzle pieces coming together. How many times did Winter and I hypothesize that maybe Briar's shiftiness was her sneaking away to see some boyfriend? Turns out, she was.

Some religions call this day in January the Epiphany. Maybe for good reason.

Savi does her food thing. The five of us eat. We laugh. The last time we did something like this, after the Halloween battle, it was a far more somber occasion. Winter's grandmother had died. Everyone was shell-shocked.

This is better. This feels like that new world Ty and I saw before us under the full Wolf Moon.

"I'm going to move in with Ariel for the foreseeable future," Winter announces when we're all stuffed and happy. She grins. "We can pretend it's for my safety. It's not."

Across the living room, Ariel allows his lips to form one of his infrequent smiles. "It's not *not* about your safety."

Winter's grin widens, but she continues. "But I can't stand to think of Gran's house empty. Or getting rid of it when Augie might want to come back here someday." She lifts her brows at Savi. "Are you sure you really want to do this?"

"You're moving in?" I study her. "I'm not sure Jacksonville is a *minion* sort of place."

"I don't think that living in such dramatic isolation is necessarily good for me," Savi says. She slides a look at me. "And I don't *need* minions, Maddox. They need me. It will be good for them to soldier on alone."

I don't really know what to say to that, so I ignore it. "You're just going to live here? All by yourself?"

"I see it as more of a halfway house," Savi says.

Winter nods. "That night at the crater, while you were busy getting married, or whatever you call it—"

"I am mated and claimed, actually," I say. "And a queen, lest you forget. Peasants that you are."

Savi actually smiles. Winter laughs, then continues. "We were talking about the fact that whatever the ulterior motives were at play here last fall, we all kind of needed a place to get back on our feet. Maybe Briar too, for better or worse. I spent three years of the Reveal doing it all myself, and it sucked. Now I've spent the past three months understanding how much bigger the world is than just my own misery. And I have to think there are more magical creatures—"

"Magical women," Savi interjects. "If we're being honest."

"I want this house to be a way station," Winter says. "My grandmother would have loved it. After she got finished bemoaning the presence of strangers in her house, that is."

We all smile at that.

"Ultimately, that's what she did with her life. She tried to help people, whether they wanted her help or not." Winter looks at our sorceress friend. "Savi can run this place without having to have everything steel plated and locked up tight, with an arsenal strapped to her at all times. Savi *is* the arsenal."

"That you think so is the greatest weapon of all," Savi says with a smile.

"And if you need another, I'm your wolf," I say with a grin.

I realize then what seems different about Winter today. She's not wearing her weapons. Maybe we're all finding our way to who we really are. Maybe all these battles really were worth it if they led us here, to the places we needed to go.

When it's time to leave, Ty and I walk hand in hand into the woods.

"I want to show you something," he says.

I smile at him, still feeling that song—our song—within me. "Whatever you want to show me, I want to see."

"Run with me," he invites me.

We shift and take off, galloping higher into the hills above Jacksonville, then looping around to the road that stretches across the crest of Jacksonville Hill. It straddles the road out of town that leads off into the Applegate Valley. Ty leads me farther up into the deeply forested hill that rises behind Jacksonville, following what appears to be a little-used road all the way to the top.

When we're nearly there, he shifts back and indicates I should do the same. Then he takes my hand in his, leads me out of the woods, and into a clearing where a grand house sits.

The grounds are covered in snow, but I can see the outlines of raised gardens and flower beds. There are terraces cut into the side of the mountain, some with patios, one with a pool. The view from here is practically the whole of the Rogue Valley—our valley—stretching down toward Ashland.

The house itself makes me think of pictures I've seen of places like France. It's sprawling and beautiful. And obviously abandoned.

"Ty . . ." I shake my head at him. "What are we doing here?"

"I heard what your mother said," he tells me, his dark gaze intent. "What wolf gets to look at the sky—or something like that."

He takes my shoulders in his hands. I can see the indigo that rings his irises.

"I've made my peace with the den," I tell him.

"You don't have to make your peace with shit," he says with a short laugh. "Every star in the sky, every cloud, every scrap of blue and moonlit night is yours." He nods toward the house. "And so is this."

I can't take it in.

He keeps talking. "It's maybe ten minutes from the den. It's strategically placed. I'm going to encourage all the lieutenants to find their own places away from the den, because I want wolves in houses all over Jacksonville. I don't want us hiding in a den. I don't want us hiding anywhere." His hands tighten on my shoulders. His thumb grazes my crown tattoo. "Just in case you think I don't listen to you."

"I never said you didn't listen," I tell him, melting against him. "But this . . . Ty. This is dreaming big."

"That's who we are, baby," he says. "Remember?"

Then he kisses me, deep and hard, before we go explore our new home.

And christen it, too. More than once.

And when we settle into our new home, despite the mutterings from the usual places, I know deep in my bones that this was the right choice. Wolves will think twice before bothering Ty—or me—with the small things. But if we're needed, we'll be right there.

Meanwhile, we get to breathe.

Over the next few months, more wolves—not only Ty's lieutenants—claim places to live in the hills above Jacksonville, honoring both parts of who we are. As spring creeps in, it's not unusual to hear howls from all over. I notice that the humans don't flinch as much as they used to.

This pleases me too. Ty and I agree that the more connection we have with humankind, along with the rest of the Kind, the better.

I think about all the creatures who showed up at Crater Lake on New Year's Eve. All of us fought to hold on to the world the Reveal gave us. It shouldn't take fighting to keep it. It's dancing in ruins at the Manor. It's playing pool with gorgons at Gold Rush. It's learning how to bake cookies with the human librarians who taught me how to read.

It's one step—foot or paw, claw or tentacle—at a time, and a lot less eating each other.

This is how we build the world I want to give to my children someday. One conversation at a time, even if it's awkward.

Until then, Ty and I get to sing the song that made us.

We get to take every breath as ours, sing it out into the world as we remake it, and make it shine like new.

29.

I don't have the bad dreams I expect, no matter how many times I think something will trigger me and bring me back to my time at the bottom of that thirsty crater. Ty and I sleep too wound up and tangled around each other for that.

Some moons later, I dream that a raven that is not anything so simple as a bird lands in the house Savi left behind.

It should not be able to land. It should not have been able to find the house at all.

Yet it cocks its head to one side as it peers around into all sorts of places it shouldn't be able to locate—much less perceive.

When it leaves, it flies straight up, like a bullet.

Then disappears.

It disconcerts me well into the next day.

Moons upon moons later still, I have another dream.

Down beneath the frigid cold water of a still-full and serenely blue Crater Lake, buried beneath a stone that was once used as an altar, the charred, mangled fragments of something that was once a heart . . . twitch.

But I'm no oracle. My dreams are barely nightmares, and no one needs more than their share.

I keep them to myself.

ACKNOWLEDGMENTS

Thanks to Selena James and everyone at Montlake—especially the outrageously talented art department—for all their hard work and enthusiasm. To Keyren Burgess for going on this ride with me, getting deep into the details, and making it all sing. Thanks to Jon F. for truly deft and thoughtful copyedits twice now. To the marvelous Holly Root, for all the things, all the time, including my phone's desire to endlessly butt-dial her. And to Jeff for saving me from myself on more than one occasion during the writing of this book, and also providing snacks.

ABOUT THE AUTHOR

Megan Crane is the *USA Today* bestselling, multi-award-nominated, and critically acclaimed author of more than 150 books and shows no sign of slowing down. Megan has a master's and PhD in English literature and has taught many creative writing classes, including through UCLA Extension's prestigious Writers' Program and in a great many workshops. She has a black belt in Krav Maga and a blue belt in jiujitsu, and spends more time in martial arts studios than she ever imagined possible. Megan lives in the Pacific Northwest with her comic book artist husband, though, at any given time, she is likely to be either huddled in a coffee shop somewhere or off traveling the world. Preferably both. You can find out more than you ever wanted to know about her at www.megancrane.com.